Murder Never Takes a Holiday

Murder, She Wrote

Murder Never Takes a Holiday

Murder, She Wrote

Manhattans & Murder

and

A Little Yuletide Murder

BY

JESSICA FLETCHER & DONALD BAIN

Based on the Universal television series created by
Peter S. Fischer, Richard Levinson & William Link

AN OBSIDIAN MYSTERY

Obsidian
Published by New American Library, a division of
Penguin Group (USA) Inc., 375 Hudson Street,
New York, New York 10014, USA
Penguin Group (Canada), 90 Eglinton Avenue East, Suite 700, Toronto,
Ontario M4P 2Y3, Canada (a division of Pearson Penguin Canada Inc.)
Penguin Books Ltd., 80 Strand, London WC2R 0RL, England
Penguin Ireland, 25 St. Stephen's Green, Dublin 2,
Ireland (a division of Penguin Books Ltd.)
Penguin Group (Australia), 250 Camberwell Road, Camberwell, Victoria 3124,
Australia (a division of Pearson Australia Group Pty. Ltd.)
Penguin Books India Pvt. Ltd., 11 Community Centre, Panchsheel Park,
New Delhi - 110 017, India
Penguin Group (NZ), 67 Apollo Drive, Rosedale, North Shore 0632,
New Zealand (a division of Pearson New Zealand Ltd.)
Penguin Books (South Africa) (Pty.) Ltd., 24 Sturdee Avenue,
Rosebank, Johannesburg 2196, South Africa

Penguin Books Ltd., Registered Offices:
80 Strand, London WC2R 0RL, England

Published by Obsidian, an imprint of New American Library, a division of Penguin Group (USA) Inc.
Manhattans & Murder and *A Little Yuletide Murder* were previously published in Signet editions.

First Obsidian Printing, November 2009
10 9 8 7 6 5 4 3 2 1

Manhattans & Murder copyright © 1994 Universal City Studios Productions LLLP
A Little Yuletide Murder copyright © 1998 Universal City Studios Productions LLLP
Murder, She Wrote is a trademark and copyright of Universal Studios. All rights reserved.

OBSIDIAN and logo are trademarks of Penguin Group (USA) Inc.

Set in Minion
Designed by Ginger Legato

Printed in the United States of America

Manhattans & Murder

Chapter One

*I*t was his eyes.

Not that his eyes caused me to stop and look at him. The red Santa Claus suit, shiny black boots and fake, grizzled white beard did that. But it was his eyes that sparked recognition in me.

He was one of a dozen solicitors of charitable contributions on Fifth Avenue that crisp, sunny day in December. Some employed loud musical accompaniment as they attempted to woo hordes of pedestrians passing each hour, a few hopefully imbued with the Christmas spirit of giving. The Santa Claus I stopped to observe had only a small, cheap bell, whose tintinnabulation could barely be heard over the blaring, out-of-tune brass ensemble of an adjacent Salvation Army unit.

He didn't seem to notice me as I stood in front of Saks Fifth Avenue's festive holiday windows. Why would he? I was only one of countless faces on the street at that hour.

Besides, it had been at least ten years since Waldo Morse and I had last seen each other. It probably wasn't even Waldo.

Still, I couldn't resist having a closer look. I pulled a dollar bill from my purse, navigated the stream of foot traffic at the risk of being bowled over, and dropped the money into a cardboard box decorated with shimmering red and green paper that sat at his feet.

"Thank you," he mumbled, his eyes looking beyond me.

"Merry Christmas," I said loud and clear. I didn't move, and my presence compelled him to acknowledge me. He stopped ringing the bell and frowned. "Waldo?" I said.

The mention of his name seemed to rattle him. He glanced away, rang his bell one more time, then looked at me again. "Jessica Fletcher." He said it in a hoarse whisper as though trying to keep others from hearing.

"Yes, it's me, Waldo. What an incredible surprise. No, shock is more like it."

It suddenly occurred to me—too late, as is usually the case—that I'd been imprudent in openly approaching him. His expression confirmed it. He was overtly uncomfortable, and I wished I could reverse my actions of the past few minutes, run the movie backward.

I was now as awkward as he was uncomfortable. I said cheerily, "Well, Waldo, they say you always bump into someone you know in this big city. I guess they're right. Nice to have seen you."

I was about to rejoin the stream of pedestrians moving uptown when he said, "Mrs. Fletcher. Wait."

I turned. Was he smiling beneath the white beard? Hard

to tell, but I felt better thinking he was. I moved closer as he said in that same whisper, "I'd like to talk to you."

He looked left and right; he seemed anxious to keep our conversation private. No need to worry about that, not with the Salvation Army brass orchestra groaning loudly through *Adeste Fideles.*

"Come back tomorrow," he said. "Meet me here at two."

"Two? Oh my, I'm afraid I—" I stopped myself. The plans I'd made for the next afternoon could be juggled, even shelved. I would not, could not, pass up the chance to talk to Waldo Morse. "I'll be here at two sharp," I said.

I walked to the corner of Fiftieth Street, stopped, and looked back over my shoulder. As I did, a priest who'd come from the direction of St. Patrick's Cathedral approached Waldo. The transaction didn't go the way I assumed it would. Instead of the priest's putting money into the box at Waldo's feet, Santa Claus handed the priest something.

The priest quickly disappeared into the crowd. Waldo snapped his head in my direction and saw that I'd observed what had taken place. I rounded the corner and headed east. Somehow, I felt I should not have witnessed the exchange between them. Why? I wasn't sure. Maybe because of who Waldo Morse was, and the reason he'd departed Cabot Cove.

Tomorrow at two. I'd be there.

Chapter Two

"Well, Jessica, how was your first full day in Gotham?"

"I'd forgotten how exhausting walking around Manhattan can be," I replied to my publisher of many years, Vaughan Buckley, in whose spacious apartment I sat, stockinged feet propped up on a blessed ottoman, a glass of sparkling mineral water with lime in my hand. Vaughan's wife, Olga, was in the kitchen making canapés. Their dogs, Sadie and Rose, were curled up together on a cushioned window seat.

"Accomplish all your shopping?" Buckley asked as he pulled a tufted red leather chair to the other side of a glass coffee table.

I laughed. "Heavens, no. I haven't even begun my own shopping. When friends in Cabot Cove knew I'd be in New York this Christmas, they all wanted me to bring something special back to them. I told them I was staying through New Year's Eve, but that didn't deter them. They said a gift bought in a fancy New York shop would make up for giving it late."

"And, there's also the panache of having the world's most famous mystery writer personally buy it for them."

"No, I don't think so," I said, sipping my drink. "I just hope my feet hold up."

Olga Buckley came from the kitchen carrying our snacks on a blue-and-white Daum serving plate. Antiques and gourmet cooking were her passions; she was well versed in both subjects. Their apartment, all twelve rooms of it, was as handsomely turned out as its owners. Vaughan and Olga Buckley were attractive people, Nautilus-thin, beautifully groomed, and impeccably dressed on all occasions. She'd been a successful model when she'd met the young editor who would go on to found one of publishing's most respected houses.

The apartment was on the ninth floor of the Dakota on West Seventy-second Street, famous for all the artistic community's leading lights who'd called it home since it was built in 1884. It had been the setting for the horror movie *Rosemary's Baby,* and rendered infamous when former Beatle John Lennon was murdered in its courtyard by a deranged fan in December of 1980.

I'd been to the apartment before as a dinner guest, but had never stayed there, although I had a standing invitation whenever I visited New York. This time, they'd been especially persuasive. Olga said she would not hear of me staying in a hotel, and Vaughan even threatened (in jest, I assume and hope) to shortchange me on royalties the next time they came due. I was glad they'd prevailed. Although our relationship was the result of my writing books for Buckley House, they'd become what I considered good, dependable friends.

Olga sat next to her husband. "So, Jessica, tell us what you did today," she said.

My first thought was of having bumped into Waldo Morse. I wanted to share that with them, along with the strange circumstances of Waldo's life, but thought better of it. Maybe after meeting with him the next day, but not now. Practicing discretion seemed the best thing I could do for Waldo at this point.

Instead, I told them of shops I'd visited in search of items on my Cabot Cove shopping list. I'd barely made a dent. "Our sheriff, Morton Metzger, collects toy soldiers," I said. "I think I've mentioned him to you before. He asked me to go to a shop with a funny name and buy him a certain soldier that's missing from one of his regiments."

I picked up my purse from the floor in search of the card I'd been given at the shop, but Olga quickly said "Funchies, Bunkers, Gaks and Gleeks."

"You know it."

"Yes. The owner and I are friends. I love the shop. Did you find the soldier?"

"I certainly did. One item checked off my list."

"Always a good feeling," Buckley said. "Want to nap before dinner, Jess? Our reservation is at seven, and doing the Larry King show will turn this into a very long day for you."

I stretched and let out a contented sigh. "A nap sounds lovely. Sure you don't mind?"

"Not at all," said Olga. "I think I'll take one myself."

I knew I wouldn't sleep, but an hour of solitude and quiet was appealing. My room was large and faced the central courtyard. Through my window I could see the balconies of other apartments, all the lovely oriel windows, turrets, gables, finials and flagpoles. The Dakota was a mix of architectural styles, some German, a little French, certainly English Victorian. It was now dark; patches of yellow light from other windows were warm and inviting.

My room looked much as it probably had when the building went up. It was furnished with a handsome selection of antiques to go with the carved marble mantel above my fireplace, walls of mahogany paneling and marble floor. A large, rich red-and-gold Oriental rug covered the center of the room. My king-size bed was canopied. I love the look but can never stop wondering how much dust has accumulated on top.

I slipped out of my clothes, put on a robe, and sat at an antique French desk near the window. I tried to focus upon all the wonderful aspects of this trip to Manhattan, but found it difficult. I'd always wanted to spend a Christmas in bustling New York City—although Cabot Cove, as small as it was, generated its own sense of holiday urgency and pace. I usually celebrated Christmas and the passage into a new year at home. But this year the early November publication of my latest murder mystery triggered an intense publicity effort by Buckley House. Vaughan Buckley saw the book as a perfect Christmas gift and prevailed upon me to head south for media appearances, newspaper interviews, and autographing sessions at bookstores. I was absolutely shocked, of course, when they told me I would be a guest on the Larry King Show. I'd always been a fan of Mr. King, but never thought he would be interested in having a mystery writer as a guest. I was wrong. Tonight, I would meet the talented TV host and do my best to sound intelligent.

I'd originally intended to return to Cabot Cove the day after Christmas, but the persuasive Mr. Buckley, along with other friends in Manhattan, had convinced me to celebrate New Year's Eve with them. This didn't set well with my friends in Maine.

"New Year's Eve won't be the same without'cha," Seth Hazlitt, my physician friend, said when I announced my plans. "Trudy promised to make a batch of her Chicken Roly-Poly, Ms. Haines's been promisin' a big round 'a molasses taffy, and the club says it saved enough over the year to bring up a real band from Portland. We never had real live music before."

It wasn't easy for me to break tradition and to disappoint Seth, but I was committed. My concession was a promise to call the Cabot Cove Citizen Center at midnight to wish my friends a happy new year.

I looked at the list of presents I was asked to buy while in New York but couldn't concentrate on that, either. The chance meeting with Waldo Morse dominated my thoughts. In a way, I was sorry I'd seen him. Better to let unpleasant episodes from the past stay just that—in the past. On the other hand, my natural curiosity, which friends have occasionally characterized as putting cats to shame, made me want the hours between now and two o'clock the next day to pass quickly. What would he tell me? What had his life been like all these years?

Oh, well, I thought, as I headed for the large marble

bathroom. One thing at a time, Jess. Shower, dinner, the TV show, a good night's sleep, sign books at B. Dalton in the morning, lunch with a reporter from *Newsday,* and then back to Fifth Avenue.

My curiosity about Waldo Morse would be sated soon enough.

Chapter Three

"Say something in Maine," instructed one of the last callers to me on the Larry King Show.

"Pardon?"

"You know, talk funny like people in Maine do."

"People in Maine don't talk funny," I said. "People in New York talk funny."

Larry King giggled. "Come on," he said. "You know what the caller means, Jessica. Put the cah in the garage."

I laughed. "What a strange thing that would be, putting a car—or a *cah* as you pronounce it—in a garage. In Maine, a car is a big underwater crate where lobsters are stored live until they're shipped."

"Really?"

"Yes." I didn't want to be combative, or a spoilsport, and so I was about to politely continue the conversation when the caller suddenly identified himself as Cabot Cove sheriff Morton Metzger. "Jess," he said, "I figured if Bill

Clinton's mother could call in when Clinton was a guest, I could, too."

"But you're not my mother," I replied. King laughed. Morton wanted to continue talking but the smooth, adept talk show host nicely and quickly put an end to Morton's fifteen minutes of fame. I was pleased to know that my friends in Cabot Cove were watching, and was glad Morton had called.

When the show was over, Vaughan, Olga, and the publisher's publicity director, Ruth Lazzara, assured me I'd been "a smash." I wasn't so sure they were right. It had gone by so quickly, I had trouble remembering anything that happened on the set.

I got to bed at midnight and slept fitfully. I didn't know whether it was the remnants of the heavy dinner we'd had, the tension of being a guest on a national television show, or lingering thoughts about my scheduled rendezvous the next day with Waldo Morse. No matter what the cause, a sound sleep evaded me that night.

I was up earlier than my host and hostess, quietly made a cup of coffee, and read the *New York Times* they told me would be at the door.

They joined me an hour later. Eventually Ruth Lazzara, a vivacious young redhead with a seemingly bottomless reservoir of energy, picked me up at the appointed time and took me to B. Dalton, where I was amazed to see a hundred people lined up in anticipation of my appearance, many of whom said they'd seen me on the Larry King Show. There were tall stacks of my book on a table, and I was to autograph one for each person in line who purchased a copy. Ruth whispered to me before we started,

"While you have a minute, Jessica, try and sign them all. The store can't send back signed books."

"I couldn't do that," I said. I knew what she was getting at. Books are sold to stores on a consignment basis, one of the few industries left that operates that way. A store can send back for full credit any book it doesn't sell unless, of course, it's been signed.

The publicity director laughed. "It's done all the time, Jessica."

"Yes, I'm sure it is, but not by me."

"Whatever you say." Her tone was less bubbly than before.

It all turned out nicely. They sold sixty books, and the people I met were friendly. I had one whimsical moment when I considered asking them to "say something New York," but I resisted the temptation.

Ruth escorted me to my lunch with the *Newsday* reporter, another lively young woman who obviously hadn't read my book—any of my books—but who wasn't deterred by that. I hadn't had breakfast and was ready for lunch, especially good Italian food (somehow, Hick's Leaning Tower of Pizza in Cabot Cove never satisfied my love of pasta and spicy veal dishes). We lunched at Antolotti's, a lovely Italian restaurant on Forty-ninth Street and First Avenue where my picture was taken with the owner to join other celebrity photos on the walls.

After salads had been served, I was bombarded with questions from the reporter about my work habits. By the time we got around to coffee, she told me she was working on a murder mystery and wondered if I would take a look at it, perhaps even collaborate with her.

"It's kind of you to ask," I said, "but I don't collaborate."

"Maybe you could read it and give me some advice."

I managed to sidestep that awkward situation by encouraging her to keep writing, giving her some general tips on submitting manuscripts for publication, and slipping her final questions about my personal life, my deceased husband, and whether I had any current romantic interests. I naturally thought about George Sutherland, the handsome and charming Scotland Yard Inspector I'd met in London the year before, but didn't mention him. You couldn't call our relationship "romantic," although I did think of him often, and had received some letters over the past year. A nice man. A gentleman. "Say something funny in Scottish," I thought, smiling to myself. "No," I said to the interviewer as we stood outside the restaurant, "there are no romantic interests in my life at this time."

The minute she turned the corner, I jumped in a cab. "Fifth Avenue and Fiftieth Street, please," I told the driver, whose only acknowledgment was to slap on the meter and jam his foot down on the accelerator pedal. Why he bothered to accelerate fast was beyond me. It was slow-going, the holiday season in Manhattan having brought thousands of extra cars into the city.

Hopelessly mired in traffic at Forty-ninth and Madison, I paid the driver and walked the rest of the way to my rendezvous with Waldo. Frankly, I didn't think he would be there, but I was wrong. There he was, ringing his little bell and tossing in an occasional "Ho, ho, ho."

I stood in front of the same Saks window and watched the parade on Fifth. There seemed to be even more people, if that were possible. A few passersby fought the flow and managed to drop change into the box at Waldo's feet. I was certain Waldo hadn't seen me arrive. At least he did nothing to indicate he had.

I instinctively reached into my purse and pulled out the small point-and-shoot camera that I always carried with me. For a moment—and it lasted no more than that—I questioned the propriety of taking a picture of Waldo. But it wasn't a decision I had to make. I simply raised the camera to my eye, waited for a break in the foot traffic, and took the photo. He still didn't seem to notice me. I heard the film automatically advance in the tiny technological marvel in my hands and was about to take another frame when it happened. It was instantaneous; a flash point of time. Sound. Motion. Horror.

I couldn't see the face of the person who stepped up to Waldo, pressed a revolver into his stomach, and squeezed the trigger, nor did I think to keep my eye on him or her. The mind doesn't always process information quickly enough to instantly do the right thing. At least mine doesn't.

Now, a scream from a woman who saw Waldo slump to the ground. The camera was still to my eye, and I took another picture. At this point, Waldo was lying on his side on the pavement, his fake beard pushed up and covering most of his face. Blood dripping from his mouth quickly turned the beard to pink. Other people stopped. I'd forgotten about the person who'd shot Waldo. Where had he gone? Was it a he? I'd only seen the back of a figure from a three-quarter angle. The person wore a stocking cap and scarf brought high up around his, or her, chin, masking features. The coat was black. A raincoat. And the killer was gone. Disappeared.

Waldo wasn't dead yet. His right hand clutched for something unseen. Life, perhaps. Now my mind caught up with the action. Someone had shot Waldo Morse, right there on Fifth Avenue, in New York City, at two o'clock in the afternoon at the height of the Christmas season.

"Oh, my God!" I said, attempting to push through the crowd that had stopped to gawk at the fallen Kris Kringle. I fell to my knees and reached through legs that separated me from him. "Waldo, Waldo," I said, my fingertips touching his beard. I couldn't see him, but one of his hands gripped mine. I looked up into the faces of the men and women witnessing his death. "Please, do something," I said. "Get help. Call the police. Call an ambulance." But I knew it was too late. As I implored those surrounding me to act, his grasp loosened and his hand fell to the cold Manhattan pavement.

I slowly stood and extended my hands in a gesture of utter helplessness and frustration. Then, I saw him, not the person who'd shot Waldo, but the priest I'd seen the previous day. He was short and stocky, and his complexion was swarthy.

I started to say something to him, but as I did, his face turned sour. He had black eyes that bore into me. He turned and walked away.

"Father," I shouted, "Father . . ." My words had no effect. He was gone, swallowed by the throng of humanity that was Fifth Avenue that December day.

Chapter Four

A police car arrived, and three men got out. Two wore uniforms; the other was a plainclothes detective. Fast, I thought. They must have been passing by. They moved the large crowd back, and one of them crouched and pressed fingertips against Waldo's neck. He looked up at the detective and shook his head.

"Anybody see what happened here?" the detective asked in a loud, surprisingly high voice. He was short and compact; dark, thin hair trailed upward in wispy curls.

There were no responses. Most people who'd witnessed the murder had walked away.

"Nobody saw nothing?" he asked, louder this time.

"I did," I said. The words came from me as though spoken by someone else. The detective turned in my direction and frowned. "You saw him get shot?"

"Yes, I did." I approached. "So did a lot of other people," I said.

The detective looked into other faces. Some of the people belonging to them shrugged and shook their heads. "I didn't see anything," a man said. "Nothing," said a woman. "I just got here."

"This is outrageous," I said, looking directly at those I knew had witnessed the murder. "Don't any of you have a sense of civic responsibility?" I'd heard stories of New Yorkers' penchant for looking the other way, but this was ridiculous.

They looked at me as though I were demented. Most left. Heavy with guilt, I hoped. I said to the detective, "My name is Jessica Fletcher. I was here when this man was shot."

"You saw it happen? You saw everything?"

"Well, not everything, but enough. I saw who shot him."

"You did?"

"Not to the extent that I could identify the person, but I did catch a glance. It was . . . I think, it was a man, although, I admit, it could have been a woman."

The detective's pained expression mirrored his thoughts. Of course, his expression might have passed for sweetness if he knew that not only did I know the victim, I'd come to this street corner specifically to meet with him.

I'd gone through an internal debate about telling the police what I knew about Waldo Morse but decided to wait. Not there, not with his body on a slab of cement in front of Saks. It wasn't only a question of place and time, however. Waldo's life since leaving Cabot Cove had been anything but routine. Because it involved elements of secrecy—and danger—I hadn't wanted to place him in physical jeopardy. That's why I'd been so circumspect in approaching him initially. But as I looked down at his lifeless body, I knew such concern was all academic now. Yes, I'd tell the police what I knew. But later. Time and place.

I'd also made a snap decision about the photographs I'd taken. I would have the film developed. If the pictures showed anything that might be of help to authorities, I would turn them over. Not before.

As the detective jotted in a small notebook, an Emergency Medical Services ambulance parted the heavy traffic with its piercing siren and joined the patrol car at the curb. A young man and a young woman in white uniforms jumped from the vehicle. The detective raised his hand. "Take it easy," he said. "He's a stiff."

His words assailed me. I didn't like the way he'd referred to the body. Waldo deserved more dignity than that. I didn't say anything, however. I didn't need a detective berating me.

I watched with a mixture of horror and relief as the medical personnel wrapped Waldo's body in a soiled sheet, placed it on a stretcher, and slid it into the back of the ambulance.

"All right, all right, everybody move on. The show is over," the detective said. Then, to my amazement, they climbed back into their patrol car.

I ran up to it. "Officer! Don't you want to question me as a witness?"

He looked at me with that same sour expression. "Lady, it's not like the mayor got killed here."

"I don't believe this," I said. "A man has been murdered. I was a witness. You can't just drive away."

One of the officers in the front seat laughed. I said in a louder voice, "I insist upon giving a statement." I wasn't sure I should be insisting upon anything, but didn't know what else to do. The police do not just walk away from a witness to a murder.

Do they?

The driver had started the engine. The detective told him to shut it off, opened the door, and invited me to join him in the back. I looked around. Dozens of people, most of them newcomers to what had happened, watched. I managed a weak smile and joined him in the car.

"Name?" the detective said, a notebook in his left hand, a pen in his right.

"Jessica Fletcher."

"What accent is that?"

"Accent? I'm from Maine. Cabot Cove, Maine."

"What are you doing in New York?"

"The same thing many people are doing, visiting friends and doing Christmas shopping." He wrote the words "Maine" and "Christmas shopping" on his pad.

"What did you see?" he asked.

"I saw . . . I was standing on the corner when a man . . . or, as I said, possibly a woman . . . stepped up to the Santa Claus, put a gun in his stomach, and pulled the trigger."

"Description of alleged assailant?"

"Medium height, wore a stocking cap and a scarf brought up high around the chin." I demonstrated with my hands. "He, or she, wore a black raincoat."

"You see the color of the hair? Eyes? Skin?"

I ruefully shook my head.

"Where did the alleged assailant go after he—or she—pulled the trigger?"

"I don't know. It happened so fast. The person was there, and then he or she wasn't."

"No idea?"

"No. No idea."

The detective closed the notebook and put it in his pocket. "Well, thank you, Mrs. Fletcher, for coming forward. You've been very helpful." His sarcasm was not lost on me.

"Don't you want to know how to reach me?" I asked.

"Maine. What town did you say it was?"

"Cabot Cove, but I'm staying in New York through the new year."

"Well, have a nice day. Welcome to the Big Apple."

"May I have your name and badge number, please?" I took out my own notebook and pen.

He stared at me.

"I'd like to be able to contact you to see how things are progressing with this case. After all, I did witness the murder. I think I'm entitled to that courtesy."

His sigh was deep. "Rizzi," he said. "Alphonse Rizzi. Badge number one-three-nine-zero, Detective. Narcotics."

I wrote it down and thanked him. "I'm sure you won't mind my calling to check on your progress."

"I'll really look forward to it, Mrs. Fletcher."

I was expected to leave the car, and did. I stood at the curb and watched it pull away, my mind still bewildered by what I considered to be an appalling lack of professional interest on the part of the police. It was beyond me that they could take so cavalier a position where not only had a murder taken place in their city, the victim had been a sidewalk Santa Claus collecting money for the needy. I've always understood the need for police to assume a detached, perhaps even callous attitude toward death—like doctors and nurses—but this man had carried it to extremes.

As I watched the patrol car wind its way through the heavy traffic, someone tapped my shoulder. I turned and looked into the eyes of a young man wearing a red-and-black plaid jacket and yellow earmuffs. He hadn't shaved in days; he had the Don Johnson look, which I thought had gone out with the Eighties.

"You photographed the murder," he said.

"Pardon?"

"Somebody told me you took pictures while it was happening."

"Whether I did or not is none of your business."

He smiled. "Maybe it should be. Look, I'm with the *Post*. This could be a big story, especially if we've got a dynamite photo for Page One."

"Well, that may be true, but you won't get any 'dynamite photo' from me."

I started to move past him, but he blocked my way. "Don't I know you from someplace?" he asked.

"I'm sure you don't," I said, attempting once again to leave but finding my progress impeded.

"Yeah, I know who you are. Jessica Fletcher. I saw you on the Larry King Show last night."

"That has nothing to do with whether I took pictures or not."

"Are you kidding, Mrs. Fletcher? If the famous Jessica

Fletcher, big-time murder mystery writer, actually took pictures of a Santa Claus getting iced on Fifth Avenue in front of Saks, that is a very big story." He strung out the final words.

"What is your name?" I asked.

"Johnson. Bobby Johnson."

"Well, Mr. Johnson, I admire your tenacity as a journalist, but I'm afraid we have nothing to talk about."

I walked as quickly as I could, which wasn't easy with the holiday crowds, and stopped occasionally to glance over my shoulder. Sure enough, Mr. Johnson was following. After I'd gone a few blocks, I paused at a corner, waited for him to catch up and said as sternly as possible, "Mr. Johnson, I did not take any photographs. But if I did, I would not share them with you to create a lurid front page for your newspaper. Understood?"

"Give me a break, Mrs. Fletcher. I've been dry for too long. I need a piece like this. The paper pays good for pictures. If we could get an exclusive, firsthand account from you of the murder, they'll really put up bucks. Besides, you're here promoting your new book. You could do worse than the front page of the *Post*."

"You're right," I said pleasantly, "but I'd rather never sell another book than use the murder of a . . ." I'd almost said old friend and was relieved I hadn't. "Good-bye, Mr. Johnson."

A taxi pulled up and a couple got out. I quickly got in, slammed the door, and told the driver to take me to the Dakota. Johnson stood on the curb, a big smile on his face, which said many things, including that he would find out where I was staying while in New York, which is not difficult for a good journalist with connections. I dwelled on that probability for a block or two until thoughts of Waldo Morse took over, and the grimy backseat of a New York taxi, driven by a madman with a lead foot, was filled with memories.

Chapter Five

By the time I reached the apartment and had received my customary warm, wet welcome from Sadie and Rose, the impact of the afternoon finally hit me. There hadn't been time to have a proper emotional reaction at the scene. My mind had been occupied by the arrival of the police, the conversation with Detective Rizzi, and my experience with Bobby Johnson, the *Post* reporter.

Now, in the welcome quiet of the living room, I began to tremble; my nerve endings were like exposed, sputtering electric wires. I went to the liquor cabinet and poured myself a larger snifter of Vaughan's favorite, Blanton's Bourbon, than I would have under ordinary circumstances. I took the drink to my bedroom, stripped off my clothes, put on a powder blue sweat suit I'd packed in case I had the energy and urge to walk laps in Manhattan (I hadn't), covered it with my robe, and returned to the living room where I sat in a chair that had unofficially become mine since arriving.

Waldo Morse had been born and raised in Cabot Cove. His family owned a small motel on the outskirts of town, which gave Waldo exposure to a wider variety of people than most other youngsters his age. Not that Morse's Blueberry Motel attracted a sophisticated group of world travelers. But interesting people had stayed there: some to fish the trout- and salmon-laden streams, many to enjoy the spectacular fall foliage, others just passing through on their way to other places.

Waldo was, as I recalled, a "good boy." He worked hard at the motel when he was old enough to shoulder some of the responsibility, and was an average student at Cabot Cove High School. He was best known for his exploits on the football field, an outstanding running back who'd been voted to the first-string all-Maine team his senior year.

Waldo attended a junior college for a year, maybe two, and stayed in Cabot Cove. He married a girl he'd dated in high school, and they quickly had two children. It wasn't easy for me to remember these details because I had never been a personal friend of Waldo and Nancy Morse. In fact, I only saw them once every couple of months in a store, or when passing in a car, and had virtually no firsthand knowledge of their life together. But there was the powerful Cabot Cove gossip mill that ensured that no one could ever live a truly private life there.

While taking marine biology courses in the junior college, Waldo had become fascinated with the sea and signed on as a hand on local lobster boats that left each morning from the town dock. Then, if memory serves, he bought his own lobster boat and moved south to picturesque, touristy Ogunquit, where I was told he became a relatively successful fisherman. It struck me as strange at the time because Nancy and the kids remained in Cabot Cove. His decision to move to Ogunquit had something to do, as I recall, with less competition there. But the real reason, according to more credible informants, was that Waldo and Nancy weren't getting along. That version proved out when the divorce came, evidently an amicable one because Waldo returned to Cabot Cove on a regular basis to visit his family.

While we kept up with Waldo Morse's life through the grapevine, one aspect of it suddenly became public knowledge, not only in Cabot Cove but in all of Maine, and undoubtedly beyond. He was arrested in Ogunquit and charged with drug smuggling.

According to newspaper accounts—embellished by those who claimed to have the "straight scoop"—Waldo had allowed his lobster boat to be used by drug runners from the Caribbean and Florida. These dealers would place narcotics in watertight containers in Waldo's lobster traps—lobster "cars"—to be picked up later by Waldo and delivered to other members of the drug ring somewhere in Maine. Most of the drugs ended up in Boston, said the reports, although that was never confirmed.

It was anticipated that Waldo would receive a stiff jail sentence. But a deal was struck. He turned states evidence in return for immunity and a place in the Federal Witness Protection Program. The trial ended, the major figures were convicted and sentenced to long prison terms, and Waldo vanished.

That was the last I'd heard of him until that fateful afternoon on Fifth Avenue.

Waldo's ex-wife, Nancy, was a clean-cut, rosy-cheeked, and energetic young blonde who'd been a popular cheerleader in high school. A good mother, it was said, and a woman who kept a low profile in Cabot Cove. After Waldo became a prosecution witness, there was natural and justifiable concern for the safety of Nancy and her children. But nothing happened to them, and those fears eventually dissipated.

Some of my friends speculated that because Waldo had lived in Ogunquit and was divorced, the drug dealers with whom he'd become involved never knew he had a family in Cabot Cove. If that was true, Nancy Morse and the kids were fortunate. From what I'd always heard, people involved in the drug world don't differentiate between women, children, and husband-informants.

Nancy and the kids stayed in Cabot Cove after Waldo's submersion into the famous but flawed witness protection program. The kids continued in school, and she ran her home and life quietly.

I suffered a sudden chill and walked to the center of the living room. Would the police know that Waldo had been in the witness protection program, and as a result simply bury him without notifying anyone?

What a horrible contemplation. Nancy Morse certainly should be made aware of her ex-husband's demise. My shoulders felt heavy as I realized I might be the only person in a position to break that sorry news to her. But I resolved not to let that happen. I would call Detective

Rizzi first thing in the morning and demand that an official notification of his death be delivered to the family. But then I wondered if notifying Nancy Morse that her husband had been murdered would place her and her children in jeopardy? How did the witness protection program work? Were the families of such individuals taken care of, informed of death, counseled, given some sort of insurance proceeds to help them continue with their lives? These questions, and many more, were gnawing at me when Vaughan Buckley turned his key in the door and stepped into the apartment.

"Jessica. I didn't think you'd be back so early."

"I didn't think I would, either."

He made himself a drink and settled across the coffee table from me. "Oh, before I forget," he said, pulling a scrap of paper from his shirt pocket. "My secretary took this message for you. 'Joe Charles. Tell Jessica Fletcher that Joe Charles will know.'"

"What does it mean?" I asked.

Vaughan laughed. "Beats me, but that's exactly what the message was. 'Joe Charles. Tell Jessica Fletcher that Joe Charles will know.'"

"Who left the message?"

"According to my secretary, the caller hung up without giving his name."

Until then, I hadn't said anything to Vaughan about Waldo Morse. But I wanted to share it with someone. Because Vaughan sat in front of me, he became the obvious choice. I told him everything that had happened since first spotting Waldo.

"That's a remarkable story, Jess," Vaughan said. "You know nothing about his life after the trial ended?"

I shook my head. "Nothing. Obviously, he ended up in New York, and at the time of his death was playing Santa Claus on the street."

"It sounds like those people he turned in got even," Vaughan said.

"That would seem the logical explanation, although I learned years ago to not always accept logical explanations, especially where murder is involved. My major concern is that his family be properly notified. Do you think the police will do that?"

"If they know who he is."

"Exactly what I was thinking. Someone in the witness protection program would have false identity. I can't imagine Waldo carrying anything to indicate that he has a family back in Cabot Cove. In fact, I'd be surprised if he didn't take special steps to see that they were never linked to him."

"What do you know about his family?" Vaughan asked.

"Not much. His wife and children are still there, but once Waldo left, he became an unknown person."

"Any idea of his life here in New York, aside from playing Santa on a street corner?" Vaughan asked.

"No, but I think I have an obligation to find out."

Vaughan smiled. "You can't resist getting involved in this sort of thing, can you?"

"I don't think it's a matter of satisfying personal needs. But yes, I do have a certain fascination with murder. You and my readers should appreciate that."

Vaughan stretched and stood. "All I can say, Jess, is go slow and be careful. The witness protection program is a strange world, filled with bad people and even worse motives. Sure you just don't want to forget it, finish up promoting your book and head back to Cabot Cove to start your next one for us?"

I sighed. "The idea is tempting, but I have to find out what happened. I won't burden you and Olga. Would you prefer that I move into a hotel? That would give me more freedom and . . ."

"Freedom? You make us sound like jailers. You can come and go as you please. If Olga and I can be of any help, including with this Waldo Morse business, just yell. We're both very fond of you, Jess."

The dogs, Sadie and Rose, came to my chair, one on each side, and placed their chins on my lap. I rubbed them in the groove between their eyes.

"Looks like they're fond of you, too," Vaughan said.

I stood and said, "The look in Waldo's eyes the first time I saw him was like a frightened, tired dog that's been on the run for a long time. Thank you for being such a good friend, Vaughan. I think I'll take a bath and get dressed. We are having dinner out again, I assume. Not good for my commitment to a slimmer waistline."

"Indulge yourself while you're here, Jess. Once you're back in Cabot Cove, you can diet all you want. When you're our guest in New York, indulgence is expected."

I laughed. "The problem is I'm about to indulge myself in investigating the murder of a former drug runner turned Santa Claus. While that might not put weight on me, it certainly weighs heavy. See you in an hour."

Chapter Six

We had dinner in a private room of a Japanese restaurant called Nippon. The presentation of the food was beautiful, and some of the dishes, especially something called *Sake Kawayaki*—smoked salmon skin soaked in sake and broiled to crisp perfection—were delicious to this pedestrian palate. But not to the extent of abandoning my love of lobster cookouts, homemade biscuits, corn-on-the-cob, and blueberry pie.

We sat on silk cushions on the floor (more suited to a younger person's vertebrae), and were joined around the black-lacquered table by another of Buckley House's authors, Harrison Libby, and his wife, Zelda. Mr. Libby had written a book in which he traced the sexual lineage of four-legged animals to us two-legged species. He had flowing white hair, wore jeans and a sari, and was inordinately fond of four-letter words. Zelda claimed to be an interior decorator; her choice of makeup and clothing did little to instill in me any faith in her ability to create a harmonious setting. Still, it was an interesting evening, but could have ended sooner.

To be honest, the real problem with dinner was me. As hard as I tried to focus on what Libby and his wife were saying, I had trouble shifting gears and setting aside Waldo Morse for longer than minutes at a time. Had I not thought it rude, I would have taken out a pad and pencil, and made notes about how I intended to initiate my investigation. I just hoped that time and the sake would not cause me to forget what I'd been thinking during dinner. The minute I returned to the apartment, I went to my room and wrote down every thought I could resurrect.

Had it been earlier, I would have called my physician friend in Cabot Cove, Seth Hazlitt. The message Vaughan had given me, that someone named Joe Charles would know, intrigued me. I might not have thought anything of it except that the name rang a distant bell. For some reason I connected it with Cabot Cove, although I couldn't put my finger on why. Seth, who prided himself on remembering everything about the people of the town, might have a better recollection than mine. But I didn't want to awaken him. Most people in Cabot Cove go to bed early and get up even earlier. The call would have to wait until morning.

As far as I knew (and any knowledge I had was only hearsay), Waldo's wife and children had not been financially deprived by his entrance into the witness protection program. I'd heard from the mailman, local merchants, and others in Cabot Cove that they seemed to be quite comfortable. A large addition had been put on the house, a new cherry red Volvo station wagon and a black-and-gold Jeep Wrangler sat in the driveway, and the mailman regularly delivered videotapes, compact discs, and books from clubs to which Nancy belonged. Did the authorities who managed the witness protection program take especially good care of the families of people involved in it? That was one of the things I hoped to find out.

Where had Waldo lived in New York City? He'd played Santa Claus, which meant someone had to have hired him. But he'd likely used another name because of the need for his underground existence. What identification was on his person when he was shot? I should have asked, another question to raise with Detective Rizzi.

Had Waldo been in contact with his wife and children once he'd turned state's evidence? I wasn't aware that he had, although that didn't prove anything. Maybe there were channels through which people in his circumstances maintained a relationship with family. Nancy Morse would be the best source of information about that.

I thought of his parents, but recalled that both had died in a fire at the motel. It was now a fast-food outlet.

My list was growing too long, each question leading to at least two others. I decided the best thing was a good night's sleep, provided my mind would indulge me that luxury.

I announced through a series of yawns that I was going to bed, but I'd taken only a few steps toward my room when the phone rang.

"At this hour?" Olga Buckley said.

Vaughan answered, listened intently, then glanced in my direction. "It's for you, Jessica."

Who would be calling me? Not many people knew I was there. I'd left the address and phone number with Seth and Morton Metzger in Cabot Cove, but there was no need for anyone else to have it because all my arrangements in New York were handled through Buckley House.

"Hello," I said.

"Mrs. Fletcher. Bobby Johnson from the *Post*."

"How did you . . . ?" My prophecy had been fulfilled.

"Did you see the story?" he asked.

"What story?"

"About the Santa Claus murder. It's in the edition that just came out."

"No, I have not seen it."

"It wasn't easy getting a good photo of you, but I think the one we went with looks okay."

"Photo? Of me? Why would you— How dare you run my picture?"

"Hey, Mrs. Fletcher, I know a big one when I see it. There's no sense in us being on opposite sides in this thing. Play ball with me, and we'll both make out good."

"I have nothing further to say until I see the story. Thank you for telling me about it."

"My pleasure. By the way, I've done a little digging. Looks to me like it might have been a drug hit."

I was speechless. Had he pierced the veil of secrecy surrounding Waldo? Did he know about the trial, about Waldo turning state's evidence, about his having entered the witness protection program and disappearing for all these years? If so, he was an even better reporter than I'd given him credit for. No, more than that. He was world-class.

It struck me that I could benefit from staying in touch with him, as unpleasant a contemplation as that was. I knew very little about New York City; he obviously knew a great deal. "Mr. Johnson," I said, "I'll look at the story, and then perhaps we can talk. How do I reach you?"

He gave me numbers at the *Post* and at home. "Call any time, day or night, Mrs. Fletcher. I swiped a copy of your latest novel from our book reviewer's desk. Looks like you're about to get a million dollars worth of publicity. Hope your publisher appreciates it."

"I . . . Good night, Mr. Johnson." I turned to Vaughan and Olga. "That was a reporter from the *New York Post*." I said. "They've done a story about Waldo Morse's murder and used a picture of me."

Vaughan put on his coat, "I'll run out and get a copy," he said. "Be back in a few minutes."

Ten minutes later he stood in the doorway holding up a copy of the paper. Most of the front page was taken up with the photograph of me. An insert in the lower right-hand corner was a picture of a very dead Santa Claus. The headline in large type read:

SANTA DEAD

A smaller headline beneath it said:

DRUG DEALERS RUB OUT KRIS KRINGLE. XMAS CANCELED.

Beneath my picture was the caption:

Famed murder mystery writer Jessica Fletcher, who witnessed the slaughter on Fifth Avenue, is reported to have photographed the entire event and will devote her yuletide New York holiday to solving this brutal, distinctly unseasonable crime.

Chapter Seven

Once the initial shock of the Post's front page had passed, I sat down with Vaughan and Olga to read the story that took up all of Page Three and jumped to another page deeper inside. Initially, I think, Vaughan found the situation somewhat amusing. But then when he read that I was staying with my publisher and his wife in their "palatial" apartment in the Dakota, the bemused smile on his lips turned to a hard line. "We'll be inundated with press and curiosity seekers," he muttered.

"I'm sorry about this, Vaughan," I said. "I hope you know I didn't tell the reporter I was staying here."

"Of course you didn't. The question is, how do we handle this?"

I said, "I think I should move to a hotel."

"What good will that do?" Olga asked. "They'll find you wherever you go."

"Yes, but the burden won't be on you."

"Absolutely not," Vaughan said. He paced the large room. "We'll gut this out together. Besides, as long as it's happened, we all have to admit it will help sell your book."

I felt a twinge of resentment. He was right, of course, but I wished he hadn't seen it that way.

"I suggest we all try to get some sleep," Olga said. "Looks like it could be a busy day tomorrow."

The phone rang.

"Or tonight," Vaughan said, answering. It was a local radio station wanting to interview me. Vaughan cupped his hand over the mouthpiece and told me the nature of the call, his eyebrows arched into question marks. I shook my head. "Sorry, Mrs. Fletcher isn't available at the moment," he said.

The phone rang again. And again. All media, and all wanting interviews with me.

"This is horrendous," I said. "I cannot subject you to this. Have your publicity people find me a secure hotel tomorrow."

Olga protested again, but Vaughan held up his hand. "Maybe Jessica is right, Olga. Not for our sake, of course, but she might feel better handling this in the impersonal atmosphere of a hotel suite. We'll talk about it in the morning." He put on the answering machine, smiled smugly, and said, "You can call them back tomorrow, Jess—if you choose to."

I lay on my bed stiff as a board, eyes wide open, ears picking up the ring of the telephone and the faint sound of Vaughan's voice informing callers that the phone couldn't or wouldn't be answered at the moment. "Leave your message after the beep and . . ."

I needed sleep. But when I was still awake at four the next morning, I gave up, clicked on the light next to the bed, and sat against the pink tufted headboard. Seth Hazlitt usually got up a little after five. He wouldn't be too upset—would he?—getting started an hour earlier. He answered on the first ring, the result of years of calls at odd hours from pregnant women about to deliver.

"Awful early to be callin', isn't it, Jess?"

"I know, and I apologize, but I had to. Seth, have you heard what happened to me yesterday?"

"Happened to you? Haven't heard a thing."

"There hasn't been news there about the murder I witnessed?"

He was now fully awake. "Run that by me again," he said.

I told him as succinctly as possible what had happened to me on Fifth Avenue, and its aftermath. When I finished my capsulized tale, I was met with silence. "Seth? Are you there?"

"Ayuh, I'm here. Waldo Morse? Sure, I remember him. I remember even better him gettin' involved with drug pushers from down south. You sure it was him?"

"Positive."

"You say they claim you took pictures of it?"

"Yes. Because I did. I have the roll of film in my camera."

He groaned. "Don't talk about things like that on the phone, Jess. You should know better."

"You asked, Seth and . . ."

"Let's get off that subject," he said. "What do you want me to do?"

"Nothing. No, not true. I received a mysterious message. It came through my publisher. The caller, who didn't give his name, said that Joe Charles would know."

"Know what?"

"I don't know, but the name is familiar. Maybe it has something to do with Waldo's murder. Maybe not. Does the name Joe Charles mean anything to you?"

"Nope, but I'll give it some good thought once I'm showered and garbed up. Got plenty of time to do that this particular mornin'."

I didn't apologize again because there was an unmistakable chuckle in his voice. I said, "I really would appreciate that, Seth. I'll be out all morning, but I'll be back here this afternoon. I might check into a hotel."

"Don't do that, Jess. Better to be with friends at a time like this."

"Yes, I know but . . ."

"You listen to me, Jessica Fletcher. I've never steered you wrong. You stay away from those New York City hotels. Heah?"

I smiled. "Yes, I hear. I'm signing books this morning at a store that specializes in murder mysteries, and I have a radio interview at eleven. I don't think I have a lunch appointment, so I'll be back here at noon, maybe a little later. If you come up with anything about Joe Charles, call me. If you get the answering machine, leave a message and I'll get back to you."

"I hate those answering machines, and you know it. I always hang up on 'em."

"Don't hang up on this one. Thank you, Seth. You're a dear."

Talking to him had a medicinal effect on me. I quickly fell asleep, only to be awakened at six by Olga's rap on my door. I wasn't due at the store until nine-thirty. "Sorry to get you up so early, Jess, but the number of calls that came in during the night is overwhelming. The doorman says there are at least thirty members of the press downstairs and an even bigger crowd watching them."

"Oh, goodness, what have I gotten me—and you—into?"

She smiled broadly. "Don't worry about it. Things were getting dull around here anyway. Come, have some breakfast."

The limousine provided by Buckley House was waiting in front of the Dakota. Ruth Lazzara, more ebullient than she'd been on the previous day—if that were possible—sat inside. On her lap were a half-dozen copies of the *Post*. She said before I even had a chance to fully enter the limo, "Fantastic! You are amazing, Mrs. Fletcher."

"I didn't do anything except have the misfortune of witnessing a murder."

"But how perfect. The world's most famous mystery writer being the key witness in a sensational killing."

I wanted to debate the issue but decided not to bother. Each person has his or her private prism through which events are refracted. This young woman was charged by her publisher with getting maximum publicity for its au thors. The fact that this bonanza was the result of a tragic circumstance meant little. As the old saying goes, "Say what you want, but spell my name right."

If I'd been impressed by the line of people waiting for my previous book signing, this morning's crowd was staggering. Hundreds of people milled about outside Dastardly Acts, a small bookstore specializing in books about murder and other antisocial behavior. Joining them was a caravan of media vehicles that followed us from the Dakota, including a car containing the *Post* reporter who had started all the hoopla, Bobby Johnson. He'd shaved, and wore a suit and tie this morning. His celebrity status had obviously risen along with mine.

Ruth and I were ushered into the store by the owner, Winston Whitlock, and two uniformed private security guards. Once safely inside, Mr. Whitlock, a tall, skeletal man with white hair and gray cheeks, and wearing a string tie whose clip was a copper disc on which was etched "MURDER PAYS," said anxiously, "I'm afraid we're going to have to cancel this, Mrs. Fletcher. The crowd is too big. There's no way we can assure your safety and the security of our customers."

"I hope you realize this was not my intention," I said. "I looked forward to a quiet book signing in this lovely shop."

"I know, but that's all a thing of the past."

Ruth said, "Why cancel? This is the best thing that could ever happen to this store. How many copies of Mrs. Fletcher's new book do you have?"

The manager shrugged. "Fifty, I think."

"Where's the phone?" Ruth asked. Whitlock pointed to his desk. She dialed a number and said in a semi-hysterical voice, "We need two hundred copies of Fletcher's book for the signing at Dastardly Acts. Get a messenger. Bring them yourself. Just get them here."

"I think Mr. Whitlock is right," I said.

Ruth hung up. "I'll make that decision, Mrs. Fletcher." Before I could respond, she said to Whitlock, "If you're concerned about security, hire more guards. Bucklev House will pay for them."

Whitlock looked at me in confusion, then told an assistant to call the security firm and order more men.

"Perhaps I should just leave and . . ."

Ruth responded by taking my elbow and moving me to a table that had been set up for the autographing. "Why don't you just sit down, Mrs. Fletcher, and start signing books."

My expression reminded her that I didn't sign books ahead of time. "All right, sit and make yourself comfortable." To the manager, she said, "Could you get Mrs. Fletcher coffee, maybe some Danish."

I said I wasn't hungry.

One of the guards stationed at the front door came to where Whitlock was perched on the edge of the table next to me. "Sir, the police are here."

"I don't want any trouble," Whitlock said, his voice flighty, his hands flapping in the air as though he wanted to fly south.

"It's a detective named Rizzi. He wants to talk to Mrs. Fletcher."

I looked up at him. "Detective Rizzi. I intended to speak with him today. This would be as good a time as any."

The guard ignored my words and looked to the man who was paying him. "Let him in," Whitlock said, abject despair in his voice.

Rizzi came through the door with another man, a much taller and more corpulent detective wearing a green raincoat. I stood. "Good morning, Detective Rizzi."

"Good morning, Mrs. Fletcher. This is Detective Ryan."

"Good morning to you, Detective Ryan. Would you like coffee?"

Ms. Lazzara interjected, looking at her watch, "Could we make this quick? We're due to start autographing in ten minutes."

"Who are you?" Rizzi asked.

"This is Ms. Lazzara. She's in charge of publicity for my new book."

"Yeah, well, I don't think there's going to be any autographing today." Rizzi looked directly at me.

"Mrs. Fletcher, we want you to come downtown with us."

"I intended to do that later in the day. I have a number of questions I'd like answered."

Rizzi and Ryan looked at each other. "*You* have questions to ask *us*? I think it's the other way around, Mrs. Fletcher. You're a material witness to a murder."

I suppose my face mirrored everything I was thinking. His expression didn't change, however, nor did that of his colleague. I said haughtily, "I am well aware that I was a witness to a murder. I came forward, which is more than I can say for anyone else who was there. I actually had to pursue you in order to give you my name and where I was staying. You were totally disinterested. Now you come in here and announce to me that I am a material witness, as though you had to track me down. Are you about to arrest me?"

Rizzi winced. "Calm down, Mrs. Fletcher. It was a busy day, people getting zipped all over town. Anyway, I didn't know who you were. I don't read much, but my wife, Emily, reads all the time. She saw the *Post* story and got excited. She says you're one of the best mystery writers in the world."

"That's flattering, Detective, but I don't know what it has to do with your change in attitude about my being a witness."

"It has nothing to do with it. Just come with us."

I shrugged at Ruth and Whitlock.

"The signing will only take an hour," Ruth said. "Surely, you can allow her that."

"I got my orders," Rizzi said.

I said to the others, "Sorry, but I think I have to go with the gentlemen."

"This is outrageous!" Ruth said. "Give me your name and badge number."

Rizzi winced again, an expression I was to see often over the ensuing days. "You, too?" he said to Ruth. He mumbled his name and number.

As I started to put on my coat, Rizzi said, "Before we go, maybe you could sign one of your books to Emily. Make it to Emily and her mother, Mrs. Wilson.

"The nerve," Ruth said.

"You certainly do have a different approach to things, Detective," I said, picking up a copy of my book, opening it, and writing: "To Emily and Mrs. Wilson." Under it I scribbled, "It must be very exciting having a New York City detective in the family." I signed and handed it to him. He muttered a form of thanks and led me from the store.

The crowds had swelled outside. Bobby Johnson, the

Post reporter, was right up front. "Mrs. Fletcher. Where are you going?" he yelled.

"To police headquarters, I think I'm being detained, if not arrested." I added, "Thanks to you and your story."

Johnson ignored my comment and asked the detectives where they were taking me. They didn't answer. Ryan held open the back door of an unmarked car.

Ruth came running from the store and shouted, "Don't forget the interview at eleven." She shoved a piece of paper with the address of the radio station through the partially opened rear window. I dropped it to the floor. Somehow, I knew that particular radio show would be minus one guest that morning. Hopefully, the host was comfortable with soliloquizing.

Chapter Eight

The few individuals who end up in Morton Metzger's Cabot Cove police headquarters are usually impressed with how clean and cheerful it is. Of course, it doesn't get a great deal of use—an occasional drunk given a cell in which to sleep it off, an out-of-state motorist speeding through town and demonstrating too much big-city bravado for Morton's taste, or occasionally someone who's committed a more serious crime like poaching blueberries. Or murder.

The police headquarters to which I was taken by detectives Rizzi and Ryan looked as though it had been created by a Hollywood set designer for a documentary on poverty. Pea green walls hadn't been painted in years, and what paint was left hung in flaky sheets. The furniture was battered and scarred, and the windows were dirty to the extent that I couldn't see through them. A heavy, pungent cloud of tobacco, body odor, and urine hung palpably over everything.

Most disconcerting, at least for me, was the noise level. Back home, Sheriff Metzger plays tapes he's made from his collection of Kostelanetz and Montovani recordings, which he claims is the largest in Maine. But there was no music in this New York City precinct. Dozens of people milled about, all yelling at each other. A long wooden bench was crammed with men and women under arrest and waiting to be processed. They looked as though the predicament wasn't new to them or, in some cases, even unpleasant.

I wished I were somewhere else.

"Come on, Mrs. Fletcher, we can talk better in one of the interview rooms."

Interview? Interesting genteel euphemism for interrogation, or grilling. No matter. I was relieved to enter the room and have the door close behind me; the outside din was muffled by half.

"Have a seat, Mrs. Fletcher," Rizzi said. He picked up the phone and said, "Get in here!" Minutes later a young female uniformed officer appeared carrying a courtroom stenographer's machine. She didn't acknowledge me, nor I her.

"Make yourself at home," Rizzi said to me.

Make myself at home, I thought. Not easy to do in such surroundings. I pulled out a wooden chair with one arm missing and sat in it. It was uncomfortable not because the arm was missing, or because the seat was hard, but because it seemed to lean forward. "I think the legs on this chair are broken," I said.

Rizzi uttered what might be characterized as a laugh. "The front legs are cut off an inch, Mrs. Fletcher. Keeps suspects leaning forward and off-balance."

"Am I sitting in this chair because I am a suspect?" I asked.

"You didn't whack Santa Claus."

"You're quite right, Detective Rizzi. I did not 'whack' Santa Claus. Now, could we get to the point of bringing me here? I intended to call you today and arrange for a time to meet, but you usurped that prerogative."

"Whatever you say, Mrs. Fletcher." Rizzi sat in his own shaky chair across the table from me. "Let's see the pictures."

"Pardon?"

"The pictures, Mrs. Fletcher. I can read. The *Post* says you took pictures of the murder. I'd like to have them." I started to say something but he quickly added, "Strike that, Mrs. Fletcher. I want them."

He sounded like he meant it. I still didn't want to turn over the roll of film until I'd had a chance to have it developed, which I intended to do that day. I'd pushed a little button on my camera that allowed me to rewind the film before the roll was finished and had placed it in my purse. I smiled. "Detective Rizzi, I'm surprised that someone in your position would believe everything they read in the press, especially a paper like the *Post*."

"Nothin' wrong with the *Post*, Mrs. Fletcher. I suppose you're the *Times* and *Wall Street Journal* type."

"I read those papers, but I wouldn't classify myself as a 'type.'" I waited. The stenographer looked up and waited, too. Rizzi was slumped in his chair, his chin on his breastbone, his dark eyes looking at me from beneath heavy brows. He said in a gruff voice without raising his chin, "Mrs. Fletcher, *finita la commedia.*"

"I don't know what that means," I said.

"It means the game is up. The farce is over. You don't speak Italian?"

"No, I don't."

"Yeah, well, I forget a lot of it because I'm not married to an Italian woman, but when I visit my mother, she talks Italian and some of it sticks. By the way, thanks for the book for Emily. She'll really appreciate it, probably send you a note. She likes writing notes to people."

"That's a nice trait."

"Yeah, I suppose it is. The film, Mrs. Fletcher. Where is it?"

While the sparring had been almost enjoyable, I also knew that the time for bantering was over. As much as I wanted to have the film developed myself, I decided I was asking for big trouble by continuing to withhold it. "All right," I said, "I never intended to not give you the prints. I wanted a chance to see them first. Obviously, I won't be able to do that." I opened my purse and reached in. The roll of film did not immediately fall under my fingers, and I began to rummage. When that didn't produce a result, I opened the bag wide and used my eyes, as well as my fingers. Nothing. It wasn't there.

"Something wrong, Mrs. Fletcher?"

"Yes. I put the film in this purse last night. It seems to be missing."

"Missing? What did it do, develop itself and take a walk?"

"No, I don't think it did that. I can't explain it, but I did take the roll of film from my camera last night and put it in this purse. I could not be mistaken about that."

He narrowed his eyes and snorted.

I shrugged and extended my hands. "I'm not lying to you. The film was here. Now it isn't, and I am as distressed as you are."

"Don't count on it, Mrs. Fletcher. This is a serious matter. I could charge you with withholding state's evidence."

"But I didn't do anything with the evidence. I'm trying to be cooperative, but the film simply isn't here."

He expelled an impatient, exaggerated sigh. "Okay, Mrs. Fletcher, we'll skip the photographs for now and get a statement from you about what you saw yesterday."

My personal debate over telling the police of what I knew about Waldo Morse now turned into an internal shouting match. I was on thin ice and knew it. Rizzi had been pleasant enough, but I didn't harbor any illusions that he couldn't—wouldn't—turn tougher if he thought I was playing games. I had to be honest.

"Detective Rizzi, I knew the man in the Santa Claus costume who was killed."

I'd gotten his attention. He sat up straight, leaned forward, elbows on the table, and opened his eyes wide. "Is that so, Mrs. Fletcher? Suppose you tell me more about that."

It was my turn to sigh. I sat back as best I could and collected my thoughts. "The victim's name was Waldo Morse."

"Morse? That's not what his ID said."

"No, I'm sure it didn't. You see, Waldo Morse grew up in Cabot Cove, the town in Maine where I've lived for a long time. He was a lobster fisherman in Ogunquit until he was accused of using his boat to help smuggle drugs into New

England. He became a witness for federal authorities in return for being taken into the witness protection program.
I hadn't seen or heard of him since that happened, which
was at least ten years ago. Then, as I was walking down
Fifth Avenue, I thought I recognized the Santa Claus. I was
right. It was Waldo. What name was he carrying on his
identification?"

"Mrs. Fletcher, *you* just keep answering *my* questions."

I stiffened. "I don't see why this should be a one-way
street," I said. "I think I have a right to ask questions of my
own."

I detected a slight smile on the stenographer's lips, and
was glad Rizzi hadn't. His response was slow in coming.
"Mrs. Fletcher, you seem like a very nice lady, and I know
you're a famous writer and all that. You're probably down
here in New York having a good time publicizing your new
book, and you probably look at guys like me as though
we're dirtbags."

"Dirtbags?"

"Yeah. Maybe not as good as you and the people you hang
out with. Emily, my wife, sometimes sees me that way. She's
a WASP. She grew up in Jersey where the worst thing ever
happened was the garbage man didn't put the cover back on
the can. She meets me, an Italian from Brooklyn, and falls in
love because she never met an Italian from Brooklyn before.
All she knew were wimpy guys from Jersey. My mother-in-
law, Mrs. Wilson, looks at me funny, too."

"I don't know why she would," I said, wanting to make
him feel better. "Do you always call your mother-in-law
Mrs. Wilson?"

"Yeah. She told me to. She went along with the marriage because she didn't have a choice, but she told me to always call her Mrs. Wilson."

"You don't sound especially fond of her," I said.

"What's to be fond of? She looks down her nose at everybody, especially me, but I have to put up with it. I mean, she is my wife's mother."

"Why are you telling me this?"

He stood, his face hard. "Just to let you know, Mrs. Fletcher, that I'm not what you probably think I am. I know a lot about a lot of things. I know my wines, and I spend a lot of time in museums. You know much about art? You ever hear of Domenikos Theotokopoulos?" He didn't give me a chance to say that I hadn't. "That was El Greco's real name. I like Matisse and Chagall, but I never did like the Cubists. What's your favorite wine?" Again, no time for an answer. "I prefer the softer Burgundies of the côtes de Beaune, and I find a Puligny Montrachet satisfying at certain times."

"Of course," I said.

"You see, Mrs. Fletcher, people like you and Mrs. Wilson underestimate people like me, which can be good because it gives me an edge."

I looked into his black eyes and tried to fathom the psychology behind what he was saying. He was obviously a man who felt there were two worlds—his, and a much larger one made up of people who scorned him. Sad, I thought. I also reminded myself that what he'd said was undoubtedly true. He was a man who always looked for the edge and used it, especially with people "like me."

"So you knew this Waldo Morse. Did you talk to him? Before he was killed, I mean."

"Yes. The day before."

"The day before?"

"That's when I first recognized and approached him. He told me to come back the next day at two. I did, and he was murdered. That's why I was there and saw it happen."

"Did you talk to him yesterday, just before he was shot?"

I shook my head.

"What did you talk about the day before?"

"Nothing." I looked across the table at a stone-faced Rizzi, and my resolve waned. I drew a breath and said, "Again, may I ask what name he was carrying."

"No. Witness protection program? You say this guy was in it?"

"That's my understanding."

"We'll check the Feds on that. What else can you tell me?"

I pursed my lips. "Nothing. Is there anything further you can tell me, Detective Rizzi?" I glanced at the stenographer.

"You're going to be in New York for a while?" Rizzi asked.

"Yes. Through New Year's Eve."

"Good. Tell you what, Mrs. Fletcher. You go on promoting your book, and I'll go on trying to solve this murder. Give me a call now and then. If I think its okay, I'll tell you how I'm doing. Fair enough?"

"I suppose it has to be. Am I free to go?"

"You were always free to go. I didn't cuff you, did I?"

"You also didn't tell me I didn't have to come with you this morning. I'm afraid there are a lot of people at that bookstore who have been disappointed. So is a radio talk show host who's sitting in his studio at this moment reading from the Manhattan phone book." Rizzi's expression said that if anything in this world concerned him, disappointed book buyers and radio hosts were not on the list.

He escorted me from the room. As we passed through the squad room, he was stopped by a uniformed officer who said, "You got a call, Al. It's the Feds about the Marsh case."

Marsh? Feds? Could he be talking about Waldo Morse, who'd perhaps changed his name to Marsh? I would have assumed that anyone in a witness protection program would go further afield in choosing a new name—Symington, or Wolinoski, or Buttafucco—but that represented only my logic.

Marsh. I kept that name with me as Rizzi took me to the door. I extended my hand; he took it with uncertainty. "I hope your wife enjoys the book, Detective Rizzi."

"She will. Thanks."

"And Mrs. Wilson, too. Have a nice day."

"It'll be a lot nicer when you find that film."

It had grown sharply colder. I looked up into a low sky the color of lead and pulled my coat collar up around my neck to shield against a brisk wind. It looked, and smelled, like snow.

The film!

Who could have taken the roll of film?

Vaughan or Olga Buckley? No.

Their housekeeper, Gina? Unlikely.

Someone at Dastardly Acts? Possibly.

But why?

Maybe it fell out of my purse when leaving the bookstore.

Maybe . . . maybe lots of things.

I reached the corner and looked down at a homeless man who'd established himself on a grate. He'd spread out cardboard and had wrapped himself in a heavy blanket, his possessions in shopping bags at his side. He looked up and extended a hand. "Just money to eat, lady. I don't drink."

As I handed him a dollar bill, I was able to look closely at his face. What I saw were Waldo Morse's eyes—frightened, defeated, life drained from them.

Poor man, I thought as I spotted a cab discharging a passenger a half block away. I ran for it and said to the driver through the open back door, "I'm going to the Dakota apartments."

He barked that he was off-duty and told me to close the door. I did and he drove off, leaving me with a distinctly bitter taste in my mouth. It wasn't so much from tasting too many plates of New York taxi drivers. I could deal with that, as unpleasant as it might be.

It was the death of Waldo Morse that was upsetting me.

I knew one thing for certain.

I had to find out the real story.

Chapter Nine

The press was camped outside the Dakota when I arrived. I waved off their questions and went to the apartment where Gina polished silver.

"Did the Buckleys leave messages for me?" I asked.

"*Sí,*" she said, handing me a yellow ruled legal pad containing a number of entries. The one I immediately responded to was a call from Seth Hazlitt.

"Where have you been?" he asked.

"Where I said I was going to be, at the—no, that isn't true. My appearances at the bookstore and the radio interview were canceled. I've been with the police."

"I already know that, Jessica. The all-news station from Bangor just ran an item sayin' you'd been arrested."

"I wasn't arrested, Seth. They just wanted to ask me some questions."

"Where are you now?"

"Back at the apartment. I'm fine. The police were very nice to me."

"If you say so. Looks like your memory is pretty good, Jess."

"What do you mean?"

"Rememberin' the name Joe Charles. He's a local boy."

"He is?"

"Ayuh, except Joe Charles wasn't his name when he was growin' up here. He's Flo Johnson's boy from up north of town. Called him Junior. Remember?"

"Flo Johnson. Yes, I do remember she had a son they called Junior. Junior Johnson. That's Joe Charles?"

"Sure is."

"But why would the name Joe Charles ring a bell if I knew him as Junior Johnson?"

"'Cause when he became a musician, he changed his name to Joe Charles. He had a band that used to work in these parts."

"Now I remember. Is he still in Cabot Cove?"

"Nope. Not much work for a musician here, so seems he headed for the big city, Los Angeles first. His mother says he ended up in New York."

"As a musician? Performing under the name Joe Charles?"

"She isn't certain about that. Seems the boy doesn't have much contact with her. Just like young people these days, leave your roots and forget they're still planted. Not hard to pick up a phone, drop a postcard to your mother once in a while. At any rate, Jess, he might be the same Joe Charles that came over your answering machine."

"Seth, this has been extremely helpful. Anything else?"

"Nope, 'cept Mort got a nice letter from Parker Brothers this mornin' 'bout his board game. Seems like they're interested."

"That's wonderful. He must be thrilled."

"Not so's you'd notice."

Our sheriff had been working on a murder mystery board game for years. Every time he thought he had it ready to submit, one of us would come up with another flaw and he'd start over. Two months ago he decided he'd made enough changes and announced he was sending it off to Parker Brothers.

"I have to run, Seth. Lots to do. Thanks again."

"If I was you, Jessica Fletcher, I'd pack my bags and come back home. New York City's bad enough without you witnessin' murders and endin' up a news item on the radio like some common criminal."

"You know something, Seth? I just might do that. But not right away. Plans still proceeding for the New Year's Eve party?"

"Sure are. The only thing lackin' will be Jessica Fletcher. You think about what I said."

"I promise I will. Congratulate Mort for me."

I perused other messages on the page. Three were from Ruth Lazzara asking me to call the minute I returned. There were calls from media, including a London tabloid anxious to interview me because I'd been involved there a year ago investigating the murder of a dear friend, the *grande dame* of mystery writing, Marjorie Ainsworth.

I called Ruth Lazzara. Her assistant told me there had been a change in schedule that afternoon. Originally, there were only two interviews, one with *Publishers*

Weekly, the "Bible" of the publishing industry, the other with the *Village Voice.* Now, they'd sandwiched in four more.

"Impossible," I told her. "I made it clear that I need some time for myself during this trip. I don't want to be uncooperative but . . ."

"I'll have Ms. Lazzara call you."

Did I dare skip out? Obviously, I would honor the two interviews that had originally been arranged, but if I didn't know the specifics of the others, I couldn't very well show up.

I put on my coat and headed for the door. "Please tell the Buckleys I'll be back sometime this evening, Gina, but not to plan on me for dinner."

"*Sí,* Mrs. Fletcher."

I heard the phone ring and paused at the door to listen to the incoming message. It was Ruth Lazzara. She sounded positively frantic.

My *Publishers Weekly* interview was at three, and the *Village Voice* reporter was to meet me at Buckley House at six. They could count on me. The others could wait.

There was something else I had to do.

Local 802, the New York office of the American Federation of Musicians, was located far west on Forty-second Street. There was a lot of activity in a large room at the end of a hallway. A hundred people, musicians I assumed, milled about in what appeared to be a shape-up hall. I scanned the crowd for someone who looked official, and who might direct me to member records. Before I succeeded, a paunchy little man wearing a shirt opened to his belly, and sporting Fort Knox around his neck and on his fingers came up to me. "You a singer?" he asked.

"Me? Heavens, no."

"You sure you don't sing? I need a singer tonight at Roseland."

"I'm afraid I'm no singer. Only in the shower, and pretty bad at that."

"You got a costume? Play maracas, cowbell?"

"Excuse me," I said, walking to a desk in the corner at which a sullen gentleman sat. "Excuse me, sir, I'm trying to locate a musician."

"You come to the right place." He grinned and took in the men and women on the floor with outstretched arms.

"I don't want to *hire* a musician. I'm trying to locate a certain individual. Where would member records be?"

"Upstairs."

The woman in charge of member records was middle-aged and pleasant. I told her I was anxious to contact a musician who worked under the name Joe Charles.

"Why do you want to find him?" she asked.

She was obviously concerned I might be a process server, or from a collection agency. "Nothing bad, I can assure you," I said. "He comes from my hometown in Maine. I have good news for him."

That seemed to satisfy her. She went to a large bank of file drawers, pulled out a folder, and returned to her desk. "Let's see," she said. "Yes. Joe Charles is a paid-up member." She placed the folder in front of me. I took the address and phone number from it, thanked her, and left the building, my heart pounding. Things had worked quickly and smoothly. Here I was with the address and phone number of the person I assumed had been referred to me by my mystery caller. Good old Seth. He'd really come through for me, as he usually did.

Junior Johnson, a.k.a. Joe Charles, lived on Crosby Street, of which I'd never heard. I had no idea where in Manhattan it was, but assumed cab drivers would know. I was wrong. The first two drivers shook their heads and said they didn't know any Crosby Street. I suggested to the second that he consult his map. "No map, no map," he said, speeding off. I was luckier with the third, an older man who was nicely dressed, and who actually seemed to display pride in being a taxi driver who knew his city.

"Not a very nice neighborhood you're going to," he said, activating the meter.

"It won't be a problem in daylight, will it?"

"No, but it's not my favorite part of New York. Just keep your eyes open."

I sat back in his refreshingly clean cab and watched the city slide by. It had started to snow. Fine, delicate flakes swirled about the windows and gave me a sense of security. Maybe that's why they call it a blanket of snow. I've always liked it when it snows in Cabot Cove. I love the crackling wood and aroma from the fireplace, the crunch beneath my feet when I walk outside, the pristine tranquility it drapes over the town. Would it snow enough to accomplish the same thing for me in Manhattan? I'd never been in New York City when it snowed. Another life experience.

We stopped for a light at the intersection of Bowery and Houston streets where two disheveled men rubbed dirty rags on the windshield despite my driver's attempts to wave them away. Another man, tottering from alcohol, knocked on my window and shook a paper cup at me.

"Sorry about that, ma'am," the driver said as the light changed and he pulled away.

"I feel sorry for them," I said, "I was thinking how pleased I was to see the snow, but I'm sure they aren't happy about it."

We pulled up in front of a beautiful old office building at the north end of Crosby Street, at the corner of Bleecker. I said to the driver, "What unusual architecture."

He replied, "I'm really not up on architecture, ma'am, but I do know this building was designed by someone named Louis Sullivan. Pretty famous in his day."

"I feel better already," I said.

"Why?"

"I know this isn't a very nice neighborhood, but if a lovely building like this can survive here, it can't be all bad."

He drove off, leaving me to admire the twelve-story building with its terra-cotta leafy designs that drew the eye to six angels above the cornice, their wings outspread as though to welcome visitors.

The address I'd been given at the musicians union was two doors up from the office building. It looked like a warehouse or factory. Why would someone live in a factory? I wondered. I heard music coming from inside—dissonant, loud, grating electronic sounds that had the quality of long fingernails dragged across a blackboard.

I went up a few steps and stood at the front door, which was slightly ajar. Doorbells had been attached to the side of the door but the wires connecting them had been cut and dangled free.

I looked back at the street. The delicate flakes had turned fatter and wetter, which usually meant to us in Maine that the snowfall would not continue as long as it would have if the flakes remained small and dry. But maybe rules of nature like that didn't apply in New York City. I pushed open the door and stepped into a large foyer. The walls were covered with graffiti, much of it patently offensive. The music was louder now, and came from above.

Startled by the sound of heavy shoes on a metal staircase, I looked up and saw a young man round the corner and continue toward me. He wore high military boots, shorts, and a purple-and-yellow Day-Glo tank top. His long hair was tied in a ponytail.

"Excuse me," I said. He stopped. "I'm looking for an old friend of mine, a musician named Joe Charles."

"Upstairs, third floor. His name is on the door." He turned and was gone. Shorts in this weather? Maybe I was missing something.

I slowly ascended the stairs, my heels clanging on the metal with each step. As I got higher, the volume of the music increased. It came from behind the door on which "JOE CHARLES" had been scribbled on a piece of cardboard. I'd never heard such music before. I call it music because the alternative was to label it "sounds from a construction site."

I knocked. Whoever was inside certainly wouldn't hear me above the level of the music. This time, I banged on the door with the fleshy portion of my palm. The music stopped. "Who is it?" a man yelled.

"A friend of Waldo Morse," I shouted back.

Although I couldn't see inside the room, I had the

feeling that the person in it, presumably Joe Charles, was debating whether to respond. I waited what I thought was an appropriate amount of time, then raised my hand again and was prepared to knock when the door opened. Facing me was a short, chubby young man, but old enough to have seen much of his hair recede. His round face was covered with stubble, and his pale blue eyes had a watery quality to them. He wore coveralls over a bare torso. Rubber thongs were on feet in need of a bath.

"I'm sorry to interrupt your practice," I said pleasantly, "but I came here about something pretty important. My name is Jessica Fletcher. I'm from Cabot Cove, Maine, and . . ."

"Sure, the mystery writer. My mother knew you, didn't she?"

"Mrs. Johnson? Yes, I know your mother. Not well, but I certainly remember that she had a son everyone called 'Junior,' and who became quite a musician under the name Joe Charles. That is you, isn't it?"

He nodded. "You said you were a friend of Waldo Morse. Why did you say that?"

"Well, I might not have been a close friend, but I was a witness to his murder. You probably read about that in the paper."

He shook his head. "I don't read the papers. Maybe *Rolling Stone, Downbeat.* Sure, I heard what happened to Waldo. A real bummer."

I raised my eyebrows. "Yes, I suppose it was a bummer, as you say. May I come in?"

He'd been cordial, but there was now conflict written

on his face. "I promise I won't take much of your time," I said, "but it is important that I speak with you."

He stepped back to allow me to enter.

The room was very large; furniture was obviously not on the list of priorities. A mattress with a flowered sheet was on the floor in one corner. His clothing, what there was of it, hung from hooks along a wall. The kitchen was part of the main room, a small sink, stove and refrigerator tucked into a corner. There was a door which, I assumed, led to the bathroom. All of this was contained in the north end of the room.

The southern end was chockablock with musical instruments. There was a rack on which four keyboards of different sizes were mounted. A set of drums sat in a corner. A large instrument that appeared to be a marimba stood in front of the drums. Another rack, from which bells, tubes, and wooden sticks dangled, was in the center of the area. A computer completed the paraphernalia.

"I've never seen so many instruments in one place," I said.

"I use them all sometimes."

"Do you use them outside of the apartment? You must need a truck to take them to work."

"Sometimes. I have a couple of groupies who help me."

"Groupies? Women who follow you around?"

He smiled. "Yeah. Fem Lib at work. As long as they're going to hang around, they might as well make themselves useful."

"That's pragmatic," I said. I looked around the room. "May I sit down?"

"Okay." He pointed to a black hydraulic chair in front

of the rack of keyboards, pulled a plastic milk crate from the kitchen, and sat on it, facing me. "Who told you about me?" he asked.

"I don't know. That sounds silly. Someone left an anonymous message with my publisher in which you were mentioned. I checked friends back home, and they reminded me about you. The message said you would know."

"Know what?"

"I don't know. That's why I'm here. I must admit, I'm very confused about Waldo. I remember when he got into all that trouble in Cabot Cove."

"Ogunquit," Charles corrected me.

"Yes. Ogunquit. Have you been in touch with Waldo since he went into the witness protection program?"

"A little. Not much."

"Had he been in New York City all this time?"

A shake of the head. "No, Waldo was relocated—I think that's what they call it—he was relocated out in Colorado."

"Did you know him when he was there?"

"I knew him from Cabot Cove, Mrs. Fletcher."

"Of course. You lost all contact with Waldo while he was in Colorado?"

"Yup. We were never real good friends in Maine. We hung around a little together. I was into music, he was a football player, but we got along. I remember the last conversation I had with him there. He told me he was marrying Nancy. I told him I thought he was nuts."

"Nuts? To marry Nancy?"

"To many anybody. He was a young guy. I felt trapped in Cabot Cove and couldn't wait to get out, but he seemed to want to keep himself in that trap, get married, have kids, try to make a living there."

"So you went to Los Angeles to find fame and fortune."

It was a gentle, self-effacing laugh. "I'm afraid I didn't find much of that in L.A. Kind of ironic, Mrs. Fletcher. I gave Waldo a lecture about staying single, but six months after I get to L.A., I meet a chick and marry her. It lasted almost a year."

"I'm sorry."

"No big deal. We didn't have any kids, so when we split, nobody got hurt. She was okay. I still talk to her once in a while if she's in New York, or if I make it out to the West Coast."

I stopped asking questions and glanced toward windows that overlooked Crosby Street. It was snowing harder now; a strong wind rattled the panes.

"Want a cup of coffee or something?" he asked.

"That would be lovely. I prefer tea."

"I have to go get it. Only be a minute."

"Please, don't bother. I thought you had it here."

"There's a Korean deli up the street. Want something to eat? A donut? Candy bar?"

"No, thank you. Just tea will be fine. A little milk." I watched him put on a green army surplus overcoat that reached his ankles, and a black stocking cap. "Can I buy?" I asked.

"If you want to. I'm a little short of cash. I have a gig tomorrow night."

I handed him a five-dollar bill. He thanked me, left, and I heard the sound of his feet on the metal stairs.

I stood and surveyed the room with more scrutiny than when I'd first entered. Junior Johnson, alias Joe Charles, had certainly been open enough with me. I liked him. He had a way about him that was appealing. He was probably not the best of sons, judging from his lack of communication with his mother, but who was I to pass judgment about something like that?

I went to the rack of keyboard instruments from which tiny red lights shone. I touched a key and an eerie, wailing, earsplitting scream came back at me from large speakers. Whatever happened to a good old acoustic piano? I wondered as I took a closer look at the other instruments. I picked up a mallet off the marimba and ran it across a set of wooden chimes that hung from the other rack. The sound was Oriental, or Middle Eastern, and pleasant. I did it again but wondered if I might be disturbing others in the building. I put the mallet down and smiled. If Joe Charles hadn't been disturbing others in the building when I arrived, no one ever would.

I perused the rest of the room. As I was looking at a photograph over the mattress of him performing with a musical group, the door to the bathroom slowly opened. Every muscle in my body tensed, and I braced. Then, I looked down and saw a large, fat, black-and-white cat come through the now open door and rub against the edge of it.

I breathed a sigh of relief and said the sort of silly things we always say to cats. True to its nature, the cat looked at me, then walked away with its back arched, stepped up onto the mattress, stretched, and curled into a ball.

I peeked in the bathroom. One of those portable plastic shower enclosures was in a corner. A chipped white-enamel sink was stained with rust. Beneath the sink was a low cardboard box that functioned as a litter box. Strips of newspaper lined its bottom. I leaned forward to better see the ripped-up newsprint. Looking back at me was an eye; my eye. One of the strips had been torn in such a way that my eye from the front page of the *Post* was visible. Other strips from that same page were in the box, too.

I straightened and returned to the main room. Strange, I thought. Charles had said he knew Waldo was dead, but had not read about me. He said he didn't read newspapers, yet here was the edition of the *Post* on which my face was plastered all over Page One. Why would he lie about something like that?

The phone rang, a muffled sound; the instrument must have been smothered beneath something. I looked at the mattress and saw a black cord leading under pillows. The ringing stopped, and Joe Charles's voice said, "I split this scene for a while, but I'll make it back soon. Lay your message on me when you hear the A-flat, and I'll return the favor when I get back. *Ciao!*"

Then, the caller's voice was heard: "Eleven tonight," a man said. "Usual place. Don't be late." There was the sound of the phone being hung up, a series of beeps, and the room was silent again.

I cocked my head and narrowed my eyes as though that would help me think, the way I have to turn off the radio in a car when looking for a house number. Always someone else's car, of course. I don't drive.

I'd recognized the voice of the caller. Detective Alphonse Rizzi. I wasn't certain it was him, at least not enough to testify under oath, but it certainly sounded like him. Why would *he* be calling Joe Charles?

I contemplated replaying the message but the sound of footsteps on the metal stairs sent me back to the black chair. Charles came through the door carrying a brown paper bag. He took off his coat, opened the bag on the plastic box on which he'd been sitting and, on his knees, looked up at me. "Sure you don't want something to eat?" he asked. He'd bought, along with his coffee and my tea, two packages of chocolate cake filled with a gooey white substance, undoubtedly terminally sweet.

"No, thank you. Just the tea will be fine."

He handed me my cup, opened one of the packages, and eagerly ate its goopy contents. He finished it in seconds and opened the second. I'd bought him a meal, maybe the only one he would have that day. He didn't mention change from my five dollars; I didn't ask.

"That's a pretty cat," I said.

"Yeah, only he's getting fat. His name is Thelonious."

"Interesting name."

"I named him after Thelonious Monk."

"The jazz musician," I said, glad to demonstrate a little knowledge of his world. "Did he play all these instruments?"

Charles laughed. "Nah. This kind of electronic stuff wasn't around when he was working. He probably wouldn't have liked it anyway." He looked at his watch. "Look, Mrs. Fletcher, I was in the middle of a composition that I have to have ready for tomorrow night. I'm afraid I have to cut this off."

"Of course, I didn't mean to take from your composing

time. Let me ask you this before I go. How did you and Waldo end up getting back together in New York?"

"He looked me up when he came from Colorado."

"Why did he come to New York? If he was in the witness protection program, it would seem safer in Colorado."

"Mrs. Fletcher, I really have to get back to work."

I stood. "Waldo was accused of drug smuggling in Maine. Was he involved in drugs here in New York?"

"Not that I know of."

"The police say Waldo was murdered by drug dealers."

"I wouldn't know about that."

"Did he live here with you?" I asked.

"No."

"Where did he live?"

"I really don't know. Somewhere around."

"I promise I'll leave in a minute, but I have so many questions. What name did you call him?"

"Huh?"

"Waldo Morse, or Waldo Marsh?"

"How do you know . . . ?"

"That he used the name Marsh? It was on his ID the day he died. That was his name under the witness protection program."

"Right." Charles pulled my chair over to the keyboard rack, sat in it, and played a chord that reverberated throughout the room.

I went to the door. "I would love to hear you perform, Joe. Where will you be tonight?"

"I don't have a gig tonight."

"I'm afraid I don't know very much about jazz, but I thought I might learn a little while visiting New York. Can you recommend a good jazz club? I'm having dinner with business associates, but I'll be free by eleven and . . ."

He said quickly without looking at me, "All over the city. Lots of jazz clubs in the Village, some fancier joints uptown."

"Well, I wish I could hear you play. You said you had to have your composition ready for tomorrow night. Could I hear you then?"

I knew I was pushing it; the scowl on his round face confirmed it. "You wouldn't enjoy my music, Mrs. Fletcher. The kind of music I'm into is for young people. I figure you're more comfortable with Tommy Dorsey and Benny Goodman."

I smiled. "I loved those bands, but I'm not so old that I can't appreciate new things."

"Thanks for the coffee and pastry."

I wouldn't have called it pastry, but I suppose the word would do. I said as an afterthought, "Do you have a phone? I would like to be able to call you."

"It's out of order."

"How do you get calls from people who want you to perform?" I asked.

"I use a service. Sorry, Mrs. Fletcher, but I really have to get back to this."

"Yes, and I apologize for not taking my cue earlier. You've been very kind."

I was on my way down the metal stairs and had rounded the corner at the second level when a young woman raced up from the foyer and almost bumped into me. She mumbled an apology and kept going. I stepped back against the wall so that I could see the third floor and saw her run directly to Joe Charles's door, open it, and disappear inside. Charles had started playing his keyboard instruments the minute I was out of his apartment, but the music stopped abruptly. I lingered as long as I thought I could; I was tempted to go up and press my ear against the door, but was afraid I couldn't navigate the metal stairs in silence.

I went back out to Crosby Street, now covered with a dense, white layer of snow. It was beautiful; all the hard, dirty concrete that had been there when I'd arrived was hidden. I was struck with a sudden touch of nostalgia. Was it snowing in Cabot Cove?

Chapter Ten

The *Publishers Weekly* interview ended a little before five, which gave me an hour until my appointment with the *Village Voice* at Buckley House. Ruth Lazzara, who wasn't happy that I'd been unreachable, but didn't make too much of it, suggested a drink or a cup of coffee, but I told her I had errands to run.

I needed a walk to clear my head. The snow had tapered off, and the city was aglow with the lights reflecting off its crystalline ground cover. I walked slowly, enjoying store windows that were showcases for their owners' holiday wares. I stopped to admire a collection of cut glass. As I did, a shop I'd passed a few doors away came to mind. I'd considered going in but talked myself out of it. Silly, I'd told myself. Too cloak-and-dagger. You're a grown woman, Jessica. Forget it.

I retraced my steps and stood in front of the other window once again. A few deep breaths and I was inside where a chubby young woman wearing clothes too tight for her figure, and chewing gum with enthusiasm, asked without enthusiasm if I needed help.

"Yes, I think so. I'm not quite sure the style I want. Perhaps if you show me a few models, I'll be able to decide."

She didn't seem happy about having to get up from a stool behind the counter, but did and went to a wall on which the shop's merchandise was displayed. "We have all these in stock," she said.

"Quite a selection," I said. "I think what I'm after is something contemporary, modern. 'With it,' I suppose is the phrase. Could I see that one?"

She removed a coal black wig from a plastic, featureless head, and handed it to me. Her pained expression testified to what she was thinking. I ignored her, took the wig to a mirror, and put it over my short, *piccolpasso* red hair. It was a full wig that reached my shoulders and made my head appear twice as big, my face half its normal size. I cocked my head left and right, smiled at my image in the mirror, and turned to her. "Yes, I think this is perfect. What do you think?"

"It's the last one I figured you'd pick," she said. "It's not you."

"Exactly," I said. "Yes, I'll take this one." I removed the wig and handed it to her.

As she put my purchase into a small shopping bag and started to write out a sales receipt, I went to a revolving display stand of large, garish sunglasses, pulled a pair from the rack, checked myself in a mirror attached to the stand, and handed them to her. "Please add these to the bill."

She looked at me with that same pained, quizzical expression. As I left the shop, she quickly placed a "CLOSED" sign in the door. I could imagine her conversation that night with friends about the kooky woman who was her last customer.

Originally, the interview with the *Village Voice* was to be on the subject of the mystery genre and my views of it as an emerging force in mainstream publishing. But because of the hullabaloo about the Waldo Morse murder, the literary critic for the *Voice* was accompanied by an investigative reporter whose specialty was the Manhattan police beat. I parried their questions as best I could, falling back time and again on the impropriety of discussing an ongoing murder investigation.

When I'd arrived at Buckley House, three members of the press were in the reception area. They'd been there all day, according to the receptionist, and must have been half-asleep. By the time they realized who I was, I was on my way through a door to the conference room. They were more alert when Ruth Lazzara and I came out of the interview. I fended off their questions as politely as possible, knowing that Ruth preferred that I sit with them.

She asked about my plans for the evening.

"A hot bath, a drink, a light dinner, and early to bed with a good murder mystery," I said.

"See you in the morning, then, Jessica."

"Yes, I have tomorrow's itinerary. Have a nice evening."

Vaughan and Olga were at the apartment when I arrived. I changed into comfortable clothing, and we enjoyed a drink in the living room, Sadie and Rose flanking my chair. "I've made a decision," I said. "I'm moving to a hotel tonight."

They expressed their usual reasons why they didn't want me to do that, but I persisted. I'd stopped at a phone booth during the day and made a reservation at the Sheraton-Park Avenue, a small, European-style jewel at Park and Thirty-seventh Street that was my favorite whenever I visited New York. Eventually, the Buckleys accepted my decision. Vaughan said he would drive me.

As I packed, the phone rang several times, each a call from a reporter. Bobby Johnson of the *Post* called twice; Vaughan said Johnson had left several messages on the machine during the day.

"See?" I said. "At least the phone might stop ringing, and you can have some peace. All I ask is that you tell no one where I'm staying."

"Of course," Olga said.

"I'll have to inform certain people at the office," Vaughan said.

"I realize that, but please keep the list to a minimum and ask them to be discreet. I'd like to consider myself purely altruistic in leaving you, but I think being in a neutral space will be good for me, too. You do understand?"

"Yes," Vaughan said. "Just as long as you promise you'll be at our Christmas Eve party."

"I wouldn't miss it." It was Wednesday, December eighteenth. Christmas was a week away.

"Well," Vaughan said with a sigh, "if you're set on going to the hotel, let's do it."

We left the Dakota by a back entrance and went to a garage where Vaughan housed his Lincoln Town Car. A short time later I checked into the hotel. I explained my need for privacy to a clerk at the desk, who assured me that all calls would be screened, messages taken, and that no calls would be put through with the exception of the people I'd listed—Vaughan and Olga, and Ruth Lazzara.

Instead of a single room, I was given a small suite. It was lovely, decorated in antique reproductions chosen to complement the muted hues of the walls and thick carpeting. I unpacked my bags, carefully hung clothing in the closet, took a Manhattan Yellow Pages directory from the nightstand, and found the listings under "LIMOUSINES." I chose the one with the largest display ad and asked to be picked up at ten.

After an invigorating hot shower, I went to the hotel dining room where, at a partially obscured table, I satisfied my hunger with a cold lobster salad preceded by hot consomme, and indulged myself in a glass of white wine. I felt two things: First, I was more relaxed then I had been since arriving in New York. And, second, I would go through with my plan for the evening.

I returned to my suite and changed from the cosmopolitan, conservative clothing I'd worn to dinner into a pair of black slacks and black turtleneck sweater. I carefully adjusted the wig in front of the bathroom mirror, applied makeup heavier than usual, and put on the oversize sunglasses that had tiny silver chips in the upper corners. I leaned closer to the mirror: "Is that you, Jessica?" I asked. I shook my head. If I couldn't tell it was me, no one else would.

Roy, my driver, was a handsome young black man in a

black uniform, white shirt, black tie, and black peaked cap. Had he looked at me strangely when opening the door? Of course he had. I looked like a fool, at least in the genteel lobby of the Sheraton-Park Avenue. Hopefully, I would just be one of the crowd where I was going.

We headed for Crosby Street, near the corner of Bleecker, which was as much of a surprise to Roy as my appearance had been. But he was too much the courteous professional to overtly indicate his reaction, and drove slowly and skillfully down Park Avenue, sitting ramrod straight as the derelicts of the Bowery tried to solicit money from us. We finally pulled up to the curb at the designated spot. Roy waited a few moments before turning and asking, "Ma'am?"

I leaned forward. "I'd just like to sit here awhile if you don't mind."

"Whatever you say."

"I'm waiting for someone to come out of that doorway." I pointed to the entrance to Joe Charles's building. "If he does, I would like to follow him, but I don't want him to know it."

"Yes, ma'am."

"I suppose this represents an unusual assignment," I said. "I assure you we aren't breaking the law."

His laugh was low and warm. "Never entered my mind," he said.

As I sat in the backseat and waited for Joe Charles to exit the building, I had trouble concentrating. How difficult it must be for law enforcement officers to conduct a stakeout hours on end. It's brain-numbing, to say nothing of the numbness that invaded other parts of my anatomy.

I played all sorts of mind games to stay alert and to make sure no one came through that door without my knowing it.

My patience paid off. At twenty minutes to eleven, Joe Charles came through the door. He was accompanied by the young woman I'd seen going into his apartment. They got into a battered tan Honda Civic parked in front of the building. They had trouble starting the car. I hadn't wanted to alert them that we were there, so I waited until they'd finally managed to get the Honda up and running and had pulled away. "That's the car I want to follow," I told Roy. We fell into a comfortable distance behind them.

"I've never done this before," Roy said over his shoulder. "I mean, never followed a car."

"You're doing just fine," I said.

We eventually ended up on a very busy street in what looked to me to be Greenwich Village. Roy confirmed that's where we were. We hadn't traveled far. We were on Seventh Avenue South, between Bleecker and Grove streets.

The tan Honda pulled up to a vacant parking meter in front of a restaurant whose sign read "SWEET BASIL." "What an interesting name," I said.

"A good jazz club," Roy said. "They book only top musicians."

I watched Charles and his female friend get out of the car and stand together on the sidewalk as though unsure of their next move. He had a manila envelope beneath his arm. We'd parked at a hydrant at the end of the block, far enough so as to not be seen by them, but close enough to observe their actions. They seemed to be arguing; I wished

I had one of those exotic microphones to point at them and hear their words. Finally, after much debate, they entered Sweet Basil.

I had a real decision to make now. It was easy following them from the backseat of a chauffeured car. But that wasn't good enough. If I left it at that, it would have been a wasted exercise, to say nothing of expensive. I had to enter the club. Would my costume, wig, and uncharacteristic makeup keep them from recognizing me? I had a feeling it would. I said to Roy, "I'm going inside. I probably won't be more than a hour. Will you wait for me?"

"Of course," he said. "If the police make me move, I'll be in the vicinity. Look for me."

"I certainly will," I said, touching his shoulder. "Thank you for being so indulgent."

"Indulgence is what I'm paid for," he said. "Enjoy the music."

"I hadn't even thought about music," I said, laughing. "I'll finally get to hear some New York jazz."

The music, loud and vibrating, hit me in the face as I opened the door. There were horns and drums, and the musicians playing them attacked their mission with zeal. A sign outside said the group was known as the Harper Brothers. I'd never heard of them, but I was certainly hearing them now.

One of my suppositions was correct. I did not seem out of place in my garb and wig. No one looked askance at me. An attractive young man asked if I wished a table in the music room. I said I preferred to sit at the bar, and he led me to a vacant stool at the far end of it, which gave me a perfect view of the music room that was at the rear of the club. The only problem was I couldn't see very much through my dark glasses. I lowered them. Joe Charles and his female companion had taken a table in the barroom, next to the music room entrance. I'd been right about the voice on Charles's answering machine. Seated at their table was Detective Alphonse Rizzi.

I tried to analyze the overall mood at the table. It wasn't anger, but it wasn't a backslapping get-together either. Rizzi did most of the talking, and Joe Charles listened intently, seeming to agree with what the detective was saying. The girl's dour, angry expression indicated something else.

It had become unbearably hot. Sweet Basil's heating system would have handled the entire State of Maine outdoors. I sipped from the Pink Lady I'd ordered, and dabbed at perspiration on my forehead and nose with a bar napkin. What made the heat even worse was the wig. It was like being under a hair dryer, and I had this driving obsession to rip it off my head. The collar of my black turtleneck seemed to have shrunk three sizes. All in all, I was uncomfortable, and considered getting up and leaving. There was nothing more to be gained by staying because I couldn't hear what they were saying. But my mission had been accomplished; Joe Charles and Detective Rizzi knew each other, and obviously had some sort of business between them.

Rizzi waved the waitress over and handed her money. Good. They were leaving, which meant I could, too.

"Hey baby, what's happening?"

The questioner was a gaunt, older man on my left

wearing glasses even darker than mine. His smile revealed a dentist's pension. "Pardon?" I said.

"What's happenin', baby," he repeated. "I haven't seen you here before. You dig the scene?"

"Dig this scene? Do I like it? Oh, yes, very much. Do you?"

"It wigs me, baby."

"Wigs you?" For a moment, I thought he was referring to my wig. Then I realized it must be a jazz lover's expression that meant he liked it.

"Yeah, it's bad. Real bad."

I fought my confusion and looked to where Charles, Rizzi, and the girl were making their way toward the door. I quickly put money on the bar and stood. Now, from a higher vantage point, I could see beneath the vacant table. The envelope Joe Charles had carried into the club was on the floor next to his chair. Did I dare scoop it up, examine its contents, maybe learn something more about him that might relate to his relationship with Rizzi, perhaps even to Waldo Morse's murder?

"Excuse me," I said to the gentleman to my left.

"Bags is at the Blue Note," he said, grasping my wrist. "What say we make it over there?"

I removed his hand from my wrist, headed for the empty table, and sat in one of the chairs. I took off my sunglasses and wig, shoved them into my purse, reached down and picked up the envelope. It was sealed with tape. Open it there or take it with me? I decided on the latter and was about to head for the natural air conditioning outside when Joe Charles burst through the door and came directly to the table. He looked at me, his eyes wide, his expression angry. I didn't know what else to do, so I smiled. He snatched the envelope from my hands.

"Hello," I said.

He seemed to want to say something, but words didn't come. He pressed his lips together, his eyes turned hard and he left, almost knocking over other tables on his way.

"Nicely done, Jessica," I said aloud. "Smooth. Real smooth."

Chapter Eleven

After a jittery night's sleep at the hotel—one recurring dream had me naked, except for my wig and sunglasses, standing in front of a large audience that laughed long and loud—I awoke with a start at six. "How could you have been so stupid?" were my first words as I went to the window and drew open the drapes. It was dark, not because dawn hadn't broken, but because the sky was heavy and low. It looked like snow; if I were outside, I knew I would smell it.

I called the hotel operator for messages.

"I have seven for you, Mrs. Fletcher, and there are a lot of reporters in the lobby. They all keep asking me to call your room, but I told them I wouldn't."

"Thank you. I appreciate that." She gave me the seven messages, two of which were from Seth Hazlitt in Cabot Cove, and two from *Post* reporter Bobby Johnson. How did they know I'd moved to a hotel? How did anybody know aside from the Buckleys, and Ruth Lazzara? I thought the Cabot Cove gossip mill was a threat to personal privacy, but I'd never seen anything like this. People say that the best place to lose yourself is in a large city. You couldn't get me to testify to it.

I showered and dressed, then ordered half a grapefruit, an English muffin, and a pot of tea from room service. While I waited for it to be delivered, I called Seth. "Seth, it's Jessica. How in the world did you know I was here at this hotel?"

"I called the Buckleys. They said you were out, but after I said it was important that I talk to you, they told me where you were. I guess they know you and I are pretty good friends."

"I talk about you often. What's so important?"

"Gettin' you to come home. I keep hearin' news reports about Waldo's murder and how you witnessed it. 'Course, they don't say his name, keep sayin' the Santa Claus was an unidentified drifter sorta fella, but I know. They say he was killed by a bunch of drug runners, and you know what they're like, Jess. They don't care that you're a nice woman and a famous writer. I want you to pack up your bags and get home here." Before I could respond, he added, "It's one thing for Jessica Fletcher not to be here for New Year's Eve, but it don't seem right you won't be here for Christmas, either."

The timing of Seth's request was perfect. One of the things I'd contemplated while showering was going to Cabot Cove to see whether Nancy Morse knew about her husband's death. If not, I'd break the news.

There was more than altruism behind my decision,

however. Nancy might be able to fill some holes, answer questions I'd been formulating since witnessing the murder. I wanted a chance to speak with her face-to-face. Informing her of Waldo's death would be as good an excuse as any.

"I am coming home sooner than planned," I told Seth.

"Good to hear you talkin' sense again, Jessica." He'd adopted a fatherly tone, as he often did when dismayed at something I was doing, or not doing. I loved him for it, but it could also be annoying.

"I won't be there for Christmas, Seth, but I am coming home tomorrow. Here's what I'd like you to do. I'll grab the first shuttle in the morning and fly to Boston. Would you be good enough to have Jed Richardson pick me up at Logan Airport and fly me home?" Jed Richardson owned Jed's Flying Service in Cabot Cove. I hate small planes. Come to think about it, I don't like big ones much, either. But I trusted Jed. And because I was trying to compress time, having him pick me up in Boston would save many hours.

"Ayuh," Seth said. "I'll call Jed as soon as I get off the phone. You say you'll take the first shuttle tomorrow morning. That'd be Friday. What time does the first shuttle arrive?"

"Friday? No, I'm coming on Saturday."

"But you said tomorrow. Today's Thursday. Tomorrow's Friday."

"God, I'm losing days already. Make it Saturday morning. I'll check what time the first shuttle leaves and get back to you."

"You are stubborn, Jessica."

"I know."

He sighed. "How long will you be stayin'?"

"It won't be long. Be a dear and be at Jed's hangar when we arrive."

"You don't have to ask. I already made a note to pick you up. Now, about how long you're stayin'. My advice is to pack all your belongin's and have them with you when you honk on up here on Saturday. Heah?"

"Yes, I hear you, Seth."

I was happy to get off the phone. Seth had a tenacious side that dictated not letting go when he was adamant about something, especially when it concerned me. On the other hand, as I dwelled on his advice, the thought of leaving New York and being in Cabot Cove for the holidays was fiercely appealing.

I didn't have a lot of time to think about it, however. I was due to be picked up by Ruth Lazzara within the hour for a television talk show. I ate breakfast and read the *New York Times* that came with it. Unlike the *Post*, the *Times* had covered Waldo's murder as a small item deep inside. I didn't see any mention of it this morning, for which I was grateful.

The first face I saw as I stepped out of the elevator into the lobby was Bobby Johnson.

"Good morning, Mrs. Fletcher." He immediately grabbed my arm and propelled me away from the other reporters, said in urgent, whispered tones, "We have to talk."

"I think that's the last thing we have to do, Mr. Johnson."

"Yeah?" He carried that morning's edition of the *Daily News* folded under his arm. He snapped it open and held it in front of my face. There, on Page One, blown up to gigantic proportions, was a picture of Waldo Morse in his Santa Claus costume at the moment he was shot. I stared at the picture. "Where did they get this?" I asked.

"That's one of the pictures you took, isn't it?" he said.

"I don't know. It looks like . . ."

"It has to be. I told you I could make a great deal for you with those pictures. I really feel betrayed, Mrs. Fletcher. I mean, I was the one who originally broke the story. I figured you owed me something."

"Owed you?" I was poised to argue the point but a more important question came to mind. It had to be one of the photographs I'd taken, which meant the person who removed the roll of film from my purse had given it, or sold it, to the *News.* Who would have done such a thing?

Now, other reporters pressed close, and Ruth tried to appease them. "I'm sure Mrs. Fletcher will be happy to talk to all of you at some point," she said, "but she's due for a television show and we're running late." Johnson took one of my arms, Ruth the other, and they virtually lifted me off the ground and headed for the exit to Park Avenue and a waiting limousine. Johnson started to get in the back with us, but I said in a voice that came as close to a growl as I could muster, "Leave this minute, Mr. Johnson. I don't know who gave that photograph to the *Daily News,* but I intend to find out who stole it from me. Leave me alone!"

He hesitated; would my bite be as strong as my bark? He slowly backed out, saying, "Please, give me ten minutes sometime today."

"Maybe," I said. "Maybe."

He slammed the door, leaving Ruth and me alone in the backseat that was separated from the driver by a Plexiglas partition. Buckley House's publicist said, "Mrs. Fletcher, this is getting out of hand. I know that all this media attention creates a lot of tension for you. At the same time, we have a golden opportunity to milk every avenue of publicity for your new book. That benefits not only Buckley House, but you, too, in a very tangible way. I would like to schedule a press conference."

"A press conference?" My laugh was involuntary. "Press conferences are to announce budget cuts at the Pentagon, invasions, declarations of war."

"Believe me, Mrs. Fletcher, this story ranks right along with those. Please. Let me schedule one."

"When?"

"I want to have enough time to properly notify everyone. How about Saturday? Saturday is a slow news day. We might get major space out of it."

"Sorry, but I won't be available this weekend."

"What do you mean you won't be available?" The words exploded from her lips.

"I need a day off, maybe two. I decided to hibernate this weekend, collect my thoughts, get a decent night's sleep. I need that."

Her voice softened. "Yes, I understand. I know I've been pushing pretty hard. How about Sunday afternoon? That would give you all of Saturday and Sunday morning to rest up. Could I schedule it for Sunday afternoon?"

"I'd prefer Monday, if we have to do it at all."

"Sunday is better, believe me. Come Monday and the papers and stations get too busy. Sunday is perfect. If we give them enough provocative material on Sunday, they'll give us plenty of space and time on Monday."

The thought of facing a press conference was overwhelming. But I knew I couldn't continue to disappoint her, or Vaughan Buckley. No matter how distasteful I found the experience, I did have a certain obligation, and I like to think of myself as a person who meets her obligations. Sunday afternoon would work. I would be in Cabot Cove Saturday and Saturday night, and fly back Sunday morning. One thing I was determined not to do, however, was to tell Lazzara or anyone else that I was leaving the city.

I agreed to the press conference.

The TV interview went smoothly, although it took concentration on my part to focus upon what was being asked. That had become a pattern since witnessing Waldo Morse's murder—physically being in one place, with my mind in another. As I sat beneath the glaring, hot lights of the television studio and discussed my working habits, my thoughts were really on Detective Alphonse Rizzi and Joe Charles. It was like waiting for the proverbial other shoe to drop. The first had hit the floor with a resounding thud when Joe Charles came back into Sweet Basil and saw me sitting at the table, sans wig and glasses. The second shoe, of course, was what they would do now that I'd confirmed a relationship between them. I'd reasoned during my restless night in the hotel that much depended upon the motive for their clandestine meeting in a jazz club at eleven o'clock at night. If it was for a good reason—a rational, legal, moral reason—it shouldn't bother them that I'd snuck in and observed. On the other hand, if there was something nefarious about their rendezvous, I might have more to worry about. The worst thing was not knowing which of the two scenarios was the true one. I was tempted to call Rizzi and confront him openly, but the morning was too rushed for that. Still, it was an option to consider, just as returning to Joe Charles's apartment to confront him was another.

"Pardon?"

"Oh, sorry, my mind wandered for a moment. I don't know how anyone can concentrate under all these lights and with all these wires underfoot," I said.

"You get used to it, Mrs. Fletcher. I was asking whether you always know the ending of your books before you start writing them."

I answered that question, and others. Eventually, it was over and we left, Ruth praising me too much, I thought, for my performance. Fortunately, it had been taped. The daydreaming segments could be cut away.

"What's next?" I asked.

"An interview with *Voice of America*," she said. "It's on your itinerary."

"I'm looking forward to that one," I said. "I've never been interviewed by a government agency before."

"The interviewer, Dave Hubler, will be in Washington," she told me. "You'll be sitting in the New York studio and hear his questions over earphones. When it's done, he'll take your answers and weave them into a finished show. He's terrific at it. It will be translated into many languages."

"Now I'm even more excited," I said. "Are you still planning a press conference for Sunday afternoon."

"Absolutely, which is why I have to get back to the office

the minute we leave VOA. Sorry I can't have lunch with you. You do know about the *People* interview at three?"

"Yes. I'll be on time. I'm so far behind in my Christmas shopping. I'll try to squeeze some in before that interview."

A million other people were evidently behind in their shopping, too, judging from the crowded stores. I stopped at Barnes & Noble on lower Fifth Avenue and stocked up on all the books on my list (mostly books for me; I bought a few as gifts and had them shipped home to avoid having to haul extra weight with me). My next stop was Caswell-Massey on Lexington where I bought pretty fragrances for female friends, including almond cream and cucumber soaps. I was running out of time. One more shop—F.A.O. Schwarz, and a collection of toys for the little ones on my list. If I didn't have that three-o'clock interview with *People,* I would have stayed the afternoon in the fabled toy store's fantasyland.

The reporter from *People* asked few questions about my work but many about my personal life, including romantic interests, which conjured up pleasant, unstated thoughts of George Sutherland in London. A photographer from the magazine took dozens of shots under the theory, I assumed, that if you take enough, you're bound to come up with a usable one. They also announced they wanted to photograph me at home in Cabot Cove when I returned. I agreed.

"Dinner plans?" Ruth asked as we sat alone in the conference room that had been the scene of the interview.

"No, and delighted I don't. I can't wait for a quiet evening in that lovely suite."

There were myriad messages for me at the hotel, including one from Vaughan Buckley marked "URGENT." I was immediately put through to him at Buckley House. "Jessica, glad you got back to me. I just missed you and Ruth at *People*. I received word this afternoon that the *Times* review of your book is a rave."

"How thoughtful of you to call with that news."

"It gets even better. The *Times* wants to do a profile on you for the same issue the review will appear in, a week from Sunday. I set up dinner this evening with the writer doing the piece."

"Tonight? I was looking forward to doing nothing."

"I imagine you were," he said, laughing, "considering the schedule you've been on. But Jess, this is a golden opportunity. By having an interview appear in tandem with a great review, it takes you and the book to another plateau. This was a last-minute decision on the *Times*' part. We can't disappoint them."

I sighed deeply. I knew he was right. I would go along with the interview because it was expected of me. At the same time, I had a nagging and painful desire to be transported magically from the suite and from Manhattan to my comfortable, familiar living room in Cabot Cove, a fire crackling in the large fireplace, and me dressed in my best no-visitors outfit.

"All right," I said. "Where and when?"

"Le Cirque. I'll have a car pick you up at the hotel at eight."

"I'll be ready."

With another dinner staring me in the face, true and total relaxation was out of the question. I paced the suite, becoming increasingly angry at my inability to turn off the world and to wind down. I took a fast shower, changed into what I would wear that evening, and went downstairs. I'd become paranoid enough to expect members of the press to be hovering outside the elevator door whenever I walked through it. But that wasn't the case tonight. I walked on Park Avenue to Fortieth Street and found a cab. "Crosby Street, at Bleecker."

Once again, I stood alone on the street in front of the converted warehouse in which Joe Charles lived. I watched the taxi disappear around a corner, its red taillights trailing away like a rescue ship that had missed me. It was bitter cold. I pulled the collar of my crimson cloth coat tight around my neck and the back of my head, and took deep breaths to stave off my shivering. I wasn't sure where the cold left off and fear began. It really didn't matter. I had acted on impulse, as though some force over which I had no control had dictated I be there, that I confront Joe Charles before he, or Detective Rizzi, took the initiative.

I crossed the street and looked up at the building. There were a few lights on in apartments on upper floors, but not many. The entrance door was still ajar. I pushed it open and stepped into the depressing, odorous lobby. The inner door was open, too. I placed one foot on the first step of the metal staircase and listened, hoping to hear music from Charles's floor. There was only a stagnant, unnatural silence. No people talking, laughing, arguing, and certainly no music.

I ascended the staircase slowly to keep my footsteps from ringing out, and paused at his door. I poised to knock. If no one was home, knocking on the door was academic—and safe. Another deep breath, and a rap of my knuckles.

What was the sound that came from inside? A gasp? A startled cry? I placed my ear against the door and focused on the sound. It had stopped. Quiet now. Should I knock again? No need. I placed my hand on the doorknob, slowly turned it, and pushed it open. A dim shaft of light from a street lamp outside splashed a faint yellow ribbon across the floor. I surveyed the room. I could see the end of it where the array of musical instruments had been. They were gone. Was Charles out on a playing job, a "gig" as he would call it?

In order to see the other half of the room, I had to enter. I was reluctant because of the noise I'd heard when I knocked, but what was to be gained by having again come here and not following through? Chances were he'd gone out to play his instruments in some nightclub, that the apartment was empty, and that—

I saw the source of the sound I'd heard. The cat crossed the room and sat in a corner, like one of those feline doorstops sold at art fairs. I had nothing to fear by going inside. Was it a breach of etiquette to do that? Of course it was, just as having contemplated stealing the envelope in Sweet Basil wasn't especially ladylike, to say nothing of legal. But I wasn't there to steal anything.

"Hello," I said softly.

I heard the noise again. I looked at the cat. He was still curled up in the corner.

"Hello," I repeated. "This is Jessica Fletcher. Joe? Are you here?"

Hearing nothing, I took bold steps through the door and looked to my left; a light was on in the bathroom.

I again scrutinized the main room. It was empty, no musical instruments, no bed, no chairs, nothing except cardboard boxes piled in front of the window. Charles must have moved. Because I'd bumbled upon him and Rizzi in Sweet Basil? Maybe, although there could be other reasons—maybe a sudden playing job opportunity in another city. No, that was silly. He'd bolted. Because of me.

I turned and squarely faced the closed bathroom. The light seeping under the door seemed to have intensified in brightness, as though a rheostat had been turned up.

I considered leaving, running down the stairs and finding the first transportation uptown. That would have been the sensible thing to do. But as Seth Hazlitt often accused me, I was not always the most sensible of people. Prudent in many aspects of my life, certainly reasonable in selected areas, but not always sensible, at least according to his definition.

I approached the bathroom door and, after a long, deep breath to fill myself with courage, opened it.

She came directly at me. It happened fast; all was a blur. I instinctively fell out of the way, my back smashing against the wall. Her forward momentum carried her slightly past me, a toilet plunger held high in both hands.

"I'm not here to hurt you. I'm Jessica Fletcher. I was a friend of . . ."

My words froze her. She slowly lowered the plunger and faced me. It was the girl I'd seen entering the apartment the first time I was there, and who was with Charles at Sweet Basil. She was a pretty little thing, although the fright on her face masked much of her beauty. She wore jeans and a red-and-black flannel shirt. I forced a smile and said gently, "You can put that down. I just came here hoping to see Joe again. It looks as though I'm late." I gestured to the empty room. "He's gone?"

She lowered the plunger and stared at me, helpless, confused, every muscle in her slender body coiled. Then, as though she were an ice statue that had been hit by a sudden blast of hot air, she visibly relaxed. The plunger fell to the floor. She looked down at it, kicked it across the room, and followed the path it took.

"I saw you with Joe at Sweet Basil."

She said without turning, "Yes, I know. He told me when he got in the car. He was furious."

"He had every right to be. Was Detective Rizzi angry, too?"

She laughed, her back still to me. "Mad enough to kill," she said.

"I didn't mean to upset anyone to that extent," I said, walking to the boxes piled near the window and sitting on them. "What is your name?" I asked.

She faced me. "Susan Kale."

I took in the empty room. "Joe has left?"

She nodded.

"For good? Do you know where he's gone?"

"I have no idea."

"Then what about these?" I asked, patting the boxes on either side of me. "How will you know where to send them?"

"They're my things. I packed them."

"You lived here with Joe?"

"Yes. And with Waldo sometimes."

"With Waldo? I assumed you were Joe's girlfriend."

She said ruefully, "What difference does it make? Joe is gone, and Waldo is dead."

"Yes, of course," I said. "I suppose you know I witnessed Waldo's murder."

"You should have looked the other way."

"That's what I've been thinking ever since it happened. I would like to know more about Waldo, especially his life here in New York. I thought Joe would be able to help me. Now that he's gone, would you fill me in about Waldo?"

She'd become calm, almost catatonic. Now she stiffened, her pretty, soft mouth stretched into a hard line. "Why should I talk to you or anybody else?"

"You don't have to, of course. I have no official connection with Waldo's murder."

"Then why . . . ?"

"Why am I here? Why did I go to such ridiculous lengths to follow you and Joe to Sweet Basil? Because, as my friends back in Maine say, I was born to snoop." I laughed. "Here I am snooping again, and this time it's on you. I want to be your friend, Susan. I wish you no harm, but I do need to sort this out. After all, I was a witness to a murder. That doesn't give me a legal right to ask questions, but it certainly makes my interest understandable. Don't you agree?"

"What good are answers going to be, Mrs. Fletcher? It won't bring them back."

"You make it sound as though Joe is dead, too."

"Maybe he is."

"It looks to me as though he moved. To avoid being dead? Is that a possibility?"

"You bet it is," she said.

It was the first sign of spark she'd exhibited, and I was happy to see it. "Who would he be running from?"

"Everybody."

"That's a big cast."

"Look, Mrs. Fletcher, this is all very nice but I have to get out of here, too. I need to find a place to live, a place to—"

"To hide?"

"Call it what you want." A heavy navy pea jacket was on one of the boxes. She put it on.

"I have a suggestion."

"What's that?"

"That you stay with me for a few days. I have a lovely suite in a very nice hotel. The couch in the living room opens up. You'd be safe and secure there. Besides—"

"Besides, you'd have me around to question."

I smiled. "Yes. My offer is not entirely altruistic. Will you?"

"I don't know. I don't know anything."

"It would give you time to collect your thoughts. I promise you don't have to answer any questions if you don't want to." Her eyes narrowed into skeptical slits. "I promise. I keep my promises."

"Maybe."

"That's better than a flat refusal. Tell you what. I'm staying at the Sheraton-Park Avenue. It's at Thirty-seventh Street and Park. I have to go to a very important dinner. I'll leave instructions with the desk that when you arrive, you're to be given a key to the suite. Do you have some identification that will prove to them you're Susan Kale?"

She nodded.

"Good. I know I can't force you to do this, but I urge you to. Bring Thelonious."

"I call her Miss Hiss."

"Miss Hiss is certainly welcome. I should be back to the hotel by eleven, certainly no later than midnight. In fact, I'll make sure I am. I hope you'll be there."

I rose from the boxes and extended my hand. She seemed unsure whether to touch me, but did. I took her slender hands in mine and squeezed. "I think between the two of us, Susan, things might work out just fine." I gave an extra squeeze for emphasis and left.

I stopped at the hotel, left instructions about Susan, and was ready when the limo arrived to take me to Le Cirque.

I'd expected to see Ruth Lazzara at dinner, but she wasn't there. It was just Vaughan Buckley and the *Times* writer. Again I had to force myself to focus on the conversation because my mind kept snapping back to the hotel. Would Susan Kale show up?

After dinner, Vaughan drove me back to the Sheraton-Park Avenue. As we sat in front of the entrance, the car's heater staving off the outside freeze, he said, "You have a lot on your mind, don't you?"

"Yes, I do." I paused, said, "You said you'd make this evening up to me, Vaughan."

"You name it."

"Give me tomorrow night off."

"I don't think anything was scheduled for tomorrow night. You can check with Ruth in the morning."

"Schedules don't seem to mean much these days. There's always something coming up at the last minute. I desperately need some time to myself." I placed my hand on his sleeve and smiled. "Don't misunderstand. I'm grateful for everything you've done for me and the book, but I'm afraid I'm one of those creatures—maybe just a typical writer—who needs think-time. Ruth has scheduled a press conference for Sunday afternoon, and I'll be there. There's a book signing tomorrow morning. I'll be at that, too. But after it, I'd love to hibernate, become a bear in the woods."

"Then that's exactly what you'll do, Jessica. Go on, get to bed. And thanks for being there tonight."

I opened the door to my suite and called Susan's name to an empty living room. She wasn't in the bedroom, either, or the bath.

"Damn!" I said. Foolish girl. I'd offered her sanctuary, and she'd shunned it.

It was quarter of twelve. The sensible decision would have been to simply go to bed and hope she showed up later that night, or the next day. But I knew I wouldn't sleep.

I called the car service I'd used before and asked to be picked up as quickly as possible. The car arrived fifteen minutes later. When I told the driver to take me to Crosby Street, he gave me the same strange look that Roy, my previous driver, had given me. We pulled up in front of the converted warehouse. "Please wait for me," I said.

"Here?" He looked out at the deserted, dark street.

"I won't be long." He got out and opened my door.

As I crossed the street, I saw him get back into the car like a man possessed, and heard the snap of electronic door locks.

I bounded up the stairs without concern for any noise my shoes made on the metal, went directly to Joe Charles's door, and tried it. It opened. All the lights were off but there was sufficient light from outside to see Miss Hiss curled up next to what appeared to be a person in a sleeping bag.

"Susan," I said.

The only response came from the cat. It stood, hunched its back, and curled up again against the form on the floor.

I stepped inside. "Susan," I said louder this time. Still nothing. I went to the sleeping bag and looked down. My eyes widened, a cry caught in my throat. It was no sleeping bag. It was a shower curtain wrapped around the body of Susan Kale.

I picked up the cat, left the apartment, went down the stairs, and crossed the street to where my driver jumped out to open the door. I scrambled inside and let the cat out of my arms. "Take us to the nearest phone booth."

"Is something wrong?" he asked.

"Something is very wrong. And this cat's name is Miss Hiss. She's going to need a home."

Chapter Twelve

"And that's all you know about the deceased?"

I stood in the middle of the apartment with two detectives, an assortment of uniformed police, a couple of lab technicians, and a police photographer. I'd called 911 from the first booth we came to, and the dispatcher directed me to return to the scene and wait. I followed her instructions to the extent that I went back to Crosby Street, but didn't go to the apartment. I stayed in the limo with the driver and Miss Hiss until the first patrol cars arrived, sirens blaring, roof lights tossing twisted, disorienting red pulses into the air.

The detectives were courteous and businesslike; I was disappointed Rizzi wasn't one of them.

I said to the officer who questioned me, "Yes, that's all I know about her. She said her name was Susan Kale. She was the girlfriend of a young man who lived here. Joe Charles."

The detective looked around the room, now flooded with lights powered by a portable generator. "Doesn't look to me like *anybody* lived here."

"Joe Charles has disappeared. I was here earlier today and spoke with Ms. Kale. I asked her to stay with me at my hotel because I thought her life might be in danger."

"What made you think that?"

"Because her boyfriend disappeared so suddenly. That struck me as unusual. Doesn't it strike you that way?"

He grunted. He obviously was more comfortable asking questions than answering them. I, of course, was again faced with the dilemma of how much to tell him, especially about my knowledge of Rizzi's familiarity with Joe Charles and the dead girl. They'd been together at Sweet Basil the night before. Should I mention that? I was hesitant to involve Rizzi, not out of any feelings for him but because I was afraid. Yes, afraid. To link him with Susan Kale and Joe Charles, and to further identify any possible connection between them and Waldo Morse—also a murder victim—could create a major scandal, one in which I would be hopelessly mired.

There was, of course, the possibility—perhaps even the probability—that Rizzi knowing these people meant absolutely nothing. I had no knowledge of what they talked about at the jazz club. As far as I know, there is nothing in the rule book prohibiting a detective from enjoying an off-duty night out.

This detective, whose name was Santana, lowered his notebook to his side and slowly shook his head. "You know, Mrs. Fletcher, this is the second murder you've been involved with."

"'Involved with?' I happened to be at the wrong place at the wrong time when Santa Claus was shot, and I discovered this body because I met a young girl and cared about her. I wouldn't call that 'being involved.'"

"Call it what you want, Mrs. Fletcher, but you sure do have a lousy sense of time and place."

I asked if I could leave.

"In a minute." He issued orders to a technician, then went to a corner where he perched on a windowsill and wrote in his book. I gave him a few minutes before approaching. He looked up and raised his eyebrows.

"Detective Santana, is Detective Rizzi on-duty tonight?"

"Al? No, he comes on in the morning."

"What time?"

Santana shrugged. "Eight, eight-thirty."

"Thank you very much." I started to walk away.

"Mrs. Fletcher."

"Yes?"

"Leave Rizzi out of this."

I closed the gap between us. "Leave him out of this? Why would I do that? He was involved with my first poor sense of time and place, and I . . ."

We both turned as the apartment door opened. A uniformed patrolman stepped inside and said to Santana, "The Fonz is here."

"The Fonz?" I said.

"The . . . Forget it," Santana said. He announced to others in the room, "Shape up. The commissioner is here."

The commissioner? The Fonz? They call the police commissioner of New York "The Fonz"?

A tall, heavyset man wearing an expensive black overcoat, and with a head of thick salt-and-pepper hair entered.

Why would the police commissioner be interested in the murder of a girl on Crosby Street? I didn't have to wait long for the answer. With an engaging broad smile on his handsome, tanned face, he crossed the room and extended his hand. "Mrs. Fletcher."

"Yes. You're Commissioner . . ." I had no idea what his name was.

"I'm Police Commissioner Frye, Ferdinand Frye. It's a real pleasure to meet you Mrs. Fletcher. I've been a fan for years."

Was he being honest, or trying to flatter me? He put that doubt to rest when he mentioned two of my older books, and referred to one of the characters by name.

"I really should offer an apology to you, Mrs. Fletcher. Here you are in New York promoting your latest bestseller, and all you seem to come upon are murders. Hardly the way to welcome one of the world's most distinguished writers to our city."

His charm—he dripped with it—took me off-guard. Whether he was an effective police commissioner remained conjecture, but he certainly made an engaging official greeter for the city of New York.

"I wonder if I might have a word with you in private, Mrs. Fletcher?"

"Of course."

He led me past technicians drawing diagrams on the floor to the small, shabby bathroom and closed the door behind us. "Mrs. Fletcher, I'm sure you have your share of crime in Cabot Cove, and I'm also sure that your law enforcement officers there are first-rate."

"That's true," I said.

Commissioner Frye's face twisted into a grimace. He shoved his hands deep into his overcoat pockets and said, "The problem is, Mrs. Fletcher, in a city like New York, crime sometimes gets complicated." He scrutinized me through narrowed eyes. "Do you know what I mean?"

"I don't think so. Are you talking about the murder of this young girl tonight?"

"Maybe. The point is there are forces at work that sometimes turn simple murders into complicated ones for me and my department."

He waited for my response. I didn't know what to say, so I said, "I still don't understand, but I'll accept your statement."

"Good." That big smile washed over his face again.

We looked at each other in silence. What was I supposed to say next?

He broke the quiet. "Tell you what, Mrs. Fletcher. The mayor has personally instructed me to extend to you every courtesy of the city. He's authorized me to pick up all your expenses while you're here, hotel, meals, the works."

"That's very generous, Commissioner Frye, but all my expenses are paid by my publisher."

"We thought they probably were, so we'd like to offer something above and beyond expenses. How would you like a free vacation—in the Bahamas?"

Free? Is there such a thing as a free vacation or lunch? I smiled. So did he. "Why?" I asked. "You say you've been authorized to offer me this. An offer is usually in return for a service. What service am I to give?"

"Ah, the mind of a mystery writer at work." He laughed. "Mrs. Fletcher, there are no strings. As I said, we're unhappy that your trip to the city has ended up with witnessing one murder, and discovering the body of another victim. The mayor wants to make it up to you."

"Well, that is very generous of the mayor, but I'm afraid it isn't necessary. No, I really don't need, or want, a vacation paid for by New York City."

"Suit yourself, Mrs. Fletcher. The mayor does feel strongly, however, that he does not want you to suffer any further unpleasant incidents while you're our guest. I'm assigning twenty-four-hour security for the duration of your stay."

I suppose my face reflected my confusion. "Do you think my life is in danger?" I asked.

That easy, pleasant laugh again. "No, not at all. But we know how much pressure has been put upon you by the press. I'm afraid that pressure is going to become even more intense. There must be fifty media vultures waiting downstairs."

"That's dreadful."

"But understandable, considering your fame as a mystery writer and the publicity you generated by witnessing the murder of that sidewalk Santa. We'd feel better knowing that you're under our protection day and night. You know, New York City doesn't have the best reputation with the rest of the country. Johnny Carson and other TV comics saw to that. We want to make sure that you—that *we*—don't give them any more grist for negative humor."

I shook my head. "I do not want a policeman with me twenty-four hours a day."

"Afraid you don't have much say about it, Mrs. Fletcher. I have a responsibility for the safety of the citizens of this city, including visitors."

I shrugged. "I suppose there is nothing I can do about it. I probably should be grateful. I'm not." I opened the door and looked into the living room where technicians were still at work. I said to Commissioner Frye, "I'm suddenly very tired. I'd like to go back to my hotel."

"Of course. I have a car waiting downstairs. I assume you gave a statement to the detectives."

"Yes, as brief as it was. I really didn't know anything aside from having discovered her body, poor thing."

I started to leave the bathroom but stopped in the doorway, turned, and said, "Detective Rizzi. Will he be assigned to this murder?"

Frye frowned. "Rizzi? No. He's narcotics. Why do you ask?"

"Just that he was the detective with whom I spoke after witnessing the murder of the Santa on Fifth Avenue. I felt comfortable with him, that's all. If I am to have constant contact with the police, I would appreciate having Detective Rizzi assigned to my detail."

Frye grunted. "I'll see what I can do," he said without conviction.

The commissioner and two uniformed patrolmen escorted me down the steps and to the front door of the building. An hour ago, Crosby Street had been eerily deserted. Now, it was a jumble of police cars, ambulances, media vehicles, cops, reporters, and dozens of onlookers drawn to the scene like moths to a summer candle. The moment I appeared, harsh lights controlled by television crews came to life, along with strobes from still photographers.

"Let us through, let us through," Frye said as he led me to a black, unmarked sedan. Two officers stiffened as we approached; one opened the back door. Frye said, "These two officers are assigned to you tonight. They'll be relieved in the morning."

"The quiet little hotel I'm staying at will not appreciate this," I said.

"Can't be helped, Mrs. Fletcher."

I suddenly remembered my car and driver, and Miss Hiss. "Excuse me," I said, walking away from Frye and his officers, who fell in step. My driver was seated behind the wheel of the limo, Miss Hiss asleep in his arms.

"Looks like you have a friend," I said as he lowered his window.

The driver grinned. "Nice little cat. Wish I could keep her."

"Why don't you?"

"Three dogs and a wife."

"We'll take the cat," Frye said.

"To where? The pound?"

"She'll be all right."

"Absolutely not. I'll take her with me to the hotel."

"Whatever you say." There was fatigue in his voice.

"Do you know where I can buy cat food and litter this time of night?" I asked.

Frye turned to an officer. "Go find a couple of bowls, litter, a litter box, and some cat food."

"Huh?"

"Just do it," Frye said. "Bring it to ... what hotel are you at?"

"The Sheraton-Park Avenue."

"Bring it there."

"Yes, sir."

"Thank you."

My driver handed Miss Hiss to me. She purred, and I squeezed her. We went to the police car, photographers' strobes going off with every step.

"Get some sleep, Mrs. Fletcher," Frye said through the partially open window after Miss Hiss and I were settled in the backseat. "If you need anything, call me directly." He handed me a card that included his private telephone number.

"I want you to know, Commissioner Frye, that I don't like any of this."

"Better than tripping over dead bodies. Good night, Mrs. Fletcher. Sleep tight."

"Good morning, Mrs. Fletcher," a pleasant male voice said on the phone.

"Morning?" I looked at the watch I'd worn to bed. It was seven; I'd gotten to sleep at four.

"My name is Tom Detienne. I'm the hotel's assistant manager."

I said in a thick, slurred voice, "Yes?"

"Could I have a few minutes of your time this morning?"

"This morning?" I rubbed my eyes and sat up. "I haven't had much sleep, Mr. Detienne. When did you want to see me?"

"Whenever it's convenient for you."

"I suppose if I get up now and take a shower—I need breakfast. Yes, I'm hungry. Would an hour be all right? Make it an hour and a half."

"Eight-thirty will be fine. What would you like for breakfast? I'll put in the order personally."

"That's kind of you." I told him what I wanted.

"What time would you like it delivered, Mrs. Fletcher?"

"Oh, eight."

"It will be there at eight, and I'll come up at eight-thirty. Thank you."

I stumbled out of bed, went to the bathroom, and splashed cold water on my face. I looked at myself in the mirror: "You look the way you feel, Jessica." More water on my face and over my wrists, something my mother taught me when I was a child. The blood in the wrists is cooled and goes to the rest of the body, which helps wake you up. At least that's what she said. I have no idea whether there is any physiological truth to it, but it always seems to work.

I felt better after showering. At eight sharp, a bellhop arranged my breakfast on the desk near the window.

At eight-thirty, Mr. Detienne arrived, a tall, handsome man with gray hair and horn-rimmed glasses. He wore a nicely tailored gray suit. "Sorry to intrude upon you, Mrs. Fletcher."

"Don't be silly. My life has been nothing but intrusions since I arrived in New York. Please, sit down."

Miss Hiss came from where she'd been sleeping on a couch and rubbed against his leg. He smiled and stroked her head. "Nice cat," he said.

"Her name is Miss Hiss. I hope you don't mind my

keeping her here." I'd arranged the water and food bowls, and litter pan in the bathroom and had created a bed from towels.

"No, that's fine," he said. "We don't allow pets under ordinary circumstances, but this is hardly ordinary."

"Far from it," I said.

Detienne seemed unsure, or unwilling, to say what was on his mind. Finally, he looked up from highly polished shoes he'd been examining and said, "Mrs. Fletcher, this whole thing is getting out of hand. You've seen today's papers?"

"No, I haven't."

He picked up the phone and instructed someone to bring up all the morning papers. He resumed his seat and said to me, "The lobby is crawling with press. Two uniformed New York City policemen are sitting in chairs outside your door. The phones are ringing off their hooks with calls from other media inquiring about you. Mobile TV vans are lined up in front of the entrance, which keeps our guests from getting cabs. Guests are complaining. We have a lot of regulars who come here because we are a quiet oasis in the middle of Manhattan. That's no longer true, I'm afraid."

I felt guilty and embarrassed. At the same time, I knew that none of this was my doing. Well, that wasn't entirely true. Seeing Waldo Morse shot on the street was certainly not my fault. But if I hadn't pursued the Joe Charles–Alphonse Rizzi–Susan Kale connection, I would not have ended up discovering her body in a loft on Crosby Street.

"I'm terribly sorry about this, Mr. Detienne. I was staying with friends when all this broke, and I felt it wasn't fair to have them subjected to the chaos. Now, I guess I've done the same thing to you and your guests. I'll arrange to leave immediately."

He shook his head. "No, Mrs. Fletcher. I'm not asking you to do that. We're honored to have someone of your stature staying with us. What I was going to suggest was that we move you to our penthouse suite on the roof. That would get you out of the main flow of hotel traffic. The suite has three bedrooms. Maybe your police protection could station themselves in one of them, or out on the roof. There's a lovely garden just outside the suite's patio doors, and you'll have a private elevator, and—"

"Put the police out in a garden in this weather?"

Detienne laughed. "We've already discussed that and are willing to go to the expense and trouble of putting up a tent, and to use portable heating units to keep them warm. In other words, Mrs. Fletcher, we'll go to any lengths to accommodate you, while at the same time accommodating our other guests. The move won't cost you any more."

"That's very generous," I said.

"Your bill is being paid by Buckley House, and we'll inform them, if you wish, that you'll be in the penthouse at no additional charge."

"Wouldn't it be better if I just found another place to stay?"

"Wouldn't hear of it, Mrs. Fletcher." He stood.

There was a knock on the door. Detienne answered and handed me the morning newspapers. The *Daily News* was on top. Its front page was a photograph of me exiting the building on Crosby Street at three o'clock that morning. The story began:

> *Famed mystery writer Jessica Fletcher, who witnessed the murder of the sidewalk Santa on Tuesday, discovered the body early this morning of a young woman named Susan Kale. Looks like Jessica Fletcher doesn't have to make up plots for her murder mysteries any longer. She can take all she needs from her real-life experiences.*

"This is awful," I said.

"Very upsetting to you, I'm sure."

Next came the *Post.* It had two photographs on the front page. One was of me climbing into the car provided by Commissioner Frye, Miss Hiss in my arms. The other was of the body bag containing Susan Kale's remains being loaded into a police ambulance. The *Post* headline read:

ANOTHER REAL MURDER
FOR JESSICA FLETCHER.

The caption read:

> *Mystery writer Jessica Fletcher, in New York to promote her latest murder mystery, has been promoting real murder since her arrival. She witnessed the slaying of a sidewalk Santa on Fifth Avenue, and early this morning discovered the body of a young woman on Crosby Street. Post reporter Bobby Johnson, who has been following Ms. Fletcher's bloody trail, reports on Page Three.*

I tossed the *Post* on the floor along with the *News,* and scanned the front page of the *New York Times.* There was no mention of the events of a few hours ago but Detienne suggested I look at the first page of the Metro Section. There it was, a brief story that reported the death of Susan Kale. It went on to say that I had found the body, and was the one who'd witnessed the murder of the sidewalk Santa.

"Even the *Times,*" I sighed.

"I'll leave these with you," Detienne said. "When you head off for the day, I'll have our staff move you to the penthouse. Again, Mrs. Fletcher, I hope this won't cause you any additional grief."

I heard his words but didn't digest them. I finally realized he'd been speaking to me, looked at him, and said, "Oh, my mind is elsewhere, which is probably good. Thank you for your courtesy. Please ask your staff to move Miss Hiss to the penthouse, too, and to take care that she doesn't get loose."

"I understand," he said. "I have two cats of my own."

When he was gone, I absently opened the *Post* to Page Three. Bobby Johnson was getting up in the world; there was a head shot of him along with photographs from the scene of Susan Kale's murder. My eyes sped over the page and stopped on a paragraph where a name popped out at me—Detective Alphonse Rizzi. He'd given a statement to the press:

"The deceased, a Ms. Susan Kale, was found dead in her apartment on Crosby Street. She was in the process of moving because there was no furniture in the apartment,

and there were boxes containing her possessions. We have
no leads at this time, but an initial examination of the
body by an assistant medical examiner indicates that she
was sexually assaulted, and that heavy traces of cocaine
were found in her bloodstream."

Impossible, I thought. The girl seemed perfectly lucid
when we talked. I hadn't examined the body, but from
what I could see she was fully clothed. She'd been beaten
about the head, which undoubtedly caused her death.

I didn't see any signs of what Rizzi had said. And, I
asked myself, why had he indicated that it was her apartment? Surely, he knew about her relationship with Joe
Charles, and that Joe Charles lived there. He'd called and
left a message on the answering machine confirming their
eleven-o'clock rendezvous at Sweet Basil. Not only that, I
had no doubt that he was aware that Waldo Morse was a
friend of both Joe Charles and Susan Kale. None of that
was mentioned in his statement.

Rizzi ended his comments to the press with:

"Unfortunately, a guest of our city, famous mystery writer
Jessica Fletcher, had to be the one to discover the body.
You'll recall that it was Mrs. Fletcher who witnessed the
shooting of the Santa Claus on Fifth Avenue on Tuesday.
Mrs. Fletcher evidently happened upon the body purely by
chance, but we are providing her with round-the-clock po-
lice protection for the duration of her stay in Manhattan."

Ruth Lazzara called from the lobby. She was to accompany me to a book signing at a midtown store. "Mrs.

Fletcher," she said breathlessly, "I can't believe what's happened to you. *Another* murder?"

"Afraid so, I think I'd better go home to Cabot Cove. If I stay much longer, your homicide rate will break all records."

"Are you all right?" she asked. "I mean, are you up to making appearances today?"

"I think so. I might as well. They don't murder people in bookstores, do they?" I was sorry at my feeble attempt to make light of what had happened. Somehow, it didn't lend itself to comedy high or low. "I'll be down in a minute," I said. "But, I should warn you, Ruth, we'll have a couple of uniformed members of New York's finest with us every step of the way."

"Maybe that's a good thing. There's plenty of press down here."

"You'll steer me through them, I'm sure."

Two policemen sat in the hall in straight-back chairs.

"Good morning," I said.

"Good morning, ma'am." As I started down the hall, they trailed after me. I stopped and turned. "There really is no need for you to spend the day with me."

"Orders, ma'am."

"Yes, I suppose you have no choice in the matter. Well, come on. It's going to be a busy day."

And tomorrow, too, I thought. Police escorts or not, I was going to Cabot Cove in the morning and I intended to make that trip alone.

Chapter Thirteen

When I returned to the hotel at five, I was personally escorted to the penthouse by Mr. Detienne. It was a stunning suite of rooms on the top of the hotel. A sliding glass door led to the roof garden, a vast expanse of AstroTurf stretching to the roof's edge. Nothing was in bloom, of course, but dozens of evergreens in large wooden tubs and strung with hundreds of tiny white Christmas lights defined the area.

I'd insisted that the two policemen assigned to me take one of the inside rooms, rather than being banished to a tent. There was more to my decision than altruism. The suite was served by a private elevator, which seemed to be the only access to it. I asked Detienne whether there was another exit.

"There's a small elevator that goes down to the kitchen," he said. "It's on the other side of the roof. Why do you ask?"

"No special reason," I said cheerily, "just my natural curiosity at work. I always look for entrances and exits wherever I stay, a habit I got into when placing my characters in different situations."

He laughed. "Always working, huh?"

"Afraid so. It goes with the territory of being a writer. As an author-friend of mine often says, 'Everything gets used.'"

After Detienne gave me a tour of the suite, I threw up my hands and said, "This is absolutely lovely. Thank you so much."

"My pleasure. Would you like me to make a dinner reservation for you tonight?"

"Goodness, no. As far as I know, I have the night off and intend to take full advantage of it—a long soak in a hot tub, a good book, asleep by nine."

"Dinner in your room?"

"Splendid. I'll check the room-service menu and call down a little later."

1 walked him to the door that led to the interior hall and the suite's elevator. "Might I ask you something, Mrs. Fletcher?" he said.

"Of course."

"I know the police are here for your protection, but do you feel secure having them in the suite with you?" My puzzled expression prompted him to add, "They may be police, but you never know what kind of people they really are. I mean, a single woman sharing a suite with two strange men could be—well, awkward."

I smiled. "I've thought of that, and I don't have any qualms. The bedroom they're staying in is certainly enough removed from mine, and has its own bath facilities. They know I need my privacy. Their door will be closed, and so will mine. But thank you for thinking of it. Good night, Mr. Detienne. I'll be fine."

I must admit that I was a little on edge as I soaked in the tub knowing that two strange men were in the next room. But I didn't dwell upon it. The luxurious pleasure of the hot water penetrating my skin was too delicious to let anything mitigate the experience.

I stayed in the tub for almost an hour. Shriveled, contented, and sleepy, I wrapped myself in a thick terry cloth robe provided by the hotel and placed my dinner order— shrimp cocktail, lamb chops cooked pink, fresh asparagus, a spinach salad, a raspberry tart, and a large pot of tea. It was scrumptious, and when I climbed into bed at precisely nine, Margaret Truman's latest capital crimes mystery on the pillow next to me, I felt as though I'd been transported to a gentler, kinder place, at least for this night. I could see through the windows that it was crystal clear outside. Stars twinkled in a black sky, like the lights on the evergreens. It was windy; the windowpanes rattled, which only added to my feeling of secure coziness.

I didn't leave a wake-up call because I didn't want the phone to ring. Instead, I set a tiny travel alarm I always carry with me and awoke at five to its faint, lilting chime. I quickly turned it off, got out of bed, crossed the carpeted room to the closed door, and pressed an ear to it. A television was playing in the room assigned to the officers. I couldn't make out what they were watching, but it didn't matter. Any sound would help.

I dressed in casual clothing—slacks, sweater, sneakers—

then went to the bathroom where my black wig and sunglasses were on the vanity. I put them on and checked myself in the mirror. Hopefully, the disguise wouldn't be necessary. The officers seemed content watching Saturday morning fare on TV, and their replacements wouldn't arrive until seven. By then, I'd be long gone.

I buttoned my coat, pulled the collar up around my chin and neck, picked up a small bag I'd packed the night before, carefully opened my door, and waited. The sound of the TV was louder now that my door wasn't a barrier to it. One of the officers laughed; they were watching a cartoon. Thank you, Nickelodeon.

I stepped into the foyer that connected the suite's bedrooms, pressed my door shut, and went through the living room to the sliding doors. I undid the latch, slid the doors open just enough for me to squeeze through, and closed them.

The wind was still blowing fiercely; hopefully, it wouldn't disrupt flights out of New York's airports. It was still dark, but the tiny lights on the trees gave off enough illumination for me to make my way.

I moved toward the back of the garden and up steps into an area used for summer concerts. I turned right again until reaching the rear of the hotel and the door Detienne had mentioned. It hadn't occurred to me that it might be locked. It was. I noticed a small button next to it and pressed, heard a ringing from far below and the groan of an ascending elevator. The door opened and a young Hispanic kitchen worker dressed in whites faced me.

"I'm Jessica Fletcher, the mystery writer. I'm staying in the penthouse suite and am researching different ways my characters might move through the hotel. Please take me down to the kitchen." I added, "Mr. Detienne, the assistant manager, knows about this."

He either didn't understand much English, or the sight of a ridiculous-looking, windblown woman standing outside at five-thirty in the morning was too much of a shock. He didn't argue, simply stepped aside. I got into the elevator and rode it down to the kitchen where I received more quizzical stares. I ignored them and went through swinging doors into the empty main dining room, and to an exit onto Thirty-seventh Street. To my delight, a cab sat at the curb, motor running, driver snoozing. I knocked on the window; he awoke with a start. "LaGuardia Airport," I said through the window. He unlocked the curbside passenger door, and I slid into the seat. "The Delta Shuttle."

As we headed for the airport, I removed my wig and sunglasses, an action the driver noticed in his rearview mirror. "I just came from a costume party," I said pleasantly.

"Must have been a hell of a party," he commented.

"Oh, it certainly was. It's still going on." I stuffed the paraphernalia into my bag.

The driver kept glancing at me in the mirror all the way to the airport. Maybe I should have continued to wear my disguise. If he recognized me from all the pictures in the newspapers, it could jeopardize my determination to leave the city unnoticed. As it turned out, he didn't say another word.

As I crossed the nearly deserted terminal, I passed a newsstand on which all three New York papers were prominently displayed. There I was again on the front page of two of them. I detoured to a lady's room where

I put on my wig and sunglasses, then went to the counter and bought my ticket to Boston—under my real name, the name on my charge card.

"You're the famous writer," the pretty blond ticket agent said.

I glanced left and right before leaning across the counter and whispering, "Yes, but I prefer to keep it quiet today."

She handed me my boarding pass, wished me a pleasant flight, and whispered, "Your secret is safe with me, Mrs. Fletcher."

The 727's passenger compartment was sparsely populated. Most of my fellow-passengers read the *Times,* but a young man and woman across the aisle perused their individual copies of the *Post.* I'd intended to remove the uncomfortable wig once we were airborne, but thought better of it. I settled in my seat and, in what seemed only minutes, the captain announced we were beginning our descent into Logan Airport.

I smiled contentedly. It had worked even better than I'd hoped. No hitches, no glitches. Way to go, Jess.

Brimming with confidence, I stashed my wig and sunglasses and left the aircraft with my head high. New York City didn't exist. I was going home. I had only one moment of concern. As I reached the terminal's main entrance and looked for Jed Richardson, an unmarked green sedan barreled up to the entrance and two men jumped out. Police, I thought, turning away. Could they be looking for me? Impossible. I'd only been gone a few hours.

I looked over my shoulder and saw them run inside the terminal. Then, I heard Jed Richardson's loud, gravelly voice yell, "Jessica. Over here."

Not so loud! Jed stood next to a taxi. After a final glance at the terminal doors—the two men had disappeared inside—I quickly crossed the road.

"Sight for sore eyes," Jed said, an infectious grin on his round, tanned, deeply creased face. He wore a battered leather aviator's jacket, a white silk scarf around his neck, and a blue peaked cap with *Jed's Flying Service* emblazoned on it.

"Where's your plane?" I asked.

"Over at private aviation. I got me this cab." The driver, an older man with a large, bulbous nose, did not look happy that we were standing there talking. I suggested we get going. "You bet," Jed said. "Looks like we got us a serious weather front coming through. The sooner we get off, the better."

Our driver complained for the duration of the short trip to the private aviation area: "I could have had a fare into the city," he said more than once. To which Jed replied: "And we could have ended up with a pleasant driver."

He dropped us next to a hangar. I went through my usual debate of whether to tip him a lot to compensate for the short trip, or to tip him little for his rudeness. My choice fell somewhere in between. He looked at the money I handed him, shrugged, and drove off.

"Damn big-city attitude," Jed said.

"You should visit New York," I said.

"No, thanks. Boston's as big as I ever want to visit. Don't much like Bangor, either, no more. Come on, Jessica. Let's get outta here."

We walked to Jed's single-engine Cessna 185 Skywagon, which was parked in a row of other small planes. Jed also owned two twin-engine aircraft, and I wished he'd brought one of them. Having to depend only upon one engine increased my general nervousness about flying.

"Be the last flight in this honey," Jed said, patting the small plane's wing. "Got a fella going to pick it up next week. Got a right good price for it."

"Good," I said. I was anxious to get inside; the open area in which we stood was like a wind tunnel, its chilled air biting into my cheeks. On the other hand, getting in meant taking off. No backing out now. Jed was there because I'd asked him to be, and I certainly trusted his flying ability. He'd spent years as a top-rated commercial pilot before opening his own small airline.

I settled into the right-hand seat, and Jed got into the left. The engine turned over smoothly, and we were soon taxiing toward the operative runway that windy, cold December morning in Boston. Jed invited me to put on an extra set of headphones in order to hear the dialogue between him and the controller. I had trouble making out their words, but they seemed to know precisely what each other was saying. We were told there were two commercial airline jets cleared to take off before us. Jed leaned over to me and said, "Got to keep our distance from those babies. Damn vortex coming off their wings, and the thrust from their engines could blow us over like a piece 'a paper."

I laughed nervously: "Yes, by all means, Jed. Let's keep our distance."

I watched the two commercial jets take off and formed the same question I always did—how can anything that big get off the ground?

We were instructed to hold because a plane was landing. After it had, Jed received permission to take his position on the active runway. "Cessna six-seven-A cleared for takeoff," the controller said.

"Roger, Cessna six-seven-A rolling," Jed replied. He pushed the throttle forward, the engine roared to maximum life, and we bounced down the seemingly endless strip of concrete, the wind doing its best to blow us off to the side. We hadn't gone very far when Jed pulled back on the yoke and the plane waffled into the air. The controller instructed him to make a right turn and to climb on an assigned compass heading until reaching two thousand feet.

I looked out my window and saw the city of Boston slide away beneath me. I had to admit that while I was still nervous—my stomach confirmed that—I also found it exhilarating. I looked through the front window at the blur of the whirling propeller. Just keep spinning.

We achieved Jed's requested cruising altitude of eight thousand feet, and the small plane moved smoothly through the air. He tapped me on the shoulder and pointed to his left. "There's that front I told you about, Jess." I followed the direction of his finger and saw a wall of black clouds. "See up on top of that big one over there? See how it's shaped like an anvil?"

"Yes."

"Big storm clouds always get that shape on top. We'll stay plenty clear of that baby. Could toss us about like a tennis ball, snap the wings right off."

Stop talking about the terrible things that can happen to us, I thought. I held my tongue. Jed loved flying and took pride in pointing out such things to his passengers. Still . . .

We gave wide berth to all the unsettled weather enroute, and Jed eventually pointed out Cabot Cove to me. Try as I did, I couldn't distinguish it from any of the other towns we'd flown over; thousands of hours of viewing things from the air develop a different visual acuity in pilots, I suppose.

"There's the runway," Jed said.

I squinted. "Where?"

He laughed. "No need for you to see it, Jess. Just so long as I do."

Our relatively smooth flight had become bumpy. The small plane lurched up and down, left and right, and we once dropped what seemed like a thousand feet, although I suppose it wasn't that far. Jed saw the frightened expression on my face and patted my knee. "Always gets rougher down near the ground," he said. "Not to worry."

He approached the runway, which I could see clearly now, on an angle. When we were almost over one end of it, Jed turned the aircraft to the right and we flew parallel to the concrete strip on our left. "Got a left-hand landing pattern here," he said. "Flyin' downwind now. Always land into the wind, so we'll take a left when we get to the end, then take another left and smack into it."

"Interesting," I said.

Then it happened, suddenly and without fanfare. I didn't notice the propeller stop but I certainly heard the terminal cough from the engine.

"What's the matter?" I asked.

"Damn carb heat control acting up again. Been havin' trouble all winter. Promised to fix it before the fella who bought it picks it up next week."

There was silence now, the only sound a whoosh of air passing the cockpit. The prop was dead. So was the engine.

"What do we do now?" I asked, picturing us pitching nose-first into the woods.

"Got to dead-stick her," Jed said, his voice as calm as usual.

"But we don't have an engine."

"Don't need one. We'll just glide ourselves right on down."

Jed never varied from his planned approach. It seemed to me at the last minute that we were getting dangerously close to the ground, but we crossed the end of the runway and, within seconds, touched down for a perfect landing.

"Biggest trouble is gettin' this thing to the hangar," Jed said as he reached a taxiway using the plane's remaining forward momentum. We came to a stop halfway between the runway and hangar. "See if I can raise anybody in Unicom," he said, speaking into the handheld microphone. There was no answer. "Guess Joe Harley ain't arrived yet. You sit tight, Jess."

I watched him trudge toward the hangar that also served as the airport office. No engine meant no cabin heat, and I began to shiver. But my spirits picked up when I saw Jed leave the hangar accompanied by two familiar faces, Seth Hazlitt and Sheriff Morton Metzger. I opened my door and was outside when they arrived. After hugs all around, Jed said, "Let's go. This baby won't move on her own."

I got behind one wing with Seth, and Jed and Morton took the other. Together, we pushed the plane to the hangar.

"Sorry about that, Jess," Jed said. "Should've fixed that damn carb heat a long time ago."

"You'd better fix it before your buyer arrives," I said. "Actually, it was kind of exciting. I felt like I was in a glider."

"That's because you were. Call any time you need another ride."

"That will be tomorrow," I said. "Can you fly me back to Boston?"

"Ayuh. What time you plannin' on leavin?"

"I have to be back in New York City by noon. I suppose I should take the nine-thirty shuttle."

We set a time to depart Cabot Cove, and I went with Seth and Morton to where Morton's squad car waited. "I didn't expect to see you here," I told him.

Metzger, who wore a green down coat with a fake fur collar with his tan uniform, earmuffs, and a large Stetson hat, said, "Had nothin' else to do, Mrs. F." He started the engine. "Where to?"

"Nancy Morse's house."

Mort looked at me. I was in front with him, Seth in the back. "What are we goin' there for?" Metzger asked.

"I have to speak with her about something. Actually, I have some unpleasant news to deliver."

"About Waldo?" Metzger said.

"Yes. I assume Seth told you."

Metzger looked over his shoulder. "Can't say he told me everything, but enough for me to get the gist."

The Morse house was in a lovely community ten miles north of Cabot Cove Center. Each house was nestled into its own unique natural setting of rocks and trees. The Morse house was especially nice because it was poised on a rise that gave it the development's highest vantage point. A steep, narrow road led up to the driveway; you couldn't see the house until you were almost upon it. This day, it was also hidden behind a large moving van.

We parked in front of the truck and walked to where the driveway began. From there, I could see a figure passing back and forth behind a large picture window. I assumed it was Nancy. "Coming with me?" I asked my companions.

"Might as well," Seth said. "Judgin' from this truck, you didn't get here any too soon."

We walked three abreast up the driveway and paused in front of the entrance to the house. "Here goes," I said. I climbed the steps and, as I reached for the doorbell, the door opened and Nancy Morse looked down at me.

"Hello, Nancy. I'm Jessica Fletcher."

She scrutinized me closely. When she accepted that I was who I claimed to be, she turned her attention to Seth and Morton.

"Mornin', Mrs. Morse," Seth said. Mort grunted and tipped his Stetson.

"What do you want?" Nancy asked.

"Just a little time to talk," I said pleasantly. "May we come in?"

Two moving men carrying a couch came up behind Nancy and excused themselves. They passed, and I repeated my request.

"Can't you see I'm busy?" Nancy said.

"Gracious, yes. I certainly can see that. I can't imagine anything more disruptive than moving. Where are you going?"

She started to answer, but her words trailed off as

an angry expression crossed her face. "Please. Leave me alone," she said.

"Nancy, I don't wish to cause you any problems, but I've flown here this morning from New York because I have something important to tell you."

Her eyes widened, and she placed her hands on her hips. "So, tell me and let me get out of here."

"Nancy, Waldo is dead. He's been murdered."

"I know."

"You do? Who told you?"

"It doesn't matter. If that's why you came here, you wasted a trip."

I looked closely at her and saw two things—the gradual erosion of the youthful, blond beauty she'd been as a high school cheerleader, and the beginnings of an older woman of whom life was beginning to take advantage. Behind her defiant, angry mask was a soft vulnerability that she worked hard to keep in the background. I said, "Nancy, if you will give me just ten minutes, I promise we'll get out of your hair for good. But I *witnessed* Waldo's murder. I have some questions. Please, if you'll just give me—"

She turned and went into the house, the door still open. The moving men returned and entered. Seth, Mort, and I went right along with them.

Although the house was in disarray because of the move, the interior was every bit as beautiful as the exterior. The living room was massive and dominated by a huge natural stone fireplace that spanned an entire wall. An Indian family could have cooked in it. Lived in it.

"Jess, maybe we should . . ." Seth said.

"No. She has to talk to me."

I didn't know where Nancy had gone so I went through the first open door, which led to the kitchen. All the appliances were restaurant grade and size. Another door from the kitchen led to a large deck overlooking a lavishly landscaped yard. I was about to retrace my steps to the living room when Nancy suddenly appeared. "How dare you come in here," she said.

I extended my hands in a gesture of pleading. "Nancy, I not only saw Waldo murdered, I discovered the body yesterday of a young woman with whom he was involved. She also was murdered. I know these two horrible incidents are related."

"So?"

"So, that means that *your* life could be in danger."

Her laugh was scornful. "Don't you think I already know that? Why the hell do you think we're moving, leaving this beautiful house, yanking the kids out of good schools? Come on, Mrs. Fletcher, give me a break. Stick to writing murder mysteries and leave us real people alone."

Her words stung but I pressed on. "Do you remember a young man from Cabot Cove named Joe Charles?"

"No."

I started to ask another question but she turned on Seth and Morton. "Why are you two standing there gawking? You have no right to be in here. I haven't done anything wrong."

I wanted to keep her talking. If the presence of Seth and Morton upset her, I'd stand a better chance if they left. They knew what I was thinking, excused themselves, and departed, leaving Nancy and me alone in the kitchen.

"Joe Charles was a musician," I said. "His real name when he was going to high school was Johnson. They called him Junior. Does that ring a bell?"

She said, "Yes, I think I remember somebody with that name."

"Have you seen him since he departed Cabot Cove? He left to make a career in music."

"I don't know anything about Junior Johnson, or this Joe Charles."

"The reason I ask, Nancy, is that Joe Charles and Waldo were friendly in New York. In fact, they lived together, at least some of the time. It was in Joe Charles's apartment that this young woman, Susan Kale, was murdered. Joe Charles has disappeared, and quite suddenly." I sighed, shook my head, and leaned against a large center island above which copper pots and pans hung. "I know there's a connection between all of this, Nancy, and I came here hoping you might help me make that connection. Did you have any contact with Waldo after he went into the witness protection program?"

"Damn it, Mrs. Fletcher, don't you ever get the hint? Of course I never heard from Waldo. That's the idea of the program. People disappear in it, leaving everybody else swinging in the wind."

"But he must have sent you money." I extended my arms to take in the kitchen. "Surely, someone from the government supported you."

"That is between me and the government."

"Yes, I suppose that's the way it must be. Still, it's hard for me to conceive of a husband and father never making contact with his family again."

"That's your problem," she said.

"It's become my problem only because I witnessed Waldo's murder. Waldo was working as a volunteer Santa Claus on Fifth Avenue when he was shot. Do you have any idea why he might have taken such a visible job, considering his need to remain in hiding from the drug dealers he turned in?"

"Not so visible. Santa Claus wears a beard, doesn't he?"

"Not a very good one. Have you ever heard from any of the drug dealers who went to jail as a result of Waldo's testimony?"

She snickered. "If I had, Mrs. Fletcher, I wouldn't be standing in this kitchen talking to you. They don't play by the same rules as the rest of the world."

"But it would seem to me that they would know Waldo had a family. From what I hear about the way they do business, they wouldn't hesitate to take out their anger on the family of an informer."

"Look, Mrs. Fletcher, I know I've been rude and I apologize for that. I've been under a tremendous strain."

"I understand," I said. "I dread the day I ever have to move."

"I'm talking about the strain of having a husband leave me and his children, then be accused of smuggling drugs, and then testify against the others he was involved with in return for disappearing, a new life, one that didn't include me or the kids. It has hurt them terribly. I ask forgiveness every day for that."

"It seems Waldo's the one who should ask for forgiveness."

"That wasn't Waldo's nature. Excuse me. I need to talk to the movers."

Alone in the kitchen, I went to the window and looked outside. The movers were carrying a large dresser to the truck. Then, I heard a voice from inside the house. A man's voice. Nancy said something. They both sounded angry. I was tempted to go in search of them, but thought better of it. Nancy was upset enough. Who was the man? I had a hunch about that.

I meandered the kitchen's perimeter. Everything was obviously expensive; no cost had been spared to create a stunning and functional kitchen. On one countertop in the corner was a pad of lined, yellow legal-size paper. I glanced down at the first page. Nancy had been writing a letter using a blue ballpoint pen that rested on the pad. It started with that day's date; it began, "To whom it may concern." I started to read the first paragraph when she returned to the kitchen, saw what I was doing, and tore off the pages.

"It's possible you'll hear from Junior Johnson, also known as Joe Charles," I said.

"I doubt that. No one is going to know where we've gone."

"That may be your goal, Nancy, but it's not easy to completely disappear. My point is that if you should hear from him, I would appreciate knowing about it. Believe me, this is not to satisfy my idle curiosity. It has to do with murder ... *two* murders ... and I've found myself more involved with both than I'd like to be."

"I'll let you know if I hear from him," she said.

"Thank you. If you can't reach me—I'll be in New York

through the new year—you can call Dr. Hazlitt, or Sheriff Metzger."

"Sure."

I knew I had overstayed my welcome and that she was getting ready again to tell me to leave. I would spare her that. "Thank you for talking to me, Nancy. I wish you and the children well wherever you go. Where are the children?"

"With my mother."

Instead of accompanying me from the kitchen, she left by herself. I hesitated, then tore off a few sheets of paper from the yellow pad, leaving enough pages so that it wouldn't be noticed. I put them under my coat, walked through the living room, and rejoined Seth and Morton in the driveway.

"You should have gotten in the car and used the heater," I said. "You both look frozen."

"Not so bad with the sun shinin'," Seth said, looking up and squinting into a brilliant blue sky. "Nancy Morse certainly was some ugly."

"I feel sorry for her," I said.

"Looks like the storm they forecast missed us," Morton said.

"And a good thing it has," I said. "Know what I want to do? I would like to go to my house, get a fire going, and have some clam pie. Is Charlene Sassi still making pies and selling them?"

"Sure is."

"Splendid. Let's stop at her house and get some. The treat's on me."

I bought the last two clam pies Charlene had to sell, and we headed for my place. I felt like a little girl anticipating arrival at a special amusement park. I couldn't wait to be in my own home again, to sit around the table with friends, and enjoy Charlene's clam pie that someone once described as "like going to heaven."

"Home! It looks wonderful," I said as Mort pulled into my driveway. Joseph, a mildly retarded gentleman who made a pretty good living around town as a handyman, had shoveled my driveway and walk. Whenever I was away, he also checked on the house every day to make sure that the heat, which I left on a low setting, was still on, and took in my mail and newspapers.

I got out of the car and headed for the front door.

"Don't slip," Seth said. I looked down, saw the icy patch to which he was referring, skirted it, fumbled for keys in my purse, and opened the door. I stood in the middle of the living room and did a clumsy pirouette. "Look. Joseph has put wood in the fireplace. Put a match to it, Seth, while I set the table."

A half hour later we enthusiastically dug into the pies. "Mort," I said between bites, "I heard the news about Parker Brothers being interested in your game."

"Haven't heard another word from them, so I don't get my hopes up. I suppose they get lots of people like me inventing games and sending them to them, bein' the biggest and all."

"But your game is really very good," I said. "Take it from a mystery writer."

Seth sat back, dabbed at his mouth with a napkin, and patted his sizable belly. "So, Jessica Fletcher, you got your chance to talk to Nancy Morse. Didn't seem to me like she was likely to be any help."

"It looks that way, Seth, but I haven't had a chance to digest what she said."

"How about fillin' us in on everything's been happening to you down in New York," Mort said, taking another serving.

"I wouldn't even know where to begin. Actually, I'm not supposed to be here."

"That young lady you found?" Seth asked.

"Yes. You know about that?"

"Been on the radio this mornin'."

I sighed and shook my head. "Because of finding that young woman's body, I was prohibited from leaving New York."

"Doesn't seem right," Metzger said. "No crime in findin' a body. Causing one's another matter."

"How did you manage to leave?" Hazlitt asked.

"I'll show you." I went to the bedroom, put on the wig and sunglasses, and returned to the dining room. "Ta-da," I sang, assuming a silly model's pose.

"Who's that lady?" Seth asked Mort. They laughed heartily.

"Where did Jessica go?" Mort said, playing into the banter.

"Effective, huh?" I said.

"You look like one of those New York City cabaret singers," Mort said.

"I hope so. Just as long as I didn't look like a mystery writer named Jessica Fletcher." I pulled off the wig and glasses, and started to tell them how I'd managed to elude the New York patrolmen assigned to my suite. I didn't get very far. An automobile pulled into the driveway, doors opened, slammed shut, and footsteps were heard approaching the front door.

"Looks like you got company, Jess," Seth said.

"I can't imagine who. Did you tell anyone I was coming home?"

"Nope," Seth said. "Well, a few folks, but I was pretty choosy about it."

I threw my physician friend a skeptical glance as someone knocked.

"You sit," Mort said, heading for the door. "I'll get it."

I couldn't hear what the man said to Mort, but I did hear my name. I raised eyebrows at Seth, and we joined them.

"Jessica Fletcher?" the man said. Another man stood directly behind him. They were straight out of central casting—police.

"Yes."

"I'm Detective Pehanich, N.Y.P.D." He flashed a badge at me. "This is Detective Taylor."

"Yes?"

"I'm afraid I'll have to ask you to come with us, Mrs. Fletcher."

"Why? I haven't done anything."

"We have a warrant for your arrest."

"On what charge?'

"Leaving the scene of a crime as a material witness."

I couldn t help but laugh. "That's nonsense," I said. "I'm coming back in the morning. I just left the city to—"

"Mrs. Fletcher, please don't give us a hard time."

Mort Metzger pulled himself up to full height and stepped between me and Pehanich. "I'm Morton Metzger, sheriff of Cabot Cove," he said with authority. "Let me see that warrant."

Pehanich handed it to Metzger, who took glasses from his pocket, perched them on his nose, and studied the paper carefully. He turned to me and said, "Appears to be in order, Jess."

"Could we get going, Mrs. Fletcher?" Taylor said. "If we leave now, we can catch the last flight out of Bangor."

"Were you the gentlemen at Logan Airport this morning?"

"No, ma'am. They were Boston police. Somebody from New York called them when they discovered you missing."

I sighed. "Your efficiency impresses me."

"Please, ma'am. It's cold. We'd like to get back. The holidays and all."

"Yes, the holidays," I said wistfully. "The holidays."

Mort Metzger said, "You don't have to go with them, Jess. We can fight extradition."

"Hey, Sheriff, cool it," Detective Taylor said. "She's wanted back in New York as a witness, not 'cause she killed anybody."

"Thank you very much," I said.

"I mean it, Jess," Mort said. "We'll buzz up Cal Simons right now." Simons was Cabot Cove's leading attorney.

"No, Morton, that won't be necessary. I was going back anyway and might as well have company." I said to the detectives, "Please come in and enjoy the fire while I clean up the dishes. There might even be some food left. We were enjoying clam pie."

"No thank you, ma'am," Pehanich said, "but we will

come inside. Please hurry. We don't want to miss that flight."

I indicated to Seth that I wanted him to follow me into the kitchen. The moment we got there I whispered, "Do me a favor. Go back to Nancy Morse's house and see if there's a young man with her. Don't let her see you. Stay out on the road and just watch." I quickly described the adult Junior Johnson, a.k.a. Joe Charles.

"What do I do if I see him?"

"Tell me the next time we talk."

I sensed the presence of one of the detectives in the doorway and rinsed a dish.

"Please, Mrs. Fletcher."

"Of course. Sorry. I'm ready."

I was led to the rental car the detectives had driven from Bangor Airport.

"No cuffs," Mort Metzger said.

The detectives looked at him strangely. Taylor said, "No, no cuffs, Sheriff. Nice town you have here." He then said to me, "My wife is a big fan, Mrs. Fletcher. I wondered maybe you could autograph a book to her. Her name is Lynn."

"Sure," I said, climbing into the backseat. "And let me have your mother-in-law's name, too. I'm sure she'd enjoy a copy."

Chapter Fourteen

"Hard for me to believe, Mrs. Fletcher, but that's what they say. You're a suspect in the murder of the Kale girl."

The voice delivering this weighty message was Sergeant Dennis Murphy, one of New York's saintly Irish cops who would have made a far better Santa Claus than Waldo Morse had. He'd been assigned to me the minute I was spirited into the precinct by my two bounty hunters, and we sat in a small holding cell just beyond the booking area.

"Am I officially a suspect?" I asked, attempting to sound unconcerned.

"No. Just what I hear, ma'am. A shocker, I'd say. You, the world's most famous mystery writer—and obviously a fine lady, too—dragged into this tawdry affair. Must be a mistake is all I can figure."

"Yes, there must be. It's preposterous. I found her. I didn't kill her."

"I'm sure it will all be straightened out in short order. Sometimes when they don't have any leads, they . . ."

". . . They accuse the closest, easiest person?" I said, finishing his thought. "I have a problem with that logic."

Murphy shrugged. I poised to deliver a speech about the absurdity of that approach to crime solving, but didn't; it would have been lost on him. Besides, he'd been extremely courteous and solicitous, even allowing me to use the phone before entering my confines. I'd made two calls, the first to Vaughan Buckley. My timing was good, considering it was Saturday night; I caught him as he and Olga were preparing to leave for dinner. He told me to sit tight and that he'd be there as soon as he could, hopefully with a lawyer named Winter, who, he claimed, was the city's best criminal attorney.

My second call was collect to Seth Hazlitt in Cabot Cove to let him know I'd arrived safely. My timing was good with that call, too. He and Mort Metzger were waiting to be picked up by Jed Richardson, who would fly them to Boston where they would catch the next available flight to New York.

"Please don't, Seth. I'm fine. I spoke with Vaughan Buckley, and he said—"

"Save your breath, Jessica. Mort and I had a meeting soon's those gorillas took you away. We decided our place was at your side."

"But if you come, you'll have to . . ."

"Not another word. We'll head straight for that Park Avenue hotel you're stayin' in. Be there as soon as we can."

I stopped trying to dissuade them. They'd show up whether I wanted them to or not. Seeing them would be comforting, of course. But they could also add another complication, as had happened a year ago when they flew to London to "comfort me" during the investigation of Marjorie Ainsworth's murder. Neither of these dear friends is at home in large cities, and their penchant for getting into trouble when away from their familiar, secure Cabot Cove was only slightly less than astounding.

But I should be the last one to talk about finding trouble in strange big cities. There I was sitting in a holding cell in N.Y.P.D. headquarters as a material witness to one murder and, as I'd just learned, a murder suspect in another. Time to stop worrying about others and to start worrying about myself. As absurd as I found the entire situation, the ramifications could be serious.

That realization turned the stuffy, hot cell into a refrigerator for me. I wrapped my arms about myself and waited for what would happen next.

Which was the arrival of Police Commissioner Ferdinand Frye. He nodded for Murphy to leave. When we were alone, Frye leaned against the bars and slowly shook his head. Then he smiled. "What are we going to do with Jessica Fletcher?" he asked.

"My first suggestion is to let me out of here immediately."

"Of course. That's why I'm here, to see that you leave without further delay."

I stood and straightened my skirt. "They took my coat," I said.

"We'll get your coat, Mrs. Fletcher. But before we do, and before you leave, there's the question of where you'll be going."

"Pardon?"

"I want you out of this city."

"And I would like very much to get out of this city, Commissioner Frye. My visit has not been what you would call festive and gay. But I have an obligation to see through my book promotion activities. I owe that to my publisher."

"I'm sure Mr. Buckley would understand if you cut it short. He must know how much you'd like to be home for the holidays. There's no place like it, as the song says."

"True," I said. "And the contemplation of going home is more delicious than you could ever imagine. But no, I intend to stay as long as necessary to fulfill my obligations. My coat please."

The wide, perpetual smile faded, replaced by a slash for a mouth and hard, dark eyes. He pushed away from the bars and closed the gap between us. "Mrs. Fletcher," he said in the measured tones of an impatient schoolteacher explaining something to an especially dense student, "your presence seriously hampers my ability to solve two murders. Your involvement in them, as coincidental as it might be, has created a media circus. If I didn't have faith in your integrity, I'd wonder whether it's all been designed to help sell your books."

"I assure you that's not the case."

"Of course it isn't. But you're in my way. I don't like it when people get in my way, Mrs. Fletcher."

"Fair enough," I said. "I'll do everything within my power to stay out of your way. But now I want to leave here, return to my hotel, and go to bed. I'm very tired."

Footsteps sounded outside the cell, and Vaughan suddenly appeared. With him was a short, squat man wearing a black cashmere overcoat and black astrakhan hat. "Jessica," Buckley said. "How could they have put you in a cell like this?"

"I was just leaving," I said, smiling sweetly at Commissioner Frye.

"What is she charged with?" Winter asked Frye. He might have been short, but his voice was tall.

"Nothing, Jerry," Frye responded. "How've you been?"

Winter ignored the pleasantry. "Then why was she detained?" he asked.

"Mrs. Fletcher is—*was* a material witness to murder."

"As well as a suspect in another murder," I interjected.

"That's ridiculous," Buckley said.

"What she might be damn soon, Commissioner," Winter said, "is the plaintiff in a suit against you and the city."

"As you wish," Frye said. "I suggest we all go home."

"I went home," I said, feeling my adrenaline surge. "But you brought me back."

"Back from where?" Buckley asked.

"Cabot Cove."

"I didn't know you were going home, Jess."

"It was my secret, at least for a few hours. May I?" Frye stepped back to allow me to exit. I turned and asked, "Do your police have an unusually high number of sick days each year?"

"What?"

"There's no air in this building. Very unhealthy."

"Thank you for pointing it out to me."

Frye joined us as we walked to the front door. "By the

way, Mrs. Fletcher," he said, "since you insist upon staying in New York, you're on your own. I'm canceling your police escort, effective immediately."

"Frankly, that's good news," I said. "Thank you for your courtesies, Commissioner. Perhaps we'll meet again." I extended my hand. As he took it, his winsome smile returned.

"It's been a pleasure," he said.

"I'd like to say the same, but I really can't. Nothing personal."

"Nothing personal when she files suit, either," Winter said, a long black cigar clenched in his teeth.

"I somehow don't see Mrs. Fletcher as the litigious type," Frye said. "But do whatever you think is right. Good night."

As we watched Frye climb into the back of his limo and speed off, I drew a series of deep breaths. It was a cold, clear night. Overhead, thousands of jewellike white stars were displayed on a black scrim. Buckley said, "I should have introduced you. Jerry Winter, Jessica Fletcher."

Winter grunted something, reached in his pocket, and handed me his card. "Monday morning at ten, my office."

"Why?"

"To start the action against the city."

I laughed. "I'm afraid Commissioner Frye was right," I said. "I'm not litigious."

"Suit yourself, Mrs. Fletcher, but you've got this city where you want it. Well, whatever you decide to do, I'm glad I could help you out tonight. Lucky Vaughan caught me. I was heading out of town for the weekend."

Help me out? I wondered. What did he do? Would he send a bill?

"He wouldn't send me a bill, would he?" I asked Vaughan after Winter had departed.

"He'd better not. If he does, I won't publish his next book. Look, Jess, I think this has gone far enough, you getting involved in *real* murder. Come on. We'll check you out of the hotel and move you back in with us. You talk to no one, no press, no cops, only book people. I'll instruct Ruth Lazzara to ease up on the schedule, focus only upon major media."

I said I would think about it, but that I wanted that night in my suite to sleep away everything that had happened over the past twenty-four hours.

"Fine," he said. "But once you've done that, Olga and I want you back at the apartment."

"Let me sleep on it, Vaughan. And thanks for being such a dear." He drove me to the hotel, reiterated his wishes, wished me pleasant dreams, and drove off, leaving me to enter the empty lobby, dart into the elevator, ride it to the penthouse, and fling open the door. No room has ever looked more inviting—except for the flashing light on my telephone. A sign I'd left on my bathroom door, "DO NOT OPEN! ATTACK CAT INSIDE," was still there. I opened the door and Miss Hiss undulated through the opening, brushed against my leg, and wandered into the living room.

I called the desk and was given thirteen messages, most from media. Two were from Bobby Johnson, who invited me for brunch the next day, Sunday.

Sunday!

The press conference. A message left by what the hotel operator termed "a frantic woman," Ruth Lazzara, informed me that the conference would be held at three at the Plaza. The thought of it was depressing, but I had to go through with it. Lazzara didn't know anything about my having left the city and the ensuing madness. I returned her call; thankfully I reached her answering machine on which her frantic voice urged callers to leave a message. Which I did; I'd be there with bells on.

There was also a message from Seth and Morton. They'd called from the airport and would be at the hotel within the hour. I smiled. They'd be here in an hour provided the cab driver didn't bring them via Philadelphia.

Their pending arrival ruled out any long nap so I showered, changed into slightly more dressy clothes, and waited for their next call. It came exactly an hour later. They'd checked in and were downstairs in the Judges' Chambers, the hotel bar.

"Gorry, you look like death," Seth said when I joined them.

"Thank you for that vote of confidence, Seth."

"No offense, Jessica, but the bloom is gone from your cheeks. I don't wonder. No one in this city has bloom on their cheeks. Just gray circles under their eyes."

"It isn't *that* bad," I said in defense. "New York is actually a nice place—once you get used to it. It grows on you."

"Sort 'a like a fungus," Mort offered.

"If you say so. Hear anything from Parker Brothers about your board game?"

"Just a letter from a lawyer tellin' me they're lookin' at it."

"That's encouraging," I said.

"Maybe I ought to get *myself* a lawyer," he said.

"I know a wonderful one here in New York. Jerry Winter. So, fill me in on your trip."

"Pretty routine," Morton responded. "Seems like it's your trip that ought to be talked about. I called the police headquarters where you were held, identified myself as a fellow law enforcement officer to some ugly guy, and told 'em to put you on. They said you were gone. 'Where?' I asked. He hung up on me. I'd like to get *his* name."

"They're very busy at the precinct," I said. I asked Seth whether he'd gone back to Nancy Morse's house after I'd left. He had, of course, being the dependable person that he is. But he saw nothing, no unidentified man.

"Thanks for trying," I said. "By the way, I'm no longer a material witness to Waldo's murder, nor a suspect in Susan Kale's death."

"Good," Seth said.

"I'm famished. Feel like a walk and a quick dinner?"

"Awful late," Seth said, checking his watch, then patting his corpulent belly. "But I am a mite hungry."

We walked out onto Park Avenue and started uptown. It's a desolate part of town at night, lots of vehicular traffic but few pedestrians. We headed toward Fifth Avenue and its festive lights and decorations. As we waited at the corner of Fortieth and Madison, a homeless man stepped from a doorway and extended his hand to us. Mort spun around, grabbed the man's wrist, and announced, "You're under arrest. I'm a police officer."

"No, Morton, it's all right," I said quickly. "Here." I handed the man a dollar bill. He thanked me, looked quizzically at Metzger, muttered "weirdo," and backed into the shadows of his doorway haven.

"Just a cold, homeless person," I said. "There's lots of them in the city."

"Could have arrested him for vagrancy," Morton said.

When I'd reached into my coat pocket for the dollar, I'd also pulled out the paper on which I'd jotted down that day's telephone messages. "Excuse me," I said, stepping into a public phone booth.

"*New York Post,*" an operator said.

"Editorial department please," I said. "Mr. Bobby Johnson."

Chapter Fifteen

Before leaving the hotel Sunday morning to meet with Bobby Johnson, I talked with Ruth Lazzara about that afternoon's press conference. No, I didn't need a limousine to take me. I'd get there on my own, and on time. And no, I would not discuss Waldo Morse or Susan Kale. I was a writer of murder mystery books and intended to stick to that in any subsequent interviews. She was disappointed but agreed. She didn't have a choice.

Seth Hazlitt and Morton Metzger wanted to accompany me to my brunch with Johnson, but I stood firm. "That's why we're here, Jessica," Seth said. "Keep you out 'a further trouble."

"I assure you, Seth, there will be no more trouble for this lady. I intend to promote my book and soak up the holidays. Period. I want you to do the same." To their glum faces I added, "Let's meet here at six. Enjoy the city. We'll find a really good restaurant for dinner. And speaking of trouble, I suggest you two avoid it."

Johnson had chosen a restaurant called Ernie's, claiming it offered the best Sunday brunch in Manhattan. "An 'in' place," he'd said. "And my treat," he added as additional inducement to join him. He didn't know that I didn't need extra inducements. I'd decided while sitting in a Manhattan jail cell that the best way to get out from the middle of murders in Manhattan—but still see the web of mystery surrounding Waldo and Susan Kale resolved—was to lay everything I knew on him. He could take it from there. After all, he was an investigative reporter, and a good one from what I'd observed. Time for me to play the bystander, feed him what information I had, and watch things develop.

I arrived at Ernies early, confirmed the reservation he'd made under his name, and waited outside rather than taking the table. The air was crisp and smelled clean. Well, relatively clean. I closed my eyes and imagined I was standing on the Maine coast inhaling its invigorating ocean breezes. I was deep into my reverie and didn't see or hear Johnson. "Mrs. Fletcher," he said. "Are you okay?"

My eyes snapped open. "Oh, yes, of course. I was daydreaming."

"Didn't mean to startle you."

"That's all right. I confirmed your reservation. Shall we go in?"

After being seated at a corner table, I got right down to business. "The reason I agreed to meet with you, Bobby, is that I've decided to share with you what I know about Waldo Morse's murder, and the murder of Susan Kale."

He smiled. "Why the turnaround, Mrs. Fletcher? Until now, you've treated me like the enemy. I want to be your friend."

"In return for exclusive juicy stories," I said.

"Sure. No such thing as a free brunch. But that doesn't mean we can't be friendly."

I observed him across the table. He was a nice-looking young man, but someone who, no matter how hard he tried, would always appear slightly unkempt. He was losing his hair prematurely; an attempt to grow a beard was hampered by a lack of natural facial hair. It grew in sparse clumps. He looked perpetually tired, and I wondered about his lifestyle. Probably a night person. Did he have a special girl in his life? Maybe there wasn't time for that. So many questions fueled by my inherent curiosity. I didn't ask them, however. As much as I wanted to cooperate with him, I wasn't seeking friendship. Besides, my motives in meeting with him were as devious as his. I wanted him to get to the bottom of the murders for my sake, my self-interest. He was right. No such thing as a free brunch, no matter who paid the bill.

A pretty young waitress gave a theatrical presentation of the day's specials. An out-of-work actress, I judged, waiting tables to pay the rent until the big break came along. She wrote down our orders—eggs Benedict and a Bloody Shame for me (the British term for a Virgin Mary), and *huevos rancheros,* a Mexican egg dish, and the real thing, a Bloody Mary for Johnson—and started to walk away. She turned, narrowed her eyes at me, and said, "You're a famous actress, aren't you? Your name is on the tip of my tongue."

"Afraid not," I said lightly. "But I'm sure you'll be famous one day."

She beamed, said, "That's my goal." She handed me a business card. "If you hear of anything," she said.

"Of course." That was one of the appealing things about New York. Everyone walking around with big dreams and willing to sacrifice to realize them.

"Well," Johnson said. "Here we are. What's new in the life of Jessica Fletcher?"

"Quite a bit, Bobby. I visited Waldo Morse's wife, Nancy, in Cabot Cove yesterday. She told me some things I thought you'd be interested in."

"You went home yesterday?"

"Yes, but only for a few hours." I told him of my furtive escape from Manhattan and of my unexpected, premature return. He found it amusing, which, in retrospect and from an observer's perspective, it probably was.

"I knew Waldo Morse from Cabot Cove."

His eyebrows went up.

I told him everything I knew about Waldo, including his disappearance into the witness protection program.

"You say you talked to his wife."

"Yes. She was in the process of moving." I filled him in on Joe Charles and his relationship to Waldo and to Susan Kale. I did not, however, mention the third member of the intriguing triangle I'd uncovered, Detective Alphonse Rizzi. I'd raise him with Johnson when, and if, I felt the time was right.

"Where did Morse's wife move?" he asked.

"I don't know." I wished I did. And then I remembered the yellow pages I'd torn from the pad in her kitchen, which were back in my hotel room. If she'd pressed down hard enough when writing on the top pages, the ones I'd removed might have indentations that could be read using the old run-a-pencil-across-it technique. That was my intention when taking them, but I'd forgotten about it in the lunacy of the past two days.

Johnson had been taking notes on a small pad as I talked. He put it aside when our food was served, and we talked of things other than murder. When coffee arrived, he leaned across the small table and asked, "Do you realize what we have here, Mrs. Fletcher?"

"Please, call me Jessica. And no, I don't know what we have here. That's what I'm hoping you can provide."

"We have the makings of a bestselling true-crime book."

I sat back. "*We?* True-crime book? I'm not interested in that."

"Suit yourself, Jessica. I can write it myself. But I think it's only fair for you to share in the spoils. Make a great movie, TV miniseries."

"Thank you for thinking of me, Bobby, but no thank you." Was I acting precipitously in sharing information with him? He was obviously a young man with ambition, like our actress-waitress. Could I truly trust him? I decided on the spot that now that I'd gone this far with him, I might as well.

We parted with the understanding that we would share our knowledge of the murders with each other, but that I would no longer be actively seeking information.

"Think about my idea for a book," he said as we shook hands on the sidewalk.

"Sorry to disappoint, but I won't be giving it a second thought, or even a first one. Feel free to pursue it on your own."

"Fair enough, Jessica. Keep in touch."

Later, at dinner with Seth and Morton at a steak house near the hotel—we chose it to satisfy Morton's refusal to avoid red meat in his daily diet: "Real men eat meat," he was fond of saying, to Seth's chagrin—I was pumped for what I'd learned from the crusading young reporter.

"Nothing," I replied, "I talked, he listened. I'm afraid the reporters at the press conference this afternoon didn't learn much from me. All they wanted to talk about was Waldo and Susan Kale's murders. And I refused to discuss those things. Ruth Lazzara, Vaughan's publicity director, wasn't happy either. But I feel good about my decision to stick to what I know: writing books. I feel incredibly relieved, a heavy burden off my back. Bobby Johnson will investigate murder, and we'll investigate the wonders of this city. By the way, what did you do today?"

My question prompted a spirited replay by both men of their sightseeing. They'd spent most of the afternoon in F.A.O. Schwarz, which had brought out the child in both of them. Their faces glowed as they described the toys, and the children who marveled at them.

"Not such a bad place after all," I said.

"The store?"

"The city itself."

"I wouldn't go that far," Cabot Cove's sheriff replied.

He'd worn his tan uniform, Stetson hat, and badge everywhere since arriving, which drew considerable reactions from most people, including patrons of the steak house. "Damn near got killed by a coupla crazy taxi drivers. They wouldn't get away with driving like that back home."

"No, they wouldn't, not with Sheriff Morton Metzger in charge," I agreed. "Shall we? This lady is getting sleepy."

Which I remedied by climbing into bed soon after getting back to my suite, Miss Hiss curled at my feet. I closed my eyes and allowed sleep to quickly and quietly consume me.

Chapter Sixteen

I slept soundly but not long enough. The jangling of the phone next to my bed sent Miss Hiss scurrying for cover, and jarred me to an unsteady sitting position against the headboard. I shook my head and tried to read the time from the digital clock radio. It couldn't be. Five-fifteen? Maybe I'd slept all day and it was early evening.

"Hello," I mumbled, thankful the incessant, grating ringing had ceased.

"'Mornin, Jess. Seth here."

"Seth, it's five-fifteen."

"I know that, and I apologize for waking you. But I thought it was important."

"You're up," I said, knowing immediately it was a stupid thing to say. Of course he was up. He was talking to me.

"Couldn't sleep. Nothing but sirens and horns beeping and garbage trucks rattling cans right outside my window.

At any rate, I've been watchin' TV—CNN—quite a service to have, TV news twenty-four hours every day."

"Uh-huh."

"Just heard a report that a Catholic priest was murdered early this morning in St. Patrick's Cathedral, of all places."

"How terrible. It was on CNN already?"

"Nope. Got that on a local channel. Certainly is a terrible thing. Seems nobody's safe. No safe *place.*"

There was silence.

"Why was it necessary to wake me at five in the morning to tell me this?"

"'Cause it got me to thinkin' about this Waldo Morse mess. Seems to me Waldo was killed right next to that church."

"That's right. But how would you know that?"

"You told me the corner where Waldo got it. Mort and I stopped in the cathedral yesterday. Some imposing place. Anyway, seemed to me that it might be a useful coincidence."

"Hmmm. Maybe." My thoughts leaped back to the first day I'd seen Waldo. A priest had approached him, and I'd found it interesting that Waldo had handed the priest something rather than the other way around. "Any other details on TV about the priest being murdered?" I asked.

"Nope. I suppose you might as well go back to sleep. See you at nine for breakfast."

I was now wide-awake and craving a cup of hot coffee. I'm basically a tea drinker, but there are times when only coffee will do. "Go back to sleep?" I said, laughing. "Out of the question. See you in the dining room at seven."

I knew I wouldn't hold out until seven, so I ordered

coffee and a muffin from room service and turned on the television. The priest's murder was reported the minute the screen came to life.

"... *And, in Manhattan, a priest was shot and killed on the steps of St. Patrick's Cathedral early this morning. The priest, whose identity is being withheld pending notification of relatives, was shot three times in the chest while leaving the cathedral. It is not clear why he was there at that hour or whether he was a member of the cathedral diocese. Robbery has been ruled out as a motive, say police.*"

After enjoying the coffee and muffin, I took a quick shower, tossed on my sweats, and rode the elevator down to the lobby. Evidently my steadfast refusal at the press conference to not speak about *real* murders had had its intended effect. There was no one from the media ready to pounce on me. I went to a small store that sold newspapers. I didn't expect the priest's murder to be in early editions but bought them all anyway, scanned the headlines, and continued my morning constitutional at a brisk pace. I enjoy the early mornings. So many possibilities lie ahead. People seem hopeful as they hurry to work, purpose written on their faces, urgency in their step. Maybe that's why I've always written early in the day, using afternoons and evenings for reading, and catching up on correspondence and paperwork. I've never understood writers who write all night and sleep all day. But they wouldn't understand my schedule either. Different body clocks, circadian rhythms marching to different drummers.

After breakfast, Seth and Morton headed off for more sightseeing and shopping—remarkable, I thought, how quickly they'd adopted the Christmas spirit in dreaded

New York City—and I stayed in my suite returning phone calls, including a postmortem by Ruth Lazzara on the Sunday press conference. She'd received a number of calls that morning from the press, including offers for me to appear on afternoon television talk shows. I'd watched a few of them back in Cabot Cove and, frankly, they didn't impress me. I asked Ruth, "Why would they want me? I've never slept with anyone but my husband, never abused a child, and *never* would talk on television about those things if I had."

"But these are national shows, Jessica, with huge and loyal followings. The book will race to the top of the bestseller charts the day after you appear."

"Sorry, Ruth, but I simply won't subject myself to that type of situation."

Her deep, dark sigh said many things; I was grateful she didn't express them.

I called Bobby Johnson at the *Post* but didn't reach him. I wondered what he knew about the priest's murder that morning. Chances were it was pure coincidence. But I'd learned over many years of plotting crimes for my books, and solving them, that taking coincidences for granted could prove misleading, if not dangerous. My books may be fiction, but there's nothing fictitious in this world that hasn't actually happened to someone.

My first appointment that day was an eleven-o'clock book signing at Shakespeare & Co. a popular Manhattan bookstore. Seth and Morton insisted upon joining me, and we took a cab from the hotel. It had started to flurry; the TV weatherman predicted one-to-three inches that day, a mere dusting back home but obviously cause for major concern to New Yorkers. I wondered if the weather forecast would keep people from attending the signing. It didn't. A large crowd had already gathered on the second-floor landing of the store, and it was only ten-thirty.

To my chagrin, there were reporters and photographers in the crowd, and they were soon joined by a camera crew.

"Seems to me we should leave," Seth whispered in my ear. "They brought you here to sign books, not to put yourself in a fishbowl."

"It's all right," I replied. "Let them take pictures, as long as I don't have to answer questions."

I ignored the media and got down to signing books, which proved to be enjoyable. No doubt about it. I'd relaxed considerably since the madness of the previous week. I felt at peace with myself and the world. Contrary to popular belief, New Yorkers can be friendly and helpful. One "fan" filled me in on the best Christmas window displays in the city and offered to take me on a personal tour. Another brought me a tin of frozen homemade lasagna: "I heard you say on a talk show that you liked Italian food," she said sweetly. Mort Metzger took the lasagna from me and said after the woman had left with her autographed book, "I'll get rid of it, Jess. Never know what some cuckoo might slip in it."

The signing was scheduled to last until one, but at twelve-thirty there was still a line that descended down the stairs and wrapped around the back of the store. I'd be there another hour. I stood for a seventh-inning stretch, felt a sneeze coming on, and pulled a tissue from my purse.

"Hope you're not getting a cold," Seth said.

"I don't think so," I said. "Well, back to business." I twisted my hand to relieve writer's cramp and resumed my place at the table. The next person in line slid a book in front of me. I asked without looking up, "To whom should I sign it?"

"To Waldo."

I began to write, stopped, and looked up. He was disguised—a shaggy blond wig, heavy growth of beard, dark glasses, and a ski hat pulled down low over his forehead—but I knew I was peering into Waldo Morse's face.

"Waldo!" I said too loud.

"I've got to talk to you, Mrs. Fletcher. Two o'clock at the library's main branch. Fifth and Forty-second. The third-floor reading room."

"Two? The last time you asked me to meet you at two, terrible things started happening."

His expression was quizzical. A small smile formed on his lips. "Two-fifteen?"

"Yes. Two-fifteen."

I finished signing his book and handed it back to him. He said nothing and hurried down the stairs.

Chapter Seventeen

I've suffered shocks before but none with the impact of seeing Waldo Morse alive. How could it be? I'd witnessed his murder on Fifth Avenue. Or had I? It wasn't even worthy of a question. Obviously, and despite popular myth, there is more than one Santa Claus in the world.

As I continued to sign books, my mind raced back to that fateful day. I'd taken too much for granted, had made assumptions based upon shaky evidence and unreasonable expectations. I'd *expected* Waldo to be there and never questioned whether it was, in fact, him who had fallen. I'd been unable to see him with any clarity. So many people had stood between us. And there was that beard that covered his face. I *assumed* it was Waldo but had been fooled, like a magic show audience having its attention diverted from what the magician's hands are actually doing.

"It's Cora," the woman standing in front of me said.

I looked up. "What?"

"I said my name was Cora. You wrote 'Dear Waldo.'"

I laughed nervously. "Sorry. My mind wandered." Ruth slid another book in front of me to sign correctly.

After a few more near autographing mishaps, Ruth asked how I was feeling.

"Not well, I'm afraid," I said. "I'm a little dizzy and weak. Could we cut this short without alienating too many people?"

"Let me see what I can do." After a whispered meeting, the store manager announced to those still in line that I had to leave at one-thirty to honor another commitment. There were groans of protest. I felt predictably guilty, but not to the extent of changing my mind. I attacked my autographing task with renewed vigor.

"I knew it," Seth said when I told him I was feeling ill and wanted to return to the hotel for a nap. He's a physician after all, my doctor for years.

"Just need some rest," I said. "I'll be good as new." We stopped at a pharmacy where he bought me an assortment of over-the-counter cold remedies, which I promised to take.

"I'll stay with you in your room," he offered.

"No, please, Seth. I won't be very good company because I'll be asleep. I'll call you the minute I wake up.

By the time I reached the suite, the theory that if you lie, the lie will come true, gained credence. I *did* feel dizzy and weak. But I rationalized that it was the result of the confusion that swirled in my brain like leaves trapped in a corner on a windy day. What was going on here?

I meet Waldo Morse wearing a Santa costume on Fifth Avenue. He tells me to come back the next day at two. I return, only to see him gunned down in cold blood. But it isn't him. Someone else is killed. The police, particularly a detective named Alphonse Rizzi, don't seem to care.

I befriend a young woman who knew Waldo, and offer her shelter. She's murdered, too.

I receive a strange message informing me that someone by the name of Joe Charles "will know." I find Joe Charles, who lies to me about his telephone. Despite my bumbling attempts at disguise, I discover that Charles knows Detective Rizzi well enough to meet with him at a jazz club. Susan Kale is there, too, one night before she's murdered.

Joe Charles disappears.

Waldo's wife, Nancy, hurriedly packs up her lovely home in Cabot Cove and takes off for points unknown.

A priest is slaughtered on the steps of St. Patrick's Cathedral. I'd seen a priest take something from Waldo on Fifth Avenue.

And now this. Waldo Morse stands in line to have me sign his book, which means he's very much alive. No Santa costume this time, but a different approach to incognito.

And yet another scheduled rendezvous.

I knew one thing. This meeting would result in answers to the myriad questions twisting in my brain. I would find out what I needed to know.

The main reading room of the New York Public Library was spacious and majestic. I'd taken the stairs at a fast clip and had to catch my breath at the top. I surveyed the room for Waldo. At least he hadn't changed costumes again. He was seated at a table, his face obscured by a large book. Most tables were occupied by more than one person. Fortunately, Waldo was alone. I quietly sat next to him, clasped my hands on the table, and stared straight ahead. His acknowledgment of my arrival was a guttural grunt.

Without turning my head, I said quietly, "I don't understand."

Another grunt; he continued to pretend to read.

"To say I am in shock is a major understatement, Waldo."

He turned his head slightly in my direction and shifted his eyes to take in surrounding tables, a hungry dog assuring that no other animal was about to take its food. His eyes locked on mine. "I'm sorry you had to get involved in this, Mrs. Fletcher. But I didn't ask you to recognize me. I didn't ask you to come up to me on Fifth Avenue."

"Of course you didn't. Frankly, I'm sorry I did. But now that I have—now that I am involved—there are questions I would like very much to have answered."

"Go ahead. I'll answer what I can."

"Let's start with the obvious. You and I are sitting here together in the public library. But I saw you shot. Murdered."

"It wasn't me."

"I've concluded that. Who was it?"

"George Marsh."

"Marsh," I muttered. The name I'd heard at police headquarters. I said, "I assumed that was a name you were using. I thought maybe you carried that name on a piece of identification because—well, because you're in the witness protection program."

"Not anymore, I'm not. Marsh wasn't a phony name I used. It belonged to a friend of mine who was out of work, broke and desperate."

I sat back and looked up at the ornate ceiling. "Why would someone shoot such a person?"

He said flatly, "They thought it was me."

He saw the confusion on my face—it was hard to miss—and so he leaned close. "When you came up to me on the street, Mrs. Fletcher, I panicked. I said I'd meet you the next day just to get rid of you. I went home that night and decided it was time to get away for a while. It isn't healthy in my line of work to be recognized. While I was deciding what to do, George Marsh stopped by. He looked like hell. He hadn't eaten in days and said he was ready to pack it in."

"Commit suicide?"

"Yeah. So I came up with the idea of having George stand in for me for a couple of days. He and I were about the same height and weight. I figured that when you came back and found out it wasn't me, you'd just forget about it and I wouldn't have to worry about you. George agreed. I even told him to pocket the donations."

"That's terrible," I said.

"Not when you're hungry, Mrs. Fletcher. Anyway, I wasn't in the mood for a debate on morality. I gave Marsh my Santa suit and split."

I felt a sudden pang of anger. I'd been defrauded in being led to believe that Waldo had been the one killed that day. "And I thought it was you," I said, unable to filter exasperation from my voice. "Do you know what pain this has caused me, Waldo?"

"Sure. Sorry about that. But don't feel stupid thinking it was me. Like they say, everybody in a Santa suit looks the same." His laugh was rueful.

I drew a deep breath. "All right," I said, "this George Marsh person was shot because the killer thought he was you. Why?"

"Why what?"

"Why did someone want to kill *you*?"

"Sure you want to know?" Waldo asked, his eyes narrowing.

"I assume it's because of what happened to you back in Maine," I said. "The drug charge, the trial."

"You got it, Mrs. Fletcher. That episode turned my life around. I've been on the run ever since."

"The drug dealers you testified against tried to kill you?"

"Maybe."

"If not them, who?"

"I'm not sure. I have my ideas."

"Waldo, I saw Nancy recently. Last Saturday as a matter of fact. I went to her house to inform her of your death, and to ask if she had any idea who might have wanted to kill you."

"You did?"

"Yes. I didn't get there any too soon. Moving men were emptying the house."

Until this moment, his expression and voice had been passive. But when I told him about Nancy's move, his face sagged as though a blast of hot air had hit a wax mask. "Moving?" he said in disbelief. "Where was she going?"

"I don't know. She wouldn't tell me."

I could feel his body tense. He looked around the cavernous room, a cornered person seeking an escape route.

"I'm sorry to have to upset you with this news, Waldo."

"They won't hesitate to kill her, Mrs. Fletcher. They'll kill her and the kids if it suits their purpose."

His frightened look now turned to sadness. His lips quivered. What a terrible life to be leading, I thought. I felt profoundly sad for him at that moment, and for Nancy and the children who'd suffered, too, as a result of his foolishness years ago. In retrospect, he probably would have been better off standing trial and paying for his crime. At least when it was over, he'd be free to pursue a normal existence, hopefully with Nancy and the kids. But the deal he'd cut with authorities had condemned him to a life of fear and suspicion, shadows and darkness.

He remained in his pensive mood a moment more, then turned and said, as though reading my thoughts, "Mrs. Fletcher, I made a stupid mistake years ago getting involved with drug dealers. I was young and trying to build a fishing business. It was hard, real hard. The money just wasn't there, and there was Nancy and the kids to support. I didn't intend to run drugs for long, just enough to build a stake. I couldn't make payments on the boat I'd bought, and the bank was threatening to repossess it."

Which was no excuse for what you did, I thought. But I said only, "Yes. It must have been difficult."

He continued his introspective monologue. "I've been trying to make it up to them—hell, to me—ever since. When I accepted the Feds' deal, I did it for my family. But they lied to me. They told me that if I testified and went into the witness protection program, I'd be settled in some pretty, quiet place where Nancy and the kids would eventually join me. Nobody would know where we were. The money wasn't great but we probably could have lived on it."

He chewed his cheek, his hands became fists on the table. "I talked to Nancy about it, and she agreed it was the best thing to do. All we cared about was getting back together."

"But they didn't live up to their promises?"

He slowly shook his head. "No, they didn't. They kept pressuring me to testify against others."

"There were other drug dealers you knew about?"

"No. They wanted me to infiltrate other drug rings. I refused. Then they got tough and reneged on some of the things they promised me and Nancy. That's when I told them to take their witness protection program and shove it." He checked to see whether I was offended. I wasn't. He continued. "I was out in Colorado when I decided to get out. I came to New York and got involved with the cops here as an informant, making friends with guys they wanted a line on and reporting back to them. I'll tell you this, Mrs. Fletcher. It may not have been honorable, but the money sure was good. It meant Nancy and the kids could live nice. I sent them plenty. I didn't like snitching on people I'd gotten to know, but I did it."

That Detective Alphonse Rizzi was a narcotics detective crossed my mind. I asked, "Was Detective Rizzi your police contact?"

"Control," Waldo corrected. "He's been my control ever since I got involved. I was working for him the day you spotted me on Fifth."

My eyebrows went up. No wonder Rizzi was so quick to arrive on the scene. He must have been close by observing Waldo. "You were working for the police but pretending to collect charitable contributions as Santa Claus?" I asked, incredulous.

"I sure was, Mrs. Fletcher. The cops were investigating drug dealing going on at St. Pats. They put me there because it gave me a good view of the action."

Drugs in St. Patrick's Cathedral? The contemplation was shocking. Could it possibly be true? Was the priest I saw receiving something from Waldo a drug dealer? And there was the shocking story that very morning about a priest being shot at the cathedral.

Again, Waldo seemed to read my thoughts. "Mrs. Fletcher, the church—the cathedral—isn't involved in drug dealing. But a group in the city decided it was a perfect cover, wearing priests' garb and doing their dealing in and around the church."

"I saw a priest approach the first day I saw you. Was he a priest, or a drug dealer?"

"An undercover cop."

Of course, I thought. How silly of me not to know.

"Waldo, you know about Susan Kale."

"Sure I do. That's one of the reasons I decided to make contact with you. I read about how you found her and all."

"She was living with Joe Charles. Did you know that?"

"Yup. That was her mistake."

"Mistake?"

"I'd call it a mistake. It got her killed."

"Whoa, wait a minute," I said. "Are you saying that Joe Charles killed her?"

"I wouldn't be surprised."

"Why? I mean, how do you know?"

"That's too long a story for now. I've already been in one place too long."

"But surely—"

He cut me off by placing his hand on my arm and leaning closer, his eyes blazing with purpose. "Mrs. Fletcher, what you told me about Nancy moving is really upsetting. I have to find out where she is."

"Do you think her life is in danger?" I thought of the male voice at her house, and my feeling that it was Joe Charles.

"Yeah, I do. Will you help me find them?"

I hesitated. But then the feelings of compassion I'd experienced earlier returned. "I don't know what I can do, Waldo, but yes, I will try to help you find Nancy. You don't have any idea where she might have gone?"

He said in a whisper, "Joe Charles. He'll know."

My eyes opened wide. "It was you who left that message."

"Yeah."

"Why? Why bother telling me about Joe Charles?"

"Once George was killed, and I knew it was me they intended to hit, I figured I wanted somebody else to be involved. If somebody else knew what was going down, it might take the pressure off. Sorry it was you I called, but I know your reputation for snooping into murders."

"I'm not sure I'm pleased with that reputation. Why didn't you just call and identify yourself to me? Why did you feel it was necessary to have me continue to believe you were dead, that it was you who was shot instead of this Marsh fellow?"

"Because it was better for certain people to think I was dead."

"Joe Charles?"

"Among others."

"Susan Kale?"

"Sure."

"But—but Detective Rizzi must have learned rather quickly that it wasn't you in the Santa suit."

"That's right. He's one of the people I'd just as soon not see for a while. He won't be happy that I split, that's for sure."

He suddenly jerked his head away, sat up tall, and looked out over the vast expanse of reading room. It was as though someone had flipped a switch that activated his antenna, set his nerve ends on alert status. "I have to go," he mumbled.

This time, I placed *my* hand on *his* arm. "Please, Waldo, don't bolt on me. You've chosen to bring me into this. You ask my help in finding Nancy, yet continue to deal with me in bits and pieces, in bursts of revelation."

He stood.

"Waldo. Sit down and listen to me," I said sternly.

He sat, but it was obvious there wouldn't be any further meaningful conversation. He opened the large book he'd been perusing when I arrived and tore off a corner of a page. I winced. He pulled out a pen and scribbled the name of a restaurant, followed by the words Sea Cliff. He handed me the scrap. "Its a little town on Long Island. I have a friend there. I think I'll hole up there a few days, probably through Christmas."

Christmas! Today was Monday. Christmas was two days away.

"What do you want me to do?" I asked.

"If you want to continue this conversation, Mrs. Fletcher,

come out there tomorrow for lunch. I'll feel more comfortable there."

I started to protest. My schedule was full through Christmas. More book signings. Interviews. A Christmas Eve party at the Buckleys'. And, of course, spending time with my Cabot Cove friends, Seth and Morton.

"Waldo, I really can't leave the city. Why not continue the conversation right here? No one knows I'm here. I certainly didn't tell anyone. In fact, I lied about where I was going this afternoon."

His response was, "I'll be at Gallagher's at noon tomorrow."

I watched him disappear down the stairs, sat back, and sighed, staring at the tabletop. My good intentions of removing myself from Waldo's twisted life now seemed distant and feeble. I looked around the reading room. I've never considered myself a paranoid person but at that moment, every person, every thing looked suspicious, posed a threat. Waldo had rubbed off on me. That cold realization prompted me to leave the library and to slowly wander back to the hotel, the holiday street scenes and festive windows obscured by the black, murky thoughts that had enveloped me.

Chapter Eighteen

B y the time I completed the short walk back to the
hotel, my somber mood had been replaced by fiery
determination. Things had gone far enough—the
furtive meetings, the disguises (including my own comi-
cal getup), people supposedly dead and then showing up
alive, the shadowy world of the witness protection program and everything else that intruded upon what was
supposed to have been a pleasant bit of book promoting, and deck the halls with boughs of holly in New York
City.

The minute I got to my suite, I called the room shared
by Seth and Morton. Morton answered. He sounded
groggy. He had obviously been taking a nap, although he
would never admit that. He was one of those people who
considered midday naps to be, at best, a sign of weakness
and sloth.

"Wake you?" I asked pleasantly.

"No. It's the middle of the day."

"Yes. Well, Mort, I want you to do me a big favor."

"Anything you say, Mrs. F."

"Did you notice the name of the moving company that was at Nancy Morse's house the day we were there?"

"Can't say that I did," he replied. "But I did take note it was from Portland."

"Splendid. Would you be a dear and call every moving company in Portland?"

"Might be quite a few, Mrs. F."

"I know, but this is important. Even urgent. I seem to remember seeing North American Van Lines on the truck. It must be a Portland mover licensed to represent that national company."

"That'd narrow it down some," he said.

"Use your law enforcement credentials to find out where the movers took Nancy. And by the way, Mort, don't worry about long-distance charges on your room bill. Buckley House will pay for it."

I was about to make the second call on my mental list when the phone rang. "Jessica Fletcher?" The operator had a distinctly British accent. I confirmed. "Please hold for Inspector Sutherland." Moments later, a delightful Scottish brogue said, "Jessica, George Sutherland here."

"How wonderful to hear your voice, George. What time is it in London?"

"Bedtime."

"How in the world did you find me? I mean, I'm in New York publicizing my latest book—things distinctly not literary have been happening—"

He laughed knowingly. "So I've been reading. From

what I gather, you're up to your neck in nasty business again. Murder, they say."

"Make that plural. I could use a distinguished Scotland Yard inspector at my side to help sort things out. But how did you—?"

"Find you? Elementary, my dear Jessica. You told me that whenever you visit New York you stay at this Sheraton-Park Avenue Hotel. A jewel in Manhattan, you said."

"You have a good memory. Actually, I started out staying with my publisher and his wife but moved here when the fur started to fly, as the saying goes."

"Wish I could accommodate you, Jessica. Be at your side. But that's out of the question." I hurriedly indicated that I was engaging only in wishful thinking. He said, "I'm leaving first thing in the morning for home. The holidays and all."

Home for George Sutherland was a tiny village at the northernmost tip of Scotland, a town called Wick. He'd been born there and, as he explained when we first met in London, his family had left him a castle of sorts overlooking a body of water called Pentland Firth. "Barren and desolate," he'd told me over tea at Brown's Hotel, but equally beautiful and inspiring. "Time Jessica Fletcher planned a visit to Wick," he'd written on a few occasions. The temptation was great, the time impossible to find. But one day . . .

"Can I be of any long-distance help?" he asked.

"Not unless you know something about our witness protection program."

"Afraid I can't help you there. Oh, now, wait a sec. Let me back up a minute. I met a chap when attending your FBI's international conference on criminal investigative techniques. As I recall, his area of expertise was that witness program. Want his name?"

"Please." I wrote "William Tomic" on a pad. George even had his direct dial number in Washington.

I thanked him for the information.

"When are you visiting us again, Jessica?"

"Just as soon as my schedule permits."

"Much too vague. We Scots have a saying. *Don't gie me the gunk.*"

"Translation needed."

"Don't disappoint me, Jessica. *I be keen o.*"

I smiled. "Yes, I'm fond of you, too." My eyes became moist. "It was sweet of you to call, George. Have a splendid Christmas at home. We'll keep in touch."

"That we will. And you be careful. Sounds to me like you're dealing with loutish people. Merry Christmas."

I called William Tomic in Washington. After being shunted between operators, he came on the line. "What a pleasure receiving a call from Jessica Fletcher," he said. "I've read all your books. At least I think I have."

"Including the new one?" I asked.

"Not yet. But now that you've called, I'll hightail it to my nearest bookstore."

"No need," I said. "I'll be happy to send you one."

"Autographed?"

Of course.

With that bit of business out of the way, I told him I was doing research for my next work and needed to know a little about how the Federal Witness Protection Program worked.

"Shoot," he said.

"Is it possible for someone in that program to decide to leave it?"

"Sure, but only if the person is crazy enough to surface after having turned state's evidence. Not an especially healthy thing to do."

"I would imagine," I said. "I'm creating a plot in which someone in the program decides to leave, and then becomes an informant for local police. Is that reasonable?"

He paused. "Yes. I've personally known a few who've done that."

"Why would anyone do that?" I asked.

"A couple of reasons. Tired of the clandestine life and wanting to get back into the mainstream. Family considerations. But mostly, money is the motivator."

"Uh-huh. When someone goes into the witness protection program, is he paid enough to live well, to support a family?"

"No. Well, I suppose it depends upon your definition of 'living well.' Nobody gets rich in the program, that's for certain."

"But could a person get rich by coming out of the program and turning informant for some law enforcement agency, say the New York City police?" I realized the minute I asked the question that I'd tipped my hand. Tomic's change of tone confirmed it.

"You know, Mrs. Fletcher, I've been following your escapades since your arrival in New York. Are you sure you're researching a book, or are you trying to get some answers to the murders you've witnessed?"

I had to smile. He didn't miss much. "Let's just say a little of both," I said.

"Okay. A little of both. To answer your question. Yes, a good informant can make a lot more money than what the Federal Government pays in the program. I've known snitches who've become millionaires. Of course, that depends upon the quality of the information they provide."

"I see. I don't have any other questions at the moment, but I would appreciate being able to get back to you."

"Any time, Mrs. Fletcher." I took down mailing information to send the book, thanked him again, and hung up.

I was glad I'd made the call. Obviously, Waldo was being straight with me, at least concerning having left the program and becoming an undercover informant for the New York City police. That was comforting considering all the lies (disinformation is the politically correct term these days) I'd received since this whole affair started.

The phone rang again. It was the hotel operator informing me that Ms. Lazzara was on her way up to the suite. I was scheduled to be interviewed in twenty minutes by a writer doing an article for *Parade*. I quickly herded Miss Hiss into the bathroom, gave her a fresh supply of food and water, closed the door, and awaited Ruth's arrival.

She was in her usual state of high anxiety, talking fast, hands fluttering like birds in search of a perch. "*Parade* wants to focus on the Marjorie Ainsworth murder you were involved with in London. Why, I don't know, but that's what the writer wants, so we'd better give it to her."

"Goodness," I said, "I'd better spend a few minutes remembering the details of that."

"Talk in generalities," Ruth said, fluffing pillows on the couch. "By the way, Oprah still wants you, and I think I can get Donahue to go with it. Sure you won't change your mind?"

I sighed. She certainly was tenacious. "No, I really would prefer not to."

"Suit yourself." As she started to straighten magazines on a glass table next to the couch, I noticed she was poised to toss scraps of paper on which I'd made notes into a basket. "Oh, no," I said, taking them from her. Included were pages from the yellow legal pad I'd confiscated from Nancy Morse's house in Cabot Cove. "You don't happen to have a pencil, do you?" I asked.

She quickly pulled a ballpoint pen from her purse.

"No, I need a pencil. An old-fashioned number two lead pencil."

"Can't help you."

The phone rang; the writer from *Parade* had arrived. I put the papers in my purse, placed it in my bedroom closet, and returned to the living room as Ruth opened the door for the writer, Carolyn Dobkin, an older woman wearing a gray suit as severely cut as her gray hair. The interview, which took an hour, was pleasant and went smoothly. But answering questions about the murder of the world's greatest mystery writer, Marjorie Ainsworth, whom I was privileged to have befriended and in whose English manor house I was unfortunate to have been a guest the night she was murdered, was both pleasurable and painful. It turned out Ms. Dobkin had written a book analyzing Ainsworth's writings. Small wonder she wanted to focus upon that.

After Dobkin had left, Ruth went over my schedule for that evening and the following day. I was to be a guest at an agent-author cocktail party at the Mercantile Library hosted by the New York chapter of the Mystery Writers of America. Immediately following that was another party for Buckley House's sales force, which, Vaughan had impressed upon me, was perhaps the most useful group I would meet while in New York. And then there was dinner—another dinner—this one with the head of a German publishing conglomerate that had recently purchased a major stake in Buckley House.

The following day, Christmas Eve, was no less hectic. A morning book signing, lunch with the head buyer from Barnes & Noble, a couple of interviews in the afternoon, and then Christmas Eve with the Buckleys at their Dakota apartment.

"You'll have to cancel the lunch," I said.

"I can't do that, Jessica."

"Sorry, but if I don't spend a couple of hours finishing up Christmas shopping, I'm going to have some very disappointed people back home. As it is, I can't get the gifts to them in time for Christmas, but at least I can call with conviction to tell them presents are on their way. Please, I've been cooperative, I think. Do me this favor."

Ruth exhibited a rare smile, nodded, put her hand on my shoulder, and said, "Of course. I've dealt with a lot of authors. You are undoubtedly the best I've ever worked with. Do your shopping."

Her words warmed me. Of course, I wasn't being truthful about my reason for canceling the luncheon. I'd decided to head for the small town on Long Island to meet Waldo Morse. Call it throwing good money after bad. Call it an obsession. Call it what you will. He'd asked for my help in finding Nancy and the children. If anything happened to them and I hadn't expended every effort, I'd have trouble living with myself.

"Ready for the mystery writers' party?" Ruth asked.

"I will be in a few minutes. I brought a special red dress with me to wear over the holidays. I think it would be perfect for tonight, provided it still fits after all these meals you've insisted I eat. Give me ten minutes."

I rejoined her in the living room wearing the dress which, strangely, seemed to have shrunk an inch.

"You look lovely," Ruth said. "Come on, time to head out."

I was closing the door behind me when I heard the phone ring. We looked at each other. "Should I?" I asked.

She shook her head. "They'll take a message. We're running late."

I decided on the ride down in the elevator to stop at the desk to see who the most recent caller had been. But by the time we reached the lobby, I'd forgotten about it. Had I stopped, I would have been handed this message written by the operator:

> *Nancy Morse called.*
> *Urgent she speak with you.*
> *Will call again.*
> *Left no number.*

Chapter Nineteen

"I'd never been so disappointed in my life," said one of the hundreds of guests at the Mystery Writers of America's cocktail party. "Marjorie had promised to personally accept her Edgar Award. It was the best-attended awards dinner we'd ever had. And then she sent that telegram at absolutely the final, last minute expressing her regrets. Did she ever tell you, Jessica, the *real* reason she didn't attend? I mean, after all, you were so close to her."

"No. I don't recall her saying anything about it," I replied.

I'd been on the receiving end of countless questions about Marjorie Ainsworth, the acknowledged grande dame of the murder mystery genre unless, of course, you belonged to the Agatha Christie school.

"At least Agatha shared herself with her public," said one of those.

I was surrounded by a dozen people, most of them authors, a few agents. Discerning the difference didn't depend upon the different-colored badges they wore. The variation in dress was sufficient. The agents tended to wear business suits. The writers dressed like—well, like writers.

"Marjorie was a quintessential recluse," I said, slightly annoyed that I'd been put in the position of having to defend my dear departed friend. "Excuse me," I said.

My agent, Russ Checkett, had just arrived. I was delighted, relieved, and somewhat surprised to see him. He'd returned that afternoon from an extended stay in the Czech Republic, where he'd conferred with his newest client, a Nobel Prize–winning novelist. The fatigue on his face testified to his lack of sleep. "Russ," I said above the drone of party blatherskite.

He gave me a hug and a kiss on the cheek. "Holding up?" he asked.

"Better than you, I would say. You look exhausted."

"Getting a little too old for this kind of frenetic globe-trotting," he said. "Buy you a drink?"

"A little white wine."

He returned from the bar with my wine and a large, amber Black Label on-the-rocks for himself.

"Frankly, you've arrived in the nick of time," I said. "Like the cavalry. If people aren't asking me about Marjorie Ainsworth, they all seem to have ideas for a locked-room mystery to out-Poe Poe."

Russ laughed and clinked his glass against mine. "I've been out of touch, but the office has kept me up-to-speed about what's been going on with you. My secretary says you've single-handedly boosted the Manhattan murder rate above the national average."

"I wish you wouldn't put it that way," I said. "But yes, it has been an interesting visit. Vaughan and his people are delighted, I suppose, at the publicity. I could do without it."

"Could we grab a couple of quiet minutes?" Russ asked. "I need to talk to you, but don't know how long I'll last."

"You're a real trouper, Russ, to be here after being on an airplane all night."

"All part of the service to my favorite author." He led me by the elbow to a relatively quiet corner of the room. "So, tell me about this new book of yours," he said.

My face reflected my puzzlement. "What new book? I haven't started it yet. I don't even have a plot."

His was a skeptical smile. "As I understand it, the plot has already been written for you."

"What are you saying to me?" I asked.

"That I think it's a wonderful idea for you to do a true-crime book based on your experiences in New York."

"But I—"

"It could be a blockbuster, Jessica. The world's most famous mystery writer turns to solving real crime. I love it."

Bobby Johnson!

Russ confirmed it. "My only concern is to what extent this Bobby Johnson from the *Post* can contribute to the work. It's your name that will sell the book. But we can't brush him off. After all, he did contact the office. And the proposal was pretty good."

"Proposal?"

"Yes. Surely you've seen it. I was impressed with its thoroughness. He's a good writer."

"And the proposal is for a book by Mr. Johnson and me, sharing authorship?"

The pleasant glow on Russ's face turned serious. "You aren't telling me that you haven't agreed to this with Johnson, are you?"

"That is exactly what I'm telling you." I told him about my brunch with Johnson and his suggestion that we do such a book together. "I turned him down flat," I said.

"Well, that does put a different spin on things. But don't discount it out-of-hand, Jess. Could be a pleasant respite to be writing about something real. We have other novelist clients who occasionally turn to nonfiction to change pace. Let's talk more about it. Free tomorrow?"

"Tomorrow is Christmas Eve. I have some appearances to make. There's a party at Vaughan's house in the evening."

"I know. I'll be there."

"Splendid. Maybe we can continue this conversation then."

Russ stayed another twenty minutes, excused himself, and left.

"Jessica Fletcher, I must speak with you immediately," said a wisp of a man with shoulder-length mouse-colored hair.

"I'm just about to leave," I said. "I have another engagement."

"It will only take a moment. Please. It is very important."

I internalized my sigh and leaned closer to better hear him. Not only was he short, he had lips that didn't move when he spoke. Lip-reading was out of the question. "I've just finished reading your new book, and there is a serious error in it."

I stifled a smile. Every book I've ever written elicited mail from "experts" taking me to task for missing an important point of fact. I prefer to receive those objections by mail. Having to face my accuser proved more difficult.

"You have the victim dying within twenty-four hours of mushroom poisoning," he said. "That doesn't happen. It usually takes two or three days for *amanita phalloides* to destroy the liver."

I replied, "I appreciate your comment but I disagree. Yes, it often takes longer for poison mushrooms to kill the victim, but not always. My victim died of a collapse of his circulatory system. I checked it very carefully with a forensic pathologist, a friend at the University of Maine Medical Center."

He wasn't deflated by my response. Instead, he puffed up to an inch taller and said through clenched teeth, "I respect the credentials of this person you consulted, but I've studied the field of mushroom poisoning extensively, as well as other poisons. Every one of my books is totally accurate."

"I don't doubt that at all," I said, desperate to escape. "I would enjoy reading one of your books."

"I'll be happy to send you a manuscript."

"Manuscript? Haven't they been published?"

He stood on tiptoe and said in a voice dripping with anger and frustration, "The publishing industry is corrupt. No one is published without paying off editors. I will never stoop to that."

I considered pointing out that I had never paid off

anyone, but realized it was futile. Instead, I said, "I think you're probably right about mushroom poisoning. I'll be more careful next time." And I was gone, moving past him with the fluid skill of a premiere football running back.

I rounded up Ruth Lazzara and suggested we head for our next appointment, the cocktail party with Buckley House's sales force. She seemed happy to be rescued, too. Once word got around the party that she was head of publicity for Buckley House, she was inundated by fledgling authors seeking an in with the prestigious publisher. We retrieved our coats—not an easy task considering there was one young man trying to keep track of hundreds of garments—bid farewell to a few people, and headed down the stairs. We were halfway to the lobby when I spotted Bobby Johnson coming through the front door. "Jessica," he said loudly, wedging his way through knots of people. He reached the foot of the stairs. "I have to talk to you," he said.

"Yes, I certainly think you do."

"We have to go," Ruth said, pulling me by the arm. Johnson took my other arm. I felt like I was on a medieval torture rack. Eventually they pulled in the same direction and we ended up in a corner.

"Mrs. Fletcher doesn't have time for interviews right now," Ruth said.

"I don't want an interview," Johnson replied. "Please, just two minutes."

"Would you excuse us, Ruth," I said. When she was gone, I said to Johnson, "How dare you approach my agent and suggest I'm interested in doing a book with you?"

I couldn't read whether his expression was contrite

or smug. His tone, however, said he considered my upset to be unjustified. "Mrs. Fletcher—Jessica—you are some hard lady to track down these days."

"And I intend to keep it that way. Why did you go to Russ Checkett with your fraudulent claim that we intend to work together?"

"Hey, calm down. I figured there was nothing to lose by contacting your agent. I didn't tell him you agreed. I just said we'd talked about it and that I thought it would make a bestseller."

"You had no right."

"Okay. I had no right. But hear me out. You'd like to know the whereabouts of this mysterious Joe Charles character. Am I right?"

"Yes. I would like to know where he is." My matter-of-fact expression of interest hardly reflected how anxious I was to receive that information. If Waldo was right—that Joe Charles had been behind the attempt to murder him on Fifth Avenue—and if I was right that it had been Joe Charles at Nancy Morse's house the day I visited—finding Charles could be the key to Nancy's survival.

"Well?" I said.

A smirk crossed Bobby's face. "Hey, Jessica, tit for tat, as they say. If I tell you how to find Joe Charles, what do I get in return?"

There goes that free lunch again, I thought. I asked, "What is it you want from me?"

"The go-ahead to your agent for us to do this book together."

"Absolutely not."

"Suit yourself," Johnson said, shrugging. "But finding

Joe Charles might answer all your questions about why your buddy, Waldo Morse, got killed."

Ruth frantically waved for me to join her. "Where will you be later tonight?" I asked.

"At the paper until ten, ten-thirty. Then home. You have both numbers."

"Yes, I do. I'll call you later."

"I'll be waiting with bated breath," he said.

As Ruth and I went to the street, I realized how dramatically my perception of Bobby Johnson had changed during those few minutes. When we'd first met, I disliked him and his groveling for a story. But then he put forth a different, less predatory face. Now, my feelings were what they'd been initially. He was not to be trusted.

It also occurred to me as we climbed into the waiting town car that he still thought Waldo Morse was dead. That information could prove to my advantage, depending upon how I chose to dispense it.

"Where are you?" Ruth asked.

I snapped back to the here and now of the backseat. "Just reeling from all the conversation," I said. "So many people writing books, so few opportunities for them to see their work published."

"It's a tough business."

The party for the sales force was held in the Wings Club, in what used to be the Pan Am Building on Park Avenue. How could there be an aviation industry without the airline that opened the world to travelers? I wondered as we rode the elevator. But nothing is forever, as they say, which I hoped would prove to be true where the party was concerned.

"Your book is breaking all sales records, Jessica," the vice president of sales, Bill Kelly, told me.

"That's wonderful news," I replied. "You and your people have obviously been busy."

"Can't sell a bad book," he said. "I'm looking forward to your next. Interesting idea turning to true crime."

"What?"

"The true-crime book about the Santa Claus murder. Will that be the title? The Santa Claus Murder?"

"I don't think so. I mean—excuse me."

The party didn't last long, for which I was grateful. No matter who I talked to, the subject of my "new book" came up. The publishing gossip mill was evidently more potent than even Cabot Cove's.

We left the Wings Club with a larger contingent than when leaving the mystery writers' party. Vaughan and Olga Buckley, Bill Kelly and three Buckley House executives would also attend dinner with the German businessman, Wolfgang Wurtzman, who now controlled, to some extent, the publishing house's future fortunes. Our chauffeur-driven limousines were parked on a ramp at the side of the building. Olga and I stood on the sidewalk and chattered as the group decided who would ride in which car. I glanced beyond her to a walkway across the ramp. A man in a tan raincoat and dark knitted watch cap observed us. I hadn't noticed him at first. Now that I had, he quickly turned and walked south in the direction of Park Avenue.

"Your dress is lovely," Olga said.

My eyes remained on the man as he continued to distance himself. "Thank you," I said absently. He disappeared around a corner.

"Anything wrong?" Olga asked.

"No, just a little battle-weary. Sorry."

The Buckleys and I would ride together. Olga got in, and Vaughan waited for me to do the same. I was about to when a car suddenly appeared from the direction in which the man in the watch cap had disappeared. It approached slowly—very slowly. I looked into the driver's window as it came abreast. I didn't recognize the driver, but I certainly knew the man in the front passenger seat. Detective Alphonse Rizzi. No question about it, not with his memorable profile. He looked directly at me, then snapped his head away.

"You'll love the view of Manhattan from the River Café, Jessica," Olga said. "It's Mr. Wurtzman's favorite restaurant when in New York."

Another fancy restaurant held little appeal for me. I glanced through the rear windshield to see whether Rizzi's car was following, but it was impossible to tell with so much traffic. By the time we had crossed to the Brooklyn side of the East River, had been ushered to our window table, and I'd been introduced to Wolfgang Wurtzman as "the pillar of Buckley House," I'd almost forgotten about having seen my detective friend again. But not completely. Seeing him had created a gnawing sense of apprehension that would stay with me the entire evening.

Chapter Twenty

"*D*a *klatscht keiner Beifall—das ist das Ungeziefer, das mit den Flugeln schlagt.*"

. . . One of Buckley House's executives laughed heartily at the punch line of Mr. Wurtzman's joke. The rest of the table, including me, also laughed but only because our host's delivery was so animated.

"Wolfgang told the actress that it wasn't applause she was hearing. It was insects flapping their wings," the German-speaking member of our party explained. We laughed a little harder and louder this time, although it didn't strike me as especially funny. But I didn't want to be impolite.

I tried to dismiss having seen Detective Rizzi, and the call I was to make later that evening to Bobby Johnson. It wasn't easy, but focusing upon the view of Manhattan's twinkling lights, and the food—my appetizer of fresh oysters with a mignonette sauce, and an entree of perfectly prepared red snapper—helped.

A great deal of wine was consumed by everyone at the table with the exception of Olga and me. Wurtzman, a gregarious, heavyset gentleman with round red cheeks, small green eyes, and thinning hair, became even more expansive as the long, thin bottles of *Trockenbeerenauslesen*, expensive German white wine, disappeared.

As we left our table and headed for the lobby, Wurtzman, who spoke perfect English when he wasn't telling jokes in German, said to me, "Jessica Fletcher, you are one of the reasons I invested in Buckley House."

"That's very flattering," I said.

"I want you to know that every resource under my control will be available to help sell your books. Might I also say that not only are you one of the world's best writers, you are a beautiful and charming woman."

I flushed a bit and thanked him for his kind words. "*Auf Wiedersehen*," I added, coming up with the only German phrase I knew.

He took both my hands and said, "Yes, until we meet again."

We were about to leave the restaurant when a hostess grabbed my arm. "Mrs. Fletcher? You are Jessica Fletcher?

"Yes."

"There's a telephone call for you."

Who would be calling me at the River Café? I wondered. Probably Seth or Morton. The hostess handed me a phone at the desk. "Hello?" I said.

"If you want a merry Christmas, Fletcher, butt out." The man hung up.

I stayed at the desk a few moments to regain my composure before joining the others outside. Ruth Lazzara and I shared a car back to the Sheraton-Park Avenue. She offered to buy me a nightcap, but I declined, said good night, and entered the hotel. As I crossed the lobby and waited for the elevator, the warning voice on the phone at the restaurant repeated in my head like a tape loop playing it over and over. The elevator took what seemed to me to be an inordinate amount of time to arrive, and ascended slower than usual. I watched the light for each floor come and go: *"If you want a merry Christmas, Fletcher, butt out."*

Miss Hiss greeted me by rubbing against my legs. I tossed my coat on a chair and went to pick up the phone to call Johnson. The message light was flashing. I'd call down for my messages later. I dialed his number at the *Post*, but was told he'd left for the evening.

I called his home number. He picked up on the first ring. "I figured you wouldn't call," he said.

"Why would you think that?" I asked. "I'm sorry it's late. I was at dinner and—"

"Do you want to know where Joe Charles is?" He sounded angry.

"That's why I'm calling."

"He's performing in a little joint tonight."

That surprised me. If he was serious about disappearing, why would he make a public performance? Then again, I reasoned, he had to eat. And, of course, appearing in a tiny, off-the-beaten-track jazz club did not necessarily translate into a "public performance."

"Where?" I asked.

"Not so fast," Johnson said. His voice still had a nasty edge. "I'm not giving you this information out of the goodness of my heart, Jessica. I can run with this story on my own."

"Then why don't you?" I asked.

"Because I think you and I could make one hell of a score by working together. But you have to back off on this attitude about not collaborating with me on a book."

I was being blackmailed, and that made *me* angry. There was nothing that would cause me to work with him on a book. I'd made that clear, and my resolve had not changed.

But someone's life was at stake here: Nancy Morse and possibly her children. If I summarily shut Johnson off, he would pursue the story without having a clue that her life was in jeopardy. Would that be sufficient motivation for him to cooperate with me without having to make a commitment to a book? He didn't seem like an especially sentimental person. Ambition was written all over his sleeve, and I've learned over the years that people driven to that extent by ambition seldom care whose body gets in the way. But it was worth a try. I said, "Nancy Morse, Waldo's wife, is in danger, Bobby. That danger might come from Joe Charles. There's more at stake here than a story—or any book. Please, tell me where he is. If I can talk to him, it might save her life."

I waited for him to digest what I'd said and to respond. Finally, he said, "Are you being straight with me, Jessica?"

"Yes, I am."

"Why would his wife be in danger? Joe Charles? The guy is just a musician."

"Maybe, maybe not." I'd debated during his silence whether to tell him that Waldo Morse was, in fact, alive. I decided to, and did.

"What? Santa Claus is alive?"

"Yes."

"How do you know?"

"I spoke with him."

"Jesus. I mean—what a story!"

"Where is Joe Charles appearing?"

"He's—"

"I won't ask again, Bobby, and I won't grovel. I assure you I will not commit to doing a book with you. You'll have to make your own moral judgment. If Nancy Morse ends up dead, it will rest on your conscience. Maybe you can write in your next story how you indirectly helped bring about the death of a woman—and her children."

I knew I was being melodramatic but didn't care. The negotiation had gone on long enough. Either he agreed, or he didn't. If he didn't, I was in a quandary because I would not learn how to contact Joe Charles. All I could do was hope that he would see things my way, if only to find out more about Waldo being alive.

"Okay," he said. It brought a smile to my face. "But don't do an end-run on me, Jessica. We'll go see him together. Remember, we're a team."

I ignored his comment. "Where will I meet you?"

"Come to my place." He gave me his address, an apartment building on the Upper West Side.

"Can't we just meet where Joe Charles is appearing?"

"No. Come here. We can talk a little bit before going there."

I didn't like having to go to his apartment, nor did I see the need for any further talks between us. But he held the cards, as they say. Unless I chose to toss in my hand, I had to go with what I'd been dealt. I told him I'd be there as quickly as I could.

I threw on my coat, took a fast peek into the bathroom to make sure Miss Hiss had water, and raced from the suite, rode the elevator down, heart pounding, quickly crossed the lobby and got into a cab. I gave the driver Johnson's address and sat back, my mind functioning at a gallop. Had things happened at a more leisurely pace, I might not be in the cab, might not be going to an apartment somewhere in Manhattan and then to an unnamed jazz club in search of a musician who possibly was a murderer.

But things hadn't happened slowly. They'd taken on their own pace and urgency, and I was swept up in the current, feeling very much like an unfortunate insect in a swimming pool about to be sucked into the skimmer.

Chapter Twenty-one

Every taxi driver I'd had since arriving in New York drove as though he (in one case a she) was competing in the Indy 500. But now that I wanted to get to my destination as quickly as possible, I ended up with a driver who, when it came time to sell his vehicle, wanted to claim it had been driven by a little old lady from Pasadena. But we eventually reached Bobby Johnson's apartment building, a decaying structure I assumed had once been a magnificent home. It was located in the low hundreds, a few doors from Riverside Drive. What a magnificent neighborhood this must have once been. I paid the driver and thanked him for a sane ride.

He smiled. "Life's too short to get yourself killed," he said.

How right you are, I thought as I approached the steps leading up to the front door. Unlike the building in which Joe Charles lived, this door was secured, and buzzers to apartments were connected. I found Johnson's name-plate and pushed the button. A sharp buzz was returned. I pushed open the door and stepped into the foyer. Another door gave me access to the first-floor hallway. A small elevator was to my right and waiting. I pushed Six. When I stepped out on to the sixth floor, Bobby stood in his open doorway. "Hi," he said.

"Hi," I said.

"Come on in."

I'd expected the worst. Why, I don't know. The address, I suppose, and a preconceived notion of the sort of lifestyle he led. But there I was assuming things again, as I'd done that day on Fifth Avenue when I *assumed* it was Waldo Morse who'd been shot.

The apartment was spacious, nicely decorated and spotlessly clean. I was immediately drawn to a room at one end that overlooked the Hudson River. "What a beautiful view," I said.

"Better than looking out on to somebody's air shaft."

I surveyed the rest of the apartment. Its only disconcerting aspect was its dim lighting. A few small lamps cast ominous shadows as their low-wattage light fell on objects in the living room. Samuel Barber's *Adagio for Strings*, one of the most somber pieces of music ever written and played at virtually every state funeral, came from unseen speakers, adding to the room's funereal atmosphere.

"Well, are we ready to go?" I asked, injecting cheer into my voice.

"In a few minutes," Johnson said. He went through a doorway to another room. I wondered what I was supposed to do next. When he didn't return, I followed to where he'd gone. It was his office, or study. He sat behind a small desk. The light from a single desk lamp was the room's only illumination aside from the eerie glow from a color computer monitor. He looked up at me and said, "Come here, Jessica. Sit down. I want to discuss something with you."

I continued to stand in the doorway. "What is it you want to discuss?" I asked.

"This." He pressed a few keys on his keyboard, and a dot matrix printer went into action. When it had completed its task, Bobby tore off the document it had printed, carefully removed the perforations from the edges, and laid it on the desk. "Come on, Jessica. Sit down and read this."

I sat in a leather club chair on the other side of the desk, picked up the printout, and held it up to catch the scarce light. It was an article. The headline read:

STARTLING DEVELOPMENT IN SANTA CLAUS MURDER.

I glanced up at him. He'd leaned back in his high-back leather chair, fingers laced on his chest, a satisfied smile on his face.

I started to read the article itself.

The brutal murder of a sidewalk Santa Claus on Fifth Avenue a week ago has taken a sudden and dramatic turn. In an exclusive interview with world-famous mystery writer, Jessica Fletcher, this reporter has learned that the individual thought to have been killed that day, Waldo Morse, is, in fact, very much alive.

I slowly shook my head. "I don't believe you're doing this, Bobby."

"Keep reading. It gets even better."

Mrs. Fletcher, whose novels about murder have sold in the millions and have been translated into dozens of languages, knew Waldo Morse from her hometown of Cabot Cove, Maine. Morse had run a lobster fishing business out of Ogunquit, Maine, until being arrested for aiding drug smugglers bringing their wares into New England. He copped a plea and, in return for helping convict members of the drug cartel, was placed in the Federal Witness Protection Program. He was in that program when Mrs. Fletcher first spotted him across from St. Patrick's Cathedral. She made an appointment to see him the next day. When she returned, she not only witnessed who she thought was Morse being gunned down by unknown assailants, she took photographs of the event. Those photographs ended up in a rival newspaper, an unfortunate fact that has never been explained to anyone by Mrs. Fletcher, including the police who would like very much to get their hands on the roll of film.

"This is outrageous," I said.

"But true, isn't it? Have I misstated any of the facts so far?"

He had. Waldo had not been in the witness protection program when he was working the streets as a charitable Santa. But Johnson wouldn't find that out from me.

I tossed the pages back on the desk.

"You haven't finished," he said.

"Nor do I intend to. Why are you showing this to me? Obviously, you intend to run this story in your newspaper tomorrow."

He came forward, causing the springs on his chair to wheeze. He placed his elbows on his desk, laid his chin on a shelf made by his folded hands, and said, "I don't have to turn this story in, Jessica. That's up to you."

"If you think I'll change my mind about doing a book with you, Bobby, you've wasted your valuable writing time. I would certainly prefer that you not run this story, but I would never change my mind in order to avoid that."

"Fair enough, Jessica. But I don't have to continue sharing information with you, either. I know where Joe Charles is. You say he might be a murderer, and that Morse's wife is in danger because of him. I can nail down that linkup without you."

I stood and came around the side of the desk. "I understand how much you want to do this book with me. I don't fault you for that, and maybe I've been too rigid in how I view it. I'm sure you can understand that making such a decision is extremely difficult in the midst of the tension and pressures I've experienced since arriving in New York. I don't make snap decisions, never have. I've often complained that the biggest problem we all face is a lack of quiet, contemplative time to think things out. I promise to give the idea serious consideration once everything has been resolved, and I have an opportunity to go home and clear my head."

The expression on his face didn't tell me whether I was making an impact or not. I continued. "If that isn't enough to convince you to take me to Joe Charles tonight, let me again remind you that Nancy Morse's life might be at stake. I believe that Joe Charles knows where she is. If I'm right, confronting him might save her life and the lives of her children." I raised my hands, then slapped them to my thighs. "That's all I have to say, Bobby. You can either do what you promised me earlier this evening, take me to where Joe Charles is appearing, or go back on your word, turn in this article, and let the chips fall where they may." I returned to the living room, picked up my coat from a chair, and put it on.

"Okay," he said, standing in the doorway. "But only if you promise one other thing."

"What's that?"

"That you'll allow me to continue talking to your agent, Russ Checkett. At least give me the opportunity to sell him on the idea."

"Without me," I said.

"You said you'd think about it."

"And I will. Continue talking to him, but only on the condition that you not tell him that I've agreed to anything—yet."

"Fair enough."

We had to walk to Broadway to find a cab. When we were ensconced in the backseat of a yellow Checker and Bobby had given the driver an address in the Bronx, I asked how he'd learned where Joe Charles was appearing that evening.

"Easy," he replied. "I called the twenty-four-hour jazz line."

"What's that?"

"A service for the jazz community. You call and get a recording telling you who's appearing in clubs around New York."

"Just like that," I said.

"Yeah, just like that."

"I wish I'd thought of it."

He laughed. "But you didn't. Like I said, Jessica, we make a great team."

Chapter Twenty-two

As we left Manhattan and entered the Bronx, the change in landscape was as distinct as the change in my mood. Pure adrenaline had carried me to this stage. I'd been pumped up with a sense of mission. Forget that I'd resolved days ago to leave the digging to Bobby Johnson, and be content with learning from him what had happened. That was then. This was now, a cold, wet night two days before Christmas. I wondered whether Santa visited the Bronx. The real one, I mean. Or, the mythical one. I'm sure he did, at least in the minds of the children. I thought of Santa being murdered on Fifth Avenue, could see the blood again, hear the report of the weapon. I'd never view Santa Claus again in the same pleasant light.

Bobby said little during the ride. He was lost in thought, his attention on the passing scene as we moved through neighborhoods that looked as though they'd suffered massive air raids. I remembered seeing and hearing scenes

of the South Bronx when President Jimmy Carter visited
there in 1978. He'd promised to commit a large amount
of money to rebuilding the area, but that obviously hadn't
happened. So much rebuilding to accomplish and so little
money with which to do it. What a tragedy, block after
block of such beautiful buildings that once housed thriv-
ing families reduced to ruin.

The taxi kept swerving to avoid potholes, but not always
successfully. Once, he slammed on the brakes because a
painfully thin stray dog darted out in front of us after having knocked over a garbage can. It had started to drizzle
before we left Manhattan. The cab's windshield wipers did
nothing but smear dirt across the window's surface. The
overall impact of the ride was to cause me to almost call a
halt to the trip, to instruct the driver to return to Manhattan. Let Bobby Johnson do his stories. I'd had enough.

But then we turned off 137th Street and were on a street
called Alexander Avenue. At least there was life there. We
passed two magnificent churches and then, to my relief,
drove past a police station, in front of which were parked
a dozen patrol cars. The movie *Fort Apache* had depicted
being a cop in such surroundings. A tough job. Hopefully,
our destination wouldn't be too far from the precinct
house.

Lights from a couple of small grocery stores spilled out
onto the wet pavement. People milled about in front of
them, undeterred by the light rain. Small residential buildings dotted the avenue. It was good to know that other
people were there. I'd begun to think Bobby and I were the
only two people in the South Bronx that night.

We pulled up in front of a redbrick building. The tattered remains of a green canopy hung loosely over the span between the door and curb. Dozens of garbage cans overflowing with trash stood between us and the door as we exited the cab. Music of the type I'd heard through Joe Charles's door on Crosby Street forced its way to the street. A faint light could be seen through a dirty window, half of which was covered by cardboard. A crude sign written in some sort of pen announced: "APPEARING TONIGHT JOE CHARLES."

"This is it, huh?" I said to Bobby as the cab pulled away.

"Looks like it. Not much of a place."

I looked up and down the street. "No, it isn't. Let's go in. I'd rather take my chances inside than stand out here."

The minute we pushed open the door, the music assaulted us with the potency of a tornado. The room was long and narrow. Running along the left side was a bar. Small tables were crowded together along the right-hand side. At the far end of the room was a bandstand on which Joe Charles, surrounded by all his instruments, performed a musical composition that sounded to these untrained ears like a steel factory in full production. It was deafening.

"Over there," Bobby said, pointing to the only vacant table along the wall. We went to it and, with considerable jockeying, managed to squeeze onto small, rickety wooden chairs. A young woman with a mane of reddish hair, and wearing an extremely short skirt and low-cut blouse, came to our table. Bobby looked at me questioningly. "Soda," I shouted. "Coke or Pepsi." Bobby ordered a beer. "No glass, just the bottle," he said.

The seats we'd taken had me facing the bandstand. Bobby's back was to it. I squinted against tearing eyes. A thick blue haze of smoke filled the room, and there was the pungent odor of marijuana. A young man and woman directly behind Bobby openly passed a cigarette back and forth. I looked to my left and saw that men at the bar had turned to observe us. I suppose it was natural that we would attract attention. Aside from Joe Charles, we seemed to be the only Caucasians in the place.

The waitress placed my soda in front of me, but I didn't touch it. I'd lost my thirst. Talking to Bobby was impossible because of the music's volume, and so we sat, each chewing on our individual thoughts and waiting for Charles to take a blessed intermission.

We must have come in toward the end of his set because after a crashing finale to whatever composition he was playing, he stopped, nodded to acknowledge the few people who bothered to applaud, stepped down from the bandstand, and went to the bar where he was handed a beer by the barmaid. I was tempted to get up from the table and approach him, but I stayed seated and simply watched. He took a swig from the bottle, wiped his mouth with the back of his hand, and began a conversation with a young woman. It was obviously a pleasant conversation because they laughed a great deal.

"Should we go over to him?" I asked Bobby.

"No. Let's wait a little. I'd rather get him alone."

My concern was that he would stay with his friend at the bar until it was time to perform again. I wasn't sure my ears could tolerate another round of his music. But then he kissed his friend on the cheek, accepted another beer from the barmaid, and slowly made his way along the bar toward the front door. He was almost abreast of us when he spotted me. I read in his face a combination of surprise, and then panic. "Joe," I said, raising my hand.

He stood transfixed, obviously confused about what to do next. Bobby Johnson had turned in his chair so that he faced Charles. "Can we talk to you for a minute?" he asked.

I sensed Charles was about to turn and head back to the bandstand, or for the door. Bobby and I quickly stood, which placed each of us in the path of either escape route.

"Please, Joe," I said. "Give us a few minutes. It's important."

Our brief dialogue, and the fact we'd stood so suddenly and had him wedged between us, captured the attention of others within earshot. Charles was aware of them looking at us, which, I think, caused him to decide to listen to what we had to say instead of pushing us aside and causing a scene. "What do you want?" he asked me.

"A few answers, that's all. Please sit down." I looked about me for a third chair, but there wasn't one.

"Is there another room?" Bobby asked.

"No. Look, I don't know why the hell you came here," Charles said. "I don't know anything. I told you that when you came to my apartment, Mrs. Fletcher."

"And I came back, only to find Susan dead. How did she die, Joe?"

My question unnerved him. He started to move away. I put my hand on his arm and said, "You've got to talk to me. Only for a few minutes." I looked to the bandstand. "Could we go up there? I promise I won't take longer than your normal intermission."

"Yeah, like when you came to my place and said you wouldn't ask any more questions. But you just kept asking them."

"I'm sorry. A bad habit of mine."

Charles seemed to be suddenly aware that Bobby Johnson was there, too. "Joe," I said, "this is Bobby Johnson. He's a reporter."

From the look on Charles's face, I was sorry I'd mentioned Bobby's press affiliation. "A reporter? Jesus."

"Maybe we should go outside," I suggested.

"Sure," Charles said. "Why not?" He heaved a deep sigh, finished what was left of his beer, plunked the empty bottle on the table, and said, "I could use some air anyway."

It was raining harder now. We stood beneath the canopy, but its gaping holes afforded little protection. "Maybe we should go back inside," I said.

Charles ignored my suggestion and pointed across the street. "That bodega's open," he said. He ran across the street, and we followed. It was pleasant and warm inside the small store. A Hispanic husband and wife served customers from behind a counter so laden with items that there was only a small space through which to transact business.

We stood just inside the door. I started to ask a question when the husband behind the counter said something loud in Spanish. He sounded angry.

"Yeah, yeah, *sí, sí,*" Charles said. "He doesn't want us standing here unless we buy something."

I went to a magazine rack directly behind Charles and pulled out a copy of *El Diario,* the Spanish newspaper. I took it to the counter, paid for it, and returned to Charles and Bobby Johnson. "This should buy us a few minutes," I said. "Joe, do you know where Nancy Morse is?"

"Nancy Morse? Why would I know where she is?"

"Because—she moved from Cabot Cove. I was there the day she left. I think you were there, too."

He looked at me as though I was crazy. "You're nuts," he said. "Why the hell would I be at her house?"

"You lied to me the day I visited you. You said your phone was broken, but it rang when you were away from the apartment. It was a call from Detective Rizzi."

"So what? Where's it written that I have to be honest with you?"

"And you and Susan Kale met with him the night I came to Sweet Basil."

"You didn't *come* to Sweet Basil, Mrs. Fletcher. You followed me there."

"You're right. And then you disappeared."

"That's also my right. I don't owe you or anybody explanations."

"Unless you have something to explain."

"Like what?"

"Like Susan Kale. About why someone tried to kill Waldo on Fifth Avenue."

"Look, if you think I—Wait a minute. *Tried* to kill him?"

"Yes."

"He *was* killed."

"No, he wasn't. It was someone else that day in the Santa suit."

"That's ridiculous," he said.

"I'm surprised you don't know that, Joe. I'm surprised your friend, Detective Rizzi, didn't tell you."

"He knows?"

"That's a fair assumption."

"He would have—"

"Would have told you? *Should* have told you?"

He looked down at his shoes. "Look, Mrs. Fletcher, I don't know what to say. All I know is that I'm in a hell of a spot."

"Why are you in a spot? Knowing that Waldo is alive should be good news. You are his friend, aren't you?"

"Sure I am. How do you know he's alive?"

"Because I've talked with him."

"Where is he?'

"I'd rather keep that to myself, at least for now. After all, he's in a tough spot, too." I didn't add that I was afraid what he might do if he knew how to find Waldo.

He noticed that Bobby Johnson had pulled a pad and pencil out of his pocket and was making notes. "Hey, knock that off," he said. "This isn't like some interview."

"Please, Bobby," I said. He reluctantly returned the pad and pencil to his pocket.

"I suppose all of this has a logical explanation," I said, unable to keep the confusion and frustration from my voice. "But that isn't nearly as important right now as Waldo's wife, Nancy. Is she with you?"

"Of course not. I haven't seen Nancy since high school."

Could I believe him? For some reason, I did.

"You said she moved," Charles said. "Maybe she went out west, or to some foreign country. Why look at me like I should know?"

This time it was the wife who yelled at us in Spanish.

I reached for the closest thing, a bag of tortilla chips and held them up to her to see. *"Dinero,"* the wife said. Bobby Johnson swore under his breath, went to the counter, and dug through his pockets for change. While he was there, I asked Joe Charles, "Did you try to have Waldo killed?"

"What?" He held his hand up in a gesture of sincerity, "Me? Try to get Waldo killed? Boy, do you have it wrong. Next you'll accuse me of killing Susan. I loved Susan. When you saw me and Rizzi together, and after she was murdered, I figured it was time to split. I'd be in L.A. or Frisco if I had any bread. Why do you think I'm hiding out like this, playing this crummy joint, living in a flophouse? Don't look at me, lady, when you talk about trying to kill somebody. Look at Waldo."

Johnson returned just as Charles finished his statement. "What did I just hear, that Waldo Morse is a killer?" he asked.

Charles looked at Johnson. "I've said enough," he said.

"But what did you say?" Johnson repeated.

Charles started for the door. Johnson grabbed his arm. Charles turned and looked at me. "You are some troublemaker, Mrs. Fletcher."

"I am only trying to get to the truth, Joe, and perhaps save Nancy Morse's life. Are you sure you don't know where she is?"

"I don't know, and I don't care. I'm outta here." With that he was through the door and running across the street.

Johnson looked at me with questioning eyes. "Come on, Jessica, share with me. Don't forget I brought you here. He claims that Waldo Morse is a murderer?"

I shook my head. "I don't know what he claims, Bobby. Waldo told me that it might have been Joe Charles who tried to have him killed on the street that day. I asked him about that, which prompted the response you heard. Frankly, I don't know what the truth is."

"Let's go back and talk to him some more," Johnson said.

I shook my head. "He won't say anything else to us. He says he doesn't know where Nancy Morse is."

"Do you believe him?"

"I think I do. I'm very tired, Bobby. How do we get a cab in this neighborhood?"

"Not easy. Maybe Mom and Pop here will call one for us."

Johnson returned to the counter where he used pidgin Spanish to get across that we needed a taxi. The wife said, *"Dinero."* I browsed publications on the magazine rack while waiting for Bobby to return. The door behind me opened. I didn't turn around until the two men who'd entered began shouting in Spanish. When I did turn in response, I was face-to-face with men brandishing handguns. One stayed with me while the other moved quickly to the counter and pointed the weapon at the owners of the store.

I was frozen with fear. At the same time, I broke out into a sweat and my throat went dry. I stared at the man holding a weapon on me. As hard as I tried to avert his stare, I couldn't. His eyes were black and small, and he had the crazed look of someone on drugs.

The voices became louder at the counter. The man with me spun away and ran in that direction. I saw the husband open the register and toss bills on the counter. One of the gunmen scooped them up and shoved them in his pocket.

Then, it happened. There were two shots. I couldn't see who'd been hit. I threw myself to the floor and lay there shaking as two pair of feet ran from the back of the store toward the door. They stopped for a moment. Did they remember I was there? If they did, they decided not to bother with me because they opened the door and vanished into the night.

The next voices I heard were the husband and wife. Unlike earlier when they were demanding money, they sounded like paid wailers at a funeral. I slowly got to my feet and approached the counter. What I saw affected me as though someone had punched me in the stomach. Lying in a pool of blood was Bobby Johnson.

"Get help," I said, although I needn't have bothered. The wife had already dialed 911.

I knelt beside Bobby and placed my fingertips on his brow. He was alive; a quick observation indicated that the bullet had hit him in the left shoulder. I pulled a handkerchief from my pocket and pressed it against the wound to stem the flow of blood. "Just take it easy," I said. "Help is on the way. You'll be all right."

He responded by looking up at me and smiling, actually smiling. And he said, "Looks like we won't have any problem finding a cab now, Mrs. Fletcher."

Chapter Twenty-three

It was déjà vu all over again.

The first two policemen through the door were in uniform. They were followed by none other than Detective Alphonse Rizzi. As had happened on Fifth Avenue, he and his colleagues were there in minutes. Late at night on Alexander Avenue in the South Bronx? It was hardly an area where a detective would be routinely cruising.

"Amazing," he said.

"It certainly is," I said. "Why are you here?"

He gave me one of his patented stupid-question looks and pointed to the rear of the store where an MPD paramedic worked on Bobby Johnson. "Is that good enough reason for you?"

"That's not what I mean, Detective Rizzi. What I meant was that it seems highly unlikely that you would just happen to be in the area."

"I'm with Narcotics. This is heavy drug turf."

"I saw you when I came out of the Pan Am Building earlier this evening."

"Wrong. The Met Life Building. Pan Am went south."

"The name of the building doesn't matter. Why are you following me?"

"Don't pride yourself on being important enough to be followed, Mrs. Fletcher. I'm not following you."

"Commissioner Frye said he was withdrawing police escort for me."

He ignored my comment. "Who's your friend back there?" he asked.

"His name is Bobby Johnson. He's a *Post* reporter."

"Oh, that one, the guy who's been turning out all the stories about you."

"Yes, 'that one.'"

I went to where the paramedic was tending to Bobby. He'd stopped bleeding, and there was more color in his face. "It's dangerous hanging around you, Jessica Fletcher," he said. A laugh accompanied his comment and caused him to cough.

I put my finger to my lips. "We can talk about that later, Bobby. Right now you just do what you're told and get well."

An ambulance arrived, and he was removed from the store on a stretcher. One of the uniformed cops who spoke fluent Spanish interviewed the mom-and-pop owners of the store.

"What hospital is he being taken to?" I asked an EMS technician who'd arrived on the heels of the police.

"Bellevue," he answered.

"I'd like to accompany him," I said.

"Against the rules, ma'am."

Rizzi came up to me. "I know you like asking all the questions, Mrs. Fletcher, but I've got one for you."

"I'm listening."

"How come you and the reporter were up here on Alexander Avenue? Not exactly a tourist attraction."

I hesitated before saying, "Perhaps the same thing you were doing, Detective. Meeting with Joe Charles across the street."

I observed his face for a sign of surprise or anger. He demonstrated neither. Nor did he confirm or deny that Joe Charles had been his reason for coming to the South Bronx. I realized, of course, that it was entirely possible that he'd simply followed Bobby and me there. Judging from his actions when we'd left the Wings Club, someone had been following us all night.

"Would you be kind enough to find me a cab?" I asked.

"No need for that, Mrs. Fletcher. I'll drive you myself."

"Directly to my hotel?" I asked.

"Sure, only you'll have to give me a half hour of your time. Since I ended up catching this one, I'll have to get a statement from you."

"You personally? Why not one of the other officers?"

His face mirrored his frustration with me. "I've developed sort of an attachment to you," he said.

"Oh?"

"Yeah. Even though you're a professional thorn in my side, I respect you."

"Like Mrs. Wilson."

He sort of laughed. "Yeah, only I wouldn't give her a

ride anywhere, at least not if I could help it. Come on, let's go. No sense standing around this dump."

"It's not a dump," I said. I went to the counter where the wife was crying. Her husband looked ready to kill. "Thank you," I said. "And *buenos noches.* I think that's the proper term for 'good night.'"

"*Gracias,*" the husband said. "Sorry for the trouble."

I followed Rizzi outside into the rain. He led me to an unmarked vehicle and held open the passenger door. I looked up and down the street before getting in. The shooting had attracted dozens of people, most of whom chattered away in Spanish. It was pouring now. My hair was quickly saturated, which sent rivulets of water down my cheeks and over my nose. I got in the car, and Rizzi closed the door. I wondered if he would put on flashing lights and use his siren, but he didn't. He drove slowly and quietly through the rubble-strewn streets and into less ravaged Manhattan.

"You know, Mrs. Fletcher. I'm really not a bad guy. You just see one side of me."

"I never considered you a bad guy, Detective."

"There's a lot you don't know about me."

More than you realize, I thought. I said, "Well, I know that you appreciate and understand fine wine and art. I know that you're married, that your wife's name is Emily, and that you have a mother-in-law named Mrs. Wilson."

"I don't mean that kind of stuff. I mean about being a cop. Where is it you live?"

"Cabot Cove, Maine."

"A little town, huh?"

"Yes."

"You see, Mrs. Fletcher, this is different than what you know about. Here in New York you don't police by the book. Can't. It doesn't matter what all the knee-jerk liberals say about respecting individual rights. It doesn't work. The scum on the street look at cops like we're idiots, jerks. We arrest them, the judges let 'em go. We protect ourselves and we're brought up on charges and the public wants our heads. You understand what I'm saying?"

"I think so."

"You cut corners if you want to be a good cop—and live to write a book about it."

"Is that what you want to do, write a book about your years as a police officer?"

"I wouldn't mind."

"I'm sure it will be a very good book."

We pulled up to the curb in front of the Sheraton-Park Avenue. He turned off the ignition and faced me. "You mind if I come in, Mrs. Fletcher. I could take a statement here in the car but it's too cold."

"Of course."

I suggested we sit in a quiet corner of the empty lobby, but he shook his head. "Too public, Mrs. Fletcher. If you don't mind, I'd just as soon come up to your room."

"Well, I—"

"Not to worry, Mrs. Fletcher. I haven't raped anybody in years." He chuckled at his little joke.

Rape was the furthest thing from my mind, but I didn't express it. I said instead, "All right, let me make a fast phone call first." I went to a house phone and dialed the room shared by Mort and Seth. They didn't answer, and the operator came on the line. "This is Jessica Fletcher in the penthouse suite. Please leave a message for Sheriff Metzger and Dr. Hazlitt. Tell them I'm meeting in my suite with Detective Rizzi. And be sure to indicate the time of this call."

"I hope this will be brief?" I said when Rizzi and I walked into the suite. "I'm exhausted. Excuse me. I see that my message light is flashing, and I want to call the hospital to check on Bobby Johnson."

"Do that after I'm gone, Mrs. Fletcher," Rizzi said. "You said you wanted this quick. That suits me, too."

"All right." I removed my coat and sat in a chair. "Do you want me to make a statement, or do you wish to ask questions?"

Rizzi's response was interrupted by a violent sneeze. Then another. A third came immediately.

"Bless you," I said.

"You got a cat up here?"

I laughed. "As a matter of fact, I do. Miss Hiss. I rescued her from that apartment where Susan Kale was murdered."

He pulled out a handkerchief and wiped eyes that had begun to run. "I got a terrible allergy to cats, Mrs. Fletcher."

"We should have stayed downstairs."

"Mrs. Wilson bought two cats just to make me miserable."

"Oh."

"Where is the cat?"

"In the bathroom." The bathroom door was slightly ajar. Miss Hiss pushed through it and headed directly for Rizzi. He quickly stood and walked to the other side of the room. The cat continued in his direction. "Please, Mrs. Fletcher, get that thing away from me."

I picked her up, put her back in the bathroom, and closed the door. "Better?" I asked.

"No, but go ahead. Tell me what happened tonight, why you were there, what you saw."

Had I not mentioned Joe Charles when we talked at the scene of the shooting, I would not have mentioned him now. But since I already had, I started with an explanation of how Bobby Johnson had found Joe Charles playing in the small dive across from the bodega, and that we'd gone there to speak with him.

"Speak with him about what?"

"About—"

Rizzi went into a sneezing frenzy. He managed to ask in the midst of it, "You got another bathroom in this place? Sometimes water on my face helps."

I pointed him in the direction of the second bath. While he was gone, I decided to retrieve my messages. There were calls from Vaughan Buckley, Ruth Lazzara, Seth and Morton earlier in the evening and, finally, the message left by Nancy Morse. "Are you sure she didn't leave any way to reach her?" I asked the operator.

"Afraid not, Mrs. Fletcher. I asked, but she said she would call back."

"Thank you."

I wrote down on a pad the name of each caller and left it next to the phone. Rizzi returned from the bathroom. I excused myself to make a different use than he had of the same facility. I reached the door and looked back. He was leaning over the pad scrutinizing the names I had written.

When I returned, he had his topcoat on and was about to leave.

"I thought you wanted a statement from me," I said.

"I got enough from this visit, Mrs. Fletcher. Somebody'll get in touch with you tomorrow to take a formal statement. In the meantime, stay out of bad neighborhoods. You can get hurt in them."

Chapter Twenty-four

My call to Bellevue Hospital had confirmed that Bobby Johnson was doing nicely. His condition was listed as "satisfactory." I returned the other calls. Seth and Morton had taken in a Broadway show. To my surprise, Mort had loved it but Seth found it "lacking in artistic integrity and dramatic urgency." Usually, Mort has trouble sitting through even a half-hour television show, and invariably finds all dramatic presentations silly at best, subversive at worst.

Naturally, my call informing them that I was being interrogated by Rizzi in my suite triggered a barrage of questions about my evening and what had led up to being questioned. "Just routine," I told them. The thought of recounting my adventure in the South Bronx was too painful, so I didn't. I focused on the parties and dinner, summing up the rest of the evening with, "There are so many areas to explore in New York. You see something new and interesting everywhere you look."

Vaughan Buckley simply wanted to tell me how I'd charmed Wolfgang Wurtzman, and that he and Olga were looking forward to having me at their Christmas Eve party the following evening. Ruth Lazzara, of course, was simply confirming the next day's activities, which would begin with a ten-o'clock book signing at Macy's. I asked her for a phone number at which I could be reached at the store. She called back with it a few minutes later. I then called information on Long Island and got the number for K. C. Gallaghers in Sea Cliff. Should Nancy Morse call again, I wanted the operator to have every possible number at which I could be reached.

I slept well considering everything that had happened. I had breakfast in the room, enjoyed a leisurely shower, and felt rested and relaxed when it was time to meet Ruth in the lobby for our trip to Macy's. Because public scrutiny of my daily activities had diminished, I'd become used to arriving in the lobby without being ambushed by the press. Which accounted for my surprise when I stepped off the elevator and was confronted with cameras and reporters. I was about to retreat to the security of the elevator when Ruth, who'd been hidden behind a group of media representatives, yelled my name and ran to me. "This is incredible," she said, thrusting a copy of that morning's *New York Post* at me. The entire front page was covered with a stock photograph of me. A small insert picture in the lower right-hand corner was of the bodega's entrance. The headline—it couldn't have been bigger—read: "JESS DOES IT AGAIN!"

I pulled Ruth into the elevator and pushed the button for my floor. Reporters tried to join us, but I held them off with a steely stare.

"I can't believe this happened to you last night," Ruth said. "Why didn't you tell me when you called?"

"Because I wanted to forget about it," I said, turning to Page Three where the story began. It was bylined by, who else? Bobby Johnson "reporting from his bed at Bellevue Hospital." He recounted the details of the shooting and made much of the fact that I was witness to yet another Manhattan assault. The rest of the story was dominated by a rehash of the Santa Claus slaying on Fifth Avenue, my discovering the body of Susan Kale, and the fact that we'd gone to the South Bronx to talk to a musician, Joe Charles, in the hope of verifying that the person originally thought to have died in the Santa Claus costume had not, in fact, been that person. At least he'd fudged it. He hadn't claimed outright that Waldo Morse was alive.

When we were in the suite, I said, "This is dreadful."

"I know," Ruth said without conviction. "It must be trying for you. But the publicity is incredible. Johnson mentions the name of your new book at least three times. And he calls you 'Manhattan's Mayhem Madam.'" She giggled.

I winced.

The phone rang. It was Seth, who'd just picked up the *Post*. "You stay right there, Jessica. Mort and I are on our way up."

"I can't face the press again," I said to Ruth.

"Is there a back door?" she asked.

I thought of my previous escape from the roof and down to the kitchen, but thought better of it. There was a loud knock on the door. I opened it, and Seth and Morton came in. Seth wore his usual brown tweed jacket, forest green suede vest, and bow tie. Morton, no surprise, was in his tan Cabot Cove sheriff's uniform replete with badge, and broad-brimmed Stetson hat.

"We have to go," Ruth said.

"Where are we going?" Morton asked.

"Macy's," I said. "To sign books."

"If it was me, Jessica, I'd cancel out and stay right here," said Seth. "Not safe for you to be out on the streets of this city."

I forced a laugh. "Don't be silly," I said. "The only threat to me is the free press. If you gentlemen will run interference for me, I'm ready to leave."

They did a pretty good job of helping me navigate the crowd in the lobby and out to the sidewalk. We were followed of course, as we made our way across town to Macy's on Thirty-fourth Street, but the store's management did a good job of crowd control. They kept the press at bay while I frantically signed books for hundreds of people.

I'd ordered a car to pick me up in front of the store at eleven-thirty. Seth, Morton, and Ruth accompanied me out to the sidewalk where I found my driver, who held up a large cardboard sign with my name on it.

"Where are you going?" Ruth asked.

"A personal errand," I said.

Seth opened the back door and climbed in.

"Where are *you* going?" I asked.

"With you on this personal errand," he said. "Come on, get in."

Two things crossed my mind. The first was that there

was no way I could dissuade them from accompanying me. The second was that I welcomed their company. I was naturally concerned that their presence might upset Waldo. But it wasn't as though I was bringing total strangers. They'd known Waldo's mother in Cabot Cove. If being with me bothered Waldo, so be it. It was time I stopped doing a solo act.

"By the way," Morton said as we headed for the Queens Midtown Tunnel and the Long Island Expressway, "I got hold of the moving company in Portland that moved Nancy."

I looked at him with wide eyes. "And?"

"Seems they brought her here to New York City."

I wasn't surprised, not with the message she'd left at the hotel. Of course, she could have called long distance, but somehow I doubted it. I asked, "What address did they take her to?"

Morton pulled a slip of paper from his pocket and handed it to me. It was a building number on Sullivan Street. "Thanks, Mort," I said. "I appreciate this."

I've heard people refer to the Long Island Expressway as the world's longest parking lot. I was now a believer. It was a tortuous ride to where we exited and headed north until reaching the quaint, petite village of Sea Cliff. It was lovely, an oasis not many miles from Manhattan that reminded me somewhat of Cabot Cove. It was on the water, Long Island Sound, and the houses were gingerbready and eclectic. Our driver let us out across the street from K. C. Gallagher's, an unimposing storefront pub with small evergreens decorated with red Christmas bows in window boxes.

"Cute place," Seth said. A young couple passed and gave Mort and his uniform a second look.

"Think he'll show up?" Seth asked.

"There's one way to find out," I said.

Waldo was seated at a table for two in a back corner. He saw me come through the door and started to stand, then saw Seth and Mort and sat back down. I quickly went to him because I knew what he was thinking. "Waldo," I said, placing a hand on his shoulder, "it's all right. These are friends from Cabot Cove. We're *all* here to help you."

His expression said he wasn't sure. But he didn't leave.

"We'll need a bigger table," I said.

We took a vacant table for four in the opposite corner. Waldo obviously was no stranger to the restaurant. A waitress immediately appeared and asked if he would have "his usual." We all ended up ordering it, French onion soup and salads.

"I don't like this," Waldo said after the waitress had left the table. "Who are you people?"

I explained Mort and Seth's connection to me. "Mort learned where Nancy might have moved," I said.

"Where?"

"Seems they moved some of her things to a place called Sullivan Street," Mort replied.

I added, "Nancy tried to reach me last night, but I wasn't at the hotel when she called. She didn't leave a number. Have you seen the papers this morning?"

"The *Times*."

"There's a front-page story in the *Post* about an incident in which I was involved last night. A reporter, Bobby Johnson, was shot in a store in the Bronx. I was with him.

He wrote about it from his hospital room. He mentions in the article that there is the possibility you are still alive."

"Great," Waldo said. "That's just great. How did he find that out?"

"From me, I'm afraid. But I don't think it will matter if we move quickly. I also saw Joe Charles last night."

"Where?"

"At a small jazz club across from the store where the reporter was shot."

"Was Nancy——?"

"No, she wasn't with him. That's why I went to see him, to ask if he knew her whereabouts. He said he didn't."

"You believe him?"

"Yes."

"I hope you're right, Mrs. Fletcher. He's dangerous. He'll do anything to save his hide."

"What's he have to save himself from?" Mort asked in his best interrogation voice.

"He—he's a drug runner," Waldo replied.

"He is?" My surprise was genuine.

Waldo looked at Seth and Mort before asking me, "Are you sure I can talk freely?"

I nodded. "Trust me, Waldo. Trust us."

"Okay. I don't know why I should, but I'm running out of options. If what you say is true about people knowing I'm alive, I might not stay that way very long."

"Go on, Waldo. Tell us about Joe Charles."

He gathered his thoughts before saying, "When I split from the witness protection program and started working for New York MPD, one of my first assignments was to link up with Joe again. The cops knew he was dealing drugs, especially in the jazz community. Turns out some of his suppliers are connected with the guys I helped put away. Joe was sort of a conduit for musicians, a guy they could always come to to make a buy. Rizzi—"

"That's the detective assigned to Waldo," I explained to my friends. "And he's been assigned to me in a manner of speaking. Go on Waldo."

"Yeah, Mrs. Fletcher's right," he said. "Rizzi has been my control ever since I started informing. Anyway, when Rizzi found out that Joe and I went back to Cabot Cove together, he set me on to him. We got friendly again, only it wasn't exactly friendship. I mean, I was hanging around with him and then telling Rizzi everything about how Joe dealt drugs, who bought them, stuff like that. I was a rat, a well-paid one."

Morton's expression said he'd just tasted something sour. But Seth leaned closer to Waldo and said, "Sometimes we do what we have to do, Waldo. I got a feeling that this Joe Charles came to know what you were doin' to him."

"That's right."

"Did Joe know you'd arranged to have your friend stand in for you that day?" I asked.

"I don't think so. At least he didn't learn it from me."

"What about Susan Kale?" I said. "She told me she'd lived with you and with Joe Charles at different times. And you indicated at the library that you thought Joe might have killed her. Why?"

"For the same reason he wanted me out of the way. Susan came to know what was going on between me and Joe. Knowing too much about double-dealing isn't healthy. At least not in this case."

I told Waldo about having seen Joe Charles, Susan Kale, and Detective Rizzi together at Sweet Basil. "If Rizzi and the police were interested in Joe because he was a drug dealer, why would the detective and the drug runner be together in a jazz club?" I asked.

"Because—" Waldo looked to Mort Metzger before completing his statement. "Because Rizzi's dirty."

"Dirty?"

"Yes. Dirty."

"Careful now, accusing a law enforcement officer," Mort said sternly.

"I can't prove it," Waldo said. "But talk on the street is that Rizzi is always on the take, always with his hand out to drug dealers in return for looking the other way."

"You wouldn't see any 'a that in Cabot Cove," Mort said.

"Waldo," said Seth, "did this Detective Rizzi become aware that *you* know he's 'dirty,' as you put it?"

The soup and salads were served. Waldo answered Seth. "I have no way of knowing," he said. "I suppose the guys who told me might have told Rizzi I know about him. *I* sure never brought it up with him."

"But he knows that you dropped out of the federal program," I offered. "He might assume you're ready to do the same with him and the New York police. If you did—if you were no longer under his thumb—you might be tempted to talk to another authority."

Waldo started to respond but I quickly added, "And consider this, Waldo. Rizzi didn't know about the switch that day between you and your friend. At least he wouldn't have known about it until after the fact. Once he did realize it, it could have been the subject of the conversation

I witnessed between Joe, Susan, and Rizzi that night in Sweet Basil. I know one thing for certain. They weren't happy about something."

We fell silent. Seth twisted some of the melted cheese from the top of his soup and tasted it. Food had no appeal for me at that moment. Morton's soup and salad were almost gone.

"Excuse me," Waldo said. "Nature calls."

He went behind a partition and was out of our sight.

"What do you think?' I asked Mort and Seth.

"Hard to say," Mort replied. "Can't say I like him much. Anybody gets involved with drugs like he did doesn't sit well with me, no matter what excuses they make."

"Do you believe him?" I asked.

"That's hard to say, too," said Seth. "You get one story from Joe Charles, another from him. Some friends. Seems like they're each out to sink the other."

"Exactly what I was thinking," I said. "But what if both are telling to truth? I mean, at least from their individual perspectives? Somehow, Detective Alphonse Rizzi keeps coming to mind. No offense, Morton, but being a police officer doesn't necessarily mean he's a good person."

"Are you suggestin' that this Detective Rizzi might actually have tried to kill Waldo, and kill that girl, too?" Seth asked.

I sat back and closed my eyes, slowly shook my head. "I can't prove it, but I have this nagging feeling that he's capable of it. Waldo says Rizzi is dirty, that he takes payoffs from drug dealers. If that's true, he'd have every reason to get rid of people who knew about it and could testify against him."

"Soup is good," Seth said, taking another spoonful.

I glanced at my watch. Waldo had been gone too long. I mentioned it to Seth and Morton.

Mort wiped his mouth with his napkin. "I'll go check on him," he said, hitching up his pants and following Waldo's footsteps. He returned moments later. "I can't find him," he said.

I motioned for our waitress. "Did you see where Waldo went?" I asked.

She smiled. "Looks like he did what he usually does," she said. "I think you're stuck with the check." She handed it to Seth.

"By the old Lord Harry!" Seth muttered.

"Shiftless son-of-a-gun," Mort said.

"Why would he have run from us?" I asked aloud. "Where would he be going in such a hurry?"

I picked up the check that Seth had dropped on the table. "I'll get this," I said. "We'd better head back to the city." I took a credit card from my purse and laid it on the check. It was then that I noticed that the waitress had left a pencil with it. A plain, old-fashioned number two lead pencil.

I went back into my purse and found the sheets of paper I'd taken from the yellow legal pad in Nancy Morse's kitchen in Cabot Cove. I pushed aside the tablecloth on my side and laid the pages on the table's hard surface.

"What the devil are you doin'?" Seth asked.

"Something I've been meaning to do ever since we went to Nancys house." I held the pencil so that the side of the lead was flat and began to slowly rub it over the faint indentations on the paper. Words began to appear. They were barely readable, but when the paper was held to catch the light at precisely the right angle, they took shape.

Seth and Morton moved next to me and squinted to read what had formed on the paper. Not every word took shape, but enough had for the message to come through loud and clear.

I shoved the pages back in my purse, replaced my credit card with enough cash to cover the bill and stood. "Come on," I said. "We don't have a minute to lose."

Chapter Twenty-five

Sullivan Street, according to our talkative driver, was actually in Greenwich Village but was sometimes considered part of New York's Little Italy. It was a lovely street of row houses that had been renovated over the years. But even with attempts at modernization, it retained the look of yesteryear, a set Hollywood might build for a movie about turn-of-the-century immigrants in Manhattan.

We stopped in front of the address Morton had gotten from the moving company. "What now?" Seth asked.

"Let's see if she's put her name on one of the mailboxes," I suggested. I knew she wouldn't have if seeking anonymity, but it was worth a try. I went up the short flight of steps and checked. No Morse. I returned to the car. "No luck," I said. "I guess we just wait. Is that all right with you?" I asked the driver.

"I'm yours till six," he said. "I go off-duty then. It's Christmas Eve."

"It certainly is," I said. A wave of nostalgia swept over me. Sitting in a hired car on a Greenwich Village street was a new holiday experience for me, one I hoped would never be repeated.

"Want me to go in and knock on a few doors?" Mort asked.

"No, let's just sit here awhile," I said. "We'll give it a half hour."

As we waited, the sunshine of earlier in the day was replaced with low, angry clouds from which snow began to fall, gently at first but then whipped by a sudden wind into a horizontal whiteout. People on the street reacted predictably, walking faster, coats pulled up tight around their necks, hats pulled lower over their foreheads. Those walking into the wind leaned forward. Everyone seemed to be carrying presents wrapped in brightly colored paper. Lights on Christmas trees and wreaths in apartment windows took on their own surrealistic movement as the driven snow whipped past them. The sound of the wind, and of the car's heater, was embellished by a church bell from across the street.

"Like some Christmas music?" the driver asked, turning on the radio before we had a chance to answer.

"Wait," I said.

"Huh?" the driver said.

"Turn it off," I said.

"Sounds pretty," Seth said.

The driver clicked off the radio. I leaned forward and peered through the window. It wasn't easy to see because of the weather, but there was no doubt that it was Waldo coming up the street. He was moving fast, hunched forward into the wind, hands jammed in the pockets of his army surplus jacket, eyes narrowed against the sting of the snow.

"Here comes Waldo," I said.

Mort and Seth turned to see what I was seeing. "Ayuh, that's him all right," said Seth.

Waldo walked past us and stopped at the building into which Nancy had moved, hesitated, looked left and right, went up the steps and disappeared inside.

"Looks like you were right, Jess," Seth said. "He knew exactly what building it was." I'd told Waldo only that Nancy had moved to Sullivan Street. I hadn't given him the address. I also knew why he'd run from the restaurant in Sea Cliff. My acknowledgment that I knew where Nancy was had panicked him. The note I'd deciphered, written to him by Nancy, told me only that he and Nancy were planning to run off together. It didn't tell me when. My assumption was that the timetable would be pushed up, which proved out.

"I'll go get him," Mort said, reaching for the door handle.

"Wait," I said. "Look."

A car driven by Detective Alphonse Rizzi, the same car he'd driven me in the previous night, parked at a hydrant up the street. Rizzi got out, went straight to the building, and bounded up the steps.

"Who's that?" Seth asked.

"The infamous Detective Rizzi," I said. "Let's go."

The three of us left the car and walked quickly to where Rizzi stood at the top of the steps. He'd just pressed one of the buzzers, and the return buzz that allowed the door to be opened sounded. "Hello," I said.

He looked down at me. For the first time since I'd met him, his expression wasn't one of anger or scorn. He was surprised, pure and simple. I went up the steps with Seth and Morton at my side. "I know why you're here," I said. "Waldo Morse has already arrived. I assume he's with his wife, Nancy."

The buzzing had stopped. Now it started again. "Is that you, Rizzi?" Waldo's voice asked through a tiny speaker. "Come on up."

"Get out of here," Rizzi said to me.

"Morton Metzger, sheriff of Cabot Cove, Maine," Morton said, flashing his ID.

"Detective Rizzi," I said, "we're not going anywhere until I talk to Nancy Morse." The buzzer sounded angrier this time. So did Waldo. "Hey, is that you, Rizzi? Come on, we don't have all day."

I stepped past him and pushed open the door. If he had any thoughts of stopping me, the presence of Seth and Mort laid them to rest. I turned to him and said, "What apartment is it, Detective? We'll bang on every door if we have to."

"All right, Mrs. Fletcher. You're here. You might as well go up. But don't say I didn't warn you."

"*We'll* go up," I said, nodding at Seth and Morton.

"Two C," Rizzi said.

I led the way, with Rizzi bringing up the rear. The door to Apartment Two C was at the top of the stairs and open. Waldo stood in it. "Hey, what are you doing here?" he said when he saw me.

"Putting an end to the unpleasant part of my trip to New York," I replied. I was angry, and my voice testified to it.

"Who is it?" Nancy asked as she came to the door. "Mrs. Fletcher. How did you—?"

"It doesn't matter how I found you, Nancy. May we come in?" I looked back at Rizzi, who shrugged at Waldo and Nancy.

The apartment was virtually bare. A metal single bed was against one wall. Two directors' chairs were against another. Suitcases were piled near the door.

Waldo and Nancy didn't appear to be ready to move to allow us to enter, but when Morton stepped toward them, they backed inside. We all entered. Waldo and Nancy stood together in front of their suitcases. They held hands.

"You knew where Nancy was all along," I said to Waldo. "This was planned from the beginning, your staged murder, Nancy's sudden move from Cabot Cove, everything— except for Susan Kale."

"What do you mean by that?" Waldo asked.

"What I mean, Waldo, is that you didn't include murdering her in your plans. The only murder you arranged for was that of your unfortunate friend, George Marsh."

"I think you've said enough, Mrs. Fletcher," Rizzi said.

"I disagree," I responded. "You were in on it, too, from the beginning. You knew Waldo was setting up to disappear, and that feigning his own death was the first step."

I looked to Nancy, who'd disengaged her hand from Waldo's and stepped away from him. I asked her, "Nancy, did you know that Waldo intended to have someone killed so that people should think he'd died?"

She looked at Rizzi as though wanting him to answer my question. I, too, looked at him. "I don't understand," I said to the detective, "why you would be a part of this.

You're supposed to uphold the law, not help someone break it."

"You're in over your head, Mrs. Fletcher," Rizzi replied. "I tried to give you a lesson last night in how the real world works in New York. You and your buffoon friends here think the world works like in your little town in Maine. The fact is, I do what needs to be done to get results. You deal from theories. You write nice, neat little books about murder where the bad guys wear black hats and the good guys wear the white ones. Everything tied up at the end. Crime doesn't pay. The killer gets his, and the good guys ride off into the sunset together. Sorry. It don't work that way in real life."

I turned to Waldo and Nancy. "Is that what you're trying to do, 'ride off into the sunset together,' as Detective Rizzi puts it?"

"What's wrong with that?" Nancy asked, stepping forward, her chin jutting out at me. "Don't you think we've paid enough? You haven't lived my life all these years, Mrs. Fletcher. It's been a living hell for me and the kids. This was a chance to put it all back together, for Waldo and me and the kids to start over. Yes, I knew what Waldo planned to do."

"Shut up, Nancy," Waldo said.

"No, *you* shut up! We've been put in this position because of you and your stupidity in Ogunquit." She smiled at me. "The fact is, Mrs. Fletcher, it doesn't matter what you and your friends know because everything that's happened has the blessing of the New York City Police Department. Everything. Isn't that right, Detective Rizzi?"

"She's right, Mrs. Fletcher. Like I said, you don't understand the real world. You think of yourself as a nice person. Right? A real lady who cuddles little animals and wants everybody in the world to live happily ever after. You want these two people to live like that? Then get lost. Go back to your cocoon in Maine and take these guys with you. So somebody gets killed, like this loser in the Santa Claus getup. Because of that, Waldo and Nancy get to see that sunset. He's done a good job for us, paid his dues. But now it's time for him to move on. I like that. A nice happy ending for the book I write when I retire."

"And a life—two lives—mean nothing to accomplish this?"

"You ready?" Rizzi said to Waldo and Nancy. They answered by beginning to pick up the suitcases.

I stood there feeling more helpless than ever before in my life. It was the way I'd felt on Fifth Avenue the day George Marsh was shot, the callous attitude of witnesses to the slaying, the nonchalant air of Rizzi and the other police. Helpless. What was I to do? What *could* I do? Waldo Morse, with the blessing of his wife, had arranged for a friend to be murdered in order that he and Nancy might be free to flee their current lives for a new and better one. There they were, willing to admit it and about to head for an airport or train station—and a New York City detective was helping them.

"What about Susan Kale?" I asked, my voice reflecting how little time I had to ask anything. "What did she do to deserve to die, threaten to expose your scheme? Or did she get in the way because she loved you, Waldo?"

"Grab that other bag," Nancy told Rizzi, who did.

"You even carry their luggage," I said. "How pathetic."

I looked at Seth and Morton. "I'm an officer of the law," Mort said. "There's a murder been admitted to here."

"Cool it, Sheriff," Rizzi said. "You might be a law enforcement officer in Maine, but here you're nothin'. Get out of the way."

The three of us stepped back and allowed them to leave, saw them struggle down the stairs with their bags, watched as they put the luggage in the trunk of Rizzi's car, got in themselves, pulled away from the curb, and never looked back.

"Must be somethin' we can do," Seth said.

"I'm afraid there isn't," I said sadly. "Except to go home."

Chapter Twenty-six

My favorite day of the year has always been New Year's Day. It's a day of pure relaxation, as well as the official beginning of a new year and what it promises.

But this New Year's Day had even greater meaning for me. The previous year had ended on its sad, frustrating note on Sullivan Street in New York City. Hopefully, the new year would be full and rich enough to smother lingering memories of it.

Seth, Morton, and I had attended the Buckleys' Christmas Eve party at their apartment, although we didn't stay very long. I'd taken Vaughan aside earlier in the evening and told him what had happened that afternoon. He was shocked, of course. "Please don't let this put a damper on your party," I said. "I'd just as soon that no one aside from you and Olga know about it. And, Vaughan, I'm afraid I must change my plans. My friends and I want to go back to Cabot Cove in the morning. I know it means canceling a few promotional appearances next week, but there really aren't many."

"Of course," he said. "I do hope you'll find some time to tell me the story in more detail."

"Maybe one day," I said. "But what I really want is to forget it as quickly as possible."

Seth, Morton, and I took a flight on Christmas morning to Boston. Jed Richardson met us in one of his twin-engine aircraft, and flew us without incident to Cabot Cove.

And here it was New Year's Day. I was in my favorite sweatsuit. A fire crackled in the fireplace. I'd attended the annual Cabot Cove New Year's Eve party but hadn't stayed late at that, either. I was asleep by eleven; the new year rolled in without me.

Seth, Morton, and a few other close friends planned to stop by later in the afternoon to share in the clam pies I'd ordered from Charlene Sassi. It was noon. I was at my desk going through the last of a mound of mail that had accumulated while I was away when the phone rang.

"Hello?"

"Jessica. Bobby Johnson."

"Bobby. How are you?"

"Fine. Healing up great. You?"

"All right."

"I've got some interesting news, Jess."

"You have my undivided attention," I said.

"I took everything I have on Rizzi, Waldo, Joe Charles, the works, to my publisher. It took him a while to decide what to do, but he finally set me up with an assistant Manhattan D.A. I figured nobody would take action against a cop like Rizzi, but I was wrong. This D.A.—she's a tough lady, Jess; you'd really like her—is calling for a grand jury hearing on the whole ball of wax. She's got subpoenas out for Waldo, Nancy, and Joe Charles. Rizzi's been suspended, pending an Internal Affairs investigation. Jess, I think they're all going to go down." The enthusiasm in his voice was contagious and satisfying.

"That's wonderful news," I said.

"Yeah. I thought you'd want to know. I also called to wish you a happy new year, Jess, and to thank you for what you did with Russ Checkett."

"I didn't do anything."

"Sure you did. If it wasn't for you, I don't think he would have taken me on as a client and agreed to represent *The Santa Claus Murder*."

"I'm sure it will be a very good and successful book, especially if Rizzi and the others 'go down,' as you put it."

"Russ told me you agreed to read the manuscript and consider providing an endorsement to use on the cover and in ads."

"Yes, I did. Happy to, Bobby."

I fell silent.

"Jess?"

"Yes, sorry. My mind was wandering. I was thinking that Rizzi was right. I don't deal with the real world of crime, especially the way it's played out in New York."

"Don't feel bad about not understanding it, Jess. It isn't to be understood except by the players. Still willing to have me come up for a couple of days so I can drag all you remember out of you?"

"I have to think about that, Bobby."

"Use that quiet time you crave to contemplate?"

"Something like that. It was good of you to call, and I'm glad you're on the mend. Happy new year."

"Same to you, Jessica Fletcher. You're some special lady."

The evening was quiet and lovely. The clam pies were unusually tasty, the conversation subdued and pleasant. Everyone left by nine except for Mort and Seth. They lingered for an extra cup of coffee. As we sat in my kitchen, the subject of Waldo Morse came up for the first time that night. "The level of deception Waldo Morse practiced is remarkable to me," Seth said. "To think that he could fake his own death and then disappear indicates how unbalanced he is."

"And cruel," I added. "Having his friend stand in for him, knowing he'd be killed, was horrible. But I'm afraid Waldo has been practicing deception his entire life. In some perverted way, he meant well. He wanted to get out of the life he'd been leading and accomplish what he'd intended when he became a witness against those drug dealers in Maine. He wanted to go somewhere with his wife and children, and establish a quiet life. But he wasn't the only one practicing deception. The people he put his faith in weren't honorable or honest, either."

"I feel especially sorry for that young girl," Mort said, taking another piece of apple pie I'd baked that morning. "She just ended up in the wrong place at the wrong time."

"More important, she hung out with the wrong sort 'a fellas," Seth said. "Like I always say, if you want a good life, hang out with the winners."

"In her case, the lesson is if you want to *live*," I said.

"The amazing thing is that Waldo didn't kill you, Jess," Mort said. "When you showed up on Fifth Avenue that day and recognized him, you upset his whole misguided scheme."

"I've thought of that on occasion but I try not to dwell upon it." I told them what Bobby Johnson had told me, that it looked as though Rizzi, Waldo, Nancy, and Joe Charles would have to face a jury one day for their deeds.

"I hope so," Mort said. "Just wouldn't seem right that no justice comes out of what they did, two murders and all."

I smiled, said, "Somehow, gentlemen, I believe that justice will prevail in their case no matter how this district attorney fares in prosecuting them. I'm talking about the brand of justice in which the guilty live a life in their own private Hell."

"Like *No Exit*," Seth said.

"What's that?" Mort asked.

"A play by Jean-Paul Sartre," Seth said. "He defined Hell as being in a locked room with people you can't stand. Maybe that's what Waldo and his wife will suffer."

"I think you're right, Seth," I said. "There's no exit from the life they'll be living for the rest of their lives. By the way, Mort, how is Miss Hiss?"

"Cute little rascal. Gets along real good with Jesse." Jesse was Mort's dog. He swears he didn't name her after me, but I've always had my doubts. He'd agreed to take Miss Hiss, and the adoption was working out fine.

I started to laugh.

"What's funny?" asked Seth.

"I was just thinking of the night Rizzi came to my hotel suite and started sneezing. He's very allergic to cats, and Miss Hiss really set him off. He told me that his mother-in-law, Mrs. Wilson, who evidently is no fan of his, bought two cats just to torture him. That's how I see justice being dispensed where he's concerned. Locked in a room with a thousand cats and no exit."

They laughed, too. "I kind 'a like that, Jess," Mort said.

"So do I," said Seth.

"I thought you would. Now go home. This writer starts her new book first thing in the morning."

I learned later that charges were brought against Rizzi, Waldo Morse, and Joe Charles. Nancy Morse wasn't indicted, although she'd certainly been a coconspirator in Waldo's twisted scheme. The three of them had been found in a little town in New Mexico where they lived together. I felt bad for Nancy's children. The sins of their father would certainly impact upon their young lives.

Hopefully, Bobby Johnson's book about what became known as the Santa Claus Murder will shed light on what really happened, especially Detective Alphonse Rizzi's role in it. I fervently hope so, as much as I hope that one day I'll be able to forget about it. I think the former is realistic. As for my latter wish, only time will tell.

A Little
Yuletide
Murder

For Zachary, Alexander, Jacob, and Luke
through whose innocent eyes the mystery,
majesty, and promise of the
Christmas spirit lives.

And for the late Roy Kramer, lawyer and accountant,
who defined what friendship means,
and Billie Kramer, his partner in decency.

Chapter One

"The meeting will come to order!"

We'd gathered in the Cabot Cove Memorial Hall, built after World War II to honor those from our town who'd given their lives, literally and figuratively, defending the country. It soon became a popular place for meetings and social events, especially when large numbers of people were involved. This meeting to plan the upcoming annual Christmas festival certainly qualified. The hall was packed with citizens, most of whom came simply to listen—or to get out of the house during that dreary first week of December—and for some, to offer their ideas on how this year's festival should be conducted.

Cabot Cove's Christmas festival had started small a couple of dozen years ago, consisting back then of townspeople getting together on Christmas Eve and going from house to house to enjoy cider and cookies, singing carols all the way. But as the years passed, the festival became more ambitious. Today it unfurls over an entire week, and has become one of Maine's leading tourist attractions. People come from all over to participate in what's been billed as "America's most traditional Christmas celebration." Hotels, inns, and bed-and-breakfasts for miles around are booked as much as a year ahead. Some claimed it had gotten out of hand, becoming too commercialized. Others reveled in the town's national reputation as an oasis in a commercial Christmas world, where tradition reigns. No matter what the view, the festival had taken on a life of its own, and most Cabot Cove citizens got caught up in the excitement and were enthusiastic participants.

I was delighted to be there, not only because I enjoyed participating in the planning, but because for the first time in a few years I would actually be home during the holiday season. I'd found myself traveling on previous holidays, usually to promote my newest murder mystery, or sometimes simply because invitations extended me were too appealing to pass up. But even though I'd spent previous Christmases in some wonderful, even exotic locations, I always felt a certain ache and emptiness at being away from my dear friends, and from the town I loved and called home.

The meeting was being chaired by our mayor, Jim Shevlin. Seated with him at a long table on a raised platform were representatives from the public library, the Chamber of Commerce, the town historic society (sometimes snidely known as the "town hysterical society"), local political clubs, the fire and police departments, the volunteer ambulance corps, and the local hospital, schools, and, of course, the standing decorating committee, which each year turned our lovely small village into a festival of holiday lights.

Shevlin again called for order. People eventually took seats and ended their conversations.

"It's gratifying to see so many of you here this morning," Shevlin said, an engaging smile breaking across his handsome Irish face. "This promises to be the biggest and best holiday festival ever."

People applauded, including me and Dr. Seth Hazlitt, my good friend with whom I sat in the front row. He leaned close to my ear and said, "Jimmy always says it's going to be the biggest and the best."

I raised my eyebrows, looked at him, and said, "And it usually is."

"Hard for you to say, Jessica, considerin' you haven't been here in a spell to make comparisons."

"But from what I hear, each year tops the previous one. Besides, I'll be here *this* year."

"And a good thing you will," Seth said. "This is where Jessica Fletcher ought to be spendin' her Christmases."

I was used to mild admonishment from Seth, knowing he always meant well, even though his tone could be taken at times as being harsh and scolding. I returned my attention to the dais, where Shevlin introduced the chairwoman of the decorating committee. She went through a long list of things the committee planned to do this year, including renting for the first time a large searchlight to project red and green lights into the sky above the town. This resulted in a heated debate about whether a searchlight was too commercial and tacky for Cabot Cove. Eventually, Mayor Shevlin suggested the searchlight idea be put on hold until further discussions could be held.

As such meetings tend to do, this one dragged on beyond a reasonable length. It seemed everyone wanted to have a say, and did. During the presentation of how the schoolchildren would participate I noticed someone missing at the dais. I turned to Seth. "Where's Rory?" I asked.

Seth leaned forward and scanned faces at the long head table. "You're right, Jessica," he said. "Rory hasn't missed a holiday planning meeting for as long as I can remember."

Rory Brent was a prosperous local farmer who'd played Santa Claus at our holiday festival for the past fifteen years. He was born to the role. Brent was a big, outgoing man with a ready, infectious laugh. He easily weighed two hundred and fifty pounds, and had a full head of flowing white hair and a bushy white beard to match. No makeup needed. He *was* Santa Claus. His custom was to attend the planning meeting fully dressed in his Santa costume, which he proudly dragged out of mothballs each year, stitched up gaps in the seams, had cleaned and pressed, and wore to the meeting.

"Is he ill?" I asked.

"Saw him yesterday," Seth said. "Down to Charlene's Bakery. Looked healthy enough to me."

"He must have been detained. Maybe some emergency at the farm."

"*Ayuh*," Seth muttered.

A few minutes later, when Jim Shevlin invited further comments from the audience, Seth stood and asked why Rory Brent wasn't there.

"I had Margaret try to call him at the farm," Shevlin said. Margaret was deputy mayor of Cabot Cove. He looked to where she sat to his right.

She reported into her microphone, "I called a few times but there's no answer."

"Maybe somebody ought to take a ride out to the farm," Seth suggested from the floor.

"Good idea," said Shevlin. "Any volunteers?"

Tim Purdy, a member of the Chamber of Commerce, whose business was managing farms around the United States from his office in Cabot Cove, said he'd check on Rory, and left the hall.

"You can always count on Tim," said Seth, sitting.

The meeting lasted another half hour. Although there was disagreement on a number of issues, it warmed my heart to see how the citizens of the town could come together and negotiate their differences.

Coffee, tea, juice, and donuts were served at the rear of the hall, and I enjoyed apple juice and a cinnamon donut with friends, many of whom expressed pleasure that I would be in town for the festivities.

"I was wondering whether you would do a Christmas reading for the kids this year, Jessica," Cynthia Curtis, director of our library and a member of the town board, said.

"I'd love to," I replied. "Some traditional Christmas stories? Fables?"

"Whatever you choose to do," she said.

But then I thought of Seth, who was chatting in a far corner with our sheriff and another good friend, Morton Metzger.

"Seth usually does the reading, doesn't he?" I said.

"Oh, I don't think he'd mind deferring to you this year, Jess. It would be a special treat for the kids to have a famous published author read Christmas stories to them."

I suppose my face expressed concern about usurping Seth.

"Why don't you do the reading together?" Cynthia suggested. "That would be a different approach."

I liked that idea, and said so. "I'll discuss it with Seth as soon as we leave."

Seth and Mort approached.

"Feel like an early lunch?" Seth asked.

"Sure. Nice presentation, Mort," I said, referring to the report he'd given about how the police department would maintain order during the festival.

"Been doing it long enough," he said. "Ought to know what's needed. 'Course, never have to worry about anybody getting too much out of hand. Folks really pick up on the Christmas spirit around here, love thy neighbor, that sort of thing."

We decided to have lunch at Mara's Luncheonette, down by the water and a favorite local hangout. The weather was cold and nasty; snow was forecast.

"I hope Mara made up some of her clam chowder," I said as the three of us prepared to leave. "Chowder and fresh baked bread is appealing."

We reached the door and were in the process of putting on our coats when Tim Purdy entered. I knew immediately from his expression that something was wrong. He came directly to Sheriff Metzger and said something to him we couldn't hear. Mort's face turned serious, too.

"What's wrong?" I asked.

"There's been an accident out at Rory's place," Purdy said.

"An accident? To Rory?" Seth asked.

"Afraid so," said Purdy. "Rory is dead!"

"Rory is dead?" Seth and I said in unison.

Purdy nodded, grimly.

"Means Santa's dead, too," Seth said.

He was right. My eyes filled as I said, "I'm suddenly not hungry."

Chapter Two

Although the sad news of Rory Brent's death had taken away any appetite I might have had minutes earlier, I succumbed to Seth's insistence that I go with him to Mara's, if only to keep him company. Sheriff Metzger had immediately left for Brent's farm to investigate the situation.

By the time we got to Mara's—only ten minutes or so after learning the news from Tim Purdy—the report of Brent's death had reached every corner of Cabot Cove.

"What terrible news," Mara said as we entered her small, popular waterfront eatery. "Can't hardly believe it."

"We're all in shock," I replied as she led Seth and me to a window table.

"Any word on how he died?" Mara asked.

"Not so far as I know," said Seth, adding, "Rory was a big man, carried too much weight. Hauling around that kind of tonnage puts a strain on the heart. I told him every time he came in for a checkup to drop a few pounds, but he'd just laugh and say he liked having more of him for folks to love."

I couldn't help but smile at that reference to Rory Brent. He was perpetually jovial; people like him warm the hearts of others. He'd be missed, not only because our familiar Santa Claus wouldn't be here this Christmas, but because we wouldn't be the recipients of his sunny disposition the rest of the year.

Seth and I sat in silence after Mara left us to greet new customers. We looked out the window onto the town dock and beyond, where a heavy, wet, cold fog had settled in over the water, obscuring all but the nearest boats. I thought of Rory's wife, Patricia, as shy and reticent a person as her husband was gregarious.

Patricia Brent stayed pretty much to herself on the farm, running the household and addressing every one of her husband's needs. A dutiful wife was the way to describe her, although I was sure she had many other dimensions than that. They had a son, Robert. Thinking of him made me wince.

Robert Brent, who'd just turned eighteen, did not share his father's positive reputation around town. A brooding young man, he'd had more than one run-in with Sheriff Mort Metzger, usually after a night of drinking with his buddies. Although he lived on the farm with his mother and father, people who knew them better than I did said he seldom lifted a finger to help out, preferring instead to sit in his room, reading magazines about guns and hot automobiles and the military. I don't think I'd ever had a conversation with the younger Brent, my direct contact with him consisting only of an occasional greeting from me on the street, which was usually not returned.

He was different from his father in another way, too. Robert Brent was as thin as his father was corpulent. To further set him apart—perhaps a continuation of his teenage rebellious years—he had shaved his head, making the contrast with his father's flowing white hair that much more dramatic. But although I was not particularly fond of Robert Brent, my heart went out to him at that moment, as well as to his mother, Patricia. As traumatic as Rory's death was for the community, it was surely devastating to them.

Seth ordered his usual, a fried clam sandwich and small green salad. Mara had made clam chowder that day, and I ordered a bowl, nothing else.

"I assume it was a heart attack," I said idly, tasting the chowder which was, no surprise, superb.

"Perhaps," Seth said. "Or stroke. I suppose we'll find out soon enough."

"Will there be an autopsy?" I asked.

"I suspect so. Doc Treyz will probably be asked to do one, considerin' the sudden nature of Rory's death. Standard procedure in cases like this."

I looked up at him and said, "I didn't realize that. I thought it was standard procedure only when the cause of death was suspicious."

"*Ayuh*," Seth said, taking another bite of his sandwich, which he'd slathered with Mara's homemade tartar sauce. "We'll just have to see what Mort comes up with, whether he labels it suspicious. Eat your chowder, Jessica, 'fore it gets cold as outdoors."

We fell silent for a few more minutes until I said, "Not a very cheery Christmas for Patricia Brent."

"I wouldn't argue that with you," Seth said, sitting back and wiping tartar sauce from the corner of his mouth with a napkin. "Never easy losing someone any time of year, but especially tough around Christmas."

"I wonder who'll be chosen to be Santa this year," I said.

"Up to the committee," Seth said.

"Cynthia Curtis suggested that you and I read Christmas stories to the kids together this year."

His eyes went up. "Did she now?"

"Of course, I wouldn't think of joining you unless you really wanted me to."

"Seems like a right good idea, Jessica. I like it."

I drew a deep breath and also sat back in my chair. Funny, I thought, how quickly we return to mundane, everyday matters so soon after someone dies. Here we were discussing the Christmas festivities as though nothing had happened to Rory.

Seth evidently sensed what I was thinking because he said, "Life goes on, Jessica. That's the way it was meant to be by the good Lord up above. Festival is real important to Cabot Cove. Rory would have wanted us to get on with it, make it the biggest and best ever. Coffee?"

Mara had made pecan pie that morning. I passed it up, but Seth enjoyed a hearty serving. We finished our coffee and had stood to leave when Mort Metzger came through the doorway. He was immediately asked by others about what information he had concerning Rory Brent's death, but he ignored them and came to us.

"Cup 'a coffee, Mort?" Seth asked.

"Don't mind if I do," our sheriff said, removing his Stetson hat and sitting heavily in a third chair at the table.

Mara came to take our new order, but lingered at the table after we'd told her we wanted three coffees. Mort ignored her presence and said, "Looks like we've got ourselves a little Yuletide murder on our hands."

Seth and I looked at each other, eyes narrowed, brows furrowed.

"Rory Brent has been murdered?" Mara said loudly.

Mort nodded, looked up at her, and said, "Seems that way, Mara. Got any pecan pie left?"

She left the table. Seth and I leaned closer to Mort. Seth said, "Now, Morton, be a little more specific. Are you certain it was murder?"

"Certainly looks that way to me, Doc. Gunshot to the left temple. Didn't exit the other side, so the bullet is still in his brain. Must have dropped instantly."

I said, "Why are you so sure it was murder? Couldn't it have been suicide?"

"Surely not, Mrs. F. No weapon at the scene. Of course, I'm saying he was shot based upon my examination of him. Could be something else was involved along with a gun. Doc Treyz will have to come to that determination. The ambulance boys were out there real fast, took poor old Rory away."

"Where was the body?" I asked.

"Out in one of his barns. The big one at the back of the property." A puzzled expression crossed Mort's face. "Funny," he said, mostly to himself.

"What's funny?" Seth asked.

"Rory was out there in shirtsleeves. No coat, no hat,

no gloves. Can't imagine him trekkin' all the way from the house out to the barn in this weather without winter clothing."

"Maybe he just ran out there to get something quick," I offered.

"That barn has got to be a half mile from the house. You don't run out there to get something quick," Mort said.

I didn't argue with him.

"How's Patricia?" Seth asked.

"She wasn't there," Mort said.

"That's unusual, isn't it?" I said. "She seems always to be at the farm."

"I wouldn't know about that," said Mort, sticking his fork into the pie Mara had set in front of him. "His crazy kid was there, though."

"Was he the one who discovered the body?" I asked.

"According to Tim Purdy. Tim said he got out there just a few minutes after Robert found Rory in the barn. Robert said he was about to call my office when Tim arrived. Says he figured since Tim was coming back to town to tell us, there was no need for him to make a call."

"I assume he was upset," I said.

"You can't prove it by me, Mrs. F. That kid is a real foul ball. Just had that dumb, placid expression on his skinny little face. Hardly said a thing."

"What was he doing when you arrived?" Seth asked.

"Sittin' in his room, reading magazines."

"After just discovering that his father had been killed?" I said, unable to keep the incredulity from my voice.

"Like I said, he's a strange-o. The only thing he said was about Jake Walther."

"What about Jake?" Seth asked.

"He said I should go arrest the old son-of-a— no need to repeat his profanity," Mort said, looking at me. "He said I should arrest Jake for killing his father."

"Does he know that for a fact?" I asked.

Mort shook his head and ate more pie.

"Everybody knows Rory and Jake Walther had bad blood between them," Seth said.

"But that doesn't matter," I said. "What would cause Robert Brent to immediately accuse Jake of having killed his father?"

"Beats me," Mort said. "I told the boy I'd be back to question him."

"Did he mention his mother?" I asked.

"Says she went to visit somebody. A cousin. Well, I'd better get back there and get answers to some questions I didn't get around to asking. I suppose seeing good ol' Rory lyin' dead in his barn shook me up a little. Not supposed to, being an officer of the law and all that. But I'm human."

"Mind if I come along?" I asked.

"I suppose not, Mrs. F., although there's not much to see. My boys took pictures of the scene and did all their measuring before the ambulance took Rory away. Just a crude sketch on the dirt floor where he was found."

"I'd like to go," I said. "Maybe Patricia Brent is there and could use some comforting. You know, woman-to-woman."

"Sounds like a good idea," Seth said. "I'd come with you, too, except I've got a full slate of patients this afternoon, starting—" He looked at his watch. "Starting ten minutes ago. Excuse me. Call you later at home, Jessica."

Chapter Three

The landscape of Cabot Cove has changed quite a bit over the years I've called it home. It still retains a small-town charm, but is no longer the sleepy little coastal Maine village it once was.

The change isn't especially apparent downtown because most of the shops continue to be owned by individuals, rather than chains and large corporations. The best coffee shop is not a Starbucks, and the largest clothing store is called Charles, not the Gap or Eddie Bauer or Jos. Bank.

But as you leave the center of town and proceed north on an extension of Main Street, the effects of "progress" become readily apparent. All the major fast-food companies have an outlet along that stretch of road, and there are now two strip-malls housing a couple of major department stores and trendy boutiques. However, unlike many towns and villages across America, the opening of the malls did not put local downtown merchants out of business. Cabot Coveites are a resilient lot, one of many things I love about living here.

I sat in the front seat of Mort's sheriff's car and watched the sights go by as we continued north until the malls, hamburger places, and gas stations faded from view and we were in tranquil farm country. The area doesn't support the farming industry as it once did, but there are still plenty of hearty souls who, having had their farms handed down from generation to generation, continue to work the soil and take from it both enough money to live, and a psychic pleasure only farmers understand.

As we approached Rory Brent's spread, Mort said, "I just keep thinking of poor ol' Rory no longer being alive. I really liked that man. I suppose everybody in town did."

"That's a fair assessment, Mort. Not only was he likable, I was always impressed at his skill at farming. It's not an easy way to make a living, but he certainly seemed to have the knack."

"No thanks to that worthless kid of his," Mort grumbled, turning into the long treelined road leading up to the Brent house, which sat majestically on a rise, affording views in every direction of the hundreds of acres surrounding it.

Not that there was much to see that day. The clouds had lowered, obscuring the horizon.

We pulled up in front of the house and got out. The Brent residence looked the way a farmhouse should look. An inviting covered porch spanned the front. The main part of the house was painted a pale yellow, the shutters and front door a forest green. It was more than a hundred years old, but had been meticulously maintained. The paint was fresh, the grounds manicured. The only artifact giving away its twentieth-century occupants was a huge satellite dish off to one side.

We stepped up onto the porch, and Mort knocked. When no one responded, he knocked again, louder this time. A chill went through me as I stood there, and I pulled my coat a little closer about me. Eventually, the door opened, and we faced Rory and Patricia's son, Robert.

"I said I'd be back," Mort said. "Did your mom return yet?"

"No," he replied flatly, the morose, sullen expression never changing on his thin, sallow face.

"You haven't heard from her?"

"No."

"Well, Mrs. Fletcher and I are going back out to the barn. You aren't planning to go anywhere, are you, Bob?"

"No."

With that, he closed the door, leaving us standing on the porch. Mort mumbled something under his breath—I assumed it was just as well that I didn't hear what he said—and we came down off the porch, went around the side of the house, and headed for the barn that was partially veiled by the low clouds. Two vehicles were parked in front of it, one a marked police car, the other a vehicle without markings.

"The boys are still going over the scene," Mort said as we trudged along a narrow path. We'd almost reached the barn when one of Mort's deputies stepped outside.

"Just wrappin' things up here," the deputy said.

"Who belongs to that other car?" Mort asked.

"County police," the young deputy replied. His name

was Tom Coleman; he'd been a Cabot Cove police officer for less than a year.

"How'd they get involved so fast?" Mort asked, leading the way into the barn.

"Didn't ask 'em," Coleman said, closing the door behind us. Not that it mattered whether the door was open or closed. It was as cold in the barn as it had been outside.

Two men in suits stood by the crude outline of where Rory's body had been. Mort introduced himself, and they did the same.

"I wish you hadn't had the body moved so quickly," one of them said.

"Didn't see any need to leave him lying on the ground," Mort said. His attempt to keep annoyance out of his voice was unsuccessful. "I *hustled* him right out of here."

The two county officers looked at each other. One asked, "Did you personally examine the body before it was removed?"

"Of course I did," Mort said. "Took a real close look at it. Checked the area for any physical evidence, weapons, notes, things like that. Nothing there. Checked for footprints. Didn't see any that wouldn't have been made by the deceased."

"Was the door to the barn open?" one of the men asked.

"Yes. I wasn't the one who discovered the body."

"You weren't?"

"No. The son did. A guy named Tim Purdy came back into town and reported that Mr. Brent was dead. That's when I came out here. Didn't know whether it had been an accident or what. When I got here, I took a close look at Rory's head. Single bullet hole to the left temple. No exit wound. No weapon. Checked for rigor. Body was getting cold, but still had a little heat left. Rigor was just setting in. I pegged time of death between two and four hours earlier."

Mort had obviously done the right thing when investigating the scene, and I was proud of him. There are people who sometimes view the Cabot Cove police department as being run by country bumpkins, but that certainly isn't true. Although Mort occasionally comes off as being unsure of himself, he'd kept pace with scientific advancement in police work ever since he became our sheriff years ago, and has a mind that is a lot keener than is sometimes apparent at first meeting.

The men had been talking to Mort as though I didn't exist. Suddenly, they seemed to discover I was there and looked at me.

"This is Jessica Fletcher," Mort said.

"The famous mystery writer," one of the county officers said, extending his hand.

"I don't know about famous, but I do write murder mysteries," I said.

"Any special reason you're here?" the other officer in civilian clothes asked.

"No. Mort told me what had happened out here, and I came along. Rory Brent was a friend of mine, a much loved individual in Cabot Cove."

"I just thought you might be out here getting material for your next mystery novel," the officer said, smiling.

"Never entered my mind," I said.

They turned their attention again to Mort. "Interview any suspects?" he was asked.

"Talked to the son, Robert. He's up in the house. The wife, Patricia, went downstate to visit a cousin, according to the son. Says she was due back a couple of hours ago."

One of the men said to the other, "Let's go up and talk to the kid."

"Now hold on a second," Mort said. "This murder occurred in my jurisdiction, and I'm responsible for the investigation. Perfectly fine for you county fellas to get involved with the autopsy, that sort of thing. But when it comes to questioning people, I'll take care of that."

Mort and the men looked at one another without another word being spoken. Finally, one of them said to the other, "Let's go," then turned to Mort. "We'll be back."

"I'll be looking forward to seeing you again," Mort said.

As we prepared to leave the barn to return to the house, Mort instructed his deputy to remain there until relieved. The front of the barn had been cordoned off with yellow crime-scene tape. "Nobody comes in here unless he's official. Got that, Tom?"

"Yes, sir."

"Come on, Mrs. F., let's go have a chat with Mr. Robert Brent."

When we were outside, I asked, "Are you sure you want me with you when you question him?"

"I wouldn't if I was about to *question* him. But I just intend for him and me to have a little chat. Nothing wrong with you being there while we chat, is there?"

"I suppose not."

A few soft snowflakes had begun to fall from the leaden

sky. We'd just rounded the corner of the house when Dimitri Cassis pulled up in his taxi. Dimitri is a Greek immigrant who'd settled with his family in Cabot Cove after buying the local taxi service from Jake Monroe, who'd retired. He is a handsome, hardworking man who'd been readily accepted into the community. Because I don't drive, I use his service often, to the extent that I have a house account I pay monthly.

He jumped out of the taxi and opened the rear door, through which Patricia Brent exited, carrying a small tapestry overnight bag.

"She doesn't know," I said quietly to Mort. "My God, what a shock this will be."

Patricia was as small a person as her deceased husband had been big. She was birdlike and wore old-fashioned long, flowered dresses. She kept her graying hair up in a tight bun. When she spotted us approaching, a puzzled frown crossed her face.

"Hello, Patricia," I said. "Jessica Fletcher."

" 'Afternoon, Mrs. Brent," Mort said, tipping his Stetson.

"My goodness," Patricia said, suddenly smiling. "What are you doing here?"

"Afraid we have some bad news," said Mort.

"Bad news?" She said to Dimitri, "I'm sorry. I forgot to pay you."

We watched as she fished money from her purse and handed it to him. He appeared to not want to leave, now that he had heard there was some bad news being reported. But he also instinctively understood that as long as he was present, that bad news was probably not going to be voiced. He thanked her, said hello to Mort and me, got back in his taxi, and drove away.

Patricia took a deep breath, pulled herself up to her maximum height, which was not more than five feet, and said, "Well, now, what is this bad news you have?"

"Maybe we'd better go inside," Mort said. "Starting to snow. Catch a chill out here."

"Of course," she said. "I'll put on a pot of tea—unless you'd like something stronger. We always keep a few bottles in the house, although neither Rory nor I drink."

Mort and I thought the same thing, that their son certainly didn't fall into his parents' teetotaling habits.

We followed her into the house and stood in a large foyer. She placed her bag on the floor, removed her coat, and looked in the mirror, touching hair that had been blown during the taxi ride. "Please, take off your coats," she said.

"Ma'am, I don't think we will be having any tea," Mort said. He looked at me; I gave him a look that said we should take off our coats and go to a more comfortable setting to break the news. He picked up on my silent message, removed his jacket, helped me off with my coat, and we went with Patricia to the living room, a large, pleasant space, dominated by a huge hooked rug, antique pine furniture, and hundreds of knickknacks.

"Please, sit," she said. "Tea will only take a minute."

"Mrs. Brent, I—"

Mort's words were lost in the room as Patricia suddenly disappeared in the direction of the kitchen.

When she was gone, Mort turned to me and said, "Something strange going on here, Mrs. F."

I nodded.

"Here poor ol' Rory is shot dead not more than six or seven hours ago. I say we got bad news, and she just sits us down in the parlor and goes in to make tea. The son knows what happened, but he doesn't even bother coming down to be with his mother when she finds out."

"I suppose people handle these things in different ways," I said, not really meaning it, but groping for something to say in defense of the Brent family.

"I'm glad you're here," Mort said. "Hate to be breaking the news to her alone."

Patricia returned from the kitchen, now wearing an apron.

"Only take a minute for the water to boil," she said, sitting primly in a straight-back chair across from where we sat side by side on the couch. "Now, what is this bad news you have to give me? It has to do with Rory, doesn't it?"

An uncomfortable glance passed between Mort and me before I said, "Patricia, Rory is dead."

She lowered her head and looked at hands clasped in her lap. She remained in that position for what seemed a very long time, and neither Mort nor I said anything to intrude. Finally, she looked up and said, "What happened? Did he have a heart attack?"

Mort cleared his throat before saying, "Not exactly, ma'am. You see, Rory died out in the barn. He was . . . well, no sense beating around the bush. He was shot dead."

A tiny involuntary gasp came from Patricia Brent. Her eyes went into motion, looking, it seemed, for some answer in corners of the room.

"You say Rory was shot," she said. "Did he kill himself?"

The directness of the question took us both aback. Mort answered, "No, ma'am, it looks to me as though someone killed your husband."

"Oh, my God," she said so softly we barely heard her. "Who would want to do something like that to Rory?"

"That's what I intend to find out," Mort said, injecting official tone into his voice.

"Does Robert know?" she asked.

"Yes, he does," Mort replied. "He's upstairs. At least, he was."

"Poor boy," she said. "Terrible to lose your father that way."

I was becoming increasingly uncomfortable at her demeanor. She was without affect, her voice a monotone, her eyes seldom blinking.

"Mrs. Brent, Robert told us you were downstate visiting a relative," Mort said.

"Yes. My cousin Jane."

"Down there overnight?" Mort asked.

"No. I took the bus first thing this morning. Jane fell and hurt her ankle. In a big cast. I went down to help out a little bit, but really wasn't needed."

"Where does your cousin live?" Mort asked.

"Salem."

"Salem's only about forty-five minutes from here," Mort said.

"That's right," Patricia said. "Forty minutes exactly on the bus. I timed it."

"What time did the bus leave?"

"Seven."

"So you got down there close to eight," Mort said. "What bus did you catch back?"

"The one o'clock. Took longer to come back. An accident tied things up in every direction. Dimitri was at the bus station and drove me home."

"So I saw," Mort said.

"Any idea who might have done this to Rory?" I asked. She slowly shook her head.

Mort followed with, "Robert told me I should check into Jake Walther."

"Jake? Do you think he killed Rory?"

"I don't know, Patricia, but that's what Bob said."

Patricia thought for a moment before saying, "Rory and Jake never did get along. But then again, I don't know of anyone in the area who gets along with Jake."

"Yes, he is a disagreeable sort," I offered. "Did Rory and Jake have a feud going, some sort of conflict that perhaps became more intense lately?"

"I wouldn't know about that," she said.

She was interrupted by the shrill sound of the teakettle's whistle. "Excuse me," she said, going to the kitchen.

Mort said to me, "I think it's time I had a talk with the son, don't you, Mrs. F.?"

"I suppose so," I said. "But frankly, I'd just as soon not be with you during *that* conversation. Any chance of running me back into town before you question him . . . have your chat?"

"I suppose so, although I want to make sure he doesn't leave here. Come to think of it, maybe he'd be willin' to come with me down to headquarters. Question him in a little more formal surroundings. Might get more done."

"Can you do that without charging him?"

"Yup, provided he comes willingly. I'm not accusing him of anything, just looking for information. If he wants a lawyer, he can have one."

"Whatever you say, Mort," I said as Patricia returned, carrying a tray with tea, milk, and sugar, and a small plate of cookies.

Mort stood. I did, too. "Patricia, I don't mean to be rude," Mort said, "but Mrs. Fletcher and I have to get back to town. Won't have time for your tea. I thought I might ask Robert to come with us. I have to start getting some information to help in the investigation, and he might be able to offer something."

"Take him to police headquarters?" she asked.

"No, ma'am, not *taking* him there. Just asking him if he'd be willing. I'll be wanting to return and talk to you again, too. My deputy, Tom Coleman, is back in the barn, and he'll be staying until he's relieved. I'd appreciate it if you didn't go anywhere until I have a chance to come back."

"I won't be going anywhere except—"

"Except what?" I asked.

"Except to make funeral arrangements, I suppose. I'll have to do that, won't I?"

"Eventually," Mort answered. "But Doc Treyz will be doing an autopsy on Rory. That's the law."

"Of course. Thank you for coming," she said. "I have a few phone calls to make. Family to be told. You understand?"

"Of course we do," I said. I crossed to where she stood and put my arms around her frail body. She was as rigid as an oak, and I quickly backed away.

"Would you be good enough to ask Robert to come down?" Mort said.

"Yes. I'll go up to his room right now. He spends a lot of time there, you know, reading. He likes to read. He's very intelligent."

Chapter Four

Judging from Robert Brent's loud, angry voice, which was clearly heard in the living room, he wasn't keen on coming downstairs. But Patricia prevailed. Five minutes later, he followed her into the living room. He wore jeans, ankle-high military-style boots, a blue sweatshirt with gold figures on it that looked like some sort of military ranger group's, and a blue baseball cap worn backward.

"Robert, you know Sheriff Metzger and Mrs. Fletcher," Patricia said.

His response was to glare at us.

Mort said, "Thought you wouldn't mind coming down with me to town, Robert. You know, just to have a little chat about what happened to your dad."

Robert looked at his mother, who smiled demurely and nodded.

"Won't take very long," Mort added. "Of course, if you'd rather not, we can talk here."

"About Jake Walther?" Robert asked.

Mort looked at me before saying, "Sure. We can talk about Jake. Talk about anything you'd like."

"I'm not being arrested or anything, am I?" Robert asked. "I didn't do anything. Jake shot my father."

Mort's chuckle was forced. "Of course you're not being arrested for anything, Bob. Like I said, you could help me understand a little bit more about what happened. I'd be right interested in hearing about Jake Walther and why you think he might have shot your father."

"Not *might* have shot my father," Robert said angrily. "He did it."

"You saw him do it?" I asked, surprised at how adamant he was.

Robert ignored my question and said to Mort, "I don't mind going with you. Are we driving in your car?"

Mort nodded. "Unless you'd rather come in your own."

Robert shook his head. "I'll come with you." He looked at me. "Are you coming, too?"

"Yes," I said. "Sheriff Metzger drove me out here and will bring me home. But I won't be with you when you and the sheriff have your talk."

That seemed to satisfy him.

While the conversation was taking place, I observed Patricia Brent. Living in a semirural part of the country had put me in contact with many farmers, men and women who live off the soil and were not unduly touched by the world's modern thinking. They tend to be a stoic lot. I don't mean that in a disparaging way. It's just that it has been my experience that such people are not glib, much to their credit. There is too much glibness in the world as far as I'm concerned.

But at a time like this, when a loved one has been found murdered, you would expect even the most dour of individuals to display some emotion, some sign of deep pain and hurt. Not so with Patricia. She was as calm and placid as though we were there picking up her son to take him to a basketball game. I had to remind myself to not be judgmental. Each of us handles grief in his or her own way. When my husband, Frank, died years ago, I fought to retain my composure and to deal with the death of this man I loved very much in a rational and controlled manner. Did people look at me the way I was looking at Patricia at this moment, wondering why I was not displaying the emotion *they* expected of me? Of course, there were countless moments alone when I broke down and allowed my grief to pour out in a torrent of tears. Perhaps that's what would happen the moment we left. Patricia Brent would go to her room, close the door, and cry her heart out.

"Ready?" Mort asked Robert.

"I have to get my coat," he said.

"Good idea," Mort said. "Nasty day out there, and gettin' worse."

Robert returned from the vestibule, wearing a black-and-red wool mackinaw.

"You take care, Mrs. Brent," Mort said, touching Patricia on the shoulder. "Just give a yell if there's anything I can do for you."

"And that goes for me, too, Patricia," I said. "Please don't hesitate to call if I can help you with funeral arrangements, or anything else."

"You're both very kind," she said.

We went to the front door, opened it, and stepped out onto the porch. As Patricia was about to close the door behind us, she said wistfully, "Rory is dead. Hard to believe. I expect to see him walking in here any minute."

I swallowed the lump in my throat and managed a small smile. I was glad to see some sign that she'd recognized the grim reality of the situation.

Mort opened the front passenger door of his car for me, but I sensed that Robert was disappointed at being relegated to the rear.

"Perhaps you'd like to ride up front," I said.

My suggestion brought a hint of pleasure to his face.

Mort started to protest, but I said, "No, I'll be very comfortable in the back."

I was glad I made the decision to give up my front seat to Bob Brent. As we proceeded toward town, he became almost animated, questioning Mort about the array of electronic communications gear wedged between the two front seats. Mort readily answered all the questions, and even demonstrated the use of the radio by calling headquarters. "This is Metzger," he said into the handheld phone. "On my way back in with Robert Brent. Should be there fifteen, twenty minutes. Over."

A voice came through the speaker. "Roger. I read."

"Over and out," Mort said. We both sensed that Robert would have liked to use the mobile phone, too, but Mort was not about to go that far.

As we pulled into the main part of Cabot Cove, Mort turned and asked, "Straight home, Mrs. F., or drop you some other place?"

"Home, if you don't mind."

As we approached the street on which I live, I noticed two cars parked in front of my house.

"Looks like you've got company," Mort said.

"Appears that way."

He turned into my driveway. I got out and came around to where Mort sat behind the wheel. He lowered his window. "Thanks for the ride," I said. I looked across to where Robert sat and said, "I'm very sorry about your father, Robert. Please tell your mother again to call if I can be of help."

His response was a glum nod and to turn away from me.

Strange young man, I thought as I approached my front door. To my surprise, it opened, and I was greeted by Seth Hazlitt. Seth and I have keys to each other's houses and don't hesitate to make ourselves at home in either one.

"Hello," I said. "I thought you had a waiting room full of patients this afternoon."

"*Ayuh*, I did, but a couple of 'em canceled last minute."

As I stepped inside, I saw Cynthia Curtis, our head librarian and member of the town board, standing in the archway leading to my living room. "Hello, Cynthia. What a pleasant surprise."

"Seth insisted I come," she said. "I just put water up for tea. Hope that's all right."

"Sounds good to me," I said, hanging my coat up on a row of pegs and leading them into the living room. Seth had made a fire. I stood before it and rubbed my cold hands. "Feels wonderful," I said. I turned and asked, "What's up?"

Seth did the talking.

"Jessica, Cynthia came to me with a problem having to do with Rory Brent's murder."

I looked at Cynthia, a vivacious, energetic mover-and-shaker in the Cabot Cove community. "A problem concerning you, Cynthia?" I asked.

She looked to Seth to continue, which he did.

"It seems that everybody in town has already convicted Jake Walther of killin' Rory."

"That's terrible," I said. "How could people come to that conclusion so quickly?"

Now Cynthia spoke. "I suppose it's because of Jake's reputation, Jess. You know how it is. Doctors with a pleasant bedside manner get sued less than the arrogant ones."

We both looked at Seth. He smiled and said, "I certainly agree with that. Never been sued in my professional life, and proud of it."

"Jake has made so many enemies over the years," Cynthia said. "You know, he has that mean streak in him that seems to come out at the worst possible moments. I don't suppose there's anyone who's lived here for any length of time who hasn't been crossed by him. At any rate, all everyone is talking about is that Jake murdered Rory Brent."

I sat in a chair in front of the fireplace and looked into flames that were building. I understood her concern. Once a rumor gets legs, as they say, it's like the proverbial snowball rolling down hill. It suddenly struck me that Cynthia might be worried that townspeople would take matters into their own hands. I asked her if that was on her mind.

"Oh, no, I don't think so, Jess. People here aren't like that."

"You never know," Seth said sternly.

"Certainly not at this time of year," I said. "It's almost Christmas. Peace on earth. Goodwill toward men."

"And women," Cynthia added.

"And women," I said.

"You might be forgetting one thing," said Seth.

"What's that?" I asked.

"It wasn't just Rory Brent, a farmer, who's been killed. It was Santa Claus."

Initially, his comment struck me as funny. But it occurred to me just as quickly that there was a certain metaphorical truth to what he'd said. Rory Brent had become synonymous with Santa Claus in Cabot Cove. He was an icon, a man loved throughout the year, but revered once he donned his red Santa costume with its furry white trim, floppy red-and-white hat, and shiny black boots.

I stood and paced the room. "If what you say is true—and I agree there could be a problem having people running around already convicting Jake Walther—then what we have to do is come up with a quick plan to put it to rest. Any suggestions?"

"Maybe you should tell us what happened out at Rory's farm when you and Mort went out there," Seth said.

I thought for a moment, then said, "Well, there isn't much to say. The county police were there. It seems there's a little jurisdictional dispute between Mort and them. Patricia arrived while we were there. She was down visiting a cousin in Salem. She hadn't known about Rory's death. It wasn't pleasant being the ones to break the news. I came back in town with Mort and Robert Brent."

"You did?" said Cynthia.

"Yes. Mort wanted to interview him and thought

headquarters was the best place to do it. He came readily enough."

"A bad seed, that boy," said Seth.

"Not terribly friendly, I agree, but I don't want to jump to conclusions about him the way you say others are ready to hang Jake Walther. Bob Brent has been telling Mort that he's convinced Jake killed his father. Not that that means anything. Mort asked him whether he had seen Jake do it, and Bob said he hadn't. He and Mort are at police head-quarters as we speak."

"I was thinking of calling an emergency meeting of the town board," Cynthia said. "Make it an open meeting, in-vite the public. What do you think?"

I shrugged. "I'm not sure it would accomplish much, Cynthia. It might even fan the flames. Maybe it's better to let it settle down on its own."

"Seems to me the only thing will settle it down is if Mort's investigation rules out Jake," said Seth. "Until that happens, people will be looking at him like he's a mur-derer."

"Has anyone seen Jake since this happened?" I asked.

Seth and Cynthia shook their heads.

"I'm sure Mort will make interviewing Jake one of his top priorities, especially since Robert Brent is so adamant about pointing a finger at him. Maybe the best thing is to make Mort aware, if he isn't already, of the sentiment in town, and urge him to work as quickly as possible to either clear Jake or arrest him."

"Good suggestion," said Cynthia. "Would you call Mort?"

"Of course," I said. "Let me give him a little time with Bob Brent before I do."

Our conversation was interrupted by the whistling tea-kettle. After I'd served them and myself, I said, "Anything else on the agenda?"

"Matter of fact, there is," said Seth.

My arched eyebrows indicated I was waiting to hear what it was.

"We've got to decide who's going to play Santa Claus this year, now that Rory is gone."

"A good question," I said. "Any suggestions?"

"I've had some discussions with a few people from the festival committee," Cynthia said. "An interesting idea came up."

"I'm all ears," I said.

"You!"

I looked at Seth. "Me?"

"Interesting notion, wouldn't you agree?" Seth said. "Politically correct, as they say. Might be a real good thing for Cabot Cove to have the first woman Santa."

I couldn't help but guffaw. "That's ridiculous," I said. "Not the concept of having a woman as Santa Claus, but *this* woman? I hate to be vain, but I really don't think I look the part."

"That wouldn't be a problem," Cynthia said. "Always easy to make somebody look heavier than they are. You know, pillows strapped around the waist, that sort of thing."

"Absolutely not," I said. I glanced at Seth. "Have you ever considered being Santa Claus, Dr. Hazlitt?"

"No, and I don't intend to at this stage in my life. Too old to have all those little kids jumping up and down on my bad knees. You think about it, Jessica. Probably get us lots of media attention, having a female Santa and all. You know, television shows, maybe a reporter from a big paper. Would give everybody in Cabot Cove a boost."

"Well," I said, "I will not think any more about it because it is absurd. I think we're much better served focusing our attention on how to defuse this situation concerning Jake Walther. There are many good candidates in this town for taking Rory's place as Santa. I'm not one of them. I'll call Mort as soon as you leave."

I didn't mean to say it in such a way that I wanted them out of the house, but I suppose it came off that way because they both stood, thanked me for the tea, and said they'd get back to me later after I'd had a chance to talk with Mort.

I was happy when they were gone, not because I didn't love being with them, but because it had been such a hectic, traumatic day. I needed some quiet time to think about what had transpired.

I made another cup of tea and went into my den that also serves as my writing room. I was between books, as they say, which was a pleasant change. Too often, I was facing deadlines around the holiday season, and swore every year I wouldn't allow it to happen. This time, things fell right, and I was free to enjoy the holidays.

I called Mort a half hour later and was told he'd returned to the Brent farm with Robert Brent. I left a message and decided to spend an hour catching up on correspondence I'd let slip over the past week. I'd just settled down to respond to a letter I'd received from an old friend and former mayor of Cabot Cove, Sybil Woodhouse, who'd moved earlier that year to California with her husband, Adrian, when I heard a knock at the door.

I glanced out my den window. I hadn't noticed that snow had now begun to fall with conviction, and a wind had picked up, sending the flakes swirling. A bad night to be out, I thought, as I got up from my writing desk and went to the front door, where I pulled aside a curtain on one of the side windows.

Standing there was Mary Walther, Jake Walther's wife.

Chapter Five

Mary Walther's arrival took me by surprise. I don't know how to explain it, but seeing her standing at my front door was unsettling. I suppose it had to do with the conversation I'd just had with Seth Hazlitt and Cynthia Curtis about Jake Walther and the rumor he'd murdered Rory Brent.

But as these thoughts went through my head, I had a parallel realization that I was being terribly rude. The weather outside had turned truly foul. There she was, standing in the snow and wind, while I peered through a window from the warm comfort of my home.

I opened the door. "Hello, Mary."

She didn't move, nor did her stern expression change.

"What a nice surprise," I said, standing back to allow her to enter. "Please, come in."

She looked as though she wasn't sure what to do next, but then entered the foyer. I closed the door behind her.

"Can I take your coat and hat?" I asked, extending my hands.

"All right," she said. Large, thick fingers unbuttoned her plain gray gabardine coat. I helped slide it off her shoulders. She reached up and removed her artificial fur hat and handed it to me. I hung them on pegs and said, "Come in. I'll make tea. Unless you'd prefer coffee."

"Neither, thank you, Mrs. Fletcher."

I led her into the living room, aware of what a large woman she was. She stood six feet tall, and her body was boxlike, her face broad and square, too. Once, when I was in a shoe store, looking for winter boots, Mary came in looking for a new pair of moccasins. They had nothing in a woman's style large enough to fit her feet, which, I noticed, were measured at size twelve. She settled for a man's moccasin, saying as she paid at the counter, "Big feet, big heart, they say."

To which the sales clerk replied, "I'm sure that's true, Mrs. Walther. Have a nice day."

A big woman—everywhere.

I've always respected Mary Walther. Despite marriage to a difficult and unpopular man, she was active in the larger Cabot Cove community, quick to respond to charity events to help out someone who'd fallen on hard times. She was aware of the occasional snide, sometimes cruel comments behind her back, but seemed able to put them aside. Mary wasn't a leader; there always seem to be too many leaders and not enough soldiers to do the grunt work on a project. But you could depend upon her to follow through and get the job done.

Like Patricia Brent, Mary Walther married a farmer

and lives on a farm. But there is a dramatic difference between both families.

While Rory Brent had been a successful farmer, Jake and Mary Walther seem always to be on the brink of insolvency. And the family's living arrangements are strange, to understate it. There isn't just one house on the property. There are three, each in decrepit condition and not larger than what might be termed a shack. The three houses are lined up one behind the other, starting a dozen or so feet from the road. Jake Walther, at least according to those who claim to know, lives in the house closest to the road. Mary lives in the next house up the hill, perhaps 200 feet from the first, with their only child, Jill, who was away at school. And in the third house lives Mary's mildly retarded young brother, Dennis, a sweet, pleasant man who earns his keep by helping Jake on the farm. I can't attest to it from personal knowledge, but people say that Mary would ring a bell just outside her door at mealtimes, and Jake and her brother would come to her house for breakfast, lunch, and dinner, then return to their respective houses.

Unconventional? Without a doubt. Then again, there are undoubtedly those families who live in the same house without having any interaction. The older I get, the less critical I'm determined to be.

A number of merchants in Cabot Cove had complained about not being paid by Jake and Mary, and a few had taken legal action against them. The bank, I'd heard, had been threatening for a long time to repossess their farm and home.

The problem is, as Cynthia Curtis had put it, unpleasant people are sued more often than pleasant ones. Compounding the Walthers' financial problems is Jake Walther's sour, combative personality. He is a tall, thin man with a craggy face and salt-and-pepper hair that looks as though it hasn't been combed in years. His clothing is always dirty and in need of repair, and his face is set in a perpetual scowl, to the extent that children express fear of him just because of the way he looks.

Mary sat ramrod straight in a chair I indicated, clasped her gnarled hands in her lap, and planted her feet firmly on the floor.

"Sure you don't want something?" I asked. "Perhaps some wine?"

"No, thank you, Mrs. Fletcher. I'm afraid this is not a social visit."

"Please call me Jessica," I said. "We know each other well enough for that."

Mary Walther and I established a bond of sorts two years ago when her daughter, Jill, was about to graduate from high school. I'd taught a workshop that spring for students who'd achieved honor status in their senior English class, and Jill Walther was one of them. She was a shy girl, with a head of frizzy hair and who wore very thick glasses. When I read her first short story, I was immensely impressed with her talent and insight. This was a young woman who was definitely college potential, and who could, if she followed the right path, become a fine writer.

I encouraged her; she seemed to respond to my praise. One day she lingered after class, and we had a chance to discuss her future. She wanted to go to college, but her father didn't have the money to send her. Although she didn't state it, I sensed that even if Jake Walther had the funds to pay for her college education, he wouldn't do it.

I decided to help. I wrote to the dean of creative writing at New York University, where I'd taught on occasion, sent him copies of Jill's stories, and urged him to consider a full scholarship for her. He came through. Jill was thrilled at the news, although her father's reaction was not as positive. Eventually, Mary Walther managed to choreograph things so that Jill could go off to New York City and begin her college studies. She kept in touch through letters, and whenever she was home made it a point to visit me.

Mary Walther, not a terribly demonstrative person, was relatively lavish in her gratitude to me, and we'd maintained that good relationship ever since, not a close friendship by any means, but a warm feeling for each other.

"Not a social visit?" I said, taking a chair across from her and leaning forward to indicate my interest in what she was about to say. When she didn't speak, I said, "Would I be correct in assuming you're here because of what happened to Rory Brent?"

She closed her eyes for a second, opened them, and said, "Yes."

"Well, suppose you tell me what's on your mind."

She said flatly, "I'm afraid there is going to be big trouble."

I sat back and sighed. "Oh, I'm sure there will be. We don't have many murders here in Cabot Cove. My hope is that Rory was killed by someone passing through, not anyone who lives here."

"They're saying Jake did it," she said in that same low voice bordering on masculine.

"Yes, I've heard the rumor. People shouldn't jump to such conclusions."

"Jake isn't much liked in these parts," she said.

I wasn't quite sure how to respond. "I suppose people consider him to be ... well, consider him to be a little angry at times."

"People don't give him a fair chance to be liked," she said.

I didn't necessarily agree with her, but didn't want to get into a debate.

She continued. "Jake's always been a hardworking man, Mrs. Fletcher. Hard work and not much to show for it. He gets bitter at times, mad at what the good Lord has dealt him."

I thought of other people I knew who'd been dealt a losing hand in life, too, but who, if they were bitter, didn't wear it on their sleeve the way Jake Walther did.

"Jake can be down right *jo-jezzly* at times. I wouldn't deny that."

Jo-jezzly was a popular Maine term for someone who was ornery or cussed. It seemed an apt description of Jake Walther.

"Not always easy living with him. I would say that for certain."

"Mary, you said there was going to be big trouble. Do you want to explain that a little further?"

She replied, "Jake knows what folks are saying about him and Rory, that they didn't get along and that Jake was the one who shot him. Jake says nobody is going to take him away from the farm because he didn't do anything wrong. He didn't, Mrs. Fletcher, I can swear to that."

I didn't know how she could be so certain, but decided that was something for Mort Metzger to examine.

"Mary, you say Jake won't allow anyone to take him away from the farm. Do you mean he won't subject himself to questioning by Sheriff Metzger?"

Now she showed her first sign of animation. "Mrs. Fletcher, Jake's back at the house, got the door locked. He won't talk to anyone, not me, not Dennis. All he says over and over through the door is that nobody's going to take him away."

"Doesn't he realize that if he didn't kill Rory, he has nothing to fear from Sheriff Metzger or anyone else?" I asked. "All the sheriff would want to do is ask him some questions. Maybe he has an alibi, someone who can say he wasn't anywhere near Rory's farm this morning. But if he refuses to cooperate, he'll end up in terrible trouble that he doesn't deserve."

"Exactly, Mrs. Fletcher. That's the big trouble I was talking about. I can't talk sense to him. I tried. Had Dennis try, too, but he runs us off his part of the farm. I don't know what to do. I surely don't."

I thought for a moment before saying, "My only suggestion would be to go to Sheriff Metzger, tell him the situation, and see what he suggests."

She slowly shook her head. "Jake won't talk to the sheriff. But maybe he'd talk to you."

"Me? Why me? I don't have any relationship with your husband."

"Jake read all about how you saved Jed and Alicia Richardson over in London. Read it in the paper and saw it on TV. He was real impressed. Said you were a brave and decent woman."

I had to stop and think for a moment to sort out what she'd said.

A year or so ago I'd traveled to England and Scotland with a contingent of friends from Cabot Cove. The trip had been arranged by my dear friend, George Sutherland, a chief inspector with Scotland Yard in London, whose family had come from Wick, Scotland. He still owns the family mansion there, used most of the year as a hotel for tourists. He insisted I visit his homestead. When I told him I was making the trip with a number of friends, he said that wasn't a problem because he would simply close the hotel for the week we were there and accommodate everyone.

We started the trip in London, where I had a few days' business to attend to before heading north. While in London, Jed Richardson, who owns Jed's Flying Service, a two-plane airline operating out of Cabot Cove, and his new wife, Alicia, were abducted by a madman and held hostage in the infamous Tower of London. I ended up negotiating their release. I hadn't planned on doing that, nor did I aspire to the task. It just seemed to evolve into that situation. The London press played it up big, and it eventually found considerable space in American newspapers.

"Mary," I said, "that was a unique circumstance. I'm not a negotiator and don't pretend to be. As a matter of fact, I don't *want* to be in that role. I don't think I would have any influence on your husband."

Her expression seemed to soften as she said, "I know I'm imposing, Mrs. Fletcher."

"Jessica."

"Jessica. I'm not the sort of person who imposes on

other people. I think you know that. I guess because you're the sort of woman who's always ready to help others in trouble, I figured you'd help out in this situation. I guess I was wrong." She stood.

I, too, stood. "Mary," I said, "of course I want to help you and Jake. As a matter of fact, if there is the sort of trouble you're indicating, I would want to do anything in my power to head it off. But I can't do it unilaterally. I can't do this alone. It would be taking the law into my own hands, something I am firmly opposed to. If you really think I could be instrumental in convincing Jake to cooperate in the investigation, I'll be happy to do it, but only in conjunction with Sheriff Metzger and his department. I'm waiting for a call from him now, as a matter of fact. If you agree, I'll tell him the situation and suggest we all go together to talk to Jake. That's the only way I can be involved."

"I'm just afraid, Mrs. Fletcher, that if Jake sees the sheriff and his car, he'll do something crazy."

"Maybe I can convince Sheriff Metzger to use a plain car, and to stay out of sight until I've had a chance to talk to Jake. Frankly, I don't think this will work. There is no reason for your husband to trust me, or to listen to my advice."

"But maybe he will. I know one thing for certain, Mrs. Fletcher."

"What's that?"

"He sure won't listen to me or anybody else I can think of."

Chapter Six

Mary Walther wasn't gone more than a minute when Mort Metzger returned my call.

"How did it go with Robert Brent?" I asked.

"All right, I suppose, although he's a strange young fella. Didn't have much to say except for repeating over and over that Jake Walther killed his father."

"Did he offer anything tangible to support that claim?"

"No, he did not. Well, maybe he did in a way. He said his father and Jake had a real altercation about a month ago or so. He says Jake came to the farm and confronted his father over something having to do with land and money. The kid says he didn't know the details of what the argument was about, just that Jake threatened to kill Rory. Said he'd be back to 'blow his brains out.'"

"That's something tangible, I would say. A direct threat of bodily harm."

"True, provided you believe what young Robert says. I'm not sure I do."

"Based upon what?"

"Based upon . . . well, gut instinct. You do what I do long enough and you develop a pretty good sense of whether people are tellin' you the truth or not."

"I wouldn't argue with that. Mort, Mary Walther just left my house."

"She did?"

"Yes. She was very distraught when she arrived. She's afraid that something really bad is going to happen because of the rumors about Jake having killed Rory. She told me Jake has holed up in his house on the property. He won't talk to her brother or Mary. Poor thing, it must be so difficult for her being married to Jake. I've always admired her determination to become involved in the community while knowing what people in town are saying about him."

"A good woman, Mary Walther," Mort said. "Sounds like Jake is actin' like a damn fool."

"Sounds that way to me, too. I told her I'd get your advice on what to do."

"Doesn't seem to be much question about what to do," he said. "Because of Robert Brent's accusation, my next move is to go out there and talk to Jake. But I sure don't want to walk into a war."

"No one wants that," I said. "I assume you intend to call the house before going."

"Sure, except the only phone is in Mary's house in the middle. You know that setup out there. She lives in the middle house—more like a shack, it seems to me—Jake lives in the one by the road, and her brother lives up the hill in the third house. Calling out there will just reach Mary. And if Jake won't talk to Mary or Dennis, doesn't seem I have much chance to reason with him except in person."

I asked, "Did Jake have any friends in town, Mort? Anyone he spent time with, trusted, maybe would confide in?"

There was silence while he pondered my question. Finally, he said, "None I can think of, Mrs. F., 'cept for maybe Doc Hazlitt."

"Seth? I didn't know Seth was friendly with Jake Walther."

"He's not. But Jake had a couple of medical problems over the last few months and went to Seth for treatment. From what I hear, Jake was pretty pleased with the way Seth handled things. Somebody told me—I can't remember who—that Jake said Seth was probably the only honest doctor in Maine. I don't think Seth charged him, at least not much."

"Then maybe Seth would have success talking sense to Jake, to get him to realize that the only sensible course is to cooperate with you, answer your questions, and put to rest any accusations that he killed Rory. Provided, of course, that he didn't."

"Maybe you're right, Mrs. F. I'll call Seth and run it by him, see if he'll come out to Jake's place with me."

"Good idea," I said. "If Seth agrees, would you have any objection to my coming along?"

"I don't see any," Mort said. "You might be helpful, considering Mary Walther came to you."

"I'll be waiting for your call."

I heard from him five minutes later. "I got hold of Seth just as he was leavin'. Told him the situation. He says he didn't charge Jake for treating him because he knew he was down on his luck and didn't have any money to speak of. Jake seemed real appreciative, according to Seth."

"Did Seth agree to go out to Jake's house with you?"

"Yup. He suggested we not go in my car. Might set Jake on edge. We'll go in Seth's."

"That makes sense," I said. "You'll pick me up?"

"Be there in a half hour."

Seth pulled into my driveway exactly thirty minutes later. By then it had really begun to snow, the flakes big and wet and sticking to the ground. At least the wind had abated, lessening the effect of the cold.

I got in the backseat and we headed for Jake Walther's farm.

"Seems to me an unusual way for the sheriff to interrogate a witness," Seth said grumpily, both hands on the wheel, eyes focused straight ahead.

"No rule about how I approach a suspect in a murder," Mort replied from the front passenger seat. He'd pulled his Stetson down low over his eyes and tucked his chin against his chest. "Seems to me we're doing it exactly the right way, considering what might happen if I did it by the book. No sense adding to the problems of having a leading citizen murdered here in Cabot Cove by ending up in some stupid standoff. Better to try and get Jake to cooperate. I'd hate to have to go out there, guns drawn, and drag him off. More people might get hurt."

"I think you're right," I said from the backseat. "The impact of Rory's murder is just really settling in on me. These kinds of things just don't happen in Cabot Cove, especially at Christmas."

Seth grimly reminded me of a couple of other murders that had occurred in our idyllic Maine town, although they had happened a number of years ago.

"Now tell me, Morton, how you want me to proceed with this," Seth asked.

"Depends on how brave you are, Doc."

Seth glanced over at the sheriff. "What in hell do you mean by that?"

"Well, according to Mrs. F., seeing me will only set Jake off, and we sure wouldn't want to send *her* up there to knock on the door. The way I figure it, we'll park out on the road a little bit away from the house. You'll go up to the door and tell Jake who you are and why you're there."

I leaned forward and placed my hands on Seth's shoulders. "That could be dangerous," I said. "If Jake is in as tormented a state of mind as Mary says he is, he's liable to panic. He might have guns with him."

"Somehow, no matter how mean-spirited Jake Walther is, I just can't see him shooting anybody," said Seth. "I don't think I'll have a problem getting him to talk to me. He's one of those fellas who's got a gruff exterior, but down deep there lurks a decent person. At least, that's the way I read him."

"What kind of medical problems did he have?" I asked.

"Can't discuss that," Seth said. "Doctor-patient privilege."

I didn't press him, but he volunteered, "Man has wicked

arthritis. Neck, shoulders, hands, back. In lots of pain. Maybe that's why he's so *jo-jeezly* all the time."

I silently thought that Seth was probably right, and felt a twinge of compassion for Jake.

As we approached the Walther property, Seth slowed down, eventually stopping fifty yards from a narrow, rutted dirt driveway leading up past the three separate houses.

"Might as well get to it," Seth said, shutting off the lights and engine.

"I don't like this," I said. "I think we should go with you."

"But if Jake sees me, he might—"

I interrupted Mort. "I don't think Seth should simply go up there by himself, Mort. If the three of us go up, we'll have each other to lean on. You and I can stay back and let Seth do all the talking. If he's successful, and Jake opens the door, then you'll be right there to take advantage of it."

Mort chewed his cheek while he thought. He turned to Seth and asked, "What do you think?"

"Jessica is probably right," Seth said. "Of course, I don't mind goin' up there alone. But maybe we should be together. If I get him to cooperate, no sense having to come back down here and bring you up. Besides, if I'm going to stand out in the cold, you might as well, too."

I didn't think that was a particularly good reason for us to accompany Seth, but didn't express it. We got out of the car, slowly walked down the road to where the driveway intercepted it, and looked up at the first house where Jake lived. It wasn't much of a house, nor were the other two.

"Here we go," said Seth, leading us up the driveway. We reached a stone path that twisted up to the front of Jake's house, we took it, but paused at the two small wooden steps leading up to the porch.

Mort whispered, "Mrs. F and I will stand over there on the porch while you talk to him through the door."

"*Ayuh,*" said Seth. He drew a deep breath; his lips were pressed tightly together. I said a silent prayer that this wouldn't backfire. Bad enough Rory Brent was dead without having someone else fall victim to violence.

We stepped quietly up onto the porch. Mort and I moved to our right, approximately six feet from the door. Seth knocked. There was no response. He knocked again. This time Jake Walther's raspy voice growled, "Who the hell is it?"

"Doc Hazlitt," Seth said loudly.

"What the hell are you doing here?" Jake asked. We judged he'd moved closer to the door because his voice had grown louder.

"Want to talk to you," said Seth.

Jake said, "Talk to me? About what?"

"About . . . about what happened to Rory Brent."

Silence.

"Jake, you listen to me," Seth said. "Folks in town are saying you had a spat with Rory, a pretty serious one, and some of 'em are even saying you might have shot him. Now I know you didn't shoot him, and the best way to make that point with everybody is for you to sit down with Sheriff Metzger, answer his questions, and put it to rest."

"Can't do that," Jake said.

"Why not?"

" 'Cause nobody'll believe me. Nobody ever does in

this town. People would just as soon hang me and get it over with."

"Now, Jake, that's nonsense. Don't you trust me? You said you did."

"As a medicine man? Sure. Best damn doctor I've ever known, only I don't know many. But that's just you, Doc. Others in town got their own agenda, and it includes getting rid of me."

Seth looked to where we stood, our eyes open wide. I noticed Mort had unzipped his jacket and had rested his hand loosely on a holstered handgun on his right hip.

Seth said, "You can trust me, Jake, with anything, not just medicine. My word is good. You'd better believe that."

Jake didn't respond.

"You hear me, Jake? I'm telling you that nobody is going to do anything to you just because they don't like you. That's not the way things work in this country, certainly not in Cabot Cove. Sheriff Metzger doesn't think you killed Rory, but he has a job to do. He has to ask questions, and you're one of the persons he's gotta ask 'em of. I assure you all that will happen is that you and the sheriff will sit down, he'll ask his questions, you'll answer them truthfully, and that will be the end of it."

Unless he did shoot Rory Brent, I thought.

Walther responded, "Can't trust nobody in this town. Nope, can't trust nobody."

Seth tried another tack. "Your wife is right worried," he said. "She came to see Jessica Fletcher earlier tonight, told her how worried she was about you. You don't want to cause trouble for her and Jill, do you?"

"Mary had no right goin' to nobody."

"Not true," said Seth. "Mary is a good woman. Thought she was doing the right thing."

"You talked to Mrs. Fletcher?" Jake asked through the closed door.

"*Ayuh,*" said Seth. "She's with me right now, on the porch."

That bit of news seemed to stun Jake into another moment of prolonged silence. He eventually asked, "Who else is with you?"

I knew the internal debate going on within Seth. Does he tell Jake that the sheriff is there on his porch, or does he lie and hope to get Jake to expose himself so that Mort could act. I knew the answer. Seth would not lie.

"I've got Mrs. Fletcher and Sheriff Metzger here with me on the porch, Jake. Now it's getting pretty damn cold out here. If I get sick, other people aren't going to get treated, and that'll be on your shoulders. If you give me pneumonia, I'm not sure I'll ever forgive you. Now open the door and let us in."

During the dialogue through the closed door, the wind had picked up and the temperature seemed to have dropped twenty degrees. My feet were numb and my ears stung. I hoped it would quickly be resolved one way or the other. Either Seth would prevail and Jake would do as he was told, or the standoff would continue. If that happened, it would be up to Mort to take the next step, and I dreaded what that might be.

Suddenly, the sound of a bolt being lifted from a latch was heard from inside the house. Slowly, the door swung open, and Seth was face-to-face through a torn screen door with Jake Walther.

" 'Evening, Jake," Seth said. "I wouldn't mind if you'd invite us in."

Jake undid a hook and eye on the inside of the screen door and pushed it open. Seth motioned to us with his head, and we followed. It was a sparsely furnished room filled with clutter. Piles of old newspapers almost reached a low ceiling along one side. The only heat came from a woodstove in another corner. The floor was bare wood and sticky. A small table by a window contained what looked like the remnants of a number of meals, empty open cans of pork and beans the primary cuisine. Also on the table was a handgun.

It worked, I thought as Mort, who was the last one into the room, closed the inside door behind us. I looked at Jake Walther, the top of his head almost touching the ceiling. He was dressed in bib overalls over a black flannel shirt. He hadn't shaved in days, and there was a crazed look in his large, watery, pale blue eyes.

Still, I didn't feel any sense of danger until I moved aside, affording Jake his first clear view of Mort Metzger. Mort had left his jacket open, and his hand continued to rest on his revolver. Jake scowled, grunted, mumbled an obscenity, and made a quick move to the table where his handgun rested. Mort was quicker. He pushed Walther against the wall, drew his weapon, and placed it against the back of Jake's neck. "Now don't do anything foolish, Jake Walther," Mort said. "Don't make things worse than they are."

It happened so fast that I didn't have a chance to react. But now my breath came in hurried spurts, and I backed away as far as I could from the confrontation.

Jake didn't resist as Mort deftly slipped a pair of handcuffs from his belt and secured them to Jake's wrists behind his back. That completed, Mort stepped back, allowing Jake to turn and face us. He looked directly at Seth and said, "Should have known not to trust anybody, including you."

"Damn fool thing you did, making a move for that gun," Seth said. "Nobody was here to arrest you. Mort just wanted to talk to you, but you pull a dumb stunt like that."

Jake looked at Mort. "Am I under arrest?" he asked.

"Depends," Mort said. "Doc is right. If you hadn't made that move, we'd just be sitting around talking like friends and neighbors. You didn't leave me any choice. Now we're going to go downtown and leave that weapon behind. I assume you've got a proper permit for it. Once we get to my office, depending upon how you act and talk, I might just take those cuffs off and have that friendly chat I intended to have when I came here. Understand?"

Jake said nothing, simply looked at the floor as he leaned against a wall.

I motioned for Mort and Seth to come to where I stood. "Maybe I'd better go up and tell Mary what's happened."

"Good idea," Seth said, then turned to Mort. "I don't think it's a good idea to bring him downtown in my car. Should be an official vehicle."

"Right you are," Mort said. "Mrs. F., there's a phone up in Mary's place. Give a call to my office and tell whoever answers to send a squad car up here on the double."

I left Jake's house, went up the driveway to the middle dwelling, and knocked on the door. Mary Walther answered. "What are you doing here?" she asked.

I explained what had happened.

"Jake isn't hurt, is he?"

"No, but he made a sudden move that caused the sheriff to react. He had to put handcuffs on Jake and is taking him to headquarters to interview him about Rory's murder. I'm sure everything will be fine. I have to call the sheriff's office to have a car brought up here to take Jake into town. May I use your phone?"

A half hour later, Jake was in the backseat of a squad car driven by one of Mort's deputies. Mort got in the passenger seat, and Seth and I watched them drive off from Jake's front porch. Mary Walther had joined us.

"Will he have to stay in jail tonight?" Mary asked.

"No tellin'," Seth replied. "We'll just have to wait and see."

"I should be with him," Mary said.

The woman's loyalty to her husband was admirable, especially since it was pretty well known he didn't treat her with much kindness.

"No, you stay here," I said. "Is your brother up in the other house?"

"Yes."

"Maybe you should have him come down and stay with you tonight."

"I don't know if he will," she said.

"Well, give it a try," Seth said. "Ready to go back, Jessica?"

"Yes."

Before we left the porch, I looked deeply into Mary's eyes. There was profound sadness in them, and I wanted to wrap my arms about her and hug her. Which I did. Seth and I then drove back into town in relative silence.

"Come in for a drink, cup of tea?" I asked as we pulled into my driveway.

"Another time, Jessica. Didn't think I'd end up spending today the way we did."

"Nor did I. Do you have the same feeling I have, Seth, that Rory's murder is only the beginning of something worse about to happen in Cabot Cove?"

He thought it over before saying, "Matter of fact, I do. But let's not dwell on it. Good night, Jessica. Give me a call in the morning."

I felt deflated and fatigued as I approached my front door. It had been an unfortunate day, certainly one I never dreamed would occur when I got up that morning and prepared to go about my daily life.

It wasn't until I was only a few feet from the door and was about to insert my key that I noticed the large, circular green wreath with a puffy red ribbon hanging from it. I'd forgotten; the man who cut my lawn, shoveled my walk, and did minor repairs to my house always hung a wreath on my door in early December. Usually, the sight of it caused me to break into a smile. But I didn't smile this time. As pretty and symbolic as the wreath was, it only reminded me that this was shaping up to be a Christmas like no other I'd ever experienced.

Chapter Seven

My clock radio went off at seven the next morning, as it always did. I kept it tuned to Cabot Cove's only radio station, owned and operated by friends of mine, Peter and Roberta Walters. Pete did the morning show himself, weaving in interesting, often amusing tidbits of local news with pleasant music that reflected his own taste—and mine—mostly big band music and singers like Sinatra and Bennett, Mel Tormé and Ella Fitzgerald.

But this morning I was awakened to the strains of "Have Yourself a Merry Little Christmas." I stayed in bed until the song ended. Pete came on with his deep, pleasant voice and said, "Good morning, Cabot Coveites. This is your humble morning host reminding you that you have twenty-three shopping days until Christmas."

That reality caused me to sit up straight. Christmas seemed to start earlier and earlier each year, usually right after Thanksgiving, but even earlier in some instances. I wasn't sure I liked that, but since there was nothing I could do about it, I didn't dwell upon it.

I got up, put on slippers and robe, and went to the kitchen, where I turned on the teakettle and retrieved from a bag a cinnamon bun I'd bought the day before at Charlene Sassi's bakery. As I waited for the water to boil, I looked out my window at the rear patio, covered by what I estimated to be three inches of snow. You get good at judging the depth of snow after living in Maine for a while. The two bird feeders I'd hung near the window were doing a landslide business, my little feathered friends fluttering about them in a feeding frenzy.

The teakettle's whistle interrupted my reverie. Armed with a steaming mug of tea and the cinnamon bun, I went to the living room and turned on the television. The *Today Show* was on; the guest was an economist forecasting how well merchants would do this holiday season. I wasn't interested in that, so I shut it off and returned to the kitchen for the more aesthetic show being put on by the birds. But as I watched them, thoughts of Jake Walther and what had occurred at his house last night took center stage.

Judging from the way things had gone, my assumption was that Jake had been detained, at least overnight, in Mort Metzger's four-cell jail, which he was fond of referring to as his "Motel Four," the humor undoubtedly lost on those forced to spend a night there.

I also thought of Mary Walther, poor thing, having to face what had become the town's apparent consensus that her husband had murdered Rory Brent. I desperately hoped it wasn't the case, that whoever shot Rory was a stranger passing through, a demented, vile individual who had no connection to Cabot Cove. But I had to admit that Jake's sudden move toward his weapon caused me to wonder whether there might be some validity to the rumor that there was bad blood between them, and that he'd killed Rory because of it. The contemplation made me shudder.

Our local newspaper was on the front steps. I brought it inside, made a second cup of tea, and read the paper from cover to cover. Originally, it had been a weekly. But the town had grown sufficiently to prompt its publisher to turn it into a daily paper, usually dominated by news of births and deaths, local events, and the goings-on of various citizens, but with an impressive national and international section culled from wire services to which the paper subscribed. Plans for the Christmas festival occupied two entire inside pages. Rory's murder took up most of the front page.

The reporter had tried to interview Mort Metzger, but our sheriff had simply replied, "No comment."

Good for him, I thought. What could he possibly say at this stage of the investigation?

But a spokesman from county law enforcement was willing to speak, at length. I recognized the picture of the officer that accompanied the article. He'd been at Rory's barn when Mort and I arrived.

There was a biography of Rory, highlighting the fact that he'd played Santa Claus for our annual Christmas festival for the past fifteen years. A picture of him in his Santa costume was there, as well as a picture of his wife, Patricia. She, too, had declined to make a comment except to say that she was sad at her husband's death, and hoped that whoever did it would be caught quickly.

It was at the end of the article that speculation appeared about who might have killed Rory. The reporter mentioned that Robert Brent, son of the deceased, had volunteered to come to police headquarters to give a statement, and that Jake Walther, who'd been detained for questioning, was being held in the town jail. That bothered me. It would do nothing but give credence to the rumor that he was the murderer. We're innocent until proved guilty in court of law, but that doesn't necessarily apply to the court of human frailty and misconception.

I was tempted to try and reach Mort to get an update on what happened last night, but fought the temptation. It really wasn't my business, even though I'd been there when the incident with Walther had occurred. I showered and dressed. I had a nine o'clock meeting scheduled with Cynthia Curtis to discuss how we might approach the reading of Christmas stories to the children of Cabot Cove. She'd suggested the meeting when she left my house yesterday, and I'd agreed to it. She wanted Seth there, too, but he'd declined, claiming he had a busy patient load that morning.

It wasn't easy summoning enthusiasm for a meeting, which I assumed was the prevailing feeling of most people in town involved with the festival. Initially, learning of Rory's murder had put us all in shock. Now, twenty-four hours later, that shock had been replaced with a pervasive sense of gloom and depression.

But I knew that I, and anyone else, couldn't let that dominate our lives. The festival was too important to have it ruined by any single event, no matter how tragic it might have been.

Dimitri picked me up in his taxi at ten of nine and drove me to the library, where Cynthia waited in her office.

"Good morning, Cynthia."

"Good morning, Jess. Glad you could make it. Frankly, I wondered whether you'd show up."

"I said I would."

"Because of what happened yesterday, I didn't want to get out of bed this morning, I was so depressed over it."

I nodded. "I know exactly what you mean. But I reminded myself that we have a festival to put on. It might be rationalization on my part, but I think Rory would have wanted us to go forward."

"I agree. I got a call from Jim Shevlin this morning."

"How is our mayor?" I asked.

"Feeling pretty much the same as we do. He said he was going to meet with the festival committee at noon and suggest that the festival be officially dedicated to Rory's memory."

"That's a splendid idea."

She'd gotten up to greet me. Now she settled behind her desk, went through some papers, saying as she did, "At least having the murderer identified and under arrest might make things easier, provide some sort of closure."

"Pardon?"

She looked up. "Didn't you hear?"

"Hear what?"

"That Jake Walther is being charged with the murder of Rory Brent."

"No, I did not hear that."

"What have *you* heard?" she asked.

I recounted what happened the night before, and the circumstances under which Jake had been brought to police headquarters. When I finished, I added, "But Mort was simply going to question him. What happened? Did Jake confess to the murder?"

Cynthia shrugged and said, "I really don't know. You read the paper this morning?"

"Sure. But the article didn't indicate that Jake had been arrested, just that he had been detained for questioning."

"Mara says she got it from a good source that Jake is being accused of the murder."

I laughed. "The good old Cabot Cove grapevine at work, with Mara's Luncheonette as its headquarters. Mind if I use your phone?"

"Not at all."

I dialed the number for police headquarters. Deputy Tom Coleman answered, asked me to hold, and a minute later Mort came on the line.

"I was wondering when you'd get around to calling," he said.

"I wasn't going to. I didn't think it was my business. But I just heard that you're charging Jake Walther with Rory Brent's murder."

"Where did you hear that?"

"It came from . . . well, just a rumor floating around town."

"Damn Cabot Cove rumor mill," he said. "No. I had Tom drive Jake back to his house this morning. Kept him overnight and stayed up asking him questions. He admits he and Rory didn't get along. Maybe that's an understatement. But he swears he didn't kill him."

"Does he have an alibi?" I asked.

"Claims he does. Says he spent the morning fixing a crumbling stone wall with his wife's brother, Dennis."

"Believe him?" I asked.

"No reason not to, unless his alibi doesn't hold water. I was just about to go out to talk to Dennis when you called."

"Well, Mort, I'm glad the rumor doesn't have any foundation in fact. I'm with Cynthia Curtis. We're talking about the children's story program for the festival."

"Sounds like a good thing to be doing. I think Doc is a little upset at not having it all to himself again this year."

"Oh, is he? I certainly don't want that to be the case. I'd rather bow out than hurt his feelings."

"Don't give it a second thought, Mrs. F. You know Doc. Gets himself riled up over stupid things. Got to run. Talk with you later."

I hung up and told Cynthia what the true situation was with Jake Walther. When I finished, she asked, "What do you really think, Jess? You write about murders and have ended up solving some real ones."

"Too many real ones," I said. "I don't know what I think. What I'm determined to do is to not come to any conclusion until Mort and other investigators do their job."

"I wish you could instill that philosophy in everyone else in town."

"Well, maybe just expressing it to enough people will have that effect. Now let's get down to the business of the children's Christmas story hour."

Chapter Eight

My meeting with Cynthia lasted until ten. From the library I went directly to the office of my dentist, Anthony Colarusso, who was also president of the Cabot Cove Chamber of Commerce. Tony was not only a fine and caring dentist, he was an avid fisherman with whom I'd spent many pleasant mornings on some of the area's tranquil streams and rivers in search of elusive trout. We always fished with barbless hooks in order not to injure the fish we caught, enabling us to easily remove the hook from their mouths and send them back into the water for another day.

I didn't have a specific problem prompting me to make my ten-fifteen appointment, but a note on my calendar told me it was time for my semiannual checkup and cleaning. As usual, most of our conversation revolved around fishing, although the gauzy, metallic paraphernalia in my mouth kept the talk one-sided.

After agreeing we would be at a trout stream in the

spring on the opening day of the fishing season, Tony said, "Shocking what happened to Rory Brent."

"It certainly was. Poor man. How could anyone do such a thing?"

"Rory was a patient. I always enjoyed it when he came in. Never had a bad word for anybody, always laughing and joking. I'm told Sheriff Metzger is focusing on Jake Walther as the most likely suspect."

It was inevitable, I suppose, that Jake Walther would be brought up in our conversation. I could only assume his name was being bandied about all over town that morning, as it had been since the earliest moments following the determination that Rory had not died of natural causes. Amazing, I thought, how scuttlebutt takes on a momentum of its own, the mere hint of an accusation mushrooming into the assumption of truth.

I said, "I just left Cynthia Curtis's office at the library, Tony, and spoke with Mort Metzger from there. He questioned Jake, but released him. Frankly, I hate to hear this kind of rumor circulating. The man is innocent until a court of law proves him guilty. At least that's the way the Constitution says it's supposed to be."

"Rinse," Tony said, indicating the basin next to the chair. I did as I was told.

"That's the problem when people create a negative reputation, like Jake. Easy to think the worst of somebody like that."

"I know exactly what you mean," I said. "Still . . ."

"I hear Jake has a good alibi."

I sat up a little straighter in my chair. "Who did you hear that from?"

"Susan Shevlin. She was in first thing this morning to have a filling replaced."

Susan Shevlin was married to Cabot Cove's mayor, Jim Shevlin, and operated the town's leading travel agency.

I shook my head as Tony removed the bib from around my neck. "My, how news gets around. She's right, though. Jake told Mort he spent the morning of Rory's murder fixing a stone wall with Mary Walther's brother, Dennis."

Tony's eyebrows went up. I knew what he was thinking, that Dennis Solten—Solten was Mary Walther's maiden name—might not be the best source of an alibi for someone accused of murder. Anyone who'd spent any time with Dennis knew that he was someone who agreed with anything and everything said, siding with totally opposing views as fast as they were proffered. Unlike his brother-in-law, Jake, who argued with everyone about everything , you never heard a word of disagreement from Dennis. The word "sweet" was most often applied to him. I sometimes wondered whether labeling him mildly retarded accurately reflected his situation. He had the look of a beaten puppy, someone who'd been put down so often in his life that it became second nature for him to be so malleable that he came off as intellectually slow, even dim-witted. Dennis Solten was as small as his sister was big. But he was a hard worker; no one would debate that. When he wasn't helping Jake on the farm, he hired out for yard work, snow shoveling, and other odd jobs. I'd hired him last fall to split two cords of wood from an ash that had died and fallen on my property. He attacked the task with vigor and dedication, swinging the heavy sledge-hammer into the wedge he'd driven into each log with such energy that it tired me out just watching him.

"Are you saying that Dennis might be providing Jake with an alibi because Jake told him to?"

"Possibility, isn't it?" said Tony, stripping off latex gloves and tossing them into a special trash container. "Seems to me it wouldn't be hard to get Dennis to say almost anything."

I thought for a moment about what he said, then offered, "If that's true, then the opposite could occur. He could be persuaded to say something about Jake that would be incriminating."

"I guess it's a matter of who gets to him first with the most persuasive argument."

I left Dr. Colarusso's office, realizing how accurate his final comment had been. I also recognized that I, too, was feeding the Cabot Cove grapevine. I wasn't doing it for the sake of gossip. At least I hoped it wouldn't be perceived that way. I made a few more stops before heading home for lunch, including the post office, the bookstore, where I'd promised to sign copies of my latest novel, and our local fish market to pick up a bushel of clams for steaming. Everywhere I went, the conversation quickly turned to Rory Brent's murder and the suspicion that Jake Walther had done the evil deed.

Happy to be home and away from the subject of murder and murderers, I placed water, two bay leaves, and a splash of white wine in the bottom of a very large lobster pot and put it on the stove. When it started to send up steam, I dumped in the clams. In the ten minutes it took for them to open, I melted some butter, cut off two pieces of crunchy French bread, and settled down at my kitchen table for one of my favorite meals. Although it had stopped snowing, it was still gray and raw outside, a perfect day to stay indoors. Unfortunately, I didn't have the luxury of spending the afternoon there. I was due at our local community college at three to meet with Bob Roark, dean of the creative writing department. He'd approached me a month ago to see whether I would be willing to teach a minicourse in mystery writing. Under ordinary circumstances, I would have had to decline his offer because of the press of my own writing schedule. But as it turned out, I didn't plan to start my next book for at least three months, which gave me plenty of time to do those pleasurable things I too often never get around to. I enjoy teaching young writers, and have been doing more and more of it over the past few years, including New York University in Manhattan, and individual one-day seminars at other institutions of higher learning.

The clams were succulent—no surprise. After mopping up the last few drops of broth and butter with the final scrap of bread, I returned to correspondence I'd been working on the night before when Mary Walther's arrival had interrupted the process. I wrote letters until quarter of three, when Dimitri Cassis arrived with the taxi to take me to the college.

"What is new about Mr. Brent's murder, Mrs. Fletcher?" he asked once I'd gotten in the backseat and closed the door.

"I really don't know, Dimitri."

"Did Mr. Walther do it?"

"Why do you ask that?"

"Everyone says he did."

"Well, Dimitri, just because everyone says so doesn't

mean it's true. I don't think anyone knows who killed Rory Brent, although I certainly hope they find out as soon as possible."

He pulled out of my driveway, and we rode in silence for a minute before he said, "I don't like Mr. Walther."

"Have you had a problem with him?"

"Oh, yes. When I first came to Cabot Cove, I drove him to his house from town. He said he would go in the house and get money, but he never came out."

"That's not very nice," I said. "What did you do? Did you knock on his door?"

"No, Mrs. Fletcher, I did not think I could do that. I had only been here a few months, and had bought the taxi from Mr. Monroe two weeks before. I did not want to make trouble."

"Well, people should be paid when they provide a service. Is that the only time you were involved with Jake Walther?"

"Yes, ma'am, although I have seen him many times in the town. He's not nice to people."

"Yes, I know. He isn't very pleasant."

We said nothing else until Dimitri pulled up in front of the administration building on the community college campus.

"Put it on my bill," I said.

"Of course," he said. "You are my best customer."

"I'm glad to hear that."

"Mrs. Fletcher?"

"Yes?"

"I would not be surprised if Mr. Walther killed Mr. Brent."

"And I would be very sad."

He nodded and said, "I understand. You will call for me to pick you up?"

"Yes. It should be in about an hour."

I'd met Dean Robert Roark shortly after his arrival in Cabot Cove. He'd come to our community college from the English Department of Purdue University, where he'd been rated the department's most popular and effective teacher. Having been born in Maine played a major role in his decision to leave a comfortable Midwest teaching position to take over a department at a two-year community college. No matter what his motivation, he quickly became a valuable asset not only to the college, but to the community at large.

I judged him to be forty years old. He had long blond hair the consistency of corn silk, and was blessed with boundless energy and enthusiasm. My first experience with him was when he put together a conference featuring Maine writers. I remember distinctly being impressed with how many writers showed up. Maine certainly has its share of authors and journalists.

Since the conference, Dean Roark and I kept in touch, which led to his asking me to teach the course in mystery writing.

His office seemed to have boundless energy, too, if inanimate objects could generate that. Floor-to-ceiling shelves were crammed with books. Dozens of elaborately carved ducks, which he collected as a hobby, filled every space not occupied by a book. He wore a blue-and-white striped shirt, red-and-white suspenders, and a floppy yellow bow tie.

"Jessica, how wonderful of you to come. Right on time, I see, but that's no surprise. I've always suspected that mystery writers have to be punctual and organized."

I laughed. "Why would you assume that?"

"Because in order to write a good murder mystery, the writer has to have an organized mind to stay on plot, or else the reader is cheated. Don't you agree?"

"Well," I said, taking off my coat and tossing it on a chair piled with books, "I do tend to be a relatively neat and organized person, although I'm not sure that extends to my writing. At any rate, it's good to see you, too."

He realized I didn't have any place to sit and quickly emptied another chair of its books and file folders. "Tea?"

"That would be lovely, if it's no bother."

"No bother at all. Back in a jiffy."

He returned with two steaming mugs, handed me one, and settled behind his desk. "So, Jessica Fletcher, who killed Rory Brent?"

The bluntness of his question surprised me, and I didn't have a ready answer. I did say, "My guess is as good as yours, Bob, or anyone else's for that matter. A shocking event."

"Certainly was. I didn't know Mr. Brent, although I think I met him once or twice in passing. Seemed like a nice fellow. Played Santa Claus every year, didn't he?"

"Yes, and was wonderful at it. A shame you didn't know him better. He was a delightful man, not a mean bone in his body."

"A shame bad things always seem to happen to nice people."

I nodded.

"Lots of speculation in Cabot Cove about who killed him," he said.

There was no escaping it. Here I was for the purpose of discussing a class I would teach, and the conversation immediately went to Rory Brent's murder, and rumors floating around town about who did it.

"Do you know this Jake Walther fellow?"

"Yes, but not well. No one knew Jake very well because he preferred it that way. I know his wife a lot better."

"From what I hear, it's an open-and-shut case."

I looked at him skeptically. "I hardly think that, Bob. The man was questioned, but not arrested. He has an alibi."

"He does?"

"Yes. His wife's brother, who lives on the property with them."

"I hadn't heard that. Good for him. I mean, lucky for him to have an alibi."

I thought back to what Tony Colarusso had said about Dennis Solten not being a terribly reliable alibi, and wondered what conclusion Mort had reached after speaking with him.

"I was thinking just before you arrived, Jessica, about the potency of rumor, especially where murder is concerned. Have you ever dealt with that in one of your books?"

I shook my head. "I've written so many I have trouble remembering specifics about some of the earlier ones. Yes, as a matter of fact I did deal with rumors in a small town. The rumor became so pervasive that an innocent man was charged with murder."

I hadn't thought about that book in connection with

Rory Brent's murder. But now that I had, the entire plot, and many scenes dealing with it, came back to me.

"Aha," Bob said, sipping his tea. "You could have a situation here where fact follows fiction."

"I don't think one has anything to do with the other, except as a coincidence." I then decided I might as well ask, "What's the latest rumor you've heard?"

"Obviously, I'm not as up to speed as you are. I had no idea Mr. Walther had an alibi. What I heard was that he was taken into custody and retained overnight at the jail by Sheriff Metzger."

I thought back to the circumstances that led Mort to slap cuffs on Jake and bring him into town, but wasn't about to talk about it.

Bob said, "I've read a number of your books, as you know, but I don't recall the one you mentioned."

"Written a long time ago, early in my career," I said. "It was called . . . let me see . . . it was called *The Hanging Vine*. I think I originally called it *The Hanging Grapevine*, but my editor considered it awkward. He felt readers would get the connection without including the word 'grape' in it."

"I'll have to read it."

"I'll drop off a copy next time I'm here. So, Bob, tell me about this minicourse you want me to teach."

I called Dimitri Cassis forty-five minutes later and asked him to pick me up. Bob Roark walked me to the foyer of the administration building, where we chatted about the weather and the upcoming Christmas festival until Dimitri pulled up in his vintage station wagon.

"I'm excited about the course," I said, shaking Bob's hand.

"To have someone of your reputation teach at a community college is a real feather in the cap—a feather in *my* cap. I really appreciate it."

"What's the college doing concerning the festival?"

"Lots. Musical and theater groups putting on performances. Should be fun, although the murder of Santa Claus takes the edge off it."

"I know what you mean, but I'm determined it won't, if only out of deference to Rory's memory. He would have wanted the festival to go on as big and bright as ever."

The first thing I always do when entering my home is to check the answering machine. The little red light was blinking, indicating I had received a call. It turned out to be my publisher, Vaughan Buckley, calling from New York. His Buckley House had been publishing my novels for the past ten years, and I was one of those rare, it seems, writers who is blissfully happy with my publisher and the job it does publishing and marketing my books. Over those ten years, Vaughan and his wife, Olga, had become my dear friends, and I often stayed with them in New York when visiting there. I returned his call immediately.

"Jessica, how are you?"

"Fine. I got your message. I was at a meeting. I'm going to teach a creative writing seminar at our local community college."

"Good for you. Keep your eyes open for the next John Grisham."

"I'll do my best. You called. How's Olga?"

"Tip-top."

"What's up?"

"A brilliant idea from your publisher."

I laughed. "One of many."

"I read about the murder of that farmer in your town. His name—yes, here it is in the story, Rory Brent."

"A tragedy," I said. "He was a wonderful man, loved by all. He'd played Santa Claus at our annual Christmas festival for the past fifteen years."

"So the story indicates. That was the peg the writer hung the article on, that a beloved Santa had been gunned down in tranquil Cabot Cove, Maine."

"I didn't think it would interest the press outside of this area," I said.

"An AP story, out of Bangor. So, what's the latest on it?"

"No suspects," I said. "A few accusations, and many rumors, but no one arrested. At least as far as I know."

"Who's being accused?" Vaughan asked.

"A fellow named Jake Walther. Jake is another farmer. An unpleasant sort, not liked by many people in town. The deceased's son claims Jake killed his father, but has nothing to support that. Sheriff Metzger interviewed Jake at length and released him. From what I hear, Jake has an alibi, and Mort was checking it today. I haven't heard how it came out."

"What's your take on it, Jess?"

"I don't have a take on it, Vaughan. Unfortunately, I got drawn in when Mort originally went out to talk to Jake. I'm friendly with Jake's wife, Mary, and she asked me to help. Jake was acting irrationally because he's convinced everyone believes he killed Rory, and no one will believe that he didn't. I suppose I can't blame him, although he's brought a lot of it on himself because of his sour disposition. As we say in Maine, he's 'some ugly.' "

Vaughan laughed. " 'Some ugly.' Certainly descriptive enough. You folks up there do have a knack for turning a phrase."

"On occasion. Frankly, Vaughan, I'm trying to put it out of my mind and focus on the upcoming holidays. I'm going to be reading Christmas stories to children as part of the festival. You remember my friend Dr. Seth Hazlitt?"

"Of course. How is he?"

"The same as always. He usually does the reading, but this year I'm going to share the stage with him. Should be fun."

"I wish I could be there."

"You can, but hotel rooms are at a premium. You and Olga are always welcome at my place."

"I'll talk to her, maybe plan to come up for a few days."

"I'd love it. So, what's this brilliant idea you've come up with?"

"That you shelve plans for your next novel, and instead do a true-crime book based upon this murder of Santa Claus."

"That never would have crossed my mind. I'm not a true-crime writer."

"But you could be. It would be a nice change of pace, wouldn't it, dealing with fact rather than having to conjure up plots and characters? There they are, right in your lap. You know them, and you certainly know the setting in which this took place. Make a great book."

"I don't think so, Vaughan."

"Don't come to an instant decision. Promise me you'll

think about it for a day or two. Readers love murder stories that take place in small towns, involving small-town people. People getting knocked off in big cities are a dime a dozen, but not when Santa is murdered three weeks before Christmas."

"I'll think about it only because the brilliant idea came from you. But don't count on it. Talk to Olga about coming up and spending a few days during the festival. You'll love it."

I spent the next hour bringing down Christmas decorations from the attic, where I keep them from year to year. Vaughan's call had reminded me that there were, indeed, only three weeks left until Christmas, which meant I'd better get busy writing cards, making a gift list and, in general, pulling myself together for the holiday season.

I was in the midst of reviewing my Christmas card list when Richard Koser called. Richard is a successful professional photographer who'd taken the photographs of me that appear on my book jackets. He and his wife, Mary Jane, are superb chefs, adventuresome kitchen partners whose culinary expertise range from Indian to Thai, Tex-Mex to down-home New England clambakes. Once, I attended a dinner party at their home, featuring an array of Indian foods—dishes like hommos bi tahini and chicken cous cous, and a dessert called galactaboureko—none of which pleased my pedestrian palate. I'm sure the food was superb, and my reaction was not intended to be judgmental. Richard and Mary Jane understood. "Indian dishes are an acquired taste," they had graciously said.

"Just as long as you invite me to other dinner parties with more familiar cuisine," I had said.

The one to which I'd been invited that evening would feature, according to Richard, an unusual approach to New England cooking, and I'd been looking forward to it since being invited two weeks ago. Besides excellent food, parties at the Koser home were always spirited and enjoyable.

"Just making sure you'll be coming tonight," Richard said.

"Absolutely," I said. "Who else will be there?"

"The familiar and the unfamiliar," he said, laughing. "My agent from Boston and his wife are in town and staying with us. Friends from New York are also up for a few days, staying at Jim Rich's Inn. Doc Hazlitt promised to come by, and Mort and his wife are joining the party."

"Mort? I'm surprised. I didn't think he had much time for socializing these days."

"Because of the Rory Brent murder?"

"Exactly." I tried to catch myself before asking the next question, but failed. "What do you hear about the murder, Richard?"

"Not very much. I've been holed up in my darkroom all day, except for a quick trip to the barber. Word there is that Jake Walther did it."

I quickly changed the subject. "What's this special approach to New England cooking we'll be enjoying tonight?"

Another laugh. "I want it to be a surprise. And no hommos bi tahini. That's a promise. Seven?"

"See you then."

Chapter Nine

Although I enjoy cooking, I would never claim to be a particularly successful or inventive chef. That's why I enjoy being around people who are, like Richard and Mary Jane Koser. For this particular evening, they'd used a recipe for baked oysters taken from a cookbook called *The Accomplished Cook: Or, The Art and Mystery of Cookery,* published in September of 1664, more than three hundred years ago. Pages from it had been reproduced verbatim in another book called *Maine Coastal Cooking,* published more recently by Down East Books, a Maine publisher.

Our hosts parboiled the oysters in their own juices, washed them in warm water, dried them, seasoned them with pepper, nutmeg, yolks of hard eggs, and salt, wrapped them in a wonderful homemade piecrust, and baked them in the oven. It was a superb entrée; everything else served was on the same level of excellence.

Following dessert, we sat in the living room, where Richard served cordials. My antenna had been up during dinner to pick up any conversation about Rory Brent's murder, and the speculation that Jake Walther was the murderer. To everyone's credit, dinner-table conversation touched upon every subject except the murder.

But once in the living room, Seth Hazlitt raised it. "Well now, Morton," he said, "we've all been on our best behavior this evening."

"How so?" our sheriff said, sitting on a couch next to his wife.

"Not a word about Rory's murder. But I'll bet my bottom dollar that everyone here has a question for you."

Mort looked at me before saying, "I figure you're right, Seth, and I appreciate everybody holding their tongues. No sense asking me questions. I can't discuss an ongoing investigation."

"Who's Rory?" Richard's cousin asked.

"A local farmer who was murdered the other day," Seth said.

"Murdered?" the cousin said, looking at me. "I thought the only murders that happened in Cabot Cove were in your books, Jessica."

"Generally, you're right," I said, "but this time it was for real."

Richard's agent narrowed his eyes and said, "You didn't have anything to do with it, did you, Richard?"

"Me?"

"Sure. Remember the old radio series, 'Casey, Crime Photographer'?"

Seth laughed. "I'm the only one old enough here to remember it," he said. "Folks joked that it was called that because the way Casey took pictures, it *was* a crime."

"I never heard of it," the cousin said.

"You're investigating the murder?" the agent asked Mort, her eyes open wide.

"Afraid so," he replied.

"Has him out of the house day and night," Mort's wife said, patting her husband on the arm. "I prefer it when the only crime he has to investigate is somebody's lobster pot being stolen."

Although many questions were now asked of Mort, he remained adamant in his commitment not to discuss the Rory Brent murder. I admired him for that, although I admit my curiosity level wasn't exactly dormant.

The party broke up at eleven, late for midweek Cabot Cove social events. We tend to be early-to-bed, early-to-rise people. Seth drove me home.

"Come in for a nightcap?" I asked.

"*Ayuh*, don't mind if I do."

The oyster pie had left me thirsty, and I poured myself a club soda with lime. Seth readily accepted my offer of brandy.

"Pleasant evening," I said as we settled in the living room.

"Always is at Richard and Mary Jane's. Don't know if they're the best cooks in Cabot Cove, but they come close."

"I was proud of Mort this evening, not succumbing to the temptation to discuss Rory's murder."

"He is capable of keeping his mouth shut on occasion," he said, tasting the brandy and smacking his lips. "The perfect end to a nice evening."

"Seth, has Mort told *you* anything about going out to check on Jake's alibi with Dennis?"

He didn't answer, but his expression told me he had, indeed, been privy to additional information about the murder. I know Seth well enough not to press. If he wished to share it with me, he would.

"I spoke with Dr. Treyz this afternoon," he said, taking another taste of his brandy.

"Oh?"

"He finished up the autopsy on Rory."

Again, I didn't push for further details. You get from Seth Hazlitt only what he wishes to give you.

"*Ayuh,* told me it was a twenty-two that killed Rory. Bullet lodged right in his brain."

"I assume it was turned over to Mort," I said.

"I suspect it was. Probably go out to the state forensic lab down to Portland. It's official, Jessica. Somebody put a bullet in Rory Brent's head."

I felt a sudden chill, and eyed Seth's half-filled snifter of brandy. But I knew the shiver that went through me was not the result of the temperature in the room. Each time I thought of Rory Brent lying dead on the cold dirt floor of his barn, I suffered a physical reaction, as though someone had set off an electrical charge inside, or poked a knife in my ribs.

"Want some cookies?" I asked.

"Thank you, no, Jessica. Quite content."

I was heading for the kitchen to refill my glass when Seth said matter-of-factly, as though speaking to no one in particular, "Jake's alibi holds up."

I stopped midstride, turned, and looked at him. "Dennis corroborated what Jake said, that they were fixing a stone wall together?"

"That is correct," said Seth.

"I had my teeth cleaned this morning by Tony Colarusso. He questioned whether Dennis could be counted on as a reliable alibi."

"I suppose Tony is right, Jessica. But as far as Mort is concerned, Dennis gets Jake off the hook."

"Mort told you this himself?"

"That he did. 'Course, he only gave me a *scrid* of information. Just a wee bit."

"But important information, I'd say. Does this mean that Mort has officially ruled out Jake as a suspect?"

"Hard to say. I didn't get into that with him. And if I were runnin' the investigation, I'd be looking elsewhere. 'Course, I'm not runnin' the investigation."

He stood. "Much obliged for the brandy, Jessica. What's on your agenda tomorrow?"

I glanced at the grandfather clock in a corner of the room. It was a few minutes past midnight. "You mean what's on my agenda *today*? A busy schedule, but I won't bore you with the particulars. I'm sure we'll touch base again. Thanks for the ride, Seth. Careful home. Watch out for that black ice."

"*Ayuh,* I certainly will. Good night."

Although the hour was late, I wasn't tired, and sat up until after one thinking about what had occurred since that fateful morning of the Christmas festival planning meeting, when Tim Purdy arrived back from Rory Brent's farm with the grim news that he was dead. And then, of course, the tragedy was compounded after Mort visited the Brent farm and reported to us at lunch that it appeared Rory had been murdered.

Eventually, I climbed into bed and tried to read a few more pages in the book I'd started. But, as often happens, the act of reading quickly caused my eyes to lower. My final thought before I drifted off was the conversation I'd had with Vaughan Buckley about doing a true-crime book based upon the Rory Brent murder. Doing such a book held little or no interest for me. But then again, maybe it wouldn't be such a bad idea to do a little poking around in the event I changed my mind.

I knew one thing for certain: I wanted Rory Brent's murderer brought to justice before the Christmas festival. If it still hung over our heads during that joyous period of time, much of the Christmas spirit—and what it was supposed to mean—would be lost.

Peace on earth, goodwill toward men.

There would be no peace in Cabot Cove until Rory's murderer was behind bars.

Chapter Ten

I was up early the next morning and feeling remark-
ably refreshed, considering the late hour I'd gone to
bed. Maybe it was the weather; the sun was shining
brightly, and the sky was a deep, unblemished blue.

A perfect morning for a brisk walk, I thought as I prepared a simple breakfast, then took a shower. A half hour
later, dressed in my favorite sweatsuit worn over a sweater,
a scarf to keep my ears warm, and a new pair of expensive
sneakers on my feet (*Why* are sneakers so expensive these
days?), I headed out the front door and for town.

Because I'm as much a creature of habit as anyone else,
I usually find my walks taking me in the same direction
each time. Sometimes, when I think of it, I alter my route,
if only to enjoy different scenery. But this morning I didn't
bother being creative in choosing what streets to take. The
only thing on my mind was to get moving, breathe in the
cold, crisp air, and feel my blood flowing.

It takes only ten minutes to reach the center of Cabot Cove from my house. When I arrived there, I glanced at my watch. It was seven-thirty. Even at that early hour the main street—aptly named Main Street—was bustling. That is one of the reasons I enjoy taking morning walks into town. It's a chance to see friends before they become immersed in their work and daily lives.

I bumped into Sandy and Bernadette, who own the Animal Inn, a wonderful kennel where dogs and cats placed in their loving charge are treated royally.

"How are all your canine and feline boarders?" I asked.

"Making the usual racket," said Sandy. "I think they sense Christmas is coming." To which Bernadette added, "A full house, no vacancies. Not an empty run in the place, and looks like it will stay that way right through the New Year."

"That's called prosperity," I said.

"I suppose you're right, Jess," Sandy said. "We've been turning down callers from miles away who want to bring their pets with them to the festival. Hate to say no but—"

I'd traveled another half block when I was stopped by Mickey and Joan Terzigni, on their way to open up their sign shop.

"Keeping busy?" I asked.

"With the Christmas festival coming up?" Mickey said, laughing. "Can't keep up with all the signs the festival committee keeps ordering. You?"

"Not very busy at all," I said, "and loving every minute of it."

The only problem with running into so many people on my walk is that it interrupts the rhythm I try to establish, one that will benefit my cardiovascular system.

I eventually left the downtown area and headed for the waterfront. The smell of sea air was bracing, the sound of gulls overhead providing what almost sounded like a choir—were they singing a Christmas song? I smiled at the thought.

The wind off the water was brisk, and I soon regretted not having dressed more warmly, perhaps adding a jacket over my sweatsuit. People were going in and out of Mara's Luncheonette, but I resisted the temptation to stop in for a cup of coffee and whatever caloric breakfast pastry she'd come up with that morning. After pausing on the dock to take in the stunning vista of sky and water, I went to the shore, removed my sneakers and socks, and walked barefoot along the water's edge. The sand was surprisingly warm on my bare feet, at least below the surface. Many people were on the beach, some throwing sticks for their dogs to fetch, others walking hand in hand. A man combed the sand with a metal detector in search of buried treasure. The sound of children's laughter rose above the steady slap and swish of waves breaking onshore.

At first, I wasn't sure I heard correctly. Had someone called my name? When I heard it a second time, I stopped and turned. Tom Coleman, Sheriff Metzger's deputy, was waving to me from where the sand ended at a series of large boulders, behind which was a parking lot.

"Good morning, Tom," I said when I reached him. "Beautiful day for December."

"Yes, ma'am, I suppose it is," he said. "The sheriff's been looking for you."

"Looking for me? Why?"

"Has to do with Jake Walther, I think."

"How so?" I asked, sitting on a rock, brushing the sand from my feet and between my toes, and putting on my socks and sneakers.

"He didn't really say, Mrs. Fletcher, except that Mrs. Walther is at headquarters. I think she's looking for you, too."

"Has something bad happened?" I asked.

"My car is right up here," was his reply.

I accepted his hand to help me up onto the rocks and followed him to his police cruiser.

Five minutes later I was in Sheriff Mort Metzger's office. Mary Walther stood by the window, her back to me.

"Good morning," I said.

"Good morning, Mrs. F.," said Mort.

"Good morning, Mary," I said.

She turned and looked at me with red-rimmed eyes.

"What's the matter?" I asked. "I assume it must be something important to have sent Tom down to the beach to interrupt my morning constitutional."

When Mary didn't respond, Mort said, "I arrested Jake this morning for Rory Brent's murder, Mrs. F."

Mary bit her lip and turned away again.

"What happened?" I asked. "I thought Jake had an alibi."

When neither of them responded, I added, "Didn't Dennis say he was fixing a stone wall with Jake the morning Rory was killed?"

"That's what he said the first time, Mrs. F., but I had my suspicions, so I went out there first thing this morning and talked to him again. Seems he's changed his story."

"He wasn't with Jake that morning?"

"Afraid not. Dennis says Jake told him to come up with that story so that he would have an alibi. But after a little prodding, I got the truth out of him."

I thought of Tony Colarusso's comment that Dennis would testify to anything, depending upon who was most persuasive. Was that the case here? Had Mort led Dennis into this total turnabout in his story?

Mary again faced me. "I'm afraid Dennis is telling the truth this time, Mrs. Fletcher."

"Please, it's Jessica."

"Jessica. He confided in me that he'd told the sheriff he'd been with Jake that morning only because he was afraid of Jake. No, Dennis was not with Jake when Rory Brent was killed. I know that for a fact. After all, he is my brother."

"But such a drastic change in story," I said, exhaling loudly. "And why would he be afraid of Jake? He's lived with you and Jake on the farm for many years."

"I know, I know," said Mary, slowly shaking her head and sinking into a chair. "But just because Dennis wasn't with Jake doesn't mean Jake killed Rory." Having stated that seemed to perk her up. She sat forward and looked at Mort. "It doesn't necessarily mean that, does it, Sheriff Metzger? I mean, just because he wasn't with Jake doesn't mean Jake killed anyone."

"I suppose that's what a jury will have to decide, Mrs. Walther," Mort said glumly. "All I know is I have enough to hold Jake on suspicion of murder until the D.A. decides whether to indict."

"Where is Jake?" I asked.

"In jail," Mort said.

"Why did you send for me?" I asked.

"Because I asked him to," Mary answered. "I don't know, Jessica, but sometimes I think you're the only real friend I have."

Her comment struck me as strange. Although we had been friendly, we'd never socialized the way true friends do, only interacted through mutual involvement in community activities. To call me her only friend was, in my judgment, a gross exaggeration.

Still, my heart went out to her. If she viewed me that way, it meant she harbored a terrible distrust of everyone else she'd gotten to know over the years.

"Mary, what would you like me to do?" I asked. "How can I help?"

Mort answered for her. "Jake's going to need a lawyer, Mrs. F. I told Mary that we could get him a public defender, but she said she wanted to talk to you first."

"Talk to *me* about lawyers?" I said.

"Because you seem to be the one person in Cabot Cove that everyone looks up to, Jessica," Mary said. "And I know you understand something about the legal system because of the books you write. Maybe I was out of place. I shouldn't have bothered you. It isn't your concern."

I pulled up a chair and patted her hand. "Mary, you haven't bothered me at all. I want to help. Mort is right. If you don't have the money to hire a lawyer, the state will provide a public defender."

"But that would be someone I don't know, that Jake doesn't even know. We don't have the money to pay an expensive lawyer, but I have some cash saved. Not a great deal, but maybe enough to use as a down payment. I could pay off a lawyer's fee over time. Jessica, all I want is to help Jake because I know he did not do this. He did not kill Rory Brent!"

Her voice had risen in volume, causing me to sit back, as though pushed by a hand. I looked to Mort, who continued to sit behind his desk, hands folded beneath his chin, eyes narrowed as he took in the conversation.

"How about Joe Turco?" I said.

"Who is he?" Mary asked.

"A wonderful young attorney who moved here only six months ago. He's a fine young man with excellent legal training, studied law in New Hampshire and New York City. Oxford, too, I think."

"Oxford, England?" Mort asked.

"Yes. He'd been practicing in Manhattan, and handling cases in New Hampshire, too. He's moved here because he likes to fish, and wanted a more quiet life than in Manhattan. He's building his practice. Would you like me to talk to him, see what he would charge to defend Jake?"

"Yes, of course," Mary said.

"It might not even involve much legal representation," I offered. "As of now, Jake hasn't been indicted." I turned to Mort. "That's correct, isn't it?"

"Correct!" he said.

"If Joe Turco is willing to take the case, he can handle this phase of things, maybe see that Jake is released on bail, something like that. I really don't know because I'm not a lawyer. But I have a lot of faith in this young attorney, who is now a member of our community, and I'd be happy to speak with him. I'll go see him when I leave here."

Mort said, "I'm not much of a fan of attorneys, as everybody knows, but I have got to admit I'm impressed with this young Turco. Got a nice way about him, which I can't say about most lawyers. It's a good suggestion Jessica is making, Mrs. Walther."

I stood. "Unless you want me here for something else, I'll go look him up right away."

Mary, too, stood, and took both my hands in her large ones. "God bless you, Jessica," she said. "I knew I could count on you. I don't know what I would do without you."

Again, this expression of friendship made me uncomfortable, although I understood that she was doing everything she could do to express her gratitude. I hadn't done anything yet, but I did feel my suggestion about Joseph Turco was a good one. What a terrible situation for anyone to be in, I thought as I picked up my scarf from where I'd laid it on the edge of Mort's desk, and wrapped it around my neck. I said to Mary, "Will you be home after you leave here?"

"Yes. I have nowhere else to go."

"Don't give up hope, Mary," I said. "I'm sure things will work out."

Chapter Eleven

Joseph Turco, Esq., had rented the second floor of a pretty, white two-story building on Main Street, owned by Beth and Peter Mullin, who operated Olde Tyme Floral, a lovely flower shop on the first floor. They were delighted to rent to the young, handsome attorney looking for a place in which to establish a law practice.

I chatted with them in their shop before heading up a short flight of stairs to the second floor. The door to Joe's office was open. He sat behind a desk piled high with law books, and was reading one when I knocked. He glanced up. "Good morning, Jessica," he said, getting up and coming to greet me.

"Hope I'm not intruding on something important."

He said, "Not at all. Just writing a brief to present before the Supreme Court." My face must have reflected I believed him because he laughed and said, "A commercial real estate deal I'm closing on this afternoon. Should have gone smoothly, but one of the parties has thrown a last-minute wrench into the works. Please, come in. Sit down. Coffee is made."

After I'd been served and he'd refilled his cup, he said, "Don't tell me you're having a copyright or plagiarism problem with one of your books."

"Goodness, no. I've been fortunate never to have had a legal problem in my career, and I want it to stay that way."

"Good thinking," he said. "Get us lawyers involved and your problems really get complicated."

"Joe, I'm here on behalf of a friend, Mary Walther."

He frowned, obviously trying to connect with that name. When he did, he said, "Is she related to that farmer, Jake Walther?"

"I would say so. She's Jake's wife."

"Poor woman."

I couldn't help but smile. Even someone who'd been in town only a short period of time was aware of Jake Walther's reputation.

"Sheriff Metzger has arrested Jake and is charging him with the murder of Rory Brent."

Joe's eyes went up, and he whistled softly. "Pretty fast work on the part of our crack sheriff," he said.

"Yes. Mort Metzger is a lot sharper than he sometimes lets on."

"I'm not surprised to hear it."

"What? That Mort is sharper than he—"

"No, no, not surprised Walther's been arrested for murder. To be perfectly honest with you, Jess, Jake Walther is a madman."

Now it was my turn to express surprise.

"Yeah. I had a run-in with him right after arriving in Cabot Cove."

"You did? What led to it?"

"I pulled out of the driveway next to the building one morning. I suppose I should have waited for the pickup truck to pass, but it looked to me like I had plenty of room. At any rate, I pulled into the street and stopped at the light. The pickup truck came flying around on the side of my car and then turned in front of me so that I was blocked. Jake Walther was driving that truck. He leaped out, came to my side of the car, raised his fist at me, and said I was an idiot—I won't repeat all of the words he used because they were pretty foul—and said he'd kill me. I'll never forget the look on his face, Jessica. His eyes were like burning coals, and his mouth was cruel. Yeah, his whole face was that of a crazy person."

"What an upsetting thing to go through," I said. "What happened next?"

"He got back in his truck and drove off. I sat there shaking when the light turned green. I'd never had anything like that happen to me before."

"How did you know it was Jake?"

"There were two people standing on the corner who witnessed it. They came to the car and asked if I was all right. They told me who he was."

"What an unfortunate experience. Have you had any contact with him since?"

"Are you kidding? Every time I see him in town I make it a point of walking in the other direction. He's nuts, certifiably so."

I decided not to beat around the bush, and simply asked, "Would you be interested in representing him?"

"Represent him? Me? Jake Walther? In a murder case? I've never handled a murder case before."

"I don't think that's as much of a problem as your attitude toward Jake, based on your previous experience with him. You have done criminal law, haven't you?"

"Sure. In New York and New Hampshire, and I've handled a few minor criminal matters since moving here, but nothing heavy duty. Murder? Jake Walther?" His grimace said to me it was out of the question to even consider it.

"I can't say that I blame you," I said. "But Jake's wife, Mary, came to me and asked for help. I thought of you. They don't have any money, and I suppose the state will provide a public defender. But do you know something, Joe? Somehow, I'm not convinced Jake killed Rory Brent."

"Based upon what?"

I shook my head. "I have no idea, and I usually wait until all the facts are in before making a judgment. But it seems that Jake's nasty reputation—and deservedly so, I might add—might be causing too many people to rush to judgment about his guilt."

"Including Sheriff Metzger?"

"Maybe not consciously so, but it's possible. Well, you were good to let me barge in on you in the middle of your work. You look busy, and I'll get out of your hair."

He held up his hand. "No, stay a few minutes, Jess. I'd like to hear more. What do you know about Jake Walther's relationship with Rory Brent?"

I filled him in on what I'd been told, most of it coming from Rory's son, Robert, that there had been bad blood between Rory and Jake, and that they'd had a verbal confrontation during which, again according to Robert Brent, Jake threatened to kill Rory. I also told him about Mary's brother, Dennis, providing an alibi for Jake, but then with-drawing it, and further claiming that Jake had threatened him unless he provided the alibi.

"Interesting," Joe said when I was finished recounting what I knew. "From what you've told me, Sheriff Metzger really doesn't have a lot to hold Jake on."

"Unless there are things I'm not aware of."

"That's always a possibility. But a man not having an alibi isn't reason enough to book him for murder, at least not according to my legal training."

"But what about Dennis's claim that Jake threatened him if he didn't provide the alibi? That would weigh heav-ily in terms of potential guilt, wouldn't it?"

"Sounds bad, but maybe it isn't. Tell me about this Dennis."

I filled Joe in on Dennis Solten.

"And Sheriff Metzger is depending upon this guy? It sounds like he'd say anything anybody wants him to."

"That's true."

"And Brent's son claiming to have overheard Jake threaten his father really isn't very compelling, either."

"Well, Joe, as I said, there may be other factors at work here that I don't know about."

"You say you've talked to Jake's wife?"

"Yes. I just left her at police headquarters."

"Did you see Jake there?"

"No."

"I hope he didn't give any kind of statement without having a lawyer present."

"I wouldn't know about that."

"The man should have a lawyer with him every step of the way."

"Obviously a good idea. I don't know how fast Legal Aid can get a lawyer here, but—"

"Maybe I'll stroll over to headquarters."

"To talk to Sheriff Metzger?"

"Yeah. And maybe talk to Jake Walther."

"But I thought—"

"No promises, Jessica," he said, standing, taking his suit jacket from where it hung on a wooden coat tree, and slipping it on. "But I wouldn't want to rule it out without having a chance to talk to them."

I, too, stood. "Even though he threatened to kill *you*?"

Joe Turco's grin was infectious. "Maybe Jake Walther had a bad hair day that morning. By the way, what's your interest in this, aside from being friends with Mary Walther?"

I followed him down the stairs. "Nothing other than that, really," I said, not adding that I was thinking of Vaughan Buckley's call asking me to consider doing a true-crime book about the Rory Brent murder. Some things were better left unsaid. All I knew was that I'd accomplished what I'd set out to do, and what I'd promised Mary Walther I would do. Whether Joe would follow through was something over which I had no control.

"Mind if I tag along?" I asked when we reached the street.

"I was counting on it. You know, Jess, maybe you should do a book about the Brent murder. One of those true-crime books."

"Never crossed my mind," I said.

Chapter Twelve

By the time we walked to police headquarters, Mary Walther had left, telling Mort Metzger she could be reached at home if he needed her. I found it somewhat strange that she hadn't waited for us, considering I'd gone off to fetch an attorney for her husband. Then again, I reasoned, I hadn't given her any assurances that Joe Turco would agree to get involved. It was probably the smart thing to do, to return to the sanctity of her home to await further news.

" 'Morning, Counselor," Mort said when Joe and I entered his office.

"Good morning, Sheriff," Joe replied. "I understand you've made an arrest in the Rory Brent murder."

"Well, now, I wouldn't say I've made an arrest. More a matter of detaining a suspect until the D.A. makes up her mind whether to indict."

"Mind if we sit down?" I asked.

"Be my guest," Mort said, indicating matching wooden armchairs.

"Jessica tells me that you're holding Jake Walther based upon his not having an alibi, and because the deceased's son claims Jake threatened to kill his father."

Mort said nothing, but simply fixed Joe with an expression I'd often seen before, which said that although he was listening, he was not about to be swayed by anything anyone said.

"That really isn't very much to hold a man on, Sheriff," Joe said. "But maybe you know more than we do."

Mort swiveled back and forth in his chair, rubbing his eyes. He eventually stopped the motion, leaned forward, elbows on the desk, and said, "Everybody knows there was bad blood between Jake Walther and Rory Brent. And as far as an alibi is concerned, it's not so much that he doesn't have one. The problem is he threatened somebody if that person didn't give him an alibi."

"You mean Mary Walther's brother, Dennis," Joe said.

"Yeah. When a man feels he needs an alibi that bad, it means he's more than likely done something wrong. At least, that's what my common sense says to me."

"An interesting speculation," said Joe. "But from a legal standpoint, it's hardly sufficient cause to detain a man in jail."

Mort looked at me; I raised my eyebrows to say that I intended to remain neutral during this conversation.

"Mr. Turco," Mort said, "are you here as Jake Walther's legal counsel?"

Now it was Joe who looked at me. I gave him the same eyebrows-up look.

"Probably," was Joe's response. "I'd like to confer with Mr. Walther. I assume he had an attorney present when you spoke with him after . . . as you put it, 'detained' him."

"No need to," said Mort. "I didn't interrogate him, just told him why I was bringin' him in and told him to cool his heels in the cell until this thing gets straightened out."

"Still, Sheriff, there should have been an attorney present from the moment he was in your custody. May I see him?"

"I suppose so," said Mort, standing, going to his door, and yelling for Tom Coleman. A moment later Coleman appeared.

"Take Mr. Turco to see Mr. Walther, Tom."

"Mind if I go with you, Joe?" I asked.

"Sure. Why not? Okay with you, Sheriff?"

"Anything Mrs. F. wants to do is always okay with me."

"That's very sweet, Mort," I said, standing.

Tom led us to the cell in which Jake Walther was confined. I noticed that all the other cells were empty—a slow crime day in Cabot Cove, thank goodness.

Jake was sitting on the narrow, hard cot in a far corner of the cell. He appeared to be sleeping sitting up, and didn't look in our direction when we stopped in front of the door.

"Hey, Jake, wake up," Tom Coleman said, hitting his ring of keys on the bars.

Jake opened one eye and cast it in our direction. He looked horrible. His hair, which was never particularly neat, was a gray, matted mess. Stubble on his face enhanced the look of fatigue and hopelessness. He wore stained bib overalls over a wrinkled yellow shirt. I noted that his shoes had been removed, probably to ensure that he did not attempt to use the laces to harm himself.

"You got company, Jake," Tom said. "Mrs. Fletcher and a lawyer."

Now Jake opened the other eye, turned slightly on the cot so that he faced us, and frowned, saying, "I didn't ask for no lawyer."

"No, you didn't, Jake," I said, "but Mary asked me to find you one. Mr. Turco is new to Cabot Cove, but is an excellent attorney. He's agreed to at least sit down with you. He hasn't committed himself to taking your case, but—"

"Why don't the two of you get the hell out of here," was Jake's reply.

Joe Turco looked at me and shrugged.

I quickly said to Jake, "You can dismiss us if you wish, Jake, but you should talk to Mr. Turco if only out of respect for your wife. She's very upset, as one can imagine she would be. The least you can do is give Mr. Turco a few minutes so that he can better understand what's going on. Then he can decide whether he would want to represent you. You do need a lawyer, you know."

Jake slowly pushed himself to a standing position, stretched, yawned, and approached the bars. When we were only a few feet apart, he said, "I don't need no damn lawyer. Everybody's already made up their minds that I killed Rory Brent. Might just as well have the sheriff take me out front right now and shoot me, or hang me from a tree. A lawyer? All that'll do is cost money, and he ain't going to be able to do nothing to make it right. Nice you coming here and all, but there's nothing nobody can say to change nobody's mind."

"Suit yourself, Mr. Walther," Joe said. "I'm not crazy about being here anyway. The one time you and I met up before, you cut me off and threatened to kill me."

Jake squinted to better see Joe's face. "That's crazy talk," he said. "I never seen you before in my life."

"Yeah, well, it happened pretty quick. Did you threaten your brother-in-law, Dennis, if he didn't give you an alibi for the morning Rory Brent was murdered?"

Another scowl from Jake Walther. "Hell, no," he said. "Dennis has the mind of a mole. Nice enough fella, but he'll say anything anybody wants him to say. Truth is I was out fixing a wall with Dennis when ol' Rory got it. That's what Dennis told the sheriff first time around. But then he changed his mind, probably because the sheriff talked him into it. You can't believe nothin' Dennis says, and that's a fact."

"So maybe we shouldn't believe him when he first said he was with you that morning."

Jake looked at me. "See what I mean, about nobody believing me? This here young lawyer is already trying to tear apart my story."

"I'm not doing anything of the kind, Mr. Walther," Joe said. "I'm just looking at it from the viewpoint of a prosecutor. Did you ever threaten to kill Rory Brent?"

"Might have," said Jake.

Joe turned to Tom Coleman, who stood listening to the conversation. "Mind if we go in the cell with him?" Joe asked. "It's awkward standing out here. And I'd appreciate being alone with— " Joe looked at me and smiled. "With my client."

"I suppose it's okay that you go in," Tom said to Joe, "but I don't think Mrs. Fletcher ought to be in there."

Jake Walther's laugh was a cackle. "What are you afraid of, Coleman, that I'll attack her? Damn fool."

Tom's anger showed on his face, but he didn't respond.

I said, "I'd like to be with Mr. Turco when he talks to Mr. Walther."

"Suit yourself, Mrs. Fletcher," Tom said, unlocking the door and opening it. Jake stepped back to allow us to enter. The moment we were inside, Tom slammed the door shut with unnecessary force, I thought, and walked away, muttering.

"Mind if we sit down?" Joe asked, indicating the cot.

Jake's response was to shrug, go to the other corner, and lean against the wall, arms folded defiantly over his chest.

We sat on the edge of the cot. Joe turned to me and said, "Anything you'd like to ask, Mrs. Fletcher?"

"No, I'm just an interested bystander, here on behalf of Mr. Walther's wife. You're the lawyer. You ask the questions."

"Okay," Joe said. "Let's start from the very beginning, Mr. Walther. Mind if I call you Jake?"

"Suit yourself."

I was impressed with Joe Turco's questioning of Jake. He was forthright, yet gentle, and had a marvelous way of putting Jake at ease, at least to the extent that was possible, considering the circumstances.

"I'm willing to be your attorney, at least for this phase of the case," Joe said a half hour later. "I won't promise anything after that. If you want me to represent you, I'll go straight to the district attorney and demand that she either indict or allow you to go free. But if they let you go, I have to have assurance from you that you won't go any farther than your farm. Understood?"

"What's this going to cost me?" Jake asked.

"We can work that out later," Joe said. "Look, Mr. Walther, I'll be honest with you. I don't like you. The one brush I had with you, whether you remember it or not, was enough to turn me off on Mr. Jake Walther for the rest of my life. I'm here because of Mrs. Fletcher, and because I believe in the law. I don't know whether you killed Rory Brent or not. You say you didn't, and I accept that. I just don't want to see a man falsely accused because of his general reputation. That rubs me the wrong way, as it should rub every citizen the wrong way. Want me as your attorney, Mr. Walther? Speak up now, because I'm leaving."

Jake looked at me, a quizzical expression on his face.

"If I were you, Jake, I'd take Mr. Turco up on his offer," I said. "You have nothing to lose and everything to gain. Again, I remind you that you have a wife who is very worried."

For the first time since entering the cell, I thought of Jake's daughter, Jill, attending school in New York City. "And don't forget Jill," I said.

The mention of her name generated an interesting softening of Jake Walther's face. I wondered whether he might even cry.

"You did a good thing for Jill, getting her into school," he said to me.

Because I knew he'd been adamant in his objection to her attending college, especially one in a big city like New York, I found his expression of gratitude touching.

"I helped her," I said, "because she's a very bright young woman who will make a fine writer one day. Have you spoken with her?"

He averted his eyes as he slowly shook his head and said, "No. She probably don't even know this is happening." He looked up. "But she will."

He turned to Joe Turco. "Sure, go ahead and be my lawyer. How old are you?"

Joe laughed and said, "Thirty-two."

"Too young to be much good at anything, but I suppose you should know somethin' after spendin' all those years in school."

Joe closed the gap between them and extended his hand, which Jake reluctantly took, then quickly dropped.

"I'll be back," Joe said, "I hope with some good news."

I walked with Joe back to his office, where he intended to tidy up a few loose ends on his real estate transaction before seeing the district attorney. We stood on the sidewalk in front of Olde Tyme Floral.

"Do you think you'll be successful with the district attorney?" I asked.

"Probably," he said. "They either have to indict or let Jake go. I'm not certain of the Maine statutes, but I'll do some quick reading before I go over there. I'm licensed here, but still have to get up to speed on local law. Think my client is guilty, Jessica?"

"I have no idea, Joe. All I know is that Mary Walther will be extremely grateful for your agreeing to become involved. And I'll see to it that there's money for your fee."

"The last thing on my mind," he said. "Frankly, doing real estate is a lawyer's bread and butter, but it can get pretty dull. Defending the grinch who shot Santa has a lot more pizzazz."

Chapter Thirteen

"O God, whose mercies cannot be numbered; Accept our prayers on behalf of the soul of thy servant departed, and grant him an entrance into the land of light and joy, in the fellowship of thy saints; through Jesus Christ our Lord."

Father Wayne Shuttee, Cabot Cove's Episcopal priest, conducted Rory Brent's burial ritual. The Brent family were staunch Episcopalians; their generosity was well known not only within the church, but throughout the community.

Rory's funeral was held at the town's largest funeral parlor, and had attracted an overflow crowd. Patricia Brent sat stoically throughout the service, which, besides Father Shuttee, consisted of a series of eulogies by townspeople for their departed friend. Bob Brent, the son, wearing jeans with holes at the knees, a T-shirt, and hiking boots, his hair in need of washing, was out of place at such a solemn event. There were muttered comments that he might at least have dressed more appropriately for his father's funeral, but I don't think anyone said it to him directly. Funerals, like weddings, always seem to produce a certain tension within families. The trick is to not feed into it out of deference to the bride and groom, or in this case the departed.

Tears flowed easily as Rory's friends praised him for his civic-mindedness, his exemplary performance as a husband and father, and for what he meant to Cabot Cove. I'd been asked to join the eulogists, but demurred, not because I didn't have good things to say about Rory, but because I knew I would be uncomfortable in that situation. I was content to listen to the words of others, some wonderfully eloquent, others halting and awkward but brimming with honest emotion.

Now, on a dank, dark day, we stood at the grave site as Rory's coffin was about to be lowered into the hard earth.

". . . ashes to ashes, dust to dust . . ."

"I still can't believe this," Richard Koser, the photographer, whispered into my ear.

"I know," I said.

"It's like . . . well, it's like burying Santa Claus. What will kids all over the world do now?"

Richard's comment caused me to smile. Somehow, there was something comforting about the Santa Claus connection to Rory Brent, even though that link would accompany him to the hereafter.

The coffin was lowered. Father Shuttee said a few final words, and we returned to the cars that had brought us to the cemetery. As I stood chatting with friends, I saw a lonely figure approaching from the far reaches of the graveyard, growing increasingly larger as she neared.

"Isn't that Jill Walther?" someone asked.

"Yes, I think it is," I said.

I wasn't sure whether to close the gap between Jill and myself, or to simply let her reach us. I decided on the former course of action, and took purposeful strides in her direction. My concern was that the speculation that her father had murdered Rory might cause some of those gathered to take it out on her with an unpleasant comment—or worse. Even if Jake had murdered Rory, it was no reason to demonstrate antagonism toward another member of his family.

"Hello, Jill," I said when we were face-to-face on the long, narrow concrete road leading from the main entrance.

"Hello, Mrs. Fletcher."

"How wonderful to see you again. Are you home on your Christmas break?"

"Yes," she said, her eyes focused on her boots. "I left a few days early once I heard about Mr. Brent."

I didn't know how much she knew about the accusation that her father was the murderer, and didn't want to prompt her. I silently waited for her to say more.

"I came home last night," Jill said. "I guess you know that my father is in jail."

"Yes. I visited him yesterday with an attorney, Mr. Turco. I hope he'll be successful in arranging for your father to be released, perhaps on bail, although when someone is charged with—"

"Charged with murder," she said, completing my sentence. Now she looked me straight in the eye and said, "My daddy could never have killed him."

"I know how you feel," I said, not adding that no matter how much faith she might have, there was still the possibility that the rumors were true, that Jake Walther had, indeed, murdered Rory Brent.

"You don't think he killed him, do you?" she asked. Her eyes were moist, and her lips quivered.

"I certainly don't want to think he did," I said, evading a direct reply to her question. No sense in feeding into her fears at that point.

"Why did you come here today?" I asked.

"I don't know," she said. "I didn't want to stay home. Mom asked me to, but I said I needed a walk. I just headed in this direction. I knew Mr. Brent was being buried and wanted to—" Now she broke down completely, sobs racking her small, slender body. I wrapped my arms around her and pressed her face to my bosom.

"Now, now," I said, hugging her tighter. "I know this is a terrible thing that's happened, but you have to have faith, Jill. If your father didn't do it, he will be cleared in the proper way. Until that happens, you have to be strong. Your mother needs you at her side."

"I know," Jill said, her voice so faint I could barely hear her.

"How is your mother?" I asked.

"Okay, I guess."

Someone called to me that the cars were ready to leave. I waved, then looked at Jill and asked, "Would you like a cup of coffee?"

"Sure. That would be nice."

"Good. There's a new coffee shop not far from here. We can walk there in just a few minutes. Give me a minute to tell my friends I won't be joining them."

When I returned to the vehicles, I was asked whether it

was, in fact, Jill Walther. I confirmed that it was. "I sponsored her as a scholarship student at NYU," I said, "and she has some questions for me."

"Amazing how kids can turn out okay even when they have a father like Jake Walther," one of our particularly crusty citizens muttered. I ignored his comment, returned to where Jill stood, and we headed in the direction of The Swan, a delicatessen with a few Formica tables at the rear. It was good to be out of the cold. We were the only people there, and settled in a corner far from the counter. Steaming mugs of coffee in front of us, I smiled and said, "You look wonderful, Jill. New York City must agree with you."

It was evidently the right thing to say. Jill hadn't spoken a word during our walk from the cemetery. But my mention of Manhattan brought a glow to her face and animation to her voice. "I love it there, Mrs. Fletcher. New York City is so alive, so vibrant. It's filled with talented people. I've met so many wonderful writers, and my professors are terrific. I don't think I could ever thank you enough for helping me get the scholarship."

"It was my pleasure, Jill. Just seeing you so enthusiastic is all the thanks I need. Classes going well?"

"Yes. I'm having some trouble with a sociology course, but I'll get through it. I'm getting straight A's in my creative writing courses. And do you know what? I love the history class I'm taking. I hated history in high school. It all seemed so . . . well, so long ago."

I laughed.

"But now I realize that what we are today is based upon what we were back then, so I'm really digging into it. Maybe someday I'll write historical novels."

"One of my favorite types of book," I said. "How did you get home?"

"On the bus. It arrived last night after midnight."

"You must be exhausted."

"No, I'm really not. I guess with what's going on here in Cabot Cove, I won't have time to be exhausted. You said you saw my father yesterday."

"Yes."

"How was he?"

"As well as can be expected, considering he's in a jail cell. Why don't you go see for yourself?"

"Would they let me?"

"I think so. If you'd like, I'll call Sheriff Metzger and arrange it."

Her face turned glum again, and she sat back in her chair.

"Problem?" I asked.

"I'm not sure I want to see him . . . *there*. He might be embarrassed."

"That's always a possibility," I said, "but I'd still suggest you do it. I'm sure he loves you, and he can use love in return at this moment."

"I'll think about it."

"Good. Care for a donut?"

She shook her head. "I'm on a diet."

"Why would you be on a diet?" I asked. "You're a slender young woman."

"But I'm afraid I'll get fat, eating all that rich food in New York. We always ate simple at home. I guess because we never had any money."

"Things have been hard for your family, haven't they?" I said.

I'd learned how financially strapped the Walther family was when I was going through the process of getting Jill the scholarship. Family financial statements had to be submitted, and from what I saw, they lived hand to mouth. Being a poor farmer, of course, has its advantages. There's usually fresh fruit and vegetables in the good weather, and I knew that Mary Walther was an expert canner, which helped them get through the long, harsh Maine winters. But there wasn't any room for luxuries.

"Did you know Mr. Brent very well?" I asked.

My question seemed to sting her. An angry expression came and went on her thin face, and she started to chew her cheek.

"I mean, most people in Cabot Cove knew him, if only as Santa Claus at the annual Christmas festival. I just thought—"

"I didn't know him at all," she said with finality. "Why did you ask that question?" she asked defiantly.

"I'm not really sure," I said. "People say your father and Mr. Brent had a problem. Are you aware of any problem between them?"

"No." The same flat, angry tone.

"I think most of that rumor is coming from Mr. Brent's son, Robert," I said.

If she showed anger before, her face now reflected an inner rage. She took deep breaths, pursed her lips tightly together, and said, "Why would anyone believe anything *he* says?"

"I take it you know Robert Brent."

"Of course I do. We went to school together."

"I didn't mean to make you angry, Jill. It's just that now

that I've become involved to some extent with helping your father, I thought you might be able to give me a hint as to the relationship between your dad and Mr. Brent."

"They didn't get along," she said. "I *would* like a donut."

"Of course."

I returned from the counter with two cinnamon donuts on paper plates. Jill took a tiny bite and pushed the plate away.

"Any idea what the trouble was between them?"

She shook her head.

"You know, Jill, when I first met you and started to read what you were writing, I was very impressed by your keen sense of observation. Every good writer is a good observer, or should be, and you demonstrated a remarkable level of it even in high school. It seems to me that your power of observation might have been operating where your father was concerned, especially in his relationships with other people, like Rory Brent."

"Mrs. Fletcher, I know you're trying to be helpful, but do you understand how painful this is for me?"

"Of course I do. But the pain will go away if we can help your father establish his innocence. What was the problem between them?"

She paused, looked up at the ceiling, then back at me, and said, "I don't know."

"And I accept that," I said. "Eat your donut. I'd say it's getting cold, but we both know that isn't the case."

When the plates were empty except for loose cinnamon sugar, I asked, "Want me to make that call to Sheriff Metzger?"

She shook her head and stood. "I really have to get back to Mom. As you said, she needs me. Thanks for the coffee and the conversation. Oh, and the donut, too."

We parted in front of The Swan. As we shook hands, I felt an ache in my heart. Jill Walther was in obvious pain, and I was convinced it had to do with something more than her father having been accused of murder. Something very heavy was weighing on her, and I wanted to know what it was. I felt a certain proprietary interest in Jill Walther, and cared deeply. But I knew I wasn't about to find out much more at that moment, not on a cold December day on a sidewalk in front of a deli.

"I'd like to see you again while you're home," I said.

"You will. I really have to get home now. Thanks again, Mrs. Fletcher—for everything."

"Sure. Take care, Jill. Stop by the house anytime."

I considered calling Dimitri Cassis from the deli to get a ride home, but decided against it and set off at a brisk pace. A half hour later, I walked through my front door to the sound of a ringing telephone.

"Hello."

"Jessica? Joe Turco here."

"Hello, Joe. I was at Rory Brent's funeral."

"I was going to go, but decided against it. I really didn't know the man. Besides, I was sort of busy over at the D.A.'s office."

"And?"

"She's not sure she has enough to hold Jake Walther for Brent's murder. I gave her until five this afternoon to make up her mind. Frankly, I think he'll be home for supper."

"That's good news. I think."

"What do you mean, 'I think'?"

"Nothing."

What had prompted my involuntary comment was my ambivalence over whether Jake Walther should be set free. I didn't want to believe he'd murdered Rory Brent. But that didn't mean he hadn't. What if he had committed the murder, was let loose, and ran away, or worse, went on to kill someone else? Wanting something not to be, and having it turn out that way are often two different things.

Turco said, "The D.A. is a nice gal. More willing to listen than some D.A.s I met in New York. If she does let Jake go, she'll set conditions. She might want him to wear an electronic ankle bracelet so his movements can be monitored."

"A small price to pay for being home," I said. "Have you spoken with Jake again?"

"Yeah. I wish I could handle the case without ever having to spend time with him. Damn, he is an ornery type, defying everybody, including me. Must be a joy to live with."

"I'll be here all afternoon, Joe. Will you let me know how it turns out?"

"Of course. By the way, I closed on that real estate deal. Went smoothly."

"That's good to hear. Call me later."

I was immersed in writing Christmas cards when Seth Hazlitt called at four.

"Thought it strange, Jessica, you running off from the cemetery like that."

"Why was it strange? Jill Walther arrived, and I wanted to find out how things were going at NYU."

"*Ayuh,* but it still seemed strange to me. Sure you didn't go off to try and find out more about her father, and whether he killed Rory Brent?"

"Seth," I said, mock indignation in my voice, "I'm a writer in between books who has no interest in crime, real or fiction. I intend to spend the next few weeks simply getting ready for Christmas, and soaking in all the joy of the season. Started your cards yet?"

"Had them written a month ago."

I laughed. Typical Seth, doing things well in advance. Traveling with him always means arriving at the airport hours before a flight.

"Well?" he said.

"Well what?"

"What did you find out about Jake Walther and his relationship with Rory Brent?"

I sighed. "Very little," I said. "I asked, but Jill claims she doesn't know."

"Believe her?"

"Why shouldn't I?"

"How convincing did she sound?"

I thought back to The Swan; not very convincing at all. I told him that.

"I've been doin' some serious thinking this afternoon, Jessica."

"Always good to hear a doctor say that," I said. "Tough case?"

"Haven't been thinkin' about medicine. More a matter of giving some thought to Rory's murder."

"You're infringing on my territory."

"Isn't the first time."

"No, it isn't, and I must admit on those other occasions you were very helpful. Tell me what you've been thinking."

"Not especially keen on doing it over the phone."

"Oh? Something sensitive?"

"*Ayuh*. Thought you might enjoy a quiet supper over here at my place."

"What's on the menu?"

"Not to worry. I don't like Indian food, either."

"Then I'll be there. What time?"

"Make it seven. I'll pick you up."

"No need. Dimitri will do just fine."

I hung up and pondered the conversation I'd just had with my dear friend, the good Dr. Hazlitt.

Too sensitive to discuss on the phone.

That was unusual for him. My curiosity was piqued to such a level that I couldn't concentrate on writing personal messages in the cards, so I put them aside and got busy cleaning the kitchen, my favorite mindless activity.

Dimitri arrived at ten of seven. I was about to leave the house and get in his taxi when the phone rang. I considered letting the answering machine get it, but curiosity got the better of me.

"Hello?"

"Jessica. Joe Turco."

"Hi, Joe. I was hoping to hear from you again. I'm on my way out the door. Has Jake been released?"

"No."

"Oh? A snag?"

"A big one. The county police came up with a footprint in Brent's barn that places Jake there."

"But the sheriff said—"

"Yeah, I know what he said. He didn't find any prints that didn't belong there. He missed one. From what I've been able to gather, the sole print has an unusual mark on it, a break or a tear. Matches perfectly with a pair of boots owned by Mr. Jake Walther."

"Ouch."

"My sentiments exactly. I did my best."

"I know you did. Thank you."

"I still might consider representing him at trial."

"I'm glad to hear that, Joe. I have a taxi waiting. I'll call you in the morning."

"Okay. Funny, but as much as I dislike the guy, I really wanted to make it work."

"And you still may. Thanks for the update. Talk with you tomorrow."

Dimitri deposited me at Seth's house fifteen minutes later.

"How late can I call?" I asked him.

"As late as you want," he replied. "I hired another driver to work at night. His name is Nick. He's a cousin."

"That sounds like a smart move," I said. "Did he just move here?"

"Yes, Mrs. Fletcher. He's living with us. I spent all day showing him where things are in Cabot Cove. You will like him. He is a good driver."

"Just as long as he's as good as you."

Dimitri grinned. "No one is as good as Dimitri. I told him you were my favorite customer."

"That's sweet," I said, patting him on the shoulder from the rear seat. "I'll look forward to meeting your cousin later this evening."

As I stood on the sidewalk and watched Dimitri drive away, a surge of apprehension came over me. I turned and looked at Seth's front door. He'd never before expressed concern about talking to me on the telephone—about anything. What did that mean? I wondered. What startling revelation did I have in store?

The door opened, and Seth's corpulent figure filled the frame. "'Evenin', Jessica. Come in out of the cold. Scallops wrapped in bacon are just about ready, and the white wine is properly chilled."

Chapter Fourteen

S eth dropped me home a little before eleven. Dinner was good, no surprise. Although my doctor friend wasn't a particularly creative chef, he always did nicely with basic dishes. After scallops wrapped in bacon as an appetizer, we went on to a hearty navy bean soup, followed by what Seth insists is an original recipe—creamed crab meat on freshly baked waffles, a combination I never would have thought of, but admit is delicious—and filling.

But the evening's menu was not foremost in my mind once I was inside my house and had made myself a cup of tea. What did dominate my thoughts, and sent my mind racing, was what Seth had raised over dessert.

Before I could settle in my den and focus upon it, however, I had to return three phone messages that had been left on my answering machine.

The first was from Vaughan Buckley. It sounded urgent, and he encouraged me to return the call "at any hour."

"Jessica?" he said the minute he picked up the phone.

"Yes. I was out to dinner and just got your message."

"Thanks for getting back to me so soon. I just heard on the news that Mr. Walther has been formally charged with the murder of Santa Claus."

"You mean Rory Brent," I said, not sure why the way Vaughan put it nettled me.

"Yes, Rory Brent."

"Who carried the story?" I asked.

"One of the all-news radio stations here in New York. They're playing it up big, Jess. You know, a brutal murder during the holiday season, a leading citizen of a small Maine town gunned down just weeks before Christmas. On top of that, the victim was that same town's Santa Claus."

I sighed deeply and pulled up a chair. "This is all so unfortunate," I said.

"Yes, it is. Have you given any more thought to doing a book about the killing?"

"I'm really not interested, Vaughan. I'm too close to it, living here and having known both parties."

"You mean Brent and the accused."

"Exactly."

"But that's why you're the ideal person to write a book about it. You know these people, are tuned in to how they think. It's your town, Jess."

"Which is why I wouldn't want to write about something so tragic having happened here."

"We've received calls at the office concerning it."

"From whom?"

"Press. They know you're Cabot Cove's most illustrious citizen. They want to interview you."

"Tell them no."

"I can't tell them that, Jess. They have a right to ask questions, which I assume they'll do starting tomorrow."

"I refuse to be interviewed about this. You know how cooperative I am when it comes to publicity, but this is different."

"Of course it's different, and I'm not suggesting you do this to publicize anything. The publishing industry may have become crass, but not to that extent. I just thought I'd inform you that this little yuletide murder in your beloved town of Cabot Cove has taken on greater significance. It's now a national story."

"Thanks for tipping me off, but as far as doing a book about the murder, I pass."

"Your call, and I wouldn't attempt to influence you. Olga and I are still considering driving up for a few days. Is the offer still good to stay with you?"

"Of course it is. Just give me a day's notice."

The second of three calls on my answering machine was from our mayor, Jim Shevlin.

"Hope I'm not calling too late," I said to his wife, Susan.

"Not at all, Jess. We're watching television, although Lord knows why. All these new cable channels and less to watch. I'll get Jim for you."

"I got your message," I said when he came on the line.

"Good. Have you been getting calls from the press?"

"No, although I just got off the phone with my publisher in New York. He tells me some reporters have called him concerning Rory's murder."

"I've been getting calls, too. There are two TV news

crews arriving tomorrow morning, one from Portland, the other from New York."

"TV news crews! I can't believe this."

"I don't want to believe it, Jess. Of course, I suppose the story does have a certain cachet. You know, the Christmas festival, Rory having been synonymous with our Santa Claus, that sort of thing. You've heard, I assume, that the D.A. has formally charged Jake with the murder."

"Yes. Joe Turco called me earlier this evening to give me the news. Something to do with a footprint in Rory's barn."

"Right. It seems the county police picked up a print that Mort missed. It has an odd configuration in the sole, which matches a pair of work boots Jake owns. Pretty compelling piece of evidence."

"I suppose so. What do you suggest concerning the press?"

"We don't have any choice but to cooperate. This story has obviously gone public. Nothing we can do to cover anything up, nor should we. I just thought you might be willing to intercede a little on behalf of the town."

"My publisher said some of them wanted to interview me. I told him I wouldn't agree to be interviewed about something this tragic."

"Which I can certainly understand. But if you were to sort of . . . well, sort of act as the spokesperson for the town, it might take the pressure off me and some other people. We still have a festival to put on."

"Let me think about it," I said.

"Sure. I've called a meeting first thing in the morning to come up with some sort of battle plan. Will you join us?"

"I suppose so. Where and when?"

He told me.

The third call I returned was from Jack Decker, who publishes a monthly Cabot Cove magazine. Jack had been publisher of some of the nation's largest magazines before leaving the hustle-bustle of New York City and settling in Cabot Cove. I had reservations about returning his call. He did, after all, represent the press. But I also knew that he was not someone looking to capitalize on tragedy. His magazine was a loving monthly tribute to the town he'd adopted and had learned to love as much as those who'd lived there all their lives.

"Was hoping you'd get back to me tonight," he said.

"I assume you're calling about Jake Walther being formally charged with Rory Brent's murder."

"Exactly. I spoke with Jim Shevlin earlier this evening. He's concerned that the story has been picked up by the national media, and that some of them are heading for Cabot Cove tomorrow. I suggested he tap you as the official spokesperson for the town."

"That was *your* idea. Thanks a bunch, Jack."

He laughed. "Makes sense. Any reporter who shows up here will want to talk to you anyway, considering your stature. You might be able to deflect their attention."

"That's a role I'm not anxious to take on. I told Jim I'd attend a meeting with him tomorrow morning."

"I'll be there. We can discuss it then. By the way, I understand you were the one who got Joe Turco as Jake Walther's attorney."

"Word does get around. Yes. I brought Joe into the situation. He's not particularly fond of Jake Walther—but then again there aren't many Jake Walther fans around, are there? But he agreed to take the case, at least in its preliminary stages. Looks pretty bad for Jake, doesn't it?"

"I'd say so. Well, see you in the morning."

"Yes, you will. Best to Marilou."

All calls returned—and hoping no one else would call that night—I sipped my tea, which by this time had become cold, and seriously pondered what Seth Hazlitt had told me at dinner a few hours before.

What he'd related to me was shocking in and of itself. Compounding it was the difficulty he'd had in deciding to share it with me. He was appropriately circumspect, which I understood, considering the sanctity of the doctor-patient relationship. But that consideration was mitigated by the importance of the information as it related to Rory Brent's murder, and Jake Walther having been charged with it. Poor Seth, I thought. He'd found himself between the proverbial rock and a hard place. That he chose to share the information with me was, at once, flattering, yet unnerving. But now that he had, I had an obligation to follow through, whether I wanted to or not.

The problem was that I wasn't sure how to proceed, whether to have another discussion with Seth, or simply to act upon what he'd told me.

An hour later, without having come to a definitive conclusion, I decided that what was most needed was a good night's sleep. Tomorrow was another day, as the saying goes, although that contemplation wasn't especially pleasant, considering what it might hold in store.

Chapter Fifteen

The meeting started out in Mayor Shevlin's office, but quickly shifted to the courtroom because of the number of people who'd decided to attend.

Cabot Cove's courtroom doesn't get much use. It's in session two nights a week to handle traffic violations and other minor infractions, but seldom hosts anything resembling a prolonged trial. The last one I could remember was a year ago when Sheriff Metzger, working in concert with state police, broke a car theft ring operating out of an auto repair service on the outskirts of town. Stolen cars from all over the state were brought to this repair place to be painted, and to have their VINs altered. The trial lasted six days; the accused were convicted and sent to a penitentiary in northern Maine.

"Well, looks like we have a media event on our hands," the mayor said once he'd gotten everyone to settle down.

"A media circus, you mean," one citizen replied. "It's a

disgrace to be known as the town where Santa Claus was murdered."

"I second that," someone else said.

"It doesn't matter what any of us feel," Shevlin said. "The fact is a murder did take place in Cabot Cove, and the victim happened to be the person playing Santa Claus at our yearly festival. Obviously, that has piqued the interest of folks in the media, and they're coming here to report the story. Now, it seems to me that what we have to accomplish here this morning is to come up with a way to manage things so that everything goes smoothly, and that Cabot Cove comes off in the best possible light."

"I have something to say," Seth Hazlitt said. He and I sat next to each other in the front row.

"Yes, Dr. Hazlitt?"

"Rory Brent's murder doesn't have anything to do with the average citizen of this town. You know how reporters are. They'll be pokin' their noses into everybody's backyard, trying to get some dumb answer from them on how they feel about the murder. If you want to protect the image of Cabot Cove, I suggest anybody arrives here from the media be herded up and kept on a short leash. The story they're interested in is the murder. We've got a victim, and we've got the accused. The only access these folks from out of town should have is with Mort and his people, the D.A., and anyone else involved in the legal aspects of the case. After that, they shouldn't be allowed to talk to anybody."

A few people applauded.

Priscilla Hoye, chairperson of the Christmas festival, stood and faced the crowd. "I would be the last one to debate anything with Dr. Hazlitt," she said. Priscilla is an attractive middle-aged woman with short blond hair and a sunny disposition. She'd forged a successful career in public relations in the travel industry, but, like attorney Joe Turco, had become tired of the hectic pace of life in Manhattan, gave up her New York office, and moved to Cabot Cove. Her natural marketing and public relations skills had been quickly put to use by the festival committee.

She continued. "But I think we might be missing an important point. Yes, we don't want this unfortunate situation to cast a pall over the festival. At the same time, as you all know, we've pursued wider coverage of the festival than just Maine media outlets. We were delighted when that network talk show decided to broadcast from here last year during the festival. We send out news releases to all the major national media. So, having them arrive, even though it's for a different purpose, should be put to good use. An integral part of the story is that this murder occurred during the weeks leading up to the festival, and that this town refuses to be set back by it. The festival is going forward, and it promises to be the most successful in its history. I'm sure we can maneuver the press in such a way that they'll balance their reports of the murder with upbeat, positive stories about the festival and the town."

Now Seth stood. "Can't say that I agree with you, Priscilla. Seems a little naive to think the press would do anything positive. All they want is stories about blood and gore."

Priscilla, who'd remained standing, said, "I know that's the popular perception of the media, Seth, but it isn't necessarily accurate. I've been dealing with the press for many years, and I can assure you that if handled right, Rory Brent's murder will be only a part of the story, not the whole story."

"Seems like we should listen to Priscilla," a citizen said. "She's the expert when it comes to these matters."

"Nope, I go with the doc," said a gentleman from the rear. "Reporters are a bunch 'a ghouls. Let's do like Doc suggests, herd them up and make sure they don't stray."

A spirited discussion ensued, with those in attendance pretty much split on whose side of the argument they favored. As usual, our diplomatic mayor settled the matter by suggesting a committee be formed to make a decision about how much latitude to give reporters. Seth declined to be on the committee, and I was asked if I would participate. It wasn't high on my priority list, but I accepted.

"All I can say is you'd better get this committee workin' pretty fast," Seth said disgustedly. "From what I hear, the vultures will be descending on us any minute."

With that, the door to the courtroom opened, and two young men and a young woman entered. The men carried portable video equipment, including lights and a microphone dangling from a long boom. The young woman, obviously the reporter, led them up the center aisle and to the front of the courtroom.

Mayor Shevlin looked down from where he sat at the judge's bench and asked, "Who might you be?"

"Roberta Brannason, Fox News."

Shevlin straightened his tie and buttoned his suit jacket. "Welcome to Cabot Cove," he said in a voice usually heard only when he was campaigning.

"Thank you," Ms. Brannason said. "Who runs things around here?"

"Pardon?" Shevlin said.

"Who's in charge? We're here to cover the Santa Claus murder."

Shevlin looked to where Seth Hazlitt and I sat. He frowned, pursed his lips, then turned to the reporter and said, "I'm the mayor of Cabot Cove. But I suppose you'd like to speak with our sheriff, Morton Metzger."

The lights held by one of the two young men came to life, and the cameraman, the video camera propped on his shoulder, began recording.

"I'd like to speak with a lot of people," Ms. Brannason said, "starting with the person in charge of your Christmas festival."

"That would be Ms. Hoye," Shevlin said, indicating Priscilla, who went to the TV crew and introduced herself.

"We'd like to interview Jessica Fletcher, too," Brannason said.

"She's sitting right over there," Priscilla said, pointing at me.

The reporter, followed by her two colleagues, came to where I sat with Seth. "Roberta Brannason," she said, extending her hand. Seth and I stood; I shook her hand.

"I'm glad you're in town, Mrs. Fletcher," said Brannason. "I understand you travel a lot."

"Usually I do, but this Christmas I'm staying close to home."

"I understand you might be doing a book about the murder."

"I'm afraid you've received faulty information."

Ms. Brannason turned to her crew and said, "Let's get a wide shot of this room and the people in it," then turned to Shevlin. "Is this meeting about the festival and the murder?"

"Well, yes and no. Actually, we knew you were coming and—"

Brannason ignored him and instructed her crew where to position themselves.

She turned again to me and asked, "After we get some wide shots, I'd like to go where I could interview you in private, Mrs. Fletcher."

"I'm afraid I'm not about to become an interview subject, at least not where this tragic incident is concerned."

By now, with the meeting thoroughly disrupted, people had gathered around us.

"You probably know more about the case, Jessica, than anyone else, except for the sheriff and the district attorney," a woman said.

"Oh, no, you're wrong."

"Is the sheriff here?" Brannason asked.

"No," Seth Hazlitt said. "Got better things to do than hang around waiting for somebody with a camera and a microphone."

Ms. Brannason ignored him and asked me again if I would consent to an interview. Before I could answer, Jack Decker, the magazine publisher, who'd joined our little knot of people, said, "I think that's a splendid idea."

I glared at him.

"Jack may be right," Seth chimed in.

The reporter waited for the crew to join her.

"You'll have to excuse me," I said, overtly checking my watch. "I have an appointment."

"What's your phone number?" the reporter asked.

"It's . . . I'm in the book. Excuse me."

Seth followed me to the courtroom door. "Where are you runnin' off to in such a hurry?"

"I have an appointment with . . . with Dr. Colarusso."

"You just had your teeth cleaned."

"I know, but I feel a sudden toothache about to come on."

He looked at me quizzically, but didn't say anything else. I left the courtroom, walked briskly down the hall to the front door of town hall, and stepped outside. The sky was deep blue and without a cloud, the sunshine bright and glistening off the snow. I walked a block to a public phone, stepped inside the booth, pulled a scrap of paper from my pocket on which I'd written a number, and dialed it. A man answered.

"This is Jessica Fletcher. I'm calling from Cabot Cove. Dr. Seth Hazlitt called you on my behalf."

"That's right, he did," the man said gruffly.

"I'd like very much to talk to you . . . today, if at all possible."

There was a long silence.

"What time would be convenient for you?" I asked.

"I'm not sure we should be having this talk, Mrs. Fletcher."

"I know how delicate the topic is, Mr. Skaggs, but as you know, someone's life may hang in the balance."

After another prolonged silence, he said, "Noon? At my office?"

"That would be fine. Can you give me directions?"

After he had, I hung up and stepped out into the lovely December day. My temptation was to call Skaggs back and cancel our appointment. But I knew I couldn't do that, now that I'd put things into motion. I had no idea where the visit would lead, but if it would shed any light on what had happened to Rory Brent, I owed it to him, to his family, to Jake and Mary Walther—and to myself—to pursue it.

Chapter Sixteen

Thomas Skaggs lived in the town of Salem, about forty-five minutes south of Cabot Cove, just over the county line. I considered asking Dimitri to drive me there, but decided that discretion was the better part of valor in this situation. I checked the bus schedule and caught the eleven o'clock, which made a stop in Salem on its way to New York City.

I hadn't traveled on a bus in years, and found the experience enjoyable, although I suppose I might not have had the same reaction were I taking a longer trip. The ride was smooth and without incident; forty minutes later, I got off in front of Salem's small town hall.

I stopped someone on the street and asked for directions to the address given me by Skaggs. This friendly citizen gave me a big smile and informed me it was only two blocks away. I thanked her and walked slowly in the direction she'd indicated. Minutes later, I was in front of a prewar, two-story brick building in what appeared to be a residential area. I looked around; it was the only commercial building within sight.

I approached and read names on small brass plates affixed to the right side of the door. There were six occupants of the building, all of them having something to do—at least according to their names—with social work or counseling. The name at the top of the row was Here-to-Help, the organization run by Mr. Skaggs.

I stepped inside and looked at a directory on the wall. Here-to-Help was upstairs in office number six. I climbed the stairs, went to the door with the organization's name on it, and knocked. A woman's voice said, "Come in."

I stepped into a cramped reception area, where a middle-aged woman with carefully coiffed silver hair sat behind a metal desk.

"Yes?" she asked.

"I'm Jessica Fletcher. I have a noon appointment with Mr. Skaggs."

"Oh, yes, we've been expecting you. I can't tell you what a pleasure this is, Mrs. Fletcher, to actually meet you in person. I've read most of your books—Mr. and Mrs. Skaggs have, too—and we love them. Imagine, you living so close and never having met you. This is an honor." She got up, came around the desk, and extended her hand. "Let me tell Mr. Skaggs you're here."

"Before you do that, I'm a little unsure of what Here-to-Help does."

"Oh, I think Mr. Skaggs would be the best person to explain that to you. But basically, we're a resource for young men and women who've made a wrong turn in life and need some sort of restructuring."

"You mean counseling?"

"Yes, we do a great deal of that, too. But primarily we point them in the direction of other agencies that can more directly help them, depending upon the problem they bring to us."

The door opened, and we both turned. Standing in the doorway was a mountain of a man with a black beard, ruddy cheeks, and glasses tethered to his neck. He wore a rumpled tan safari jacket over a blue denim shirt, jeans, and sneakers.

"Jessica Fletcher?"

"Yes. You must be Mr. Skaggs."

"Tom Skaggs, and I would appreciate it if you would call me Tom."

"Provided you call me Jessica."

"We're already off on the right foot," he said in a deep, gravelly voice. "Please, come in."

His office wasn't much bigger than the reception area, but it had a comfortable feel to it because of the dozens of framed autographed photographs on the walls. I glanced at a few, which were pictures of him with familiar political faces.

"My personal rogues' gallery," he said. "You don't get paid a lot in this business, but you do meet a lot of important and self-important people. I keep telling the bank that holds the mortgage on my house that these pictures are worth something, but they never seem to agree."

I laughed. "I suspect there are millions of people with

that same problem, doing important good work, but not being recognized for it by bankers."

"Well said. Please, sit down."

I took one of six director's chairs that formed a semi-circle to one side of his desk. He plopped into a large, high-backed leather swivel chair and propped one sneaker—it had to be size fourteen—on the edge of the desk. "Well," he said, "I have a feeling you're about to cause me to break one of my most stringent rules."

"Which is?"

"Never to discuss anyone who's ever stepped through this door."

"I can understand and appreciate that, Tom, but I'm sure you agree that the circumstances make it the perfect time for you to break that rule."

"You may be right. From what I've been told by Seth Hazlitt, this could represent one of those extenuating circumstances. I believe in the law, but sometimes it has to be broken if the cause is great enough. Same goes for bureaucratic rules. Fill me in. Seth did his usual shorthand explanation. I suspect that you, being the great writer you are, will do a better job of weaving the tale."

"I'm not sure being a writer will help me in this situation, but I'll try to be concise. I'm a great believer in the old adage, 'If I had more time, I would have written less.'"

His laugh was as big as his body. "I like that," he said. "Go ahead. I'm all ears."

"I'm sure you've heard about the murder of Rory Brent, a successful farmer in Cabot Cove, and a man loved by everyone in town."

"Santa Claus at your yearly festival."

"Exactly. Our sheriff has made an arrest in the case, a gentleman—another farmer—named Jake Walther."

"Yes, I've heard about that, too."

"Jake Walther is disliked by many people," I said. "He's an unpleasant sort of man, rough-hewn and without what might be termed a warm and fuzzy personality. He was immediately suspected of the murder, mostly because of having rubbed people the wrong way. The deceased's son, Robert, claims that Jake Walther threatened his father, said he was going to 'blow his brains out.'"

"Sounds like the motive was there."

"Oh, yes, if the son is to be believed. At first, our sheriff only *questioned* Jake Walther in connection with the murder. Jake claimed to have had an alibi provided by his wife's brother, Dennis, who lives with them on the farm. But then Dennis changed his story and said he'd been threatened by Jake if he *didn't* provided that alibi. I should mention that Dennis is somewhat impaired. He's the sort of person who will agree with anything in order to not offend. There's speculation that our sheriff might have pressured him into changing his story, although I tend to dismiss that theory, knowing our sheriff as I do."

"I'm sure you're right in that assessment, Jessica, although it's possible, isn't it, that your sheriff influenced this fellow, Dennis, without meaning to."

I nodded. "Yes, that is always a possibility. I brought a young lawyer into the case, and he was confident Jake Walther would be released, based upon the grounds the sheriff and district attorney were using to hold him—nothing more than the deceased's son's claim that there was bad blood between the two men, and that Dennis had changed his story and says Jake threatened him. But then the county police discovered a footprint in the barn where Mr. Brent was murdered, and they further claim that Jake Walther owns a pair of work boots with a unique characteristic in the sole, some sort of tear or rip that matches the print found in the barn. Based upon that, he's being formally charged with the murder."

I sat back, confident I'd accurately portrayed the situation.

Tom Skaggs, too, leaned back and ran his hand over his beard. Finally, he came forward in his chair, placed his elbows on the desk, and cradled his chin in his hands. "I take it you aren't convinced that this Jake Walther committed the murder."

I shook my head. "No, that's not quite right. I don't know whether Jake Walther killed Rory Brent or not. Based upon this new piece of evidence involving the boot, I have to go with the sheriff's decision to charge him with the crime. On the other hand, there was such an obvious rush to judgment that I must wonder whether even our sheriff, and the district attorney, have been unduly influenced by public condemnation of Jake Walther. I'm not trying to clear him of anything. But I'm also determined that an innocent man not be charged with a heinous crime. We have the Christmas festival coming up, and you know how important that is not only to us in Cabot Cove, but to thousands of others who've come to depend upon our festival as an affirmation of the Christmas spirit."

Skaggs pondered what I'd said, stood, then went to a gray metal, four-drawer file cabinet in a corner of the office, where he withdrew a folder. He returned to his desk and opened the file.

"I understand how sensitive this is, Tom. But I also hope you see the necessity of knowing what actually happened. It could have an important bearing upon this case."

His response was to nod and flip through pages in the file, asking as he did, "Are you involved in this, Jessica, because of a professional interest? As a writer of crime novels?"

"Goodness, no," I said. "My publisher did ask me to consider writing a nonfiction book about the case, but I've declined. On the other hand—"

He glanced up. "On the other hand?"

I smiled. "On the other hand, I must admit to a certain genetic curiosity that has held me in good stead when writing my novels, but that sometimes gets me in trouble."

He returned my smile. "Curiosity killing the cat?"

"Fortunately, not yet. I just want to make you aware that I'm cognizant of the difficult position this puts you in, just as it put Dr. Hazlitt in an awkward posture."

"No need to further explain. If I wasn't going to open these files to you, I would have said so right from the beginning. I've known Seth Hazlitt for years. He's one of the most honorable and ethical physicians I've ever met, and I come in contact with a lot of them because of what we do here. No, I'm willing to share this with you and answer your questions, provided we keep it between us, in this room. In other words, you can use what you learn, but can't tell anyone where you learned it. Fair enough?"

"It will have to be."

"Okay, here's what happened. Jill Walther was referred

to this agency by Dr. Hazlitt a year ago. She was a senior in high school, and I understand was a very good student. I'm also led to believe that she was not the sort of young woman who might be termed 'promiscuous.' "

"I certainly would concur with that. I got to know Jill pretty well because of her writing talent. I arranged for a scholarship for her to New York University."

"I didn't realize that. A nice thing you did for her."

"I did only what I thought was justified."

"Does Jill know everything going on with her father regarding the murder?"

"Yes. She came home on Christmas break a few days early once she heard about it. She's with her mother at the farm."

"You say you got close to her. She never mentioned any of this?"

I shook my head. "Not a word."

"I suppose I'm not surprised," he said. "The reason she was sent here, after all, was to get her out of your county. I was reluctant when Seth Hazlitt first called about her. My experience has been that when a young person messes up, it's better to face things right where they are, with the people they know. But there seemed to be some additional pressure involved, and I certainly wasn't about to say no. We seldom do when a young person is referred to us."

"I know that Dr. Hazlitt referred her to you," I said. "I also know the reason she went to him."

"A sad thing when a high school girl becomes pregnant. It's a national epidemic. For some reason, these young women think having a baby will give their lives something worthwhile, something to love and to love them back.

They never stop to realize that they've put their entire lives on hold, never consider the tremendous financial responsibility having a child entails."

"I certainly agree with that," I said. "Tragic when a young woman forfeits her future by becoming pregnant before she's ready emotionally and financially to raise a child in the proper way. But my understanding from Seth Hazlitt is that this was not the result of a deliberate act on her part. There was the question of whether she was raped, and became pregnant by virtue of that."

"That's right. Frankly, I honestly don't know the circumstances that led to her pregnancy. She told me she'd been raped, but it wouldn't be the first time I've heard that from a girl suffering guilt, and trying to lay the blame off on something, or someone else. Did Dr. Hazlitt indicate what he felt had actually happened?"

"No. He told me she claimed when she went to him that she'd been raped. She wanted him to arrange for an abortion, even do it himself. Of course, he refused and urged her to go to the police. She said she couldn't do that."

"Exactly the same thing she told me when she was here. Does Dr. Hazlitt have any idea who the alleged rapist was?"

"Not that he told me. Did she give a name to you?"

He shook his large, shaggy head. "I urged her to bring charges, too, but she was adamant about not doing it. I have the feeling she was afraid that if she named the person, there might be serious repercussions. I didn't press; it's not my job to press."

I thought for a moment, then asked, "Did she come here seeking an abortion?"

"Yes."

"And you refused as well, I assume."

"We're not in the abortion business. I wanted her to stay in our group home for a few days and receive some counseling before making up her mind about what to do. She refused that as well. I gave her the names of two respected abortion clinics. That's protocol with Here-to-Help. I pointed out other options—delivering and keeping the child, or putting it up for adoption. All I could do."

"Did she come here alone, Tom? I mean, was she accompanied by anyone?"

"Not that I'm aware of. I asked her whether someone had brought her, and she said no. I felt very sad seeing her walk out of this office after the brief conversation we had. She seemed like an extremely intelligent and decent girl. I think I could have helped her if she'd stayed."

"Do you know if she went on to get an abortion?" I asked. "I mean, I suppose I have to assume she did since I'm not aware she had a child. If she did have a child— no, that's impossible. I spent a great deal of time with her throughout her senior year. She must have aborted the baby."

"I'd say your assessment is correct."

"Do you have any idea *where* she had the procedure performed?"

"Not a clue."

"Did she pay for your services?"

"No, nor was she asked to. We're funded by the state, some federal funds, and charitable donations. We don't take money from the young people we serve, although there are times when a family member will insist upon making a donation to the agency. We never turn them down." He laughed.

"Did anyone offer such a contribution on her behalf?"

He grunted as he searched for an answer. "Not that I can recall, although sometimes such contributions are made long after the young person has been helped by us, and made anonymously."

"Do you keep records of contributions made according to their source? I mean, would you have a list of contributors to this agency from, say, Cabot Cove?"

"Mrs. Witherspoon is a fanatical record keeper. She makes a note of everything. I wouldn't be surprised if she has the height and weight of every contributor in her files, along with eye and hair color. Want me to ask her?"

"If you would."

He left the office, leaving me with some time to consider what he'd said. That Jill Walther had become pregnant in her senior year of high school was certainly a shock, not because I'm unaware that such things happen, but that it happened to her. Of course, her claim that she'd been raped cast a very different light on her situation—if that claim was true.

I was still digesting what he'd told me when he poked his head in the door and asked, "How far back do you want me to go?"

"Not too far," I replied. "Maybe the period immediately following her visit to you."

When he returned, he carried with him a computer printout. He sat behind his desk and scrutinized it while I waited. "Yeah, there were a couple of donations from Cabot Cove during the three months following the date of my meeting with Jill. A couple of small contributions, but one impressively large." He laughed again. "We could use more people like this. Interesting donor, based upon what you've told me."

"May I see the list?"

"Sure."

He positioned the printout on his desk so I could peruse it. The name came off the page with physical force. Rory Brent had made a contribution of five thousand dollars shortly after Jill Walther sought the counsel of Here-to-Help.

Chapter Seventeen

I had to wait two hours for a bus back to Cabot Cove, and spent the time browsing quaint shops and enjoying a tuna salad sandwich in a pub that seemed to be a popular gathering spot for Salem's business community.

I was virtually alone on the bus, for which I was grateful. I've always found traveling, whether on a plane, an ocean liner, or even a bus, to be good thinking time. The problem was the bus ride was so short that I'd barely began to codify what I'd learned from Tom Skaggs when we pulled up to the small, two-bay bus station in Cabot Cove.

It was four-thirty. Although the sun continued to shine, albeit with less intensity as it neared the horizon, the weather had turned colder, the sort of bone-chilling, dry cold that seems to occur only on clear winter days in Maine.

Dimitri's cousin, Nick, was parked at the curb. I got in the back of his taxi and he drove me home.

"How are things working out?" I asked as I signed the

small chit that would become part of my monthly bill for cab services.

"Very good, ma'am," he said. "I like it here. This is a good place."

"Cabot Cove? Yes, it certainly is," I said, getting out of the taxi as he stood holding open the door. I'd reset the timers on my outdoor lights to go on earlier, and the one in front did as we stood in my driveway, illuminating the pretty wreath on my door.

"Are you getting ready for Christmas?" I asked.

"Oh, yes, but there is so much to do. America is a busy place, especially when a holiday comes."

"It certainly is," I said. "Thank you for the ride. Say hello to Dimitri."

I brought in the mail, turned up the heat, which my frugal New England heritage has me turning down to the lowest possible level whenever I'm not there, and made a fire in the fireplace.

I sat at the kitchen table and started going through my mail. Most of it consisted of bills, although there was an envelope with only my handwritten name on it. I opened it and read:

Mrs. Fletcher—I want very much to interview you about the Santa Claus murder. I'll make myself available any hour of the day or night—you name the time and place. Other people in town have been very cooperative all day, and I was hoping to meet up with you again. We're staying at Morton's Boardinghouse—it was the only place we could find rooms in town. Please call me the minute you get this message—Roberta Brannason.

She included Morton's phone number.

I put the note aside; I was in no mood to talk to Ms. Brannason, or any other member of the press for that matter.

The phone rang.

"Hello?"

"Jessica. Seth here."

"Hello, Seth. I just came back from Salem."

"Yes, I know. Tom Skaggs called. You'll have to fill me in on what transpired between you."

"Well, he basically confirmed that—"

"Not on the phone, Jessica. Free for dinner?"

"Yes, although I'd prefer to have a quiet dinner alone right here at the house."

"As you wish. Heard from the reporters?"

"Only Ms. Brannason, the reporter from Fox News. I take it more have arrived."

"*Ayuh,* they certainly have. You'd think the president of the United States was holdin' a summit meeting in Cabot Cove. Got to hand it to Priscilla Hoye. She seems to have them all pretty much in hand. Knows how to deal with them, somethin' I wouldn't want to do."

I laughed. "They can be an aggressive lot, that's for certain."

"By the way, Jessica, seems to me we ought to start pickin' the stories we'll be readin' to the children at the festival."

"You're right, although I thought we should confer with Cynthia before making any decisions."

"My thinking exactly. Well, if I can't get you to agree to let me buy you dinner, I'll wish you a good evening."

"And the same to you, Seth. Please understand. I'd love to, but not tonight."

"Of course. But I do think we should meet up tomorrow, say at my office at ten? I don't have patients till one."

"Fine. Put me in your appointment book."

Although I wanted to settle down for the evening, content myself with some snacks for dinner, and get back to writing Christmas cards and answering correspondence, I was too restless to accomplish any of that. I found myself pacing the house, the events of the past few days flooding my brain. So I did what I often do when faced with such mental confusion. I took out a yellow legal pad and pen, sat at my desk, and listed everything I'd learned to date:

- The victim, Rory Brent, successful farmer and beloved figure in town, found murdered in his barn a half mile from his house wearing only shirtsleeves. Killed sometime in the morning.
- Brent's wife, Patricia, away visiting her cousin, Jane, in Salem, Maine. (Just occurs to me that Tom Skaggs and his Here-to-Help organization is located there, too.)
- Patricia says she took an early bus, the trip took forty minutes, and she returned on the one o'clock bus.
- Brent's son, Robert, seemingly untouched by his father's death—claims Jake Walther threatened his father. Known that bad blood existed between Rory Brent and Jake Walther. Walther disliked by many people in town.
- Walther initially claims his brother-in-law, Den-

nis, was fixing a stone wall with him the morning of Brent's murder. Dennis confirmed that. Then, Dennis changes his story and says Jake threatened him unless he provided that alibi, and that he was *not* with Jake the morning of the murder. Question is, can Dennis be trusted in what he says?

- Jake's wife, Mary, seeks help for her husband. I bring attorney Joseph Turco into picture. Looked like Jake would be released until county police determine that a footprint on the barn's dirt floor, missed by Mort Metzger, had a unique sole print matching boots owned by Walther. Walther now charged with Brent's murder.

- Jill Walther, Jake and Mary's daughter, pregnant in senior year—referred to a social agency in Salem by Seth Hazlitt. Tom Skaggs confirms that a pregnant Jill Walther came to him, and that he gave her names of two abortion clinics. Also says he counseled her on other options, including giving birth and keeping the baby, or putting it up for adoption.

- Jill Walther claimed she was raped, but refuses to name the person. Who was it?

- Shortly after Jill's visit to Here-to-Help, Rory Brent makes a big financial contribution. What connection does the Brent family have with Jill's pregnancy?

- My next move? Confront Jill Walther with my knowledge she'd become pregnant? To what end? I have no right knowing that information— unless it bears directly upon murder, it should remain her business. Still, could be a valuable piece of information. Possibility: discuss it with Mort Metzger. No!!!! If I do anything, must be face-to-face with Jill.

I'd no sooner written that last line when the phone rang. It was Roberta Brannason, the Fox News reporter.

"Glad I caught you, Mrs. Fletcher," she said brightly.

I wish I could say the same.

Instead, I said, "Well, you have. I was gone for the day."

"Mind if I ask where?"

My guffaw was involuntary. "Of course I mind. Where I go is none of your concern."

"I just thought it might have to do with the Santa Claus murder."

"Ms. Brannason, Santa Claus was not murdered in Cabot Cove. Mr. Rory Brent was, a leading citizen. Frankly, I think treading upon the fact that he played Santa Claus at our yearly festival is distasteful."

"Hey, Mrs. Fletcher, don't jump on me. I'm just developing a story the way my bosses want me to."

"Well, maybe you should tell your bosses they're on the wrong track. Now, what can I do for you?"

"Give me a half-hour interview."

"Out of the question. I told you I would not grant an interview having to do with this tragedy."

"I talked to your publicity director at Buckley House in New York. She said she hopes you'll cooperate. Help sell books, you know."

I am normally a very patient person, and I understand the need of reporters to press as hard as they can to get a story. After all, that is their job, and I respect it. But there are times when the press has strained my patient nature, and this was developing into one of those times.

I tried to divert her attention by saying, "I understand a number of your media colleagues have arrived."

"Yes. It's a big human interest story, Mrs. Fletcher. I understand how you feel, but the public has an insatiable appetite for stories like this, especially when they involve a major holiday—like Christmas."

"That may be, but—"

"Were you in Salem today following up on some aspect of the murder?"

"Was I in—? How did you know I went to Salem?"

"By asking a few simple questions around town. My network has sent up two investigative reporters to help me develop the story. Someone at the bus station said you'd bought a ticket to Salem."

"I must say, I'm impressed, Ms. Brannason."

She laughed. "We're pretty good at what we do. Isn't Salem where Mr. Brent's wife went the morning he was murdered?"

"I'm even more impressed now."

Another laugh. Then, in a more serious tone, "Look, Mrs. Fletcher, I don't want to unduly interfere with your life. But we're going to do this story one way or the other, and it really would mean a great deal to have the famous Jessica Fletcher, the most illustrious citizen of Cabot Cove, give me an on-air interview. Please? Won't you at least consider it?"

"I'm always willing to consider most anything, Ms. Brannason."

"Call me Roberta."

"I'll think about it . . . Roberta. In the meantime, I'm busy this evening doing some paperwork. I'm sure I'll see you around town tomorrow. We can chat then." I didn't give her a chance to respond because I quickly added, "Good night. Thank you for calling," before hanging up.

I received other calls that night before going to bed, none of them having to do with the murder. Mostly they were from people wanting to discuss the upcoming festival. I enjoyed those conversations. They certainly were less weighty than murder.

But the final call of the evening, which came in just as I was preparing to go to bed, was from Joe Turco.

"Hope I'm not calling too late," he said.

"Not at all. I'm happy to hear from you. Anything new?"

"I'd say so. They're releasing Jake Walther."

"What? Why? How did that come about? I thought—"

"It seems there's some conflicting theories about that footprint found in Rory Brent's barn. The county police say it matches the sole on one of Jake's boots. But another scientist from the same lab claims they don't match. Anyway, while they're thrashing out conflicting theories, I put the arm on the D.A. I've been with her all night. I told her that she absolutely has nothing to justify holding Jake in jail. As I told you, she's a pretty levelheaded person. She finally agreed with me that there wasn't enough evidence to indict, and so he's being let go. Should be on his way back to the farm by now."

I had the same ambivalent set of feelings as when it was first anticipated that Jake would be allowed to go free. I was delighted for him and his family. On the other hand, I had that lingering question of what would happen if he had, in fact, killed Rory Brent.

But I couldn't let that color my thinking. The man was innocent until proved guilty, and up until this point no such proof existed.

"You've done a marvelous job for someone who dislikes his client so much," I said.

His laugh was weary. "Every lawyer I know has done work for clients they couldn't stomach, absolutely hated. It isn't important how a lawyer feels about a client. What *is* important is that the law be followed, and justice be served. I'm just glad it worked out this way, at least for his wife and daughter. I just learned about her. Jill, is it?"

"Yes. She and I . . . well, Joe, it was good of you to call and give me the news. You sound like you could use some sleep."

"What I could use is a drink and some dinner," he said, "which I intend to take care of right now. Good night, Jessica. Talk to you tomorrow."

Before going to bed, I added a final item to my list: Jake Walther released. What next?

Chapter Eighteen

"Hello, Mary."

I'd just finished showering when Mary Walther called.

"No, you didn't wake me. I've been up for an hour. I heard the good news about Jake. Joe Turco called me last night to tell me he'd arranged for Jake's release."

Mary Walther's voice did not mirror the sort of joy I expected. She said flatly, "I suppose it's good news, Jessica, although I have to be honest with you. I'm very worried."

"About Jake?"

I thought back to my previous conversation with her in which she'd indicated her concern that Jake was capable of doing something destructive. It was that conversation that had led Seth, Mort, and me to the farm, resulting in Mort's taking Jake into custody. Was she voicing the same concern this time?

I asked.

"I don't know how to explain it, Jessica," she said. "Naturally, I'm pleased that he's not in jail any longer. But—"

"But what?"

"Could you come to the farm today? I know it's an imposition—I've imposed upon you enough already—it is, after all, the Christmas season, and I know how busy you are, but I just thought—"

"Of course I'll come. How is Jill doing?"

"That's part of my concern. You will come?" Her voice brightened.

"Yes. What would be a good time for you?"

"Well, I'm not quite sure at the moment. Maybe midday? Yes, about noon. I'll make some lunch."

"No need to do that," I said. I knew of their dire financial situation; the last thing Mary Walther needed, with everything else on her plate, was to be making lunch for visitors.

"I look forward to you coming," she said.

I dressed, tidied up the house, and checked my personal calendar for the day. I'd promised to meet with Seth Hazlitt in his office at ten. Other then that—and, of course, with a trip to the Walther farm now on the schedule—I was relatively free, which meant I might actually get around to doing some Christmas shopping.

In previous years, when I'd been away from Cabot Cove in the days leading up to Christmas, I'd done my shopping in big cities like New York or London. Shopping for gifts in Cabot Cove would be a welcome deviation from that pattern, and I looked forward to it. With only a few exceptions, Cabot Cove's shopkeepers are extremely pleasant and helpful. Not only do they offer an array of interesting and useful gifts, there is psychic satisfaction from buying locally and supporting their efforts.

It was an overcast day, but no snow in the forecast, and I decided to walk into town. I'd put on my down jacket, hiking boots, red-and-black plaid scarf, and woolly hat, and was about to go out the door when the phone rang. Rather than pick it up, I let the answering machine do its work, and stood next to it waiting to hear who was calling. Call screening certainly comes in handy on occasion.

I wasn't surprised that it was the Fox news reporter, Roberta Brannason. "Please, Mrs. Fletcher, just fifteen minutes for an interview. I promise I won't take any longer than that. I'm not sure where we'll be during the day, but if you're in town, I'm sure we'll bump into each other."

Glad that I'd opted to not pick up, I set off at a brisk pace toward the village. I had a few minutes to kill before my ten o'clock appointment with Seth, and stopped in to visit with Peter and Beth Mullin in their flower shop. With Christmas coming up fast, Beth and seasonal helpers she'd hired for the holidays were extremely busy. Her husband, she told me, was spending most of his time making deliveries—"Cuts into his poetry writing," she said, laughing. When Peter wasn't helping run the shop, he was writing poetry for which he'd gained a sizable reputation in Cabot Cove, and gave Monday night poetry readings at a trendy, cozy coffee house that had opened within the past year.

"Anything new on Rory Brent's murder, Jess?" Beth asked, not looking up from an elaborate floral arrangement she was creating.

"No," I said, "except that Jake Walther has been freed."

That announcement stopped her in midtask. She looked at me, eyes opened wide, and said, "I hadn't heard that. I thought they'd pretty much identified him as the murderer."

"That's the prevailing understanding of most people in town, Beth, but there's evidently been a classic rush-to-judgment. Something to do with a conflict over the lab analysis of the shoe print found in Rory's barn. Jake is back at the farm."

Beth frowned and bit her lip. "I'm not sure letting Jake Walther loose was a great idea."

"Why do you say that?"

"Oh, we all know the man is irrational. And irrational people can do . . . well, irrational things."

I had to silently agree, although I worked hard at the moment to override my emotional response with a more cognitive one. I decided not to respond, but asked instead, "Is Joe Turco upstairs?"

"I think so," she said, returning to her arrangement. "He came in a few minutes before you did."

"Think I'll pop up and say hello," I said. "Save some poinsettias for me, Beth. I love them in the house this time of year."

Joe Turco was drinking coffee and munching on a Danish when I arrived at his open office door.

"Come on in," he said.

"Just stopped by to say hello, and to thank you for letting me know about Jake's release."

"I suppose I should consider it a legal victory."

I entered the office and took a chair across the desk from him. "Why do you say you 'suppose' you should consider it a legal victory. It is, isn't it? I mean, from a lawyer's perspective, arranging for a client to be released has to be viewed as some sort of triumph."

"I know, I know," he said, wiping his mouth with a paper napkin and tossing it along with the empty Styrofoam cup and paper plate into a wastebasket. "Maybe if the guy were a little nicer, I'd feel better about it. When I went down to police headquarters to give him the news and escort him out, all he did was glare at me and growl some obscenity. He's a real head case, Jess. What's that word for it? You know, that Maine slang."

"*Jo-jeezly*," I said. "I really feel bad having gotten you involved with him."

"Don't. I did what I was supposed to do as his attorney."

"What will happen now? I mean, what's the next legal step?"

"That depends on whether the labs get their story straight on the shoe print. The D.A. released Jake on his own recognizance. He's been told he can't leave the farm. There was some talk of using an electronic monitoring system, something strapped around his ankle that can be monitored from a central station."

Thinking of the concern Beth had expressed downstairs, I said, "That sounds like a sensible idea. Why wasn't it done?"

"Because Sheriff Metzger and his department don't have such a system. He could have gotten it from the county, I suppose, but the D.A. decided not to press it. Walther assured her he would abide by the rule to stay at his farm, and he promised me the same thing—when he wasn't cursing under his breath."

"I got a call from Jake's wife. She sounded concerned now that Jake is back home, and asked me to come to the farm to talk with her. I'm going there at noon."

"Well, give my best to my lovely client if you see him. In the meantime, I have to get a contract ready for a closing this afternoon. This business with Jake Walther cut into my normal routine, put me behind a little."

"Did Jake say anything about paying you?" I asked.

"No, of course not, and I wasn't looking for it. There's nothing else for me to do at this point. Unless, and until, the D.A. can resolve the dispute between the lab people and come up with more of a solid case against Jake, he'll cool his heels at his farm. I could petition the court to force the D.A. to officially remove him as a suspect, and to have the home restriction lifted. But I have to think about that a little bit. I'm not sure it's the right move to make at this juncture. Good to see you, Jess. Have a good day."

Seth Hazlitt had just finished frying up a batch of apple fritters when I arrived, and insisted I join him for one, and coffee, at his kitchen table.

"Anything new, Jessica?" he asked.

"No. Oh, did you hear that Jake Walther has been released?"

"*Ayuh*," he said, pouring maple syrup over his fritters. "Spoke with Mort first thing this mornin'. Seems the lab folks have a bit of a conflict over Jake's boot."

"That's what I was told. Enough of Jake Walther. Let's get down to choosing stories for this year's reading. By the way, the fritter is excellent."

Seth showed me a list of Christmas stories he'd jotted down on a yellow legal pad. "I especially like this one," he said, pointing to the title, " 'The Dog That Talked at Christmas.' "

"I don't think I'm familiar with it," I said.

"Lovely story. About a dog that breaks the canine code of silence. You know, all dogs can talk, but they know that if they do, they'll have to go to work."

"Who wrote it?"

"Wonderful writer named Laurie Wilson."

"Fun," I said, laughing. "What are the other stories you'd like to do?"

"Got a couple of others, Jessica. Not as well known as the standard ones. Ever hear of 'A Christmas to Remember,' by a fella named Coco?"

"Can't say that I have."

"Nice story. Santa comes to help a brother and sister fix a broken star on their Christmas tree."

"And does he?"

"And does he *what*?"

"Fix the star."

"Of course he does. He's Santa Claus."

"A happy ending. Good. That's two. I was thinking of 'Carl's Christmas.' "

"Doesn't ring a bell."

"By a wonderful writer named Alexandra Day. It's about a dog named Carl who—"

" 'Nother dog story."

"They're always the best. Carl is put in charge of a family's baby and takes the child on a Christmas tour of everything wonderful about the season. Beautifully illustrated, too."

"Speaking of illustrations, I got Cynthia to agree to

blow up pictures from the books we use, maybe even project 'em on a screen."

"That's a wonderful idea. What's next?"

We eventually decided on five stories—"Nutcracker Ballet," the Christmas staple "Rudolph the Red-Nosed Reindeer," "The Dog That Talked at Christmas," "The Lonely Snowman," and "The Littlest Christmas Elf."

By the time we finished, it was almost eleven-thirty.

"Well, this was a fruitful session," I said, "but I have to run. I'm due at the Walther farm in a half hour."

Seth fixed me in a quizzical stare. "Didn't know you were goin' out there, Jessica. What brings this on?"

"I forgot to mention it. Mary called and asked that I speak with her."

"Strange," Seth said.

"Why?"

"Now that Jake is back home, I wouldn't think there'd be any reason for you to go out to see Mary. Did she say what she wanted to talk about?"

"Just that she was worried. I suppose she needs a female shoulder to lean on. Even though Jake has been let go, this still must be a terribly stressful time for her. For all of them."

"I suppose it would be. Sure you don't want to think twice about it, Jessica?"

I stood, put on my coat and hat, and went to the front door. "I don't see any reason why I shouldn't go out there, Seth. I feel sorry for Mary and want to be as much help as possible, especially at this time of year. To be facing these sorts of troubles at what should be a joyous season makes it doubly difficult."

"Why don't you stop by here on your way back home. I'd like to hear what transpired."

"If I have time. Will you call Cynthia with the list of stories?"

"*Ayuh.* Do it the minute you're gone. How are you gettin' there?"

My laugh was involuntary. "I forgot to call Dimitri," I said. "Silly of me. Can I use your phone?"

"No need. I'll drive you."

"I wouldn't put you out like that."

"No trouble at all."

"But I don't know how long I'll be there. I don't think you should come in with me."

"I won't wait—just drive you there and drop you off. You can call Dimitri for a ride back."

"All right," I said. "But we'd better get going. I don't like to be late—to anything."

We drove slowly to the Walther farm, taking in the scenery as the village slowly melted into countryside. Seth was deep in thought; I eventually asked him what he was thinking.

"I was thinking how unsettling this whole Rory Brent business is. I mean, everybody points a finger at Jake Walther. He's questioned by Mort, then arrested. They're going to let him go, but then they discover a footprint in Rory's barn that matches one of Jake's work boots. The D.A. decides that's enough evidence to charge him with the murder. But then the lab experts can't agree whether the footprint really matches the boot, so they let Jake go. I suppose what I'm wishin', Jessica, is that it would be resolved one way or the other—right now! Either Jake Walther killed Rory Brent and is officially charged with the crime, or he's absolved of any guilt. This town needs some closure." He turned and looked at me. "You agree?"

I nodded. He was right. With the Christmas festival getting closer and closer, not having a resolution to Rory's murder made things that much worse. Which is not to say that I would want Jake Walther falsely accused in order to neaten things up. But if Rory Brent's murderer had been identified beyond a reasonable doubt, it would go a long way to putting to rest the minds of a lot of people in Cabot Cove.

Seth was the first to spot the vehicles parked on the road in front of the Walther farm. There was a television remote truck with a huge antenna protruding through its roof, and three cars. People milled about.

"Damn press," Seth said, slowing down.

"Not unexpected," I said. "Everyone knows that Jake Walther has been released and is confined to the farm. That's where the action is, at least as far as the media is concerned."

Seth pulled to the side of the road and stopped, then started to make a U-turn.

"What are you doing?" I asked.

"Heading back to town. You don't want to be in the middle of this media feeding frenzy."

I put my hand on his arm. "No, I'm going in to see Mary Walther. I promised, Seth. I suspect she needs me, and I want to be there for her."

His sigh said many things, mostly that he was frustrated with me. Nothing new there.

"Drop me in front of the farm," I said, "and go back

into town. Take care of whatever it is you have on your
agenda. They can't make me talk to them, and I won't. I'll
simply go into Mary's house and spend some time with
her. Okay?"

"You are a stubborn woman, Jessica Fletcher,'" Seth
said, turning the wheel and proceeding toward the other
vehicles.

"I know," I said. "But you're still my friend, aren't
you?"

Seth chuckled. "Can't imagine anything you could do
to change that," he said. "If you have trouble gettin' hold of
Dimitri, give me a call and I'll come back out to get you."

"Fair enough."

When I opened the door to get out of Seth's car, those
standing in front of the farm immediately headed in my
direction, led by the Fox TV reporter, Roberta Brannason.

"Mrs. Fleltcher, good to see you. Did you get my message?"

I lied. "No. Did you call me?"

"Yes. I got your answering machine. But it doesn't matter because here you are."

"Yes, here I am," I said.

"Did you come to see Jake Walther?" she asked.

"I'm here to see his wife, Mary. Excuse me. I have an
appointment with her."

I started to walk up the narrow, rutted road leading
past the first house on the property, in which Jake lived,
and to the middle house, where Mary—and, now that she
was home from college—where Jill Walther lived, too. I
glanced at Jake's house as I passed. There was no sign of
life. The curtains were closed. So was the door. Then I

noticed smoke wafting from a metal chimney pipe jutting up through the roof. Someone was there, presumably Jake.

Ms. Brannason and members of her crew fell in step behind me.

I stopped halfway up, turned, and said, "Please. Mary Walther is a friend of mine, and I'm here on a social visit. I have nothing to say to you, so I suggest you go back to your vehicles and continue waiting for something to happen. It's not going to happen with me, I assure you."

I started to resume my walk when Ms. Brannason grabbed my arm. Her action angered me; I turned and glared at her.

"Mrs. Fletcher, all I'm trying to do is my job. I don't want to intrude on your life. I know that you're a famous personality, and I respect that. But I don't understand why you won't talk to me for even just a few minutes. You probably know more about what's going on with Mr. Walther and the investigation than anybody else in town, except maybe for the sheriff and the district attorney. What are you *hiding*?"

"Hiding? I'm not hiding anything. But if I were, it is my right to do so. I understand that you are doing your job, and I'm not looking to hinder that. But it doesn't mean that I'm under any obligation, legally, ethically, or morally, to talk to you about this tragedy that has occurred in a place I love very much. Maybe later today, or tomorrow. In the meantime, I'm running late for a date with a friend. Have a good day, Ms. Brannason."

I stepped up onto the porch of the house, hesitated, then knocked on the door. I heard sounds from inside.

Eventually, the door opened, and the frame was filled by Mary Walther.

"Hello, Mary."

"Thank you for coming, Mrs. Fletcher," she said, holding open the door.

"I'll come in only if you call me Jessica, or Jess."

"I know, you've said that before. I'm sorry. Please come in . . . Jessica."

I stepped into the small, spartan living room. I didn't immediately notice that another person was present, sitting in a wooden chair in a corner to my right. I turned and looked. It was Dennis Solten, Mary's brother.

Dennis hopped to his feet and lowered his head so that his eyes were directed at my feet. He held a crumpled hat in his hands and wore soiled bib overalls and heavy boots.

"Hello, Dennis," I said.

He managed to glance at me past the top of his head, nodded, muttered something unintelligible, and returned his focus to the floor.

"I hope you don't mind that Dennis is here, Jessica," Mary said. "I thought you might be interested in something he has to say."

"I'm always happy to see Dennis," I said. "I remember the good work you did around my house, Dennis. As a matter of fact, there are some things I could use help with now."

"Yes, ma'am," he mumbled.

"Please, let me take your coat," said Mary, reaching out. I slipped out of my coat and handed it to her. As she went to another corner of the room to hang it on pegs protruding from the wall, I took the moment to glance about the room. Although it wasn't particularly attractive, there was a certain warmth and comfort to it that was appealing.

"Please, sit down," I said to Dennis. He did as he was told.

"I made some tuna salad and tea," said Mary.

"I'm really not very hungry, but if it's made, I'd love some. Tuna is one of my favorites."

"It's with real mayonnaise I make myself," said Mary. "I know I should offer some with low fat—everybody seems to be eating low-fat things these days—but I've just never gotten into that."

"Sometimes I think people are into it a little too much," I said. "Homemade mayonnaise will be just fine."

Mary went to the kitchen, leaving me alone in the room with Dennis. It was obvious he was not about to initiate conversation, so I took the lead.

"How have you been, Dennis?"

"Pretty good, I guess," he replied, not looking at me.

"I suppose you were very busy when Jake was away from the farm."

"Yes, ma'am."

"You must be happy to have him home again."

"Yes, ma'am, only . . ."

I sat forward in my chair. "Only what?"

"Jake, he's . . . he's sort 'a mad at me."

"Is he? What is he mad about?"

"About what I said to the sheriff."

"Yes, I know what you mean. The problem was that there was confusion about what you said. First you claimed you were working with him the morning of Mr. Brent's murder, but then you said something else. And if I'm not

435

mistaken, you said Jake threatened you if you didn't tell that original story."

Dennis didn't answer, just slumped a little more in his chair and nervously twisted the brim of his hat. It was then I realized that he and I were not completely alone. I turned; Mary stood in the kitchen, peering into the living room.

"Dennis and I were just chatting about Jake's being home," I said to her.

She seemed surprised that I'd noticed she was listening, and said, "That's nice. Would you like tea, or I have some raspberry lemonade."

"Tea would be fine."

"I'll only be a minute," she said, disappearing from my view.

Dennis and I sat silently until I said, "Mary said you might have something interesting to tell me, Dennis."

He squirmed in his chair and tightened his grip on the hat.

"Dennis? What was it you wanted to say?"

I glanced over my shoulder; Mary had positioned herself again so she could observe and listen.

Dennis drew a series of deep breaths, rolled his eyes around looking at everything but me, then said into the air, "I wasn't with Jake that morning."

"That's what you told Sheriff Metzger the second time. Did Jake really threaten you if you didn't originally claim that you were with him?"

I don't know what he said, but it seemed to indicate an affirmation.

"Why are you repeating this to me now?"

"'Cause . . . 'cause Mary will tell you I'm not lyin'."

I turned once again in the direction of the kitchen, but Mary wasn't there this time.

I returned to Dennis. "What do you mean that Mary will tell me you aren't lying?"

" 'Cause she knows where I was that morning. She was with me."

I sat up straight and processed what he'd said. Why hadn't Mary come forth before with information that would prove that Dennis had not been with her husband the morning of the murder?

I turned in my chair and looked up at Mary, who now stood directly behind my chair. "Dennis says that—"

"It's true, Jessica. Dennis wasn't with Jake that morning."

"Where was he?"

"Helping me tend to the chickens."

"The chickens? Here on the farm?"

"Yes."

"Why didn't you tell Sheriff Metzger this right away?" I asked.

"Because I didn't want to hurt Jake. It was better that the sheriff think Dennis was with him."

"But that's . . . that's withholding evidence, Mary. It amounts to lying to the sheriff."

"I did it because Jake is my husband. A wife should stand by her husband."

"I certainly agree with that, in most instances. But Jake was charged with murder. Whether he had an alibi was crucial for the authorities to determine who killed Rory Brent."

"I suppose you're pretty disgusted with me, Jessica."

"Not at all. I can understand the dilemma you were in. It must have been a very difficult decision to make."

"I'm a God-fearing woman, Jessica. Always have been. I was taught not to lie, and I never do. But when they said Jake had killed Rory Brent, I just knew I had to help him."

I turned to Dennis. "And you told the sheriff you were with Jake because Jake threatened you if you didn't?"

"Yes, ma'am."

"What caused you to change your story?" I asked.

"I dunno. I guess I just didn't like having to lie to the sheriff. Made me nervous. I get nervous a lot."

I understood, but didn't see the need to reinforce his sudden pang of conscience.

I turned to Mary. "Why are you telling *me*? Have you told anyone else?"

"No."

"Will you? Will you go to the sheriff and tell him this?"

"I don't want to, that's for certain."

"If you don't want the sheriff to know, why not just keep it entirely to yourself?"

Her broad face became a mass of wrinkles as she pondered the answer. Finally, she said, "Because like I said before, Jessica, I'm a God-fearing woman. I feel like I did when this thing first happened, when I had to make a decision about what to tell people. I don't know what to do, and that's the plain and simple truth. You were the one I came to right away when Mr. Brent was killed, and when Jake was acting strange. I came to you because you seem to have a level head on your shoulders, and would help me do the right thing. I feel that way now, and that's why I asked you to come here today. What should I do, Jessica?"

"I'm afraid I have only one answer, Mary, and that's for you to go to Sheriff Metzger and tell him this. No one can make you do that, but it's the right thing. It's the *only* thing, especially for someone who, as you say, fears God."

The truth was, I'd never been someone who believed in fearing any God. For me, God—whoever he or she might be—is a benevolent force somewhere out there, to be loved, never feared. But I understood that there are many people who were brought up to believe differently, and this was not the time to get into a religious debate.

"Will you go with me to the sheriff?" Mary asked.

"No, Mary. This doesn't directly concern me. I suggest you call him. If you want to do that while I'm here, that's fine. But no, I don't think it would be appropriate for me to go with you."

"But you came over with that young lawyer to help me. You were at the house the night the sheriff took Jake away. It would mean a lot to me, Jessica, to have you at my side when I go in and admit my lie, admit that I did a terrible thing."

I stood and placed my hands on her beefy arms, looked her in the eye, and said, "Mary, you haven't done a terrible thing. You've been under tremendous stress, and I'm sure the sheriff will understand that."

Her face became soft, almost childlike, and I wondered if she was about to cry.

"Yes, I'll come with you to the sheriff."

We didn't bother eating lunch that day. Ten minutes

after Mary had made her confession, we were outside and ready to climb into their battered pickup truck. The press was still camped on the road.

Dennis got behind the wheel. I was about to get in the truck when I remembered that Mary had said on the phone she was worried about Jill, whom I'd forgotten about.

"Where is Jill?" I asked.

"Sleeping."

"In your house?"

"Yes. Poor girl. She's been crying her eyes out ever since this happened."

I turned and looked at the small house. An upstairs curtain parted, revealing Jill Walther. Although I was a distance from the window, I could see the anguish etched into her pretty, young face. I raised my hand to wave, but she quickly closed the curtain and was gone from my sight.

"I'd like to see Jill again before she goes back to school," I said.

"I don't think that will be possible," said Mary.

"Why?"

"I've convinced her to go back early—day after tomorrow."

"She won't be home for Christmas?"

"Better to be away from here until all this is settled," Mary said.

"I . . . well, that's your decision . . . and hers."

As we slowly drove down the rutted access road, we had to pass the house in which Jake lived. He was on his small porch. I thought Dennis might stop, but we drove right past without acknowledgment. I looked in the rearview mirror and saw him clearly. He was leaning against the door and holding a rifle that dangled at his side. It was a chilling sight, one I would not soon forget.

Roberta Brannason and the other members of the press stood on the road. She waved; I didn't return it. What I was thinking was that I hoped she, and her colleagues, wouldn't be foolish enough to approach Jake. He looked like he meant business.

Chapter Nineteen

I accompanied Mary Walther and Dennis into police headquarters, where Sheriff Mort Metzger sat in his office, eating a slice of pizza. He glanced up, wiped his mouth with the back of his hand, and came around the desk. "What brings you here?" he asked.

"Mary has something to tell you, Mort," I answered.

"Oh?" Mort's eyebrows went up. "And what might that be?"

"Maybe we ought to sit down," I suggested.

"Sure, Mrs. F., sure thing."

Since there were only two spare chairs in his office, he yelled out the door for someone to bring in a third.

Once seated, I looked at Mary, gave her a smile of encouragement, and said, "Go ahead, Mary. It's the right thing to do."

Mary told Mort that she'd been with Dennis the morning of Rory Brent's murder.

"Doin' what?" Mort asked.

"Tending to the chickens and trying to fix a wall of the chicken coop that was falling down," she said.

Mort looked at Dennis. "That true, Dennis?"

Dennis nodded, hat clenched tightly in his hands, eyes focused on the floor.

"So, what you're saying," said Mort, "is that not only was your original story about being with Jake that morning a lie, you now have someone to corroborate your second story, that you *weren't* with him."

"Yes, sir," Dennis mumbled.

"Okay," said Mort. "But what about your claim, Dennis, that Jake threatened to hurt you if you didn't come up with that first story about being with him? You still stand by that?"

Dennis glanced nervously at Mary before replying, "Yes, sir. He certainly did."

Mort sat back in his chair, formed a tent with his hands beneath his chin and grunted. After a moment, he said, "I appreciate your coming in to tell me this. But I've got to tell you, Mary Walther, that lying to a law enforcement officer isn't taken lightly around here."

I said, "But she didn't lie, Mort. She simply didn't offer the information, and I don't think you asked her whether she was with Dennis that morning."

"Maybe lying is too strong a term," Mort said. "But it certainly involves withholding information. Wouldn't you agree, Mrs. F.?"

I didn't answer. It seemed to me there was no longer a reason for me to be there. I said, "Mary confided this in me, and we agreed to come to you, Mort. She wanted to get it off her chest because it was weighing heavy. I admire her for that."

I gave her another smile.

"Now that she has," I said, "and unless you have anything else to ask her, I suggest we all get about our business."

"No need for you to stay, Mrs. F.," Mort said. He turned to Mary and Dennis. "But I'd like you two to hang around a few minutes more. I've got a couple of questions that need answering."

A look of panic came over Mary's face. I stood, went to where she sat, placed my hand on her shoulder, and said, "There's nothing to worry about. All you have to do is tell the truth."

Mort said, "You realize, don't you, Mrs. Walther, that what you've told me this morning isn't calculated to help your husband any."

Mary agreed.

"I suppose you didn't want to tell me this in order to protect him."

"Yes, sir, that is the truth," she said. "A woman has to stand by her man. That's the way I was raised."

"Admirable enough, but sometimes when the law is involved—especially murder—that rule doesn't always hold up."

"I'll be off," I said, "I have things to do."

"Want a ride back home?" Mort asked. "Tom can—"

"No, thank you, Mort. I have errands to run here in town. Besides, a walk will do me good. Good-bye, Mary. Good-bye, Dennis."

Mary stood and thanked me for my support. Dennis didn't move from his chair, although a slight twitch of his head indicated, I suppose, that he was responding to my words.

I walked at a leisurely pace from police headquarters to the center of town. My first stop was the Post Office, where I'd heard they were selling a special edition of Christmas stamps. I bought a hundred of them on self-stick sheets, spent a few minutes chatting with Debbie and Jim, two of our friendly, helpful postal clerks, left the building, and stood on the street. It was still overcast, and a breeze had picked up from the east. Although snow hadn't been forecast, I could smell it in the air. You live in Maine long enough and your nose becomes extremely sensitive to the possibility of snow, no matter what the official forecast.

I went to the building housing Olde Tyme Floral, waved to Beth, and went up the stairs to Joe Turco's office. He didn't see me in the doorway because he was hunched over an office machine in the corner of the room. I cleared my throat. He stopped what he was doing, turned, and shook his head.

"What are you doing?" I asked.

"Trying to program phone numbers into this new fax machine I just got. Ordered it from a catalogue. Great machine, but it takes a Ph.D. in space science to program in the numbers. You've got to push one button after another, and by the time I remember to push the next one, the menu the previous button brought up is gone."

I laughed. "How are you at programming VCRs?"

"Even worse than programming fax machines."

"Well, don't let me interrupt you."

"I'm glad you did. What's up?"

We sat, and I filled him in on what had happened that morning with Mary Walther and Dennis.

His response was to shake his head and say, "Not good for my client."

"I suppose not, although the fact that Dennis can't provide an alibi still doesn't say Jake murdered anybody."

"True, but it just keeps looking worse and worse for him. Maybe the lab techs will never get together on the shoe print. That's the key piece of evidence. If they ever come to an agreement, Jake will find himself facing a jury."

"Joe, I was wondering if you would do me a favor."

"If I can."

"I'm interested in what the town records indicate about the Walther farm."

"What do you mean?"

"Well, Rory Brent's son, Robert, claims that his father and Jake Walther had a real falling-out. I remember distinctly his saying that they argued more than a month ago over 'land and money.' Yes, those are precisely the words he used. 'Land and money.' "

"So?"

"So, I've been around long enough to have seen some pretty irrational behavior where land and money are involved. What I'm wondering is why such an argument would take place between Jake and Rory Brent. Rory's farm isn't adjacent to Jake's property. What interest would Rory Brent have in the Walther farm?"

Turco chewed his cheek, shrugged, ran his index finger around the inside of his ear, and said, "I can't imagine public records would shed any light on that, Jessica, but I'm willing to take a look. Easy to do."

"I know it is, and I realize I could do it myself. But I just thought that any information contained in those records might have more meaning for an attorney."

"Could be. I'll hop over to Town Hall right now if you'd like."

"No rush. You do have that new fax machine to program."

"No, I don't. I think I'll give it up and just punch in numbers when I need to send a fax. Or, have a couple of stiff drinks later today before trying again. Where will you be for the rest of the day?"

"In town. I promised Seth Hazlitt I'd drop by his office after coming back from the Walther farm. I'll do that, get in a little Christmas shopping, and then head home."

"If I come up with anything, I'll give you a call."

I started to leave the office, but he stopped me. "You know what I've been wondering lately, Jessica?"

"What's that?"

"I've been wondering where Rory Brent got his money."

"Oh? That seems fairly obvious. He ran an efficient and profitable farm. At least that's what I've always heard."

"I've heard that, too. But I have some successful farmers as clients. While they do pretty well, none of them will ever get rich working the land."

"I suppose not. It's a tough way to make a living, as the saying goes. Maybe Rory had family money. Or Patricia."

"Maybe. Just a thought. I'll be in touch."

Seth was with a patient when I arrived at his office, located in a wing of his stately Victorian home. His nurse, Pat Hitchcock, who worked part-time for him, greeted me warmly and said he wouldn't be long.

"Any other patients due?" I asked.

"No. Slow day, Jess. Getting ready for Christmas?"

"Trying to. I thought I'd block out this afternoon for some shopping."

"My shopping was done a month ago," Pat said. "All my cards written, too."

"I envy you. Every year I promise myself to get a running start on cards, have them in the mail no later than the middle of November. But as my father used to say, 'The road to Hell is paved with good intentions.'"

"How true, how true," she said. "Excuse me, Jess. I have to get some paperwork done before I leave."

Seth's patient, a young woman named Anne Harris, who'd recently moved to Cabot Cove, was introduced to me by the good doctor.

"I've wanted to meet you since moving here," she said. "I do some writing of my own."

"Really? What sort of writing?"

"Nothing major. Some poetry, short stories."

"Short stories," I said, "the hardest form of writing."

"So I've heard. I thought I'd like to try my hand at writing a murder mystery."

"Then you should do it," I said.

Seth, recognizing a familiar scenario in my life—someone aspiring to write murder mysteries and wanting me to become involved—said, "Good to see you Mrs. Harris. You pick up that prescription and take it until it's run out, heah?"

"I promise," she said lightly.

When she was gone, I followed Seth to his study, where he was engaged in—what else?—the writing of last-minute

Christmas cards. He poured tea from a teapot Pat Hitch-cock had placed on his desk and said, "All right, fill me in, Jessica. What happened out at the Walther farm?"

I told him.

"Must have been difficult for Mary to tell that to Mort. Doesn't do her husband's case any good."

"Yes, it was difficult for her, Seth, but I'm proud that she found the courage to do it. I also stopped in Joe Turco's office before coming here."

"And how is our young attorney friend?"

"Just fine, although he's having trouble programming phone numbers into his new fax machine."

Seth laughed. "You'd think they'd come up with a way to make programming those infernal machines easier. Must be some sort of plot against consumers. Time for Ralph Nader to get involved."

"Seth, Mary told me Jill Walther is going back to college early, leaving the day after tomorrow."

"That's odd, isn't it?" he said.

"I thought so. I asked her about it, and she said she thought it was better for Jill not to be here in Cabot Cove while all of this is going on with her father. I've got to talk to her before she goes."

"Shouldn't be difficult. Just go back out there."

I shook my head. "No, Seth, there was something in Mary's tone that told me *she* did not want me to talk to Jill. She didn't state that, of course, but I sensed it."

"Why would she want to keep you from speaking with her daughter? After all, Jessica, you were the one who got her into college, got her that scholarship. Seems to me you'd be the first person welcome at the house."

"I feel that way, although what I did for Jill doesn't give me any automatic rights to spend time with her. But I have to see her, Seth. I have to clear up, if only for my own sake, this business of Jill's having sought abortion counseling, and Rory Brent's making a big contribution to the counseling center right after she was there. I'm also intrigued with what Robert Brent said."

"Which was?"

"Robert said his father had argued with Jake Walther over 'land and money.' That's why I stopped up to see Joe Turco. I asked him to check public land records to see if there was any link between Jake Walther and Rory Brent from a real estate point of view. I just know there's a relationship of some sort between those two men that goes beyond Jake's surly disposition."

"*Ayuh,* you may be right, Jessica. Funny, while I was waiting for Mrs. Harris to arrive, I started thinking about Patricia Brent."

"Rory's wife?"

"*Ayuh.* Everybody's looking to Jake Walther as the likely murderer, but no one is looking at anybody else."

"Seth, you aren't suggesting that Patricia might have murdered her husband."

"I'm not suggesting any such thing. But I am talking sense. The only suspect is Jake Walther. What about Patricia? Wives have killed husbands before. And what about that son of theirs, Robert? Barely showed any emotion about his father gettin' murdered, at least according to what I've heard."

He was right, of course. Not that I suspected Patricia or Robert Brent of being capable of doing such a dreadful thing. But with all the focus on Jake Walther, it seemed that Mort and his deputies hadn't looked beyond him. Yes, there had been speculation—no, make that *hope*—that Rory Brent had been murdered by a passer-through, a stranger, someone with no connection to Cabot Cove. We all fervently wished that.

But what if he had been killed by a Cabot Cove resident—someone who knew him well, someone whom we all knew well? Rory was a popular citizen. He knew many people, maybe the majority of Cabot Cove's population. And because he was a prosperous farmer, he'd undoubtedly had many business dealings, perhaps with someone who became angry at the way a business deal came out.

"You know all the basic reasons for someone murderin' somebody else, Jessica—passion, greed, money, family tensions. Could be somebody got real mad at Rory and flew off the handle."

I shook my head. "I don't think so, Seth, not the way Rory was killed. It was a deliberate act, well thought out in advance. Maybe not *too* far in advance, but it certainly wasn't a sudden flare-up that resulted in physical harm to him. Somebody wanted to kill Rory Brent—and did."

"I suppose you're right. Did you get a chance to talk with Mort while you were over at headquarters?"

"No. I just stayed long enough to lend some moral support to Mary. Mort wanted them to stay a little longer to answer some questions. I left."

"More tea, Jessica?"

"No, thanks. I'd better be running along. I promised myself some time for Christmas shopping."

"What will you be getting me this Christmas?"

I laughed. "I have a very special present in mind for you, Dr. Hazlitt, and wild horses could not pull it out of me. You'll just have to wait until Christmas Eve."

I'd be spending Christmas Eve, after festival activities had ended, with Seth at his home, along with twenty or so other guests.

"Got a special present picked out for you, too," he said.

"Tell me."

"Wild horses couldn't pull it out of me," he said.

I finished my tea and was about to leave when his doorbell rang. I accompanied him to the door. Standing on his wide, wraparound porch was a television crew, led by a middle-aged man. I looked beyond them and saw Mort Metzger getting out of his sheriff's car and heading up the walk.

"And who might you be?" Seth asked the reporter.

"Gary Kraut, Portland TV," the man said. "We just arrived in town to report on the Rory Brent murder. We understand you were his physician."

Seth glared at them.

Mort joined us, and they immediately turned their attention to him.

"You're the sheriff," Kraut said. "What's new in the Brent murder?"

"Excuse me," Mort said and turned to Seth and me. "Got a minute?"

"Of course," Seth said. The three of us returned inside and closed the door in the face of the television crew.

"I just left Joe Turco," Mort said, removing his Stetson and placing it on a small table in the entrance hall.

"You did?" I said, thinking of my request that Turco research public real estate records in Town Hall.

"Thought it only right to run the news past him before acting on it," Mort said.

"What news?" I asked.

"About Jake Walther."

"Stop beatin' around the bush, Mort," Seth said. "Just tell us what the news is."

"Well, seems the lab boys have gotten their act together. No doubt about it, they tell me. The footprint on Rory's barn floor is a perfect match to that boot owned by Jake."

I thought back to what Joe Turco had said, that unless that match was made, Jake would probably remain in the clear.

"Interesting development," said Seth. "What happens now?"

"I've got a call into the D.A. Hope to meet with her before the day is out," Mort responded. "Seems to me there's nothing else to do but go arrest Jake."

"Again?" Seth and I said in unison.

"Afraid so, Mrs. F.," Mort said.

"Think this time it'll stick?" Seth asked. "Folks in this town are getting downright tired of Jake Walther goin' in and out of jail."

Mort looked at Seth with a hurt expression, as though his good friend was being critical of his police work.

"Didn't mean anything by it, Mort," Seth said. "But you get my drift. Seems to me if you arrest Jake Walther again, it had better be for good this time."

"I wouldn't argue with that," Mort said. "Reason I came by was to ask you, Mrs. F., if Mary Walther, or that strange brother of hers had anything else to say when you were with them."

"No," I said. "The only thing of substance Mary said is what she told you at headquarters."

"Just checkin'," Mort said. "I'll leave you two to whatever it was you were talkin' about."

"I was just leaving when you arrived," I said.

"Got those media vultures outside," Mort said.

"Tell 'em to go away," Seth told our sheriff. "They're on private property up on my porch."

"I'll do just that. Need a lift, Mrs. F.?"

"I think I'll take you up on that, Mort, considering they're outside. Drop me in town where I can do some shopping?"

"Certainly will. Christmas shopping?"

"Yes. I—"

"Got any ideas about what you'll be gettin' me for Christmas?"

Seth and I looked at each other.

"Jessica and I have just been talking about that, Mort. You'll have to wait until Christmas Eve."

"Just remember that if it's clothing, I don't like green. Always had a funny feeling about green clothes, like they were bad luck."

I sighed, smiled, and said, "Mort, I promise the tie I buy you will not be green."

"A tie? I've got a closet full of ties. I was thinking more along the line of—"

"Come on," I said, picking up Mort's Stetson from the table and handing it to him. "If I don't get downtown, I'll never get my shopping done."

Chapter Twenty

I made a silent pledge to myself as I got out of Mort's car in the middle of town that I would blot out everything having to do with murder for the rest of the afternoon.

Although I'm not especially fond of shopping in general, Christmas shopping is another matter. I take great pleasure in finding just the right gift for those I love, and was not about to allow a self-imposed pall to taint that activity.

"I'd appreciate it, Mrs. F., if you wouldn't mention what I told you to anybody else," Mort said, leaning across the seat and speaking to me through the open passenger window.

"Count on it," I said. "You will let me know if Jake is brought in again."

"Yes, I will," he said, resuming his place behind the wheel. I started to walk away, but he stopped me. "If I were

you, I'd stay far away from the Walther farm. No telling
how Jake will react if he gets wind I'll be taking him in
again."

I nodded and said, "Thanks for the advice, Mort. Talk
with you later."

Actually, I'd already done some of my Christmas shopping. Seth Hazlitt loves miniature soldiers, particularly
those from the Civil and Spanish-American wars. He has
elaborate displays of them in his office, and I'd ordered a
set from a shop in London whose card I'd taken the last
time I was there. They would be arriving by mail any day.

I started at the far end of town, going from store to
store, consulting my list of gifts to buy as I went, and thoroughly enjoying the process. The shopkeepers were in excellent spirits, and I found the perfect gifts for a number
of people on my list.

Mort Metzger loves board games and had once in-
vented a murder mystery game that he came close to selling to Parker Brothers. But the deal fell through at the last
minute over certain changes requested by the company
that Mort refused to make. One of our local gift shops had
just received a brand-new game, a whodunit set in Los Angeles. I bought that, as well as a fancy new cribbage board
for Mort, making sure that none of the inlaid pieces on the
board or the pegs themselves were green.

I would have continued shopping except that my load
of gifts had gotten heavy. I decided to call it a day and head
for home. I checked my watch. It was almost five. Night
had fallen; it had become noticeably colder.

"Call Dimitri for you, Jessica?" the owner of the last
shop asked when I mentioned I was going to my house.

"If you wouldn't mind," I said.

Dimitri's cousin, Nick, arrived a few minutes later, helped me load the packages into the back of his vehicle, and drove me home. The timers had turned on my outside lights, one of which cast an appealing glow over the large wreath on my front door.

I thanked Nick, signed the receipt, and got out of the cab.

"I will help you in with the packages," he said.

"Thank you," I said. "I didn't realize I'd bought so much."

"Because you have so many friends," he said pleasantly, loading his arms with the bags and boxes and following me to the front door. I opened it for him. He carried the gifts into my living room and placed them on the couch.

"Thanks, Nick," I said. "That was kind of you."

"No problem, Mrs. Fletcher." He is fond of saying "no problem" in response to most comments made to him by customers.

As I escorted him back to the front door, we were both brought up short by a sound emanating from the rear of my house. It sounded as though someone had tripped over something and fallen.

"What was that?" I said.

Nick didn't answer. Instead, he returned to the living room and approached the door to my study. Another sound was heard, this time a door opening.

Someone was there!

Nick entered the study, with me bringing up the rear. I'd just reached the open doorway when I saw someone swing an object at Nick. It caught him on the side of his head and sent him sprawling to the floor.

"Who are you?" I shouted.

With that, the figure lurched across the room and ran through open French doors leading to a small patio at the back of the house. I didn't see him clearly; it was too dark, too gloomy, for that. None of the lights in the room had been on. But as he ran out to the patio, one of the outside lights caught his face and torso for a fleeting second.

It was Robert Brent!

Or was it?

I fought the urge to take pursuit. Instead, I dropped to my knees next to Nick, who now sat up and massaged the back of his neck and side of his face, groaning as he did.

"Are you all right?" I asked.

"I think so," he said weakly.

"My God, why would such a thing happen?" I asked myself aloud as I stood, went to the wall, and flipped on the overhead lights. Nick had been struck with a foot-tall metal cup, the largest of a set of four I'd purchased in Turkey many years ago. Fortunately, the set was not made of heavy metal, and the damage to Nick was minimal. He seemed more shocked than physically injured.

I helped him to his feet. He immediately went to the open French doors and peered out beyond the lighted patio into the darkness. His assailant was gone, presumably having jumped over hedges lining the perimeter of that end of the property.

"Close the doors," I said. "He's gone."

Nick secured the doors, turned, and faced me. "Who would do such a thing?" he said. "In your own house."

"I don't know."

Although I thought the person I'd seen was Robert

Brent, I couldn't be certain of it. It had all happened so fast. It looked like him, but if I were asked to attend a police lineup, I knew I would never be able to say beyond a doubt that he was the one who'd been in my house moments ago.

"You must call the police," Nick said.

"Yes, you're right. Please, sit down. Would you like some tea, coffee? A drink? Brandy?"

He shook his head. "No, Mrs. Fletcher, I am quite all right. Please, call the sheriff."

Mort Metzger and a deputy were at my house within minutes. Mort ascertained that the intruder had entered through a window in a small bathroom just off my study. Obviously, using the French doors to escape was a lot quicker and easier than retracing his steps through the window.

"You didn't get a look at him, Mrs. F.?" Mort asked.

"Well, I did, but only for a second. Not long enough to *really* know who it was."

Mort fixed me with a skeptical stare. "Sounds like you're fudging a bit. Sounds like you did see who it was, but don't want to say because you can't be a hundred percent sure."

"It looked to me like . . . I hate to say this, because you're right. I can't be sure. It looked to me like Robert Brent."

"Rory and Patricia's boy?"

"Yes. Again, Mort, it happened so quickly that—"

"Saw his face?"

"Yes. Well, not so much his face. It was his hat and jacket."

"Hat and jacket?"

"He wore a blue baseball cap backward, and a black-and-red wool mackinaw."

"Did he now? Seems to me Robert Brent wore that the day he came into town with us."

"Exactly."

Mort scribbled something on a pad he carried, looked at me, and said, "I think I'll head out to the Brent farm and have a talk with young Mr. Brent."

"I suppose that's what you have to do."

"Have you checked for anything being stolen?" he asked.

"No. I haven't even thought about that. But as you can see, whoever it was was looking for something in my desk." Drawers had been opened, and papers tossed on the floor.

"Well, Mrs. F., I suggest you do a quick inventory, see if anything's missing. You can let me know about that later. Right now, I'd like to hightail it out to the Brent farm. Want Tom to stay with you?" He indicated his deputy.

I shook my head. "No, I'm fine, just fine."

"You okay, young fella?" Mort asked Nick.

"Yes, sir, I am all right. I was glad I was with Mrs. Fletcher and could scare him away."

"Probably was a good thing you weren't alone, Mrs. F. Well, make sure you lock the doors behind me."

They all departed, leaving me alone in the house. I felt an intense chill, which had nothing to do with air temperature. More a reaction to the reality that someone had violated me and my home.

As I walked around the house, looking for signs that something had been taken, I kept hearing noises. I knew they were in my mind, irrational responses to what had just happened, but I couldn't help it.

I settled down and made myself a cup of tea before

tackling the task of picking up the papers that had been strewn about my study, and checking to see whether any documents were missing. It seemed to me nothing was gone, although it was hard to make that judgment.

I kept seeing the face I'd seen in the light of the patio. It *was* Robert Brent—or maybe it wasn't. The only thing I was sure of was that the intruder wore a blue baseball cap backward on his head and a black-and-red wool mackinaw. Hardly enough to accuse him of having been the one to break into my home. From what I'd been able to observe, wearing a baseball cap backward had become almost a uniform for teenagers. That the cap was blue wasn't helpful. Most baseball caps are blue, aren't they? A red-and-black mackinaw? Hardly a unique item of clothing in Maine in winter.

If only there had been a second more for me to observe him. The last thing I wanted was to falsely accuse someone.

Seth called a half hour later. He'd heard from Mort about what had happened and wanted to check on me.

"I'm fine," I said. "When did Mort tell you? Had he already gone out to the Brent farm?"

"I don't know, Jessica," Seth replied. "He called me from his car, said I should ring you up to make sure everything was all right. That's what I'm doin'."

"And I appreciate it, Seth."

"How about some dinner?"

"I don't know. I'm kind of beat from shopping today."

"And all shook up by what just happened to you."

"That, too. I'd love dinner with you."

"Fine. Pick you up in forty-five minutes. We'll go to

Simone's. That all right with you? I've had a yearning all afternoon for their special veal chop."

"Fine with me," I said. "I'll be ready when you arrive."

Forty-five minutes later, I had my hat and coat on and was ready for Seth's arrival. But as I stood in the foyer, I remembered I'd left my house keys on my desk in the study. I went there and surveyed the desk. They weren't there. I circled the desk to see whether I'd knocked them off. I had; they were resting on the carpet just enough under the desk to have escaped my initial attention.

When I bent down to pick them up I saw the sheet of paper jutting out from behind my wicker wastebasket. Assuming it was something that had been removed from my desk by the intruder, or was a piece of paper I'd tossed at the basket and missed, I picked it up and was about to wad it into a ball for disposition when I realized it was nothing I'd seen before.

I stood up straight and examined it in the light. It was a note made from cut-out letters from magazines and newspapers, the sort you see in kidnap ransom notes in the movies. The letters were crudely pasted on the paper, forming a jumble of letters, large and small.

But what they spelled out was unmistakable:

Butt out, if you know what's good for you.

Chapter Twenty-one

Seth and I had just finished a shrimp appetizer and were considering what to have as a main course when Phillipo Simone, the gregarious owner of the restaurant, came to the table.

"You have a telephone call, Mrs. Fletcher," he said.

"Really? Who knew I was coming here?"

"Must be Mort," Seth said. "I left a message for him that we'd be here this evening."

I followed Phillipo to the bar, where he handed me the receiver.

"Hello?"

"Sorry to interrupt your dinner, Mrs. F.," said our sheriff, "but thought you'd want to know that it *was* Robert Brent who broke into your house."

"It was? Are you certain?"

"Certain as I am that Christmas is coming," he said. "The boy admitted it the minute I confronted him."

Mort didn't know about the note I'd found in my study just before leaving for dinner. I'd shoved it into my handbag and taken it with me, and had shown it to Seth shortly after arriving at Simone's.

"Have you arrested him?" I asked.

"Yes, ma'am. He's cooling his heels in cell number three as we speak."

"Mort, there's something else you should know."

"Oh?"

"Whoever broke into my house—Robert Brent, you say—left a note for me."

"A note? What kind of note?"

"The words were spelled out with letters cut from magazines and newspapers. It said, 'Butt out if you know what's good for you.'"

"What does that mean?"

"I don't know."

"Why didn't you give it to me when I was at your house?"

"Because I didn't know it was there. I discovered it on the floor as I was leaving for dinner with Seth. I have it with me."

"I'll be right over," Mort said.

I returned to the table and recounted my conversation for Seth.

He thought in silence, then asked, "What do you make of all this, Jessica?"

I shrugged. "Obviously, Robert Brent left the note in order to intimidate me. But I can't be certain about his motivation. Does he think I've been poking my nose into his father's murder? If so—and even if I was—why would it concern him, unless—"

Seth finished my sentence. "Unless he killed his father and views you as a threat to him by proving it."

Now, it was my turn to be silent. Somehow, the idea that a son would shoot a father in cold blood was anathema to me. Granted, Robert Brent was not your average young person, at least in terms of social skills and outlook on life. Children have killed their parents in the past, and it was naive of me to rule that out based solely upon my refusal to accept the possibility. Still, I wasn't at all convinced that simple tension between a father and son would lead to such a dreadful act.

My thoughts gravitated to Jill Walther and her having sought counseling when she became pregnant in her senior year. Rory Brent, Robert's father, had made that five-thousand-dollar contribution shortly after Jill visited Thomas Skaggs at his agency, Here-to-Help. Jill Walther and Robert Brent had been classmates. When I raised his name during my coffee with her at The Swan, she'd visibly reacted, was angry that I'd even mentioned him.

Was Robert Brent the father of Jill's aborted child?

Had Rory Brent made that large donation to Here-to-Help in order to cover up his son's involvement in the pregnancy?

The problem with that scenario was that I couldn't conceive of Jill Walther and Robert Brent having had an intimate relationship. They were polar opposites—she the quiet, achieving young woman; he the brooding, marginal student with a sour view of the world.

But I'd learned long ago to never question why any two people get together. Many of my friends over the years have ended up in relationships that didn't make sense to me, or anyone else viewing it from the outside. Yet there was obviously an unnamed, mysterious attraction between them that others were not expected to fathom.

Seth said nothing.

"What are you thinking?" I asked.

"I'm thinking that Robert might have left that note on somebody else's behalf."

"I hadn't thought of that."

Phillipo Simone came to our table and asked what we wished to order as an entrée.

"Any specials tonight?" Seth asked.

"Of course," Simone said, grinning. "There is always a special dish for our favorite doctor and writer." He described a veal dish in exquisite detail, and we both ordered it, along with a salad.

"Wine?" Simone asked.

"Not for me, thank you," I said. Seth ordered a glass of Chianti; I opted for a glass of water. I considered a bottle of mineral water, but had decided a long time ago that paying premium prices for water in a bottle didn't make any sense, especially since Cabot Cove's natural water is excellent.

We changed subjects and chatted about things other than the episode at my home that evening. Naturally, the Christmas festival came up, and we discussed in greater detail how we would approach our reading of Christmas stories to the children. We were well into that topic when Mort Metzger entered the restaurant, removed his Stetson, greeted Phillipo Simone, and came to our table, followed by Simone carrying an extra chair.

Once Mort was seated, Seth asked him about the circumstances leading to Robert Brent's confession.

"I drove out to the Brent farm," Mort said. "I beat the kid there by a half hour. I'd no sooner gotten out of my car and was walking up to the house when he comes flying in like a bat out of hell in a pickup truck. He didn't see me at first, and got out of the truck. When he spotted me, he panicked and jumped back in the truck to make a getaway. I stopped him and asked where he'd been. He had guilt written all over his face, that's for certain. I asked him if he'd been at your house, Mrs. F., and he blurted out that he had. He said he went inside to get warm." Mort laughed. "Some excuse, huh? I told him I was putting him under arrest for breaking and entering, and maybe a few more things. He looked at me with that blank expression of his and said, 'Okay.' "

"Was Patricia Brent there?" I asked.

"I didn't see her. There were lights on in the house, but I figured I didn't have any obligation to go tell her what I was about to do. I put the kid in my car, and we drove back into town. Read him his rights, told him he was entitled to have an attorney present. He just mumbled a few things, so I put him in the cell."

"Will he be charged?" I asked.

"Sure. I'll take him before Judge Coldwater in the morning. You'll have to be there, Mrs. F."

"Why?"

"To testify. Tell the judge what happened."

"But I'm not the one bringing charges," I said. "You and the district attorney will do that on behalf of the state."

"We could, but it would have a lot more clout if you showed up."

I looked at Seth, who nodded.

"All right," I said.

"Now, what about this note?" Mort asked.

Before I could respond, Mr. Simone came to the table and asked the sheriff if he wished anything.

Mort looked at Seth's glass of wine and said, "Can't drink 'cause I'm still on duty. Maybe just one of your antipasto platters and a glass of that nonalcoholic beer."

Seth, who'd been looking at the note earlier in the evening, handed it over. Mort's brow furrowed as he digested it.

"What do you make of it, Mort?" Seth asked.

"Doesn't seem to be any debate about what it says, or means," our sheriff replied. "Looks like young Mr. Brent was trying to scare you off."

"We understand that, Mort," I said, "but the bigger question is scare me off from *what*?"

"Has to do with Rory's murder. Seems pretty simple to me," Mort said.

I was tempted to tell him about Jill Walther's pregnancy and the possible link to Robert Brent, but knew I couldn't do that without breaching Seth's confidence. Mort carefully folded the note and put it in the pocket of his blue down winter uniform jacket. "Wish you hadn't touched this," he said. "Could be prints on it."

"I never stopped to think. I was running out the door, spotted it on the floor, grabbed it, and brought it with me," I said defensively.

"No harm, I suppose," Mort said.

Phillipo's son, Vincenzo, who worked with his father at the family restaurant, delivered Mort's antipasto platter and bottle of Buckler beer.

"More than I can eat," Mort said. "Help yourselves."

Seth and I glanced at each other and smiled. We'd never seen a platter of any size that was more than Mort's voracious appetite could handle.

Mort stayed throughout the dinner, and we left the restaurant together. To our surprise, it had started to snow, lightly and gently.

"Weatherman didn't say anything about snow," Seth grumbled, raising the collar of his overcoat and pulling it tight around his neck.

"You folks take care, drive easy," Mort said, tipping his hat.

"Same to you," Seth said.

As Seth drove me home, I asked absently, "I wonder why it took Robert Brent the length of time it did to drive home after leaving my house."

"Probably stopped off for a Big Mac," Seth said.

"Possibly. Or, maybe he stopped to see someone."

"Like who?"

"I don't know." I turned and faced him. "Jill Walther?"

"I don't think so," was Seth's response. "Can't imagine him going to the Walther farm, considering everything that's gone on."

"Maybe he met her some other place. Maybe they had a date."

"Always a possibility, I suppose," Seth said, turning into my driveway, which now had a thin coating of fresh snow on it.

"Cup of tea?" I asked.

"Thank you, no. Sure you'll be all right alone here tonight?"

"Of course I will. Robert Brent was the one who broke into my house, and Robert Brent is sitting in a jail cell. Nothing to worry about."

"I suppose you're right. Well, Jessica, sleep tight, call me in the morning."

"I will. And thanks for dinner. It was excellent, just what I needed."

As was his custom, Seth walked me to the door and waited until I'd opened it. Before I did, however, I saw that a large manila envelope was propped against it. I picked it up. My first name was written on it in big letters.

We stepped into the foyer, and I opened the envelope. A handwritten note was attached to a sheaf of papers.

Jessica—Here's what I came up with at Town Hall re: the Walther property. Hope it's helpful. Pay particular attention to the info on Rory Brent's "other life." He had more money than anyone knew. I checked on the partnership he was involved with in Indianapolis. An eye-opener. Happy reading. Sorry I missed you. Will call in the morning. Joe.

"What's that all about?" Seth asked.

I explained that I'd asked Joe Turco to see what he could find at the town clerk's office about the Walther farm.

"Why did you do that?"

"Curious, that's all. Jake Walther and Rory Brent allegedly argued about land and money. I just thought public records might provide a hint as to what might have prompted that argument."

"I see. Well, looks like you've got some reading to do.

Frankly, I can never make sense out of legal papers. All full of gobbledygook and boilerplate legalese."

I laughed. "I'll do my best," I said. "Thanks again for dinner. Careful home. The roads are slippery."

Despite my bravado about being alone in the house that night, I found myself apprehensive once there. I kept thinking of earlier that evening: the sound of someone intruding upon my sacred place, seeing the person run out the French doors, and believing it was Robert Brent; the papers from my desk strewn all over the floor. I'd been fortunate. Evidently, the only reason Robert came to my house was to look for something in my desk, and to leave his sophomoric note warning me to "butt out." Inflicting serious bodily harm wasn't on his agenda.

Still, there was something unsettling about being where an intruder had stood only hours earlier.

I tried to put it out of my mind, turned on the television set, and settled back to watch the news, the papers Joe Turco had delivered resting unread on my lap. I surfed the channels, using the remote control, until landing upon the Fox News network, where Roberta Brannason was filing a live report on the Rory Brent case from the steps of City Hall.

"I'm Roberta Brannason reporting from Cabot Cove, Maine, where one of this charming town's most beloved citizens, Rory Brent, a prosperous farmer and a man who brought joy to the village each year as Santa Claus at the annual Christmas festival, was murdered in cold blood. We've been reporting to you on the progress of this case, which has shaken Cabot Cove to its foundation. Now, Fox News has learned that an arrest is imminent. The prime suspect all along has been another farmer, Jake Walther, a man universally disliked by most citizens of this Maine community. He's been detained, then released on two occasions. Now, reliable sources have told us that the laboratory analysis of a footprint found on the dirt floor of Rory Brent's barn does, in fact, match the sole of one of Mr. Walther's boots . . . and that the sheriff of Cabot Cove, Morton Metzger, in concert with the local district attorney, will once again arrest Mr. Walther and charge him with the murder of Santa Claus. I'm Roberta Brannason reporting from Cabot Cove, Maine."

I lowered the sound on the TV, sat back in my recliner, closed my eyes and sighed.

I thought of Mary Walther, and, of course, her daughter, Jill. What a tragedy to have a member of your family accused of having murdered another person. The pain must be unbearable.

I placed the papers on a table next to my chair, got up, went to the window, and peered through the glass. It was still snowing, although it hadn't intensified. I returned to my chair and waited for the TV weather report. Our local weatherwoman—local in the sense that she reported from a station in Portland; Cabot Cove does not have its own TV outlet—said that we shouldn't expect much in the way of accumulation, and that the snow would stop before dawn.

Although dinner had been delicious, it sat heavy on my stomach; too much food without enough time to properly digest it. I considered taking a walk, but the weather dissuaded me. Instead, I went to the cabinet in which I keep liquor and poured myself a small snifter of half brandy and half port wine.

Years ago, when coming back to the Scottish mainland from the Orkney Islands, we'd hit vile weather, so bad that I wondered halfway through the trip whether we'd make it. Obviously, we did, but I stepped ashore a shaken person, and with an extremely upset stomach. I went into a hotel near the dock and asked the bartender for a small glass of blackberry brandy, which I'd always considered good "medicine" for an upset stomach. The bartender, an older Scottish gentleman, suggested I instead try a mixture of port and brandy. "Make you feel like a new person," he told me.

His advice proved right. My stomach immediately settled down, and I enjoyed a big dinner before heading for my hotel in another village along the coast.

I took a sip of my medicinal concoction and focused my attention on the events of earlier that evening. It was obvious that Robert Brent had left the note to scare me. What I couldn't figure out was what he might have been looking for in my desk. What sort of paper would be of interest to him, so much so that he would break into my home and risk arrest?

My pondering of that question was interrupted by the ringing phone. I glanced at a clock on the wall; it was eleven-thirty, late for someone to be calling, especially in Cabot Cove, where most people lived the adage of early to bed, early to rise, including me.

"Hello?"

"Mrs. Fletcher?"

I recognized Jill Walther's voice.

"Jill?"

"Yes. Did I wake you?"

"No, although I was about to head for bed. I watched the news and the weather."

"Mrs. Fletcher, I have to talk to you."

"I'm happy to hear that, Jill. I wanted very much to see you again before you returned to school. Your mother said you'd be cutting short your vacation."

"Yes. That was her idea."

Her tone was accusatory. She didn't sound at all happy that her mother had made the decision for her to leave Cabot Cove prematurely.

"Why don't we get together tomorrow? Breakfast? My treat."

There was a long, profound silence on the other end of the line.

"Jill?"

"Yes. I'm sorry. Could you come to the farm?"

"Tomorrow?"

"No, right now. I wouldn't ask except . . . Mrs. Fletcher, I'm so scared."

"About what?"

"About everything. About my father and what might happen to him. About me. I don't think I could go back to school knowing my father is accused of Mr. Brent's murder. I couldn't face anyone. I saw the news tonight, too. They keep talking about my father having killed 'Santa Claus.' That isn't fair. I can't stand having people think of me as the daughter of someone who murdered such a popular person as Mr. Brent."

"I think you might be overreacting, Jill. Most people don't blame a family member for the act of another. Besides, your father hasn't been proved guilty of anything."

She began to sob, softly at first, then more urgently.

"Please, Jill, get hold of yourself. I don't see how I could come to your farm tonight. I don't drive and—"

"I'm sorry, Mrs. Fletcher. I never should have made this call. This isn't your concern."

"Oh, but it is, Jill. I took a very special interest in you, and that interest continues to this day. I want what's right for you, no matter what your father might have done. And I stress the word *might*. Maybe I can get someone to drive me out there—the local cab company."

Her toned brightened. "Would you?" she said. "Thank God. You're such a wonderful person and—"

"I'll call and see if they'll pick me up. It might be too late for them, although at this time of year they tend to work later. People getting ready for Christmas, that sort of thing. If you don't hear from me, I'll be there within the hour."

"Thank you again, Mrs. Fletcher. I knew I could count on you."

Dimitri answered on the first ring.

"Are you still working?" I asked.

"Yes, ma'am. My cousin worked all day, and I'm driving at night. A busy time of year."

"Yes, it is. Dimitri, could you pick me up at the house and take me out to the Walther farm?"

"Now?"

"Yes."

"Of course I can, Mrs. Fletcher, but—"

"But what?"

"Why do you want to go out there at this time of night, and in this weather?"

"Oh, the weather doesn't seem to be a problem. It isn't much of a snowfall. I have to go out there to . . . well, to deliver some Christmas things."

"I see."

I knew what he was thinking, that it was an odd time of night to be delivering Christmas gifts. But I didn't elaborate, nor did he ask me to. He simply said he would be at my house in fifteen minutes.

I used the few minutes I had to peruse the public land records Joe Turco had dropped off. As Seth said, they were loaded with legal boilerplate, and I had trouble digesting what they said. But it wasn't a completely futile exercise. I was in the process of going back to reread a section concerning ownership of the Walther farm when Dimitri arrived. I shoved the papers in my bag, left the house, and joined him in his taxi.

Although it was a light snow, it did create slippery road conditions, and Dimitri drove slowly and carefully. As we approached the Walther farm, he asked which of the three houses he should take me to.

"The middle one," I said.

He turned onto the rutted dirt driveway that led into the farm and stopped at the house shared by Mary and Jill Walther. It hadn't occurred to me to ask Jill whether her mother was there. I assumed she would be. When I thought about that, I wondered why it was Jill who'd made the call, and not Mary. Had Mary encouraged her to do it? Did Mary share in her daughter's fear?

I had a choice of asking Dimitri to wait for me, or to dismiss him and call him later. "I will wait for you," Dimitri said.

I was about to tell him not to bother, but the thought of having him outside was comforting.

"I appreciate that," I said. "Just charge me for whatever time you have to wait."

"That is not a concern, Mrs. Fletcher. I will do whatever is best for you."

I slid forward on the backseat and placed my hand on his shoulder. "Thank you," I said. "You're a good man."

I had noticed as we came up the road that there was a light on in the first cabin, the one occupied by Jake Walther, and that smoke drifted from the chimney. Lights were also on in the middle cabin. I looked beyond it to where Dennis lived. That cabin was dark.

I got out and shivered at the sudden change in temperature between the warmth of Dimitri's car and the cold outside air.

I went up the steps, stepped onto the porch, and knocked. Mary Walther opened the door.

"Good evening, Mary," I said. "I know this is late to be visiting but—"

Her tone was as stern as her face. "I know why you're here, Mrs. Fletcher. Because of my silly daughter."

"Silly? She called and asked me to come because she was frightened. That's why I'm here."

Mary Walther's large body filled the open doorway. She pressed her lips tightly together, narrowed her eyes, and said, "As long as you're here, you might as well come in."

She stepped back, allowing me to enter the living room, and closed the door behind us. It was toasty warm in the house, and the smell of freshly baked cookies wafted from the kitchen.

"A nasty night, although they say the snow will stop by morning," I said, making conversation.

"She shouldn't have called you," Mary said.

"Jill? I don't know whether she should have or not, but I didn't see any alternative but to respond. She sounded upset. Is she here?"

"Upstairs."

"May I see her? Will you go tell her I'm here?"

"She doesn't have to!"

We both turned at the sound of Jill's voice, who stood on the narrow staircase leading to the second floor, arms folded across her chest, defiance painted on her face.

Mary said sweetly, "Why don't you get some cookies and tea for Mrs. Fletcher, Jill?"

"No need for that," I said.

"As long as you're here, we might as well be good hostesses." Her voice firmer now. "Get cookies and tea for Mrs. Fletcher."

I watched as Jill made up her mind what to do. Then she slowly descended the stairs and disappeared into the kitchen.

"You're right," Mary said. "She's very upset. I suppose she's entitled to be, but that's why I insisted she leave here and go back to school. There's nothing but negative feelings because of what Jake did."

"Because of what Jake did? Are you saying he murdered Rory Brent?"

"I can't defend him any longer, Mrs. Fletcher. Lord knows, I want to. He's my husband, and I don't want to see him go to jail. What will we do here without him? We'll lose the farm. But it seems certain now that Jake did kill

Rory. I can't say that I blame him. Rory Brent, with all his so-called niceness, was not as nice as people thought."

"I'm sorry to hear that from you, Mary. May I take off my coat?"

"If you're intending to stay."

"I don't mean to intrude, and I'm not here to see you. I promised Jill I'd come and talk to her. I intend to do that."

"Suit yourself, although you won't get much sense out of her. She's just a wreck, schoolgirl sort of emotions. Crying all the time, wailing about what her life is going to be like because of what Jake did. I told her to get a grip on herself. Lord knows I've shed my tears, but I've done it in private. What we have to do now is face reality. My husband murdered another man, and they have the proof of that. He'll have to face the consequences, and so will we, but we'll do it with dignity."

I admired her staunch stand. She undoubtedly had had to exhibit this sort of inner strength throughout her adult life as Jake Walther's wife. Not only was he an unpleasant man, his efforts at farming had not resulted in much financial gain. Many woman I know would have bolted, run from such a situation. But Mary had stayed, and obviously intended to stand tall no matter what fate befell her and her daughter.

Jill reappeared carrying a plate with Christmas cookies in one hand, and a mug of steaming tea in the other. I took off my coat, placed it on a chair, and sat at a small table. Jill placed the plate and mug in front of me.

"The cookies look good," I said, thinking it must be especially hard to do anything in the Christmas spirit under the circumstances.

"Life must go on," Mary said. "Mrs. Fletcher, I—"

"Please, Mary, call me Jessica. I'm here as a friend."

"You keep reminding me to call you by your first name, but I find it difficult. You're a woman of substance and of the world. Famous and rich. I was brought up to be respectful of my superiors."

"I am not superior to anyone or anything."

I turned to Jill. "Want to sit down and tell me why you asked me to come here tonight? I'm sure whatever is causing you such concern can be worked out, and I promise I'll help any way I can."

Jill looked to her mother as though to gain permission to speak.

"Go ahead, Jill, tell her whatever it is you want," said her mother. "Get if off your chest. Maybe once you do you'll stop acting so silly."

Jill and I looked at each other.

I said, "I'm waiting, Jill."

She averted her eyes and took a few breaths as though pumping herself up for what she was about to say. Finally, she said flatly, in a statement that sounded as though she'd rehearsed it, "My father did not kill Mr. Brent."

I looked at Mary, who said, "See? Denial. Just denial all the time." She said to Jill, "You have to stop this, Jill. You have to grow up and face facts. Neither of us wants to admit that Daddy killed Rory Brent. I've been denying it to myself ever since it happened, and there's a side of me that keeps saying he didn't do it. But he did, Jill, and that's the cruel truth."

I asked Jill, "Why do you say your father didn't do it? I mean, I understand that you want it that way, but do you have a solid reason, some evidence that would prove his innocence?"

She looked straight at me and said, "Ask Dennis."

Mary guffawed. "Here you go again. Dennis told the truth when he said he was not with Daddy the morning of the murder. Dennis was with me. We were attending to the chickens and trying to fix that damn wall that keeps falling down on the coop."

"That's not true," Jill blurted, standing straight and clenching her fists, as though about to do physical combat. "Dennis would say anything that you tell him to, and you know it."

Mary extended her arms at me and said, "See? I get no help from her. She's calling me and Dennis liars. Some daughter. She's out of her mind. The best thing for her is to be away from here and back at school."

What Jill had said a few moments ago about Dennis doing whatever Mary told him to do interested me. Until then, it had been assumed that any possible influences on Dennis's story had come from either Jake—who allegedly threatened him with physical harm if he didn't tell Sheriff Metzger that they'd been together the morning of the murder—or from the sheriff himself, suggesting to Dennis that he might want to change his story. It wasn't that Mort would have done anything like that deliberately. But if Dennis was as suggestible and malleable as people said, it was possible that Mort had inadvertently led him into a different version of events.

Was Jill right? Had Mary exerted control over Dennis, helping him shape his recounting of events that morning to suit herself? Why would she do that? What would she have to gain from seeing to it that Dennis testified in a certain way?

I asked Mary, "Do you have any doubt in your mind that Dennis is reporting what actually happened that morning, Mary?"

A dark, severe expression crossed her broad face. "Are you suggesting, too, that I'm lying?"

I laughed to soften the moment. "Of course not. But Dennis has a reputation for being easily influenced. That's all I meant."

"People think a lot of bad things about Dennis because he's slow. But I assure you, Jessica . . . Mrs. Fletcher . . . that he's not a liar. He's a good and decent man who works hard and keeps to himself. That's the way we were brought up as brother and sister."

Not wanting to further anger her, I turned my attention to Jill, who'd regained her seat on the bottom step of the staircase. I wasn't sure what the reaction would be if I raised the question of her visit to Here-to-Help to obtain counseling, including the option of abortion. I certainly would have preferred to ask her about that in a private setting, just between the two of us. But I had the sinking feeling that the only opportunity I was going to have to speak to her was here and now, in this small, modest home in which she'd grown up, and in the presence of her mother who, I now realized, was more domineering than I imagined.

I decided to broach the subject obliquely.

"Jill, when you and I had coffee the day of Mr. Brent's funeral, I mentioned his son, Robert. You said you knew him because you were classmates."

I searched her face for a visible reaction and found it. It was a combination of surprise, fear, and anger.

"So?" she said.

"Do you know that Robert broke into my home earlier this evening?"

Her stutter-step response said clearly to me that she was aware of it.

"No. I mean . . . broke in? . . . No . . . why would I . . . ?"

I continued. "Robert has been arrested and is in jail now. He left me a note, Jill, warning me to, as he put it, 'butt out.'"

Nervous glances were exchanged between mother and daughter.

"Have you seen him tonight?"

"Seen who?"

"Robert Brent."

"No. I mean, why would I see him?"

Mary, who'd been sitting in a narrow ladder-back chair, now stood, placed her hands on her sizable hips, and glared at me from her elevated position. "Maybe it's time you left," she said.

I sighed, shrugged, and said, "I will leave, of course, if you want me to. But I have a feeling, Mary, there's something more going on here having to do with Rory Brent's murder than you're willing to admit."

I didn't give her a chance to respond. I looked at Jill. "Jill, I know about what happened in your senior year. I know you went to seek counseling in Salem with the Herc-to-Help organization. Mr. Skaggs? Remember him?"

I braced for a response. It came from Mary Walther.

"You obviously have been doing a lot of snooping into this family's business," she said.

"I prefer not to call it snooping, Mary. I have become involved in the investigation of Rory's murder due to circumstances that I didn't create. But now that I am, I think I owe it to myself—no, let me amend that—I think I owe it to this town to help get to the bottom of what happened so that it can be put to rest, hopefully before the Christmas festival and everything good and decent it represents."

Jill started to say something, but caught the words before they came out.

"You have no right doing this," Mary said.

"I'm not doing anything, Mary, except trying to get some answers. Which, I might add, could help your husband. I don't believe he murdered Rory Brent."

"You don't?" Mary said. "What makes you such an expert in murder? You write books, that's all. The evidence is against him, as sad as that might be. Please leave."

I stood and went to where Jill continued to sit. I placed my hands on her shoulders, brought my face close to hers, and said softly, "Sometimes, Jill, keeping painful secrets weighs too heavy on us. What happened in high school was a mistake, a tragic one, of course, but a mistake. You don't have to live the rest of your life suffering for it."

I straightened and turned. Mary held out my coat for me to slip into. I did, retrieved my hat and scarf from where I'd dropped them on a table, and went to the door.

"I wish you didn't view me this way," I said. "Believe it or not, Mary, all I want to do is help you and your family."

"I think the best way to help my family is to leave us alone," she said.

"Fair enough."

As I reached for the doorknob, I was startled by the sound of heavy footsteps on the porch outside. My hand froze in midmotion. There was no need for me to open the door because Jake Walther did. He pushed it open with such force that it almost knocked me over. He stepped inside and slammed the door behind him.

He had a crazed look in his eyes.

The smell of alcohol on his breath was overwhelming.

And the sight of the shotgun he carried was sobering.

Chapter Twenty-two

To say Jake's sudden arrival shocked me would be an understatement of classic proportions. Although he didn't physically touch me, his mere presence caused me to back up as though I'd been pushed.

"Cozy little group you've got here, Mary," he said, his words slurred.

"Go back to your house," Mary said with authority.

Jake glared at me. "You just can't keep your nose out of our business, can you?"

"I came to visit your daughter," I said, forcing calm into my voice. "I was just leaving."

"Maybe you ought to stay a spell," he said. There was a distinct threat in his voice.

"No," I said. "I have someone waiting for me outside."

He grinned and said, "He won't be missing you."

"What do you mean? It's Dimitri. He drove me here. He's waiting for me to—"

"Dimitri ain't waiting for nobody," Jake said. "I took care of that."

"You haven't hurt him, have you?" I said.

"Just made sure he wouldn't be worryin' about when you come out."

"Excuse me," I said, moving toward the door. "I'll see for myself."

He shifted position so that my path was blocked. "What's everybody been tellin' you tonight, Mrs. Fletcher?"

Realizing I was not about to be allowed to leave, I returned to the table. "What I've been told," I said, "was that Mary has become resigned to the fact that you'll be arrested for Rory Brent's murder."

"Yup. I heard that on the radio. Matched up my boot, did they, with the footprint on ol' Rory's barn floor?"

I looked directly into Jake's watery, bloodshot blue eyes and said, "I don't believe you killed Rory Brent."

My words seemed to stun him into a moment of sobriety.

I continued. "I came here only to talk to Jill. I took a deep interest in Jill and her future when she was in high school, and that interest hasn't waned."

I turned to Jill. "Jill, I know what happened to you in your senior year of high school."

Mary erupted. "I'll have none of that talk in this house."

I said to her, "I know it's none of my business, Mary, at least not personally. But I can't help feel that what happened to Jill in high school has a bearing upon Brent's murder. Do you know that shortly after Jill visited Here-to-Help, the social agency in Salem, Rory Brent made a large contribution to that organization?"

No one replied.

"Why did he do that?" I asked. "We all know that Rory was a prosperous and generous man, but what did Jill's pregnancy have to do with *him*?"

My mention of the word *pregnancy* hit the room with all the impact of an exploding grenade. Mary was barely able to contain her rage. Jake, whose rigidity had lessened, sagged against the door.

"Jill," I said, "please tell me why Mr. Brent would have done that. It's not because I'm prying into your life. I have no right to do that. But if it helps identify who killed Rory Brent, it's important that you be honest with me."

Jill said softly, "He did it because of—"

"Shut up!" Mary Walther shouted, turning, and approaching her daughter.

"Why not tell her?" Jill said, standing. Although she was considerably smaller than her mother, she now matched her in defiance. "It's all going to come out anyway, no matter how hard you try to keep it quiet."

Mary turned to her husband. "Tell her to stop it, Jake." Again to Jill, "Go upstairs to your room."

"No," Jill said.

"It was because of Robert Brent, wasn't it?" I said.

When she didn't respond, I went to her, placed my arm around her shoulders, and said, "Jill, honey, it's all right. This kind of thing just keeps festering inside us unless we face it head-on. Was Robert Brent the father of your child?"

My back was to Mary and Jake. I heard shuffling behind me, but thought nothing of it. My attention was too intently focused upon Jill, who had started to weep silently.

She pressed against me, and I wrapped my arms around her. She said in a voice so soft I could barely hear, "Yes."

"Jill, did Mr. Brent arrange your abortion?"

The noise behind me had stopped. Jill dabbed at her eyes with the back of her hands and slowly shook her head.

"Who did then?"

"No one. I . . . I had the baby."

A muttered curse from Mary Walther caused me to turn. Mary had taken the shotgun from Jake. It was pointed at me.

I was surprised at how calmly I said, "Put the shotgun down, Mary. This can all be worked out. The important thing is that the pieces be put together so that Rory Brent's murder is solved, and we can get on with our lives. All of us. Christmas is almost here. What's happened to you and your family is tragic, and I ache for you. But don't do anything to make it worse."

"You just don't understand, do you?" Mary said. "You've lived a charmed life, never had to worry about where your next meal was coming from, never had to wonder what people were saying behind your back. I know how people view Jake and me in this town. Do you think I'm stupid?"

"Of course not."

"You write your books and travel all over the world, live in a nice house, have money in the bank. Like most folks in Cabot Cove. But we've struggled just to survive ever since we bought this farm and tried to make a go of it. It's never been easy. But we always kept our dignity, always believed in ourselves as a family. And we had a daughter. There she stands, Ms. Jill Walther. All our hopes were with her, that she'd make something of herself and the Walther name. But then she went and got herself pregnant with that bum, Robert Brent, and everything we hoped for went up in smoke."

I said to Jill, "You said you had the baby. While you were in school?"

"Yes."

"I never even knew you were pregnant," I said.

"Nobody did," Mary said. "She never showed much. Couldn't even tell she was carrying. Had the child down in Salem at some home for girls like her. Was there just a few days. Called in sick to school."

"Where is the child now?" I asked.

"Adopted," Mary said. "Don't know who. They don't tell you such things."

"You poor girl," I said to Jill. "Have you seen your son since giving birth?"

"It was a girl, Mrs. Fletcher. A little girl. I named her Samantha."

"Samantha," I repeated absently. "Did Rory Brent make that donation to keep your pregnancy quiet and to protect his son?"

Mary answered for her. "Mr. Big Shot, Rory Brent, wanted Jill to end the pregnancy. He sent her to that agency, hoping they'd talk some sense into her."

"I take it Mr. Skaggs at Here-to-Help did just the opposite," I said, feeling a sudden warmth for the bearlike man who ran Here-to-Help.

"He urged me to have the baby," Jill said. "And I did."

"Was Mr. Brent angry with your decision?" I asked.

"Sure as hell was," Jake Walther said. "Said he'd bury us all if we didn't do things the way he wanted."

I smiled at Jill. "But you stuck to your guns."

"Yes, ma'am."

"But if sending you to the agency didn't result in ending your pregnancy, the way Rory wanted it to end, why did he make that large contribution?"

"Because I told him I intended to have an abortion," Jill said.

"You lied to him?"

"I didn't know what to do, what was right and what was wrong. I decided to keep my baby. He sent the money before I changed my mind."

Brent having sent five thousand dollars to Tom Skaggs at Here-to-Help was an act of supreme arrogance. He'd wanted Skaggs to convince Jill to end her pregnancy, and was rewarding him for it. Good for you, I thought, looking at Jill.

Discovering that my thesis had been wrong—that Jill had had an abortion—forced me to shift gears and to try to fit this new piece into the scenario under which I'd been operating. What took front and center in my thinking at that moment was the role this information possibly played in Rory Brent's murder.

I asked Jill, "What did Rory do after he learned that you decided to keep the baby?"

Her mother answered for her. "Oh, Rory Brent was hopping mad." She looked at her husband. "Wasn't he, Jake?"

"Yup," Jake muttered.

"Mr. Rory Brent liked to call the shots," Mary continued. "He didn't want his precious son to have to take financial responsibility, and said he'd see to it that he never had to."

"What did he mean?" I asked.

"He said that if Jill didn't give up the baby, he'd trash her so bad—trash us—we might as well be dead. We weren't in no position to argue with him. If Jill kept the baby, that would have ended her dreams, and ours, too. Another mouth to feed? We've had trouble putting food on the table just for us."

"Did you want to keep the baby, Jill?" I asked.

"Yes."

"But your parents urged you to give it up because of finances?"

Jill didn't answer. I looked to Mary and Jake, but they, too, said nothing.

Jill had again sat on the bottom step of the staircase. I sat next to her and took her hand in mine. I then said to no one in particular, to the room itself, "Why was Rory Brent killed?"

Jake and Mary Walther looked at each other. It was Jake who spoke. "The man was no good, Mrs. Fletcher. Him and that goddamn son 'a his. Raped Jill and—"

"That's not true," Jill quickly said. "Robert and I . . . we got together, that's all, sort of found each other. The other kids never liked me much, or him. A couple of nerds. It just happened, that's all. One day at his house."

"Jake," I said, "if someone was mad at Robert Brent for getting Jill pregnant, why would he kill his father?"

"For trying to use what his son did to our daughter to blackmail us, hold it over our heads," Mary said. "Jake just snapped, that's all. Had enough from that so-called saint, Rory Brent. *Mr. Santa Claus.*"

I stood and said, "You didn't kill him because of what happened between Jill and Robert."

"What are you saying?" Mary said.

I pulled the envelope from my purse that had been left at my house by Joe Turco, opened it, and removed the papers it contained. "Rory had taken your farm from you."

Mary reached for the papers, but I kept them from her reach. "You were about to lose the farm to the bank. Rory lent you the money to save it, but charged exorbitant interest and attached an impossible repayment schedule. If you didn't meet the deadline to pay it back, the farm was his. And that's exactly what happened, isn't it?"

Mary started to say something, but I cut her off.

"You weren't the only ones to have this happen," I said. "I'm not certain how it worked, but these papers indicate Rory was involved with a company in Indianapolis, a partnership of some kind that made its money identifying farmers who'd fallen on hard times, lending them money with their farms as collateral, and taking the farms when they couldn't make the payment. They've been doing it all over the country for years. It's called loan sharking in big cities."

I waited for an answer.

"You got it right," Jake said.

"So now, you know what happened," Mary said. "Can you blame Jake for wanting him dead?"

"No," I said. "I don't blame Jake at all—because Jake didn't murder Rory Brent."

Mary glared at me.

"You killed him, Mary."

Mary's response was flat, void of emotion. She slowly lowered the shotgun and said, "That's all we had left, the farm. It never gave us much, but at least we had a roof over our heads and a place to grow vegetables." Her voice gained strength. "Everybody walked around talking about what a wonderful person Rory Brent was. He wasn't wonderful, Mrs. Fletcher. Sure, on the outside he looked like a perfect gentleman, putting on his Santa Claus costume every year, giving to charity, everybody loving good old Rory. But he was an evil man. He wouldn't have cared if he put all of us in the ground. He and Jake had an argument about a month before about him taking the farm from us. I wanted Jake to do something, but what could he do? Look at him." She turned and extended her hand to her husband. "Jake's just a dirt-poor, hardworking man who drinks too much and lets the world stomp all over him. But he's always tried, for me and for her." She pointed at Jill. "But sometimes you can't let people walk on you, Mrs. Fletcher. Sometimes you have to take matters into your own hands and right a wrong."

"And you shot him to right that wrong," I said.

"Don't say nothin' more, Mary," Jake said.

"It doesn't much matter," Mary said. "I couldn't believe I did it. I went to talk sense to him, ask him to be fair and to let us stay till we found the money to pay him back. When I arrived that morning, I saw him leave the house and walk to the back barn. I followed him inside and pleaded with him, put my heart in my hand and offered it to him. All he did was laugh, Mrs. Fletcher. Oh, excuse me. Jessica. I forgot I'm supposed to call you by your first name, real friendly like. Rory said me and Jake were losers and didn't deserve to have this piece of property. He called Jill a slut, said she seduced Robert and wasn't any better than her mother and father. He just kept saying things like that until I couldn't take it anymore. So yes, I shot him, shot him dead, and walked away not feeling guilty one bit."

I walked to where Mary stood and took the shotgun from her hand, then placed it on the table. "Mary, I'll help in any way I can. No matter what happens, it's important that Jill go on with her life, continue her education, and become the fine writer I know she will."

I turned to Jake, "You knew Mary shot him, didn't you?"

"'Course I did. I figured they'd think it was me 'cause of my reputation. We had Dennis change his story so that Mary would have an alibi. I was hoping that if nobody could prove it was me, they wouldn't ever think of her. You kind of knew all along, didn't you?"

I shook my head. "No, I didn't, although I started to suspect when I learned that your boot had once again been matched up by the laboratory to the footprint in the barn."

I said to Mary, "I remember once being in a shoe store with you. You had to buy a man's moccasin because none of the women's sizes fit you. It occurred to me that you might easily have worn Jake's boots that morning and left the footprint in the barn. Did you do that deliberately, to make Jake the suspect?"

"No," Mary said. "It just happened that way. I always wear Jake's boots when I'm out and around."

"What about Dennis? Why did he lie?"

"Like I said, to protect her," Jake answered. "Dennis and me were fixing a fence that morning, just like he first said. But after she shot Rory, we wanted folks to think it was me."

"And you were willing to go to jail, maybe even the electric chair, to save her."

"Like she said, Mrs. Fletcher, we may be dirt poor, but we know we're family. All we've got is each other."

This time, when I went to the door, no one attempted to stop me. I opened it and looked outside.

"What did you do with Dimitri?" I asked.

"Nothin'," Jake said. "Just told him to get out of here, to get off my property before I blew his brains out."

As he said it, I saw lights approaching, some of them flashing. A moment later, Sheriff Mort Metzger pulled up the road and stopped outside of the house. Dimitri was in the car with him, along with two deputies.

"You okay, Mrs. F.?" Mort asked as he ran up onto the porch.

"Yes, Mort, I'm fine."

"Dimitri came and got me. Told me he'd dropped you here, but that Jake ran him off the property with a shotgun. I figured I'd better get out here pronto."

"And I appreciate that, Mort. But everything is fine now. I think if you talk to Mary, you'll be able to put the Rory Brent murder in your file of solved cases. In the meantime, I am very tired and would appreciate a lift home."

Chapter Twenty-three

"'Who said that?'"

"The kindly old man looked around. Someone had said 'I'm hungry.' But as far as he knew, he was the only person in the house that Christmas morning."

Seth and I continued to read from "The Dog That Talked at Christmas," the story of a lonely old man who'd found a stray puppy in a snowstorm on Christmas Eve. In front of us this Christmas Eve were more than a hundred small children, their eyes bright, their attention totally focused on this charming tale of all creatures, great and small, sharing in the Christmas spirit.

"'Could I please have something to eat?' The old man spun around and looked down at the puppy. 'Did you say that?' he asked, his eyes open wide," Seth read.

I followed with, "The puppy said, 'All I said was I'm hungry.'"

Behind us on a large screen, color illustrations from the book were projected to coincide with the story's progression. Seth and I alternated paragraphs.

"'You can talk? But you're a dog. Dogs don't talk.'"

"'Oh yes we can,' the puppy said. 'We're not supposed to, but I'm so hungry.'"

"The old man sat and stared at the puppy. A talking dog, he thought. A Christmas miracle. He could become rich with a talking dog, go on television, make commercials, become famous."

"'All dogs can talk,' said the puppy. 'But we know that if we do, we'll have to go to work. Don't tell any other dogs I broke the rule. They'll be very mad at me.'"

"The old man made them a hearty breakfast, and the puppy gave him a big, wet kiss. Tears came to the old man's eyes. He'd been alone for so long. Having this Christmas puppy filled his house with joy and love. 'Your secret is safe with me,' he told the puppy. 'But you will talk to *me*, won't you?'"

"'Of course I will.'"

The final picture came to life on the screen—the puppy and the old man together beneath the Christmas tree.

"'Good night,' the old man said."

"'Good night,' said the puppy."

"Merry Christmas!" we said in concert.

The kids got to their feet and applauded. Cynthia Curtis came from the wings and congratulated us on a wonderful performance.

"Suppose I'd better get back to the house," Seth told me. "Still some preparations to go for the party."

"Yes, you have twenty guests coming."

"And you have another performance."

"I know." I raised my eyebrows and sighed. "I can't believe I agreed to do it. I'd better get dressed."

His grin was wicked. "Can't think of a better person to play Santa, Jessica. But don't let the little tykes cough in your face. Bad flu season coming up."

A half hour later, after having pillows strapped to my waist and being outfitted with a brand-new Santa costume purchased by the festival committee, I sat in a large chair, propped a steady stream of children on my lap, and heard their wishes for Christmas presents. Roberta Brannason's TV crew and the one from Portland filmed the action.

When the last child had told me what he wanted Santa to bring—some sort of expensive video game I'd never heard of   Ms. Brannason approached.

"You make a great Santa," she said.

"Thanks. But I think I'll retire from the job. Not easy."

"You made it look easy, Mrs. Fletcher, like you were born to it. Now that the Brent murder has been solved, how about an interview?"

"About the case? Nothing to say."

"No, not about the murder. About being the first female Santa Claus in Cabot Cove festival history."

I couldn't help but laugh. I'd removed my false white beard and red hat, enjoying the cool air on my face and head. I said, "Give me a minute to get this beard back on, and I'll be happy to speak with you on camera."

The interview went well, and was actually fun. It gave me the opportunity to extoll the festival, the village, and the wonderful people who made Cabot Cove a special place at Christmas.

"Thanks a lot, Mrs. Fletcher," Brannason said. "I really appreciate it."

The TV folks left, and I was about to go backstage to shed my Santa uniform when the door opened at the rear of the school gym. Jake Walther and his daughter, Jill, stepped into the gym and looked around. Jake had on his bib overalls, but wore an ill-fitting suit jacket over it. Jill was dressed in a pretty red-and-green dress suitable for the season. They slowly approached.

Hello," I said. I was about to add "Merry Christmas," but thought better of it, considering Mary Walther had been arrested and was in prison this Christmas Eve.

"Merry Christmas," Jill said.

"Merry Christmas," I said. "Hello, Jake."

"Mrs. Fletcher," he said.

"You look great in that costume," Jill said.

"And I can't wait to get rid of it. I'm surprised to see you."

"Didn't want to come," Jake muttered, "but the girl dragged me here."

I smiled. "I'm glad she did."

"Mrs. Fletcher," Jill said, "I just wanted to come and thank you for everything you've done."

"My goodness," I said, "I'm afraid there are no thanks in order. After all, I am responsible, to a great extent, for your mom being where she is at the moment."

"You did what you had to do," Jake said.

"I'm glad you see it that way, Jake."

"Mr. Turco says he'll do everything he can to help Mary," Jake said. "She's a good woman. Never been in trouble her entire life. I guess the pressure got a smidge too much for her."

I didn't respond.

Jill stepped close to me. "The reason I wanted to come here was to ask Santa for something for Christmas."

"Oh?"

"I wanted to ask Santa that he—I guess Santa is a *she* this year—that she pay a little extra attention to a little girl in Salem, Maine, named Samantha. At least I assume she's still there."

I fought to hold back the tears.

"I just know she's with a wonderful family who's giving her a special Christmas. But I thought that maybe Santa would put in an extra-good word for her."

"You can count on it, Jill," I said. "And I'm sure you're right. Samantha is having a wonderful Christmas with a family that loves her very much."

"Thanks, Mrs. Fletcher."

It occurred to me that there was a wonderful, meaningful story in what had transpired with Jill Walther, a story she could write from the heart. As fiction, of course. Maybe I'd suggest it to her at another time.

"Well," I said, "time for me to get back into my civilian clothes. I'm going to a party at Dr. Hazlitt's house."

"Don't want to hold you up," Jake said. "Much obliged for how you've helped Jill with college and all."

"It's been my pleasure, Jake. Where are you going now?"

"Back home, I reckon," he said.

I was certain they didn't have a Christmas tree, or any

other vestiges of the holiday season. I wondered if they even had any festive food.

"Would the two of you like to come to Dr. Hazlitt's Christmas Eve party?" I asked.

Father and daughter looked at each other.

"Please," I said. "As my special guests."

"I don't figure I'd be welcome there," said Jake.

"Don't worry about that," I said. "I'll see to it that you're made to feel very much at home. After all, this is Christmas."

An hour later, my Santa uniform having been shed, and dressed in my holiday finery, I went with Jake and Jill Walther to Seth's house, where the Christmas Eve party had begun. When we first walked through the door, the expression on people's faces was of surprise, even shock. But Seth broke the tension by coming to Jake and Jill, extending his hand, and saying, "Welcome, Jake. Hello, Jill. Merry Christmas. Help yourselves. There's plenty 'a food for everyone."

The party broke up at eleven, and most guests headed for their homes to spend the remainder of Christmas Eve around their own trees with family. Mort Metzger, his wife, Jim and Susan Shevlin, and Seth and I handled the clean-up chores. Once the house had been put back into some semblance of order, we sat in the living room.

"It was a nice thing you did, Mrs. F., bringing Jake Walther and his daughter here," Mort said.

"They seemed to enjoy themselves," I said. "No matter what Mary did, they shouldn't have to pay for it. How is she holding up in jail, Mort?"

"Pretty well. Prays a lot. Gives us no trouble. She'll be off to the county lockup in a few days. Better facilities there. Jake and Jill visited her this afternoon. Brought a Christmas wreath and some cookies to cheer her up. I feel bad for Jake. He really wanted to be in that cell instead of his wife. Was willing to take the rap for her, and would have, if you hadn't intervened, Mrs. F."

"The festival was a success," our mayor, Jim Shevlin, said. "Best ever."

"You always say that, Jimmy," said Seth.

"But it was the best," Susan Shevlin said, "thanks to you, Jessica."

I waved her compliment off and said, "Actually, being Santa Claus wasn't as bad as I thought it would be. I kind of enjoyed it."

"I wasn't talking about playing Santa," Susan said. "What saved the festival was having Rory Brent's murder solved before the festival. Having it hanging over the town as an unsolved crime would have put quite a damper on things."

"What do you think will happen to Robert Brent?" Seth asked our sheriff.

"About breaking into Mrs. F.'s house? Up to her if she wants to press charges." They looked at me.

"I don't intend to press any charges," I said. "Actually, it was somewhat touching the reason he broke in and left that note. He'd gotten wind that I knew about Jill's pregnancy and wanted to help her keep the secret. As he told you, Mort, he was looking for any papers I might have had concerning it. In some ways he's nicer than his father is."

"I still have trouble knowing that Rory wasn't as nice

a guy as everybody thought," Seth said. "Sort 'a challenges your faith in mankind."

"I don't feel that way," I said. "Yes, it is disillusioning that he was part of a group that preys on people like the Walthers. Hundreds of others like them all over the country. But it hasn't destroyed my faith—in anything. Peace on earth, goodwill toward men."

"And women," Susan said.

"All living things," Mort's wife said.

"Yes, all living things," I repeated.

"Deck the halls with boughs of holly, fa la la la la, la la, la la."

We went to the window and looked out at the dozen men, women, and children making the rounds singing Christmas carols. They waved; we returned the greeting. A few flakes of snow could be seen in the flickering flames of the candles they carried.

Eventually, the others left, leaving me alone with Seth. Vaughan and Olga Buckley had planned to be there, but canceled at the last minute. I wasn't disappointed, although I always love to see them. But it was nice having some quiet time for myself, shared at that moment with my good friend, Seth.

At a few minutes before midnight, he handed me a small glass of sherry, raised his glass to touch rims with me, and said, "Merry Christmas, Jessica."

"Yes, Seth, Merry Christmas."

To all.

About the Authors

Jessica Fletcher is a bestselling mystery writer who has a knack for stumbling upon real-life mysteries in her various travels. **Donald Bain,** her longtime collaborator, is also the writer of more than one hundred books, many of them bestsellers. He can be contacted at www.donaldbain.com

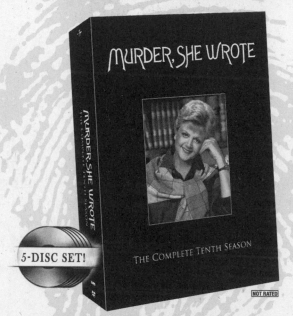